# HOOF

## Sera the Well-Adjusted Serial Killer

Carrie Lacina

To Peter who believed in me no matter what.
Even when *it* (all of it) took way too long.


And to my mom because she's the best person
ever, and I love her more than she'll ever know.

# ONE

Sera's mind was racing. She needed this to end, and she was going to end it. The curb beneath her was hard. The moon high. This was some seriously fucked-up shit. Seriously. She didn't want to be here. She wanted to be at home and do nothing. She wanted to watch TV. She wanted to eat nachos. She wanted to go back in time and never meet The Bitch. She wanted to simply be okay, but she was never okay. Not anymore. That had been taken from her.

She wanted to curl into a ball and die.

The Bitch had to come home sooner or later. She had to. She was probably out with those who had yet to fall from grace. It wasn't Sera's fault she had been unable to fully commit and worship devotedly at the feet of She-Who-Must-Not-Be-Named.

Who was she kidding? It was her fault. Not fault. *Choice*. It was her choice, and she had been right. *RIGHT,* goddamn it! So why did she feel like she was being punished?

Because she was.

She knew it.

The Bitch knew it too.

At least, Sera *thought* The Bitch knew it too. She couldn't be sure. She could never be 100 percent sure. That's how The Bitch derived her power. Those moments of self-doubt. Those moments where you gave *her* the benefit of the doubt even though *she* never gave anyone the benefit of the doubt. Those moments where your humanity made you weak. That was the problem. Sera was human. A real human, with thoughts and feelings and emotions and empathy.

*Fucking empathy—*

The Bitch was a facsimile.

Convincing? Yes. But human? Absolutely not.

*Was that unfair?* she wondered, and a guttural noise somewhere between a heart-wrenching sob and a death cry escaped from her. She squashed the sudden surge of emotion and knew with all of her being that *no.* No, she was not being *unfair.* No, she was never *unfair,* not to The Bitch. She was completely unfair to herself, always, and she was sick of it.

Sera's ass was completely numb now. How long had she been sitting here? It had to be midnight. Maybe later.

*Fucking concrete.*

She didn't know what she'd do when The Bitch arrived, but she knew it would be good. Or bad. Really bad. And that's what she wanted.

Because evil had to be stopped.

She glanced at her wrist for a watch she'd stopped wearing years ago. Sera'd switched it for an Apple Watch and then switched the annoyance of the Apple Watch for nothing. She hated a world that told her even telling time had to be wrapped up in ten-thousand tasks she was unlikely to complete. She hated a watch that could control her with a *DING* or a soft *BUZZ,* so she'd opted out. She'd been meaning to buy a new battery for her old, banged-up analog watch for years now. *It was time,* she thought.

It was time for a lot of things.

She couldn't go on like this. Wouldn't.

She was sick of herself.

She was possibly just as sick of herself as she was of The Bitch. Maybe more so. The Bitch had gone on living her life. Sure, she'd been pissed. She'd clawed and grabbed and tore and threatened Sera with a ferocity generally reserved for starving lions in the Savannah, but when Sera refused to bend to her will any longer, she'd sniped. She made her a pariah. She'd blamed, manipulated, battered, and utterly decimated Sera's self-worth because Sera couldn't be at The Bitch's beck and call 100 percent of the time. Then, she simply walked away.

That was power.

That was evil.

But apparently even when you knew the devil existed, it was impossible to fight her.

*Evil could be too harsh... Stop it!* Sera railed against herself. Her body trembled with unfettered energy. *Where the fuck is she?*

Sera should have known damn well that The Bitch was full of mind games when they'd met, but she was also enticing.

The Bitch was fun, and that was deadly.

You have no personality. You are a carbon copy of me.

You will think and feel how I think and feel.

She'd said Sera "understood things." They were "on the same page." Sera was the only one who "got it." "Got her."

You will back me up and agree with me when I talk loudly.

If you are ever silent for a full second when I ask your opinion, that means you agree.

You have slit your wrist and signed a blood oath.

This didn't happen around other people. Of course not. Who would say how much more amazing one friend is in front of another? The Bitch wasn't controlling or manipulating Sera through hours and hours of grooming, no. She was simply being nice to other people. She wasn't telling every other friend the exact same thing to see who would light up, to see who would respond to this sort of demeaning praise, definitely not.

*You are nothing without me.*

"Enough!" Sera screamed into the night, shooting to her feet just as high beams flashed into view, blinding her.

The night they'd met, after the party had begun to wind down, after most people were done and crashed or done and leaving, The Bitch led Sera outside.

"Stand right there. Eyes closed. It's a surprise," The Bitch had said.

Unseen in the dark, Sera raised an eyebrow. Then she closed her eyes and almost giggled. This was weird but invigorating. She'd just met this girl, but she felt like she was an insider. She listened to some rustling and the obvious sound of a car door opening.

Suddenly, an engine roared angrily to life, and bright lights assailed Sera. She jumped at the onslaught and opened her eyes, about to laugh at her foolishness, only to find she was directly in front of the roaring car. She quickly dodged out of the way and into the dark, but the car wasn't moving. Her heart raced. *What the fuck?* She tried to blink the halos out of her eyes, but it was no good.

The Bitch laughed and climbed out of the open driver's-side door. "Isn't it great?"

Sera smiled because Sera was *nice.* The sudden lights and the alcohol coursing through her veins were disorienting. They masked a feeling she didn't want to feel—She kept trying to blink the residual tracers away, but it was no good.

"I didn't scare you, did I?" The Bitch laughed.

Sera tried to ignore her thumping heart. *It must be the alcohol,* she told herself. "I'm okay. Totally fine."

"I knew you were tough," The Bitch said, and Sera swelled slightly with pride, heart returning to normal.

Of course, she wasn't scared.

"Only a kid would be scared by that," The Bitch jabbed nonchalantly.

Sera glanced at her, but The Bitch passed over the moment. She held her arms out like Vanna White and presented, "Silver Lightning."

"Oh. Cool name," Sera said, coming back to herself.

The Bitch gave her a condescending sort of look, but it was there and gone so quickly Sera wasn't sure she'd even seen it. "It's the color. Silver lightning. I didn't name my car."

Sera nodded, but The Bitch clearly wanted some reaction. Unsure of what to say, Sera mustered, "Silver's a good color."

"Silver lightning," The Bitch corrected and climbed in.

Was the scare planned? It couldn't be. But uncertainty stung. The Bitch popped open the passenger door, and Sera slid in. Nice. So nice.

"I'd drive, but..."

"Shots!" they yelled together.

They laughed, lifting invisible shot glasses into the air, erasing the oddness of the previous moment. Sera sat in the passenger seat, elated that she was being taken into the inner circle even before she knew there was an inner circle.

They sat in the car and talked because they were too drunk to drive. The Bitch said a lot but very little of import. Sera heard gossip about every friend, and for the first time, was told how like The Bitch she was. It was clearly a compliment. It seemed like she was being taken into the deepest of confidences. Perhaps, she was. Sera felt like she'd been invited to an exclusive club. Who wouldn't like that?

"How do you spell your name?" The Bitch asked eventually.

"S-E-R-A like that song. The one from the Nicholas Cage movie."

"Not S-A-R-A-H?" The Bitch turned her nose up a little bit. The almost imperceptible tilt delivered just a hint of disgust as if she couldn't hide it but was trying her best to be polite. Sera misinterpreted the disgust.

"Yeah. I guess my mom wanted to make me stand out." She shrugged pleased. She loved her mom.

"But not too much." A loaded pause. "I mean, she didn't want anyone to *know* you stood out other than you."

Sera twinged studying The Bitch's face in the dark. This was the first taste of distrust. Deep-seated distrust. It was different from the engine revving. It was somehow more sinister, more insidious. It was the kind of thing that picked a person apart. Sera wouldn't have used the word "distrust" though. It was like she suspected her, secretly, deep down inside. Suspected her of what, Sera didn't know, but an unease entered her frame.

"Do you mind if I spell it with an H?" The Bitch asked. Sera gave her a confused look, but The Bitch wasted no time. "Just in my mind. When do you even write someone's name anymore? It's not like I'm going to send you a letter." Sera searched for how to say "no." How to politely phrase, "no." But the briefest of non-pauses passed, and The Bitch sprung, "Good." She said practically clapping. "I knew you wouldn't mind. I think it's such a beautiful name. S-A-R-A-H. Sarah. Exactly how it's supposed to be. All the letters doing what people expect. Let's go back inside." And she hopped out of the car completely ending the conversation, cutting off Sera's ability to protest.

Dumbfounded, Sera looked after her for a moment. *What the hell?*

"Come on," The Bitch yelled back. Knowing time for thought was her enemy. "Let's do another shot."

Sera shook it off. She barely knew this girl. She couldn't have realized how rude that was. Could she? She must be too drunk, or trying to connect or wanting to give her a nickname? Sera would probably never see her again anyway, right?

Later, Sera tried to make herself feel better musing, *sure, it's weird, but how often do people write your name?*

All the time actually... the answer turned out to be all the time.

Getting people to spell her name correctly became one of S-E-R-A's biggest peeves after The Bitch had passed her misspelled contact on to everyone and assured them, even though they didn't ask, that she had asked "Sarah" how to spell her name, and it was indeed with an H - and an A. Conveniently, Sera had been left off of that text thread. That would have made it too easy to correct her. Mysteriously, she got every other text chain under the sun, and The Bitch had no idea how Sera had "missed" that one.

The high beams dipped out of view, yanking Sera from the past.

This was her. The unmistakable sports engine whirring up just a little more than it needed to for the short stretch. The Bitch did everything in a way that said, "Look at me. I'm the best." And maybe, just maybe, it stung even more because she was. The Bitch was winning at life and friends and looks and stupid fucking sports cars.

"Look at me, I'm The Bitch," Sera muttered and smirked to herself. This time she was standing her ground squarely in the car's path. It was still far enough away that The Unsuspecting Bitch probably hadn't even seen her, but every victory felt good. Every stance she took reclaimed a piece of her.

In retrospect, she'd known. She'd always known she couldn't trust The Bitch, but sometimes she missed things. Sometimes, she looked the other way. Sometimes, Sera worked very hard at not seeing how awful people were being *to her* specifically. She was blinded by friendship, blinded by society's praise of polite. Besides, she was tough, and they *couldn't* mean it, could they?

From day 1, The Bitch had been informing Sera of who she was. A gut punch wrapped in a pillow was still a gut punch.

The Bitch informed Sera of who she should be as well. Subservient. Docile. A good girl. All that was missing was a pat on the head.

Sera hated herself for not knowing to run that night. For not running many other nights. For not listening to her gut, for not standing up to The Bitch and saying, "No, actually I want it spelled—" No, for not saying, "It *is* spelled S-E-R-A." She didn't *want* it spelled any particular way. It *was* spelled S-E-R-A.

It turns out a big part of how manipulative people work is by slipping things past in small ways that make regular people feel rude for interrupting or correcting them. It turns out "Nice" is the enemy of not being trampled on and pushed-over, and Sera had, unfortunately, been a very nice person.

It wouldn't have mattered anyway.

Sera knew that now. Stand up to a sociopath and watch them do whatever they want regardless. Still, her mind clawed at her. Even with everything she knew, everything she had learned she couldn't help but wonder *what if... What if she had stood up to her? What if she had put her foot down? What if... Would they still be friends?*

She shook herself free from the intrusive thoughts. *No. Absolutely not.*

The sad truth was no.

The hard truth was no.

The reality was no.

The mindfuck was nothing was one hundred percent.

Doubt can tear a person apart.

And it had.

As the car came into focus, Sera chuckled cruelly to herself, *Silver Lightning my ass.* She had looked the color up. It wasn't even silver. It was flaked gray. Regular old gray.

The car had lightning embellishments painted on the sides. Something The Bitch would call garish for others was impressive for her. A cry for attention for others was tasteful for her. Laughable for others was enviable for her. It was "different." Sera had wanted to scream, *If something is only ever different when you do it, it's not different. It's not different at all!* But Sera was nice.

Well, Sera wasn't nice anymore. In fact, Sera was planning on working very hard at being the biggest fucking asshole she could be.

The Bitch flashed her lights, and the truth struck Sera. She was going to out sociopath the sociopath. She was going to kill The Bitch and anyone like her because that was the only way to truly eradicate evil, and Sera needed her gone. The Bitch was no good.

# Two

The bright lights barreled toward Sera where she stood, waiting. She didn't move or even flinch as the car kept its steady pace. She knew this was a game of chicken that she could lose, but The Bitch could not. If Sera flinched, she was a weakling, but if The Bitch stopped, well, that was just good driving. Sera almost hoped she'd hit her. It'd be easier to hate the concrete act of hostility than the millions of tiny pinpricks that had torn her brain apart.

The abrupt squeal of rubber biting into asphalt assaulted Sera's ears as the car slid to a stop half a foot from her. She couldn't see anything through the high beams, but she imagined she could. She imagined The Bitch's snide little smirk. Sera kept her expression steady. Flat. The lights cut out. The jump from light to dark left her blind for a moment. Another disorienting sensation she didn't allow herself to display.

As residual halos dissipated, Sera saw Levi sitting in the passenger seat. Of fucking course.

The Bitch had cultivated an overly close social circle that provided her the comfort of almost never having to face herself mano-a-bitcho. The chief benefit was an absolute lack of self-awareness. She was able to completely eliminate the possibility of perceiving any personal flaws by keeping others around her 24/7. When it was absolutely necessary to be alone, she'd call someone and continue her incessant monologuing over the phone.

In movies when people monologue, it's about the evil acts they are about to commit. Monologuing reveals their larger-than-life plans, unfurls their character, deepens insights. Unfortunately, in real life, evil monologuing consists almost entirely of complaints. Evil people could harp for hours on how a Target employee had ruined their day with an averagely handled return. They could complain for hours about pickles on their hamburger. They could cry foul about being given an extra dollar in change. These incessant, unending small complaints would wear down the listener, opening them up to attack. Because evil is insidious.

The Bitch could stay on the phone all night, never stopping for air or acknowledging that there was another person on the other end. She obliged with the cursory and required—thus non-negotiable—hello at the beginning of the call, but that was it.

It was quite the feat.

Sera barely kept herself from snarling at Levi. It wasn't his fault he'd decided to hang out with The Bitch. Well, maybe it was his fault. It was his *choice* after all, and where does fault come from if not directly from the choices we make? Still, Sera could hardly kill The Bitch with him here.

The Bitch slithered out of her car. She knew this was a standoff.

"You're lucky I stopped in time. What if I hadn't seen you there, skulking in the dark?" she asked, claiming their game of chicken as a victory for herself. There was no winning. However, Sera's expression didn't change. She didn't accept the loss, and this drained a bit of The Bitch's power. "Anyway, we're heading inside to watch a movie. Or we could play a game, if you want to come in?"

"No, I just—" Just what, Sera thought? Just came here to kill you because you're too fucked up to ever acknowledge that you screwed me over or could ever be wrong? Sera still had her power, but Levi didn't deserve to die. She wasn't going to kill a meek guy who didn't dare to leave his toxic friend. "I stopped by to see what you were doing, but I was just leaving."

"You were just standing there," The Bitch scoffed. "And now you're leaving?"

Sera regarded The Bitch with her newfound cold, flat eyes and imagined a chill running up The Bitch's spine. Did she shudder? No, it was a trick of Sera's imagination, but she did turn away first.

"Whatever, you always leave when the fun is starting. Right, Levi? Let's go. I couldn't believe that server. Could you?"

Sera heard the hesitation in Levi's voice, "Was going to call it a night..." But he went inside. How could he do anything else?

Their voices trailed into nothingness as Sera stood in front of the curb, looking past the regular gray car into the reinvigorating night.

Sera had been contemplating homicide for a while now, and not just for The Bitch. Once Sera had her eyes opened up to how poorly her "friend" had been treating her, she began to see how poorly so many people treated her. She had always been able to see when other people were wronged, had always helped them, but somehow, she'd had blinders on for herself.

What's worse, she let people get away with abusing her. All these people carving her up into little bits, treating her like nothing. Sera hadn't crawled into a hole to shrivel up and die. She'd been shoved there. She'd been held there. Bit by bit, people had torn her apart until she couldn't put herself back together again. Until she didn't even know where to find the pieces. Sera had a giant target on her back and a sign that read:

KICK ME. I WON'T DO A FUCKING THING. And she knew it, now.

It's amazing how much a person can hate themselves.

Sera had mastered the fine art of self-hate. It was a skill she had unwittingly practiced for years and years. A skill others helped her practice. She put herself down. She put herself aside. She raised others up at her expense. She thought that was how she was supposed to live. She'd help them. They'd help her. She thought that was how the world was supposed to work. If you help others, if you're a good person, if you do your best, if you're *nice,* you might not find wealth or renown, but you will be treated well. You will have friends and love and all the good things in life. All the best things Hallmark has to offer.

Hallmark is a tar pit full of lies that sucks you in and devours you whole.

Hallmark doesn't spit out your bones. No, it puts them under so much pressure that they eventually turn into oil, and then all the fuckers who drove you to the tar pit, who kicked you in and held your head under while your lungs filled with black death, all those fuckers use the petrol you've become to fuel their lives. Even after they've taken everything from you, they will take more.

Sera was going to be a serial killer.

She needed to get rid of The Bitch, yes, but she wasn't the only one.

Sera wasn't whole or well-adjusted. She wasn't working toward finding her place in this world. She didn't have self-confidence or a group of supportive friends. She had something better. She had *purpose.*

The thought filled her with a happy calm, like a soft breeze rushing over her skin in the cool mountain air. It was the same as the breath she took after she got a few miles out on a hike and realized she was completely alone. The breath that replaced all her jittery firing neurons with a real and simple calm. The breath that filled her with silence and made her one with the world. The universe. Herself.

The idea of killing lots and lots of people brought Sera that same calm.

Perhaps there was such a thing as a well-adjusted serial killer.

She hadn't planned it. She hadn't thought she'd really kill her. She had wanted to find out why, why The Bitch had worked so hard to decimate her so completely. But something clicked, and she knew what she had known for a long time. All these wrongs piled together into one gelatinous goo, they weren't a thing The Bitch did. They weren't a decision or a manipulation or even a sick game. They weren't her modus operandi. They were her mode of being.

Everyone who treated her like this, who kicked her to the side and affirmed that she was nothing had the same mode of being. She had a skill for finding narcissists, sociopaths. She was a magnet. Now, she could put that skill to good use.

Sera would free herself from The Bitch and anyone like her. She needed to protect a world of Levis from a Battalion of Bitches.

The pitch-black horizon spread before her like the most beautiful sunrise. It was the dawning of her new and improved self.

*Life is good,* she thought, *but murder is better.*

Energy coursed through her veins. There was only one issue. If Sera was going to become a serial killer, she was going to have to figure out if she could kill not just someone, but lots and lots of someones.

# THREE

*Holy shit!* Sera went into the night. *Holy Shit! Holy shit!* Her body electric. She'd never felt so good. So... *Alive* came to mind, but it wasn't right. It was too cliché. She didn't feel more alive. She'd always felt alive. Now, she felt *transcendent.* She felt like she could rise above the absolute chaos of any situation. She felt like she had just become something great. *Well,* she thought, *let's not get ahead of ourselves. After all, we haven't killed anyone yet.*

She walked down the middle of the road toward home. A car honked as it drove toward her, politely alerting her to its presence. She simply waved and kept her ground. The car swerved around, horn blaring, cutting close to the curb.

*MEOOOOOW!* A cat's cry pierced the night. It jumped back to safety as the car sped past narrowly missing it. A black cat. It was definitely an omen. A good omen. Tragedy averted, the cat licked its paw as it perched on the curb. It regarded Sera with cool confidence. Sera, in turn, considered the cat. For a moment, it seemed they had an understanding. Both of them were completely at ease with themselves. Sera hadn't felt this way in a long time—*Ever,* her mind threw at her, and it was true. Sera hadn't ever felt this way. She was 100 percent present in the moment. She was absolutely unconcerned with who others thought she was and what she presented to the world. She was absolutely herself. This is why confidence can be a drug. This is why confident people rise to the top. There's a clarity of thought and purpose that comes with absolute confidence that nothing can match.

Standing there, Sera's euphoria inevitably gave way to practicality. How was she going to become a serial killer? And, quite frankly, should she become a serial killer? She could just kill The Bitch. There was value in that. Less risk. Quick results. But it didn't feel right to her. Serial killer felt like the answer. Everyone who manipulated, used, and abused her needed to pay, so serial killer it was. Decisions felt good. But there was one problem: how was she going to make sure she had what it takes?

Subconsciously, she reached out her arm and stepped toward the cat, who intuitively darted away. They had an understanding, but the cat was nobody's fool.

*Practice.*

Sera's instincts were already taking over. *Good.* Most serial killers started with animals as kids. They were able to hone their craft in secret for years, often by catching and killing rats, squirrels, and the neighbor's cat or dog. Sera didn't want to wait years. She wanted to get good and killery ASAP. She doubted murder protégés kept their secret for long after they stole good old Fido, so Sera figured she would have to get her own animal to slay. Besides, this was the city; she didn't know her neighbors, and their animals might not like her. The cat hadn't. She couldn't get caught trying to steal some barky stranger-danger dog. Plus, introducing herself to Spot right before stealing him seemed unwise at best. *Not Spot,* she thought. *No Fido, no Spot, and no Lassie.* Whatever animal she got, whatever "it" she acquired, she wasn't going to name. It would be inhumane to name an animal and then kill it.

Back in her room, Sera stripped off her clothes and climbed into bed. She braced herself, ready to resist the urge to look at the last text from The Bitch, but the urge didn't come. She didn't need to relive every moment of every exchange. She didn't have to question each emoji or every question she had asked that The Bitch had left unanswered. She clicked the light off, prepared to battle the never-ending assault of thoughts that accompanied the night, but the assault didn't come either. She laid her trauma down to rest, and it let her rest too. She closed her eyes and, wonder of wonders, fell asleep.

When morning came, Sera woke and noticed the light filtering through the curtains. The sun was already high in the sky. Not only had she fallen asleep, but she'd slept through the night. A wave of joy bubbled up within her. Tears threatened to fill her eyes. She didn't even know that was possible anymore. She rolled out of bed, pulled an outfit from her dresser, and marveled at herself. It was possible to pick out clothes without being submerged in a cesspool of doubt and fear.

Sera was a new person, and that new person had goals. Today, she was getting a victim.

# Four

The concrete building screamed of utilitarianism. A wood sign with a sun embellishment announced it as an animal shelter, but the stack of cages under a weathered awning spoke louder. "Drop your unwanted here, and we'll figure it out... we hope," it clearly said.

To Sera, it was a glistening mecca. So many unwanted animals, so little time!

She stood in front of the animal shelter, allowing the moment to wash over her. A shudder of excitement rushed down her spine, spurring her on. A worker (likely a volunteer) with a messy bun and dog treats bulging from a tattered fanny pack walked past with a small herd of dogs on leashes. They were gorgeous. So cute, so happy.

*Shit.*

Did Sera really want to hurt them?

She looked back at the ramshackle cages, pulling strength from them. She chastised herself, if she were a real serial killer, this wouldn't be a problem. She shouldn't feel sad for the dogs. She should feel, what? Elated? Powerful? It was hard to think of how you could feel more power over another being than when you were able to tell it to sit and it sat. You literally lead them around on leashes, and they are HAPPY about it.

Clocking her stare, the volunteer smiled. "These good dogs will be back in about 15 minutes, if you want to meet any of them. Won't you? Won't you be back? Yes, you will. Where do you want to walk today?" She walked off, still talking to the dogs as she went.

Sera watched her continue down the sidewalk, unsure if the woman realized she was no longer talking to a person. It was as if she thought Sera had joined her. She asked the dogs about their days and paused as if they would answer. Sera cocked her head and wondered how lonely the woman was. *We could be friends,* she thought before shaking her head and breaking herself free from the moment of pity. Pity for who though? *Stop it. You're not here to find friends or get a pet. You're here to practice your technique.*

She walked inside the shelter, where concrete walls were completed by concrete floors. Nothing belonged here that couldn't be hosed off. Dogs barked from all sides. Some dogs cowered in the backs of their kennels. Others charged the gates, barking and snarling. Signs hung saying how much work a dog may or may not be. "Looking for an Experienced dog lover," many signs announced. This, Sera was not.

She actually wasn't much of an animal lover at all, which gave her hope. On its own, this didn't make her a serial killer. She'd have to work at that, but maybe some small part of her had always suspected this would be her path. Her lack of interest in animals could be a gift rather than a curse. Maybe it was a skill rather than her Achilles' heel. From time to time, the dreaded "Are you a dog person or a cat person?" had come up at parties. Initially, she'd honestly responded "Neither," but that answer saddled her with distrustful glances and arguments that she didn't have to own a pet to be a pet person.

Sera learned quickly, and now, she always responded with a quippy, "Why does it have to be one?" Immediately, people took this to mean that she believed she loved both dogs and cats equally. They would argue the merits of one or the other, and she would listen obligingly. No one ever believed it was possible that she legitimately cared for both the same amount, which was exactly zero, or next to it. *Let them win their own arguments,* she thought. Who wants to explain that their animal of choice is a good book?

As she walked past the kennels, she realized the dogs weren't snarling because they were ready for a fight. It was more of a test or a challenge. The dogs were demanding that they be allowed to own their own 6x4 concrete cells. The dogs were trying to hold onto some shred of dogmanity. Sera got that more than she'd care to admit. *Okay, not any of those ones,* she thought.

She kept walking along the wet concrete pathway. There were small, yippy dogs. Those she found herself imagining killing even without trying. It'd be so easy to snap those tiny, yippy necks. Did she secretly hate animals? If so, had she always hated them this much? She had thought of it as an indifference, but she did cross the street when a dog walked past, she did pretend like she was allergic if a friend really wanted her to watch their cat. Not a major allergy, mind you. She could still hang out, but being the only one around the cat for days or weeks really wouldn't be a good idea.

Rats appealed to her. They were smart, and no one expected you to cuddle them. No one demanded you like them and affirm the love with a T-shirt or a coffee mug. Maybe she just didn't want to be told how to feel anymore.

Sera stopped in front of a kennel.

In the far back corner, a sad, mangy mutt lay in a puddle of its own piss. One eye was caked over with mucus-y gunk. It had matted fur that was an entangled mesh of mud-brown, gray, and gray-white. The sign read, EXPERIENCED DOG LOVERS ONLY, with *only* heavily underlined. REQUIRES MEDICATION

AND ADVANCED CARE. NOT TO BE RELEASED UNTIL MED-
ICAL TREATMENT IS COMPLETE.

This was the dog.

Sure, it wouldn't exactly be murder. It would be a bit more like an act of euthanasia, but people had been committing murder in the name of euthanasia for centuries. It didn't make it true. Murder was murder. She could lie to herself if she wanted to, but she didn't want to. This would be murder, but it would also be an easier start. Sera was in.

"Excuse me," she said to a vapid teenager who was, no doubt, forced by some legal infraction to be here, "I'd like to adopt this dog."

The teenager looked from her to the dog and back. Judgment oozed from her. There's no way *you* can take care of *this* dog, her eyes screamed. Aloud, she said, "Sure. Down the hall." She lifted her phone back up and disappeared into a labyrinth of social suicide. Clearly getting no more direction, Sera looked at the sign again. Kennel 42. Kismet.

• • • • • • • • • •

Sera stood in a concrete office with linoleum floors that could have once been white and blue, though they were now yellow and a greenish brown. The room was no cozier than the dog kennels. The main furnishing was a metal desk from the '70s. Rust spread out from its bracing points confirming that, yes, everything did indeed need to be hosed off.

There was only one chair, and it wasn't for Sera.

"That's a special needs dog," the woman sitting behind the desk emphasized, giving Sera a look that made the teenager's feel like a hug. The woman wore her cargo shorts with a certain authority and had the kind of fit, wrinkly knees that had seen a lot of sun. She could easily be thirty-five or fifty-five. This woman could be the only actual employee the pound had.

Fear crept up the back of Sera's neck. The woman's confidence and even-keeled look immediately made Sera suspect the woman hated her. Primordial terror eased into her being like an old friend. She shrank inside herself, becoming very small. She knew she shouldn't. *This is not serial killer behavior,* she thought. Still, she shrank.

"Yeah, I, uh, I've had a lot of dogs before, and they really like me," she said weakly. *They really like me? Jesus Christ. What's wrong with you?* she thought.

She talked to herself like this a lot. She didn't know when the voice had surfaced, but she knew it was after meeting The Bitch. It began as an echo of The Bitch and the slimy little things she said. Initially, it had a friendly accompanying voice that asked if those echoes were right or wrong, but the echoes got louder. The echoes solidified. They turned into shouts, and then the shouts evened out into a kind of running inner monologue. Her inner monologue spoke to her in the second person and incessantly called her crazy. It wasn't that her inner voice pointed out all of her faults, so much as her inner voice thought she was a *clinically insane whiny little bitch.*

This type of self-talk was not okay. She should absolutely take the derogatorily gendered *bitch* out of it. She was fully aware of this defect, so she was working very hard at correcting herself. Thus, she applied great effort to call herself *a clinically insane whiny little <u>dick</u>* instead. Feminism was important. Unfortunately, her efforts rarely worked. In fact, they usually led to her calling herself a bitch, then a stupid asshole, then the repeated phrases with dick, and a whole lot of *you can't even fucking do that right, you stupid bitch. Fuck. Dick! You stupid dick. Fuck dick bitch suck fuck dammit!*

In this moment, Sera really did feel like a stupid dick.

She was going to kill that voice and, to do that, she had to kill the cause of it. The Bitch was going down. The irony of the nickname was not lost on her.

*Give me the fucking dog,* she thought, but mumbled a "I really am good with animals" as a sorry way of defending herself. It wasn't much, but it was all Sera could muster.

The woman looked her up and down and resolutely said, "If you return the dog, you don't get your money back."

"I wouldn't dream of it," Sera replied.

"It counts as a charitable donation." Full-stop. She waited for Sera to say something, to back down, to change her mind, but Sera stood there. She was either oblivious or overconfident. Either way, the woman knew that dog needed a home. "Great. We'll bring the dog to the yard so you can properly meet," she said.

"No need." Sera dismissed the idea offhand. She didn't need to meet the dog. The dog would do everything she needed, which was live, then die. No worries. The woman's eyes locked onto Sera's, weighing her. They stood there, paused for what felt like a full minute. Sera wanted to shift, to squirm under the gaze, but she forced herself to stay stock-still.

"Do you know how to do eye drops?" the woman asked suddenly, springing to life again. She walked to the medical area of the office, opening a cupboard and pulling out a variety of tonics and pill bottles.

Sera followed and nodded, yes, but she had gone into auto-nod mode as the woman droned on. SHE WAS GETTING THE DOG! Happy dance!!!! She didn't need to know the medicine or the doses. She didn't need any of this shit. She needed a knife.

*Oh, wow,* she thought. *Am I going to use a knife?* She considered it for a moment and realized yes, she was going to use a knife. *Amazing.*

Her surroundings suddenly became crystal clear. She looked at the linoleum floor. It pulled up in the corners slightly and had well-worn patches from this woman's safari boots. The boots creaked under the woman's shifting weight. There was a slight inconsistency in the fluorescent yellow light as it spilled into the room. Rather than a smooth, continual glare, it caught and flickered every now and again. The cool metal of the examination table against her palm was comforting as she leaned on it.

This was the place where she officially had plotted her first kill. This place was special. She'd stalked a victim—okay, well, close enough. She'd *selected* a victim. She was ensnaring said victim, and she knew how she was going to kill her. Him? Huh. It? It. She didn't know what sex it was, but she was going to kill it. Equal opportunity. Feminism was important. She would kill everyone equally based on the merits of their assholishness. This moment was important and would be forever etched into her mind as one of the greatest moments of her life.

"...Diarrhea."

"What?"

"Diarrhea is a common side effect of the medicine. It should only last a week or two. I'm sure you know..." This lady knew damn well Sera didn't know, but she also knew no one else was gonna adopt that poor fucking dog. Sometimes you take what you can get. "...It'll be a good idea to have her sleep in a crate because of that. Also, take her out for frequent breaks. She doesn't like to go to the bathroom in her house. And *call me* if you have any questions." She regarded Sera with the desperate look she'd come to wear so well. *Please, don't bring the dog back,* the woman thought to herself. *Please, let this idiot get lucky.*

The woman led Sera through the shelter past kennels and the dog walker, who was still talking to the four-legged friends that were bound to her. "You're sure you don't want a yard visit, in case you don't... Get along?" The woman asked again as they rounded the corner.

Sera simply shook her head no. She was too excited to trust her voice not to waver if she spoke.

"You're lucky. We don't get Wirehaired Pointing Griffons in here. No shelter does," she continued.

"Don't get whats?"

"The dog. It's a Wirehaired Pointing Griffon."

"Oh, it seemed kinda like a mutt?"

"It's mixed. There's some Collie, Staffordshire, maybe some Terrier. Probably Cattle Dog."

"So, a mutt?"

"No, it's a Wirehaired Pointing—"

"Griffon," Sera finished. *Of course it was.*

They were back. This was it. This was her first victim. Her very first. Sera stood in front of kennel 42, staring down at the dog who was indeed a she. For her part, the dog was lying in an even larger pool of her own urine than she had been before. She did not look up or even shift at their arrival. *Yeah, this dog totally hates peeing in her house,* Sera thought. All this was hers, for the low price of—

"Four-hundred and ninety-seven dollars," the woman said, standing next to her. Sera's eyes bulged, and the woman quickly added, "The adoption fee is one hundred and five, but the eye drops are sixty, and you need two bottles to do a full treatment cycle. The dewormer is—"

"It's okay," Sera cut her off. "Five hundred isn't a bad price to pay for..." *For your first kill,* she added in her mind.

"Oh, great. You'd like to round up for charity?"

Sera chuckled, but the woman was clearly not joking.

"Fuck it," Sera said. "Why not?"

The woman didn't flinch. She knew better than to look a gift horse in the mouth. *Say all the fucks you want,* she thought, *so long as the card clears.*

• • • • • • • • • •

Standing in front of the concrete prison, Sera held onto a crisp piece of bright yellow rope that was wrapped around the dog's neck like a noose. A makeshift leash. The woman had been appropriately faux surprised when Sera admitted she hadn't brought a leash.

"First-timers usually don't know," she had slipped, and had quickly covered with, "First-time adopters. I'm sure all your dogs were family pets or given to you by friends who couldn't care for them."

Holding the rope in her hand, Sera felt a twinge of guilt for all the times she'd lied about allergies to friends over the years. Then, a pinch of fear. Instinctively, she glanced up the street, a matter of self-preservation. If they saw her... *If they saw me, what?* she thought. *Then what?* But she couldn't stop the wave of relief that washed over her when no one was there.

She had tried to say no to them, hadn't she? But no wasn't acceptable. Not for her. She had to have a reason. Ironclad or nothing. A few small lies were worth keeping her sanity. Weren't they? Besides, if she was going to hell, it wasn't going to be for lying about allergies. At least, not anymore.

She looked down at the dog, a pathetic pile of fur and snot.

"Now what?" she asked aloud, and the dog perked up for about a second and a half before slumping back into the shell she was. *I'm totally doing this dog a favor,* Sera thought before she tugged on the leash. "To the car!" Sera announced, but the dog did not move. Sera dragged her half a foot, and instead of walking, the dog lay down.

Maybe the dog could sense something was up. That was a thing, right? Begrudgingly, Sera bent down and lifted the mutt up, though she was really too big to carry.

Against her better judgment, the dog nuzzled into Sera, just a tiny bit. It was so insignificant a movement Sera wasn't even sure she felt it. So, she wrote it off. *Just my imagination,* she thought and walked away, carrying her victim and whistling a new tune she was coming up with on the spot. She called it "I'm Gonna Be A Serial Killer."

It was a very happy song.

# FIVE

Sera pulled a long butcher's knife from the knife block. This was it. The dog sat like a sack of potatoes by the door, waiting for whatever might come its way. It did not expect murder, and so, while it was slightly uneasy in its new home, it did not believe it was actually sniffing around its own crime scene. The dog was looking for clues, of course, but it was looking for clues of a more edible nature.

Sera glanced over her shoulder and decided to sharpen the knife. She wasn't sure how tough dog skin was, but she figured, particularly for her first kill, she didn't want to have to stab too many times. Plus, if there was any howling it might alert her landlord, and she wasn't allowed to have pets. She wondered, *Would the landlord scold me for killing a dog since that technically did follow the "no animals" clause? He'd probably argue that it wasn't in the spirit of the rule, and I'd get evicted anyway. Fucking landlord.*

Her one-bedroom apartment was a pigsty, but she liked it. It was all *her* mess. Every pile, every scrap of paper, every takeout container. Built circa 1960s, everything was a little dated, but the kitchen's black-and-white tile floor felt more like old-Hollywood than poverty. She liked that.

The hardwood floor running down the hallway was janky and misaligned after years of settling—a problem Sera related to all too well—but it added a certain charm. She didn't know, but she suspected that hardwood was also hidden beneath the generic beige low pile carpet the living room had been updated with. She'd considered ripping the carpet out, letting the beautiful imperfections show, but she didn't dare. Besides, what if the wood was rotten underneath? At very least, they should have used the same shag that was in the bedroom. It brought the room all the way into the '70s, and like it or not, at least it had personality.

In all honesty, once she'd found out it wasn't a studio, she knew she'd be signing the lease. Now, she had no job, thanks to The Bitch. She couldn't be searching for a new apartment too.

That stupid Bitch.

*There's always Grandma's,* she thought. It was in the country, sure, but she didn't mind that. She paused, questioning her thoughts. Hadn't she planned on going straight there when her grandma had left it to her? What had happened?

"Don't expect us to visit," The Bitch had said. "Nothing against you. At all. But. I mean, no one's going to."

"It's a paid-off house," Sera said, pain still fresh, though her eyes were dry. Even then she knew it wasn't smart to cry in front of The Bitch.

"Sell it." No preamble. No "What's the house like?" No semblance of concern.

Sera shrugged. She'd love to take credit for saying nothing, but she couldn't. It was instinct. She'd shrugged and stopped talking, not because she knew she shouldn't sully her happy memories with the cascade of negativity The Bitch was sure to unleash, but because her lizard brain told her to.

The lizard brain is never wrong.

Sera knew that now.

In her kitchen, she threw open drawer after drawer searching for her knife sharpener. She'd know where the knife sharpener was at her grandma's. Why wasn't she more organized? Why wasn't she organized *at all?* Her mother had given her the sharpener in some weird attempt to connect and help her daughter be more domestic. It wasn't what Sera had had in mind, but now it seemed quite useful. Finally, she found it in the very back of the very bottom of the very last drawer she searched. It's always that way.

The dog sat completely still, by the door. It had ceased all exploratory clue missions and instead opted for a watchful tactic of wait and see. The dog didn't cower. She'd never been the terrified type. However, all the banging did lead her to believe that this particular human really needed some help and probably a game of Frisbee.

The dog had never actually played Frisbee, but she wanted to. She wanted to more than almost anything else in the world. She had seen other dogs playing with people as she scrounged for leftovers in garbage cans. It was not an easy life. Unfortunately, there had been a fence and two latched doors around the field, and no matter how much she dug, she couldn't get in to play with them.

It was there, while digging, trying with all her might to reach the coveted Land of Frisbee, that a woman had snatched her up. The woman threw her in a car, separating her from another dog, which she thought was quite rude. She didn't even get to smell him first. She soon found out the other dog was "the woman's dog." The details didn't make sense, but he assured her it was a common scenario that involved regular feedings. He asked her name, and she said dogs always described her as having sort of a nutty-lasagna butt smell. That was not what the other dog had meant. His name was Sampson. Apparently, people named the dogs rather than smelling their butts. It seemed a bit confusing, but so was the gate separating them.

When she wondered about the separation, he had explained that people have a lot of fear when it comes to dirty dogs and fleas. It seemed if people had to scratch, they might end up tearing off their skin or something.

Sampson wasn't entirely sure how it worked, but he reported that he'd gotten fleas a few years before, and the woman had torn apart the entire house, washed every sheet, towel, and clothing item, and even threw away his bed. It was a very nice bed. He still missed it. It had smelled of a steak bone he'd managed to hide for a full week—and peanut butter. She had asked him what steak and peanut butter were, but he insisted it was impossible to describe heaven.

With that, the woman yelled at both of them, and they fell silent. In a brief whisper, Sampson explained that the woman also seemed to be afraid of loud conversations, but only from dogs. She and her friends could be as loud as they wanted. The dogs rode in silence, but the dog wondered if getting picked up in this car might mean she would get a bed too. Maybe she would get peanut butter and steak. Maybe she would even get to play Frisbee.

That was before they were torn apart.

As a woman in khaki shorts drug her away, she and Sampson howled and howled. They tried to explain to the woman that the new dog didn't have fleas, but she was too afraid and sent her away anyway. Sampson explained in a yell as they were pulled apart, to act playful, and be nice and someone else, someone less afraid of fleas, would pick her. She didn't understand what this meant, but she was comforted by the fact that he must have been here. This was before she was unceremoniously hosed off with freezing cold water and thrown in a concrete cell. How in the dog bone would she act playful and nice when all she felt was miserable and abused? She raced to the bars and furiously dug, but her nails were no match for the concrete. Her paws hurt, and all she could hear were the cries for help coming from many, many other dogs. She'd even felt bad for the wailing cats!

As if being handed a ray of sunlight, she saw a Frisbee in the back corner. She raced over and snatched it up, but it cracked and broke into a thousand pieces. It had been left in the sun for too long, and now it was no good for anyone. It was too much. She was no match for the awfulness. She curled up in a ball and cried. She cried for many days and nights. She tried digging again but lost a nail and knew there was no hope. The people were not nice. They poked and prodded. She couldn't help but cry over and over again. Unfortunately, crying had certainly been the wrong choice, because no one seemed to like the howling, and the tears had dried in a thick wad over both eyes, making it hard to see. Each day, she tried to act playful and nice, but her crusted eyes and hose-matted hair seemed to convince everyone that she did, in fact, have fleas. And they were all very afraid of fleas.

Sera did not seem afraid of fleas. She didn't seem like she necessarily knew what they were either, but the dog was willing to do anything to get out of that cell. She had figured wherever Sera was taking her would be better than where she was, and at the very least, it would give her a chance to escape. She didn't much like that she'd have to live until the next rainstorm barely able to see and looking like old carpet, but you play the hand you're dealt.

As Sera threw the drawers open, the dog wondered if maybe she was afraid of fleas. This couldn't possibly be normal. The dog wanted to help, but the crazy display did not seem like something Sera would want help with. At long last, Sera pulled a small, black object from a drawer. The dog had no idea what it was, but it seemed that Sera had found what she wanted. The dog didn't know what it would do to fleas, but it certainly looked intimidating.

Sera sat down on the couch and began running her butcher knife through the black sharpener she'd finally found. It caught a few times, and Sera cursed her mom for not buying her a better one. If she wanted her to be domestic, the least she could do was give her good tools. After ten minutes, she examined the blade. It was definitely duller than it had been.

*Fuck.*

# Six

Sera held the knife high above her head. She would bring it down with all the force of her five-foot-six frame. Below her, the dog hunched sadly, not scared exactly, but looking up warily. The dog could run, could howl, could lunge at her, could attack. Sera knew all these things, but the damn dog seemed so docile. It was a little...disconcerting, to say the least. The dog looked up at Sera with her big, crusted eyes. *Maybe,* Sera reasoned, *she can't even see me.*

That was not the case. The dog could indeed see Sera. However, if there's one thing this dog had learned, it's that people are kinda shitty to dogs, but if there was a second thing this dog had learned, it was that fighting it would only make it worse.

The dog didn't imagine the drastic end Sera had in mind for her. If she had, she no doubt would have made a run for it. She was still biding her time, thinking she'd escape when the door was good and open or perhaps when she was already outside. Unfortunately for her, Sera had other plans.

Sera brought the knife down in a sharp, hard stab— but stopped after a few inches. A fake. A test. The dog flinched but didn't retreat, didn't run, didn't snarl. Still, Sera was worried that, when she plunged the knife through the air further, the dog would bolt, leaving Sera trying to catch a dog—or worse, trying to explain to her landlord why there was so much barking.

Sera resolved to tie the dog down. It didn't seem sporting, but nothing about this was exactly fair. Sera had a sneaking suspicion that she might not be made out for dogicide, but quickly dismissed it.

*Of course she wasn't ready!* Sera thought. *It wasn't about the dog. It was about the blood.* She folded a towel in half and placed it on the floor. She stared at it, examining the minimal surface area. That would never do. She had no idea how much blood a small dog would expel, but it would certainly be more than that.

She dug an old red comforter out of her cupboard. She hated to part with it. Her mom had also given this to her, and while she didn't like the rough feel of the material and never used it, somehow it always seemed slightly dirty, she still liked it. It smelled of her mother, with her classic tinge of cigarette smoke. Sera's mom had smoked for years before kicking the habit, and while Sera hated the smell of smoke, she very much liked the smell of her mother's comforting hugs, and her mom's scent happened to be wrapped up in cigs, as her mom called them. She loved the smell of her mother's smoke.

Sera hesitated as she folded the comforter in quarters to lay down. Her mom would definitely not approve of slaying the dog. Any dog. A person? Now that she might understand. She laid the blanket down and put the towel on top, trying to stop the voice nagging at her. It wasn't like it was her *favorite* blanket, but maybe it was. *Shit,* she reprimanded herself for the myriad of mental gymnastics she could no longer escape. *That's why you have to do this,* she thought. If there was a chance she could save the blanket, she would.

"Sit," she ordered the dog, pointing at the blanket. The dog stared at her, unsure for a moment, then climbed right on and snuggled in super deep. "Stay," Sera said and walked away.

A rush of emotions overtook the dog. A bed! Her very own bed. This woman was certainly on edge, but maybe it would pass.

*If I ever meet a flea, I'm going to tell them to leave humans alone,* the dog thought before relaxing further into the bed, as if that settled everything. Fleas were surely the devil.

Sera returned with the rope-leash to hog-tie the dog's feet, but she realized with a sad pang, the dog was already fast asleep. In its defense, the dog hadn't been able to fully relax for weeks, and while it didn't entirely trust Sera, she had put down a blanket, which was the first kindness the dog had had from a person in a long time, maybe ever.

Now was Sera's chance.

She lifted the knife high overhead, ready to stab ferociously, but it didn't seem precise enough. She pointed the tip at the dog's soft belly, ready to plunge, but she was worried it would only wound it inevitably leading to her eviction. There was nothing for it. Sera would have to slit the dog's throat. A quick, clean *deep* cut. Fast and painless, she hoped.

There would be more blood. The blanket wouldn't survive. Unless... unless she washed it immediately after and kept it as a souvenir of sorts. Serial killers do that all the time. It could remind her of her mom and her first kill. She immediately dismissed the thought.

She really should have planned. It's possible, the blood could come out if she washed the blanket quickly once she disposed of the—*shit*. She hadn't really thought about that either. Thank God she'd decided to start with a dog.

What if she'd made this mistake with her first human victim, or The Bitch? She paused. Hm. She hadn't considered it before, but did she want The Bitch to be her first victim, or would it be better to start with someone else? There were pros and cons to both, but— The dog twitched beneath her, bringing her back to the matter at hand. She needed to kill this dog.

She grabbed its head from behind in what she imagined would be the easiest approach, giving her the most leverage with the knife. She leaned its head further back, revealing its throat.

Unbeknown to Sera, the dog's eyes opened. Strange, crusty, sleepy slits pulled wide by her grip. The dog considered its options but was still too groggy and too inexperienced to grasp the gravity of the situation. This could be what happens to most victims as they are nabbed on the street or in the woods late at night. If you don't understand the danger, you don't know that it's time to bite.

Sera pictured The Bitch and pressed the knife close against the dog's soft neck. She was filled with the thrill of her new path. The tip pressed into the dog's fur. It let out a small whimper. Sera pushed it further into the soft fluff, bracing herself for the terrible cry to come. Instead, she was met with silence.

She paused, feeling the dog's rhythmic breath. The blade eased up slightly, but she caught herself. She pushed the knife edge against the dog's skin. Again, there was the same small whimper followed by nothing.

Sera didn't know what to do. She'd imagined a strike too fast for a response. She'd imagined doggy howls and moans. She'd imagined thrashing and biting, but compliance, compliance shook her. She looked down and saw the dog's crusted eyes upside down and now wide open with terror, well, as open as they could be.

"Bite me," she ordered, harsh and insistent. "Bite me!" The dog stared with huge, concerned eyes. *It knows,* she thought. *I'm about to kill it, and it knows.*

This wasn't right.

The dog didn't deserve this, not the way The Bitch did. Not the way so many people did. She looked down at the dirty, mangy dog and decided it didn't deserve such an unceremonious death. She didn't decide not to kill it, but she decided she shouldn't let it die like this.

# Seven

Sera slumped back onto the couch. The first kill is always the hardest. A simple enough assertion. *Is that true?* Sera wondered as she stared down at the dog. Poor, decrepit dog. She could do this. She knew she could. She wasn't going to name it. Only a monster would kill their pet, and once you name it, it's a pet. But it did seem like she should be able to call it something until it passed. So, she called it 42. It wasn't a name. It was its kennel number. It would have been like calling Sera Iowa. Not a name. Though it did roll off the tongue a bit easier than someone's hometown might. It seemed like forever had passed while she watched 42 lying on the makeshift bed/death pyre.

Sera hadn't bought any of the supplies suggested to her since she wouldn't have the dog long at all. She had figured she'd have her for less than an hour. Now, minor murder attempt notwithstanding, she found the stress of abducting a victim was a bit more exhausting than she'd expected. She stared at the butcher knife, carefully centered on her messy coffee table. She nudged the handle, repositioning it slightly. 42 looked up at her. Eyes barely open. *Is she pretending to be asleep?* Sera thought and quickly dismissed it. As soon as she did, though, the dog opened her eyes and looked up as if she knew the jig was up. 42 looked at her expectantly. Sera stared back, getting the distinct impression that she knew exactly what the dog wanted—the couch. Sera sighed. It seemed rude not to let the dog on the couch since it was going to die soon and all, but it was filthy.

"Come on," she said and got up heading to the bathroom. Sera looked around her tiny apartment and realized the dog looked more like it belonged here than she cared to admit. The sink was full of dishes. The coffee table full of takeout and discarded life—unread books, magazine quizzes she took online instead, coasters that had never been used, and general depression.

She'd let it sit on the couch—why not? She found she was more comfortable with the idea of *it* than *the dog,* given its impending demise, but she wasn't going to let it sit on the couch smelling, and looking, like death. Into the tub, the dog went. She turned on the water, and soon 42 was splashing around like a maniac. It may be a lot younger than the one-thousand-years old that it looked.

Sera reached for her "cheap" shampoo, but kinda like a last meal, 42 really ought to get the proper stuff before being snuffed out. So, Sera grabbed her "fancy" shampoo instead. It cost twenty dollars a bottle, and she didn't use it every day. She knew many wouldn't call that fancy, but it was quite a jump from the dollar bottles of Suave that were her staple.

Peaches. A light summer scent wafted through the air as she dumped more and more shampoo onto 42. The dog was entirely composed of bubbles. Its tongue flicked out and licked great swaths of them. Immediately it made a face. Sera rinsed its mouth, then rinsed pounds of dirt from its fur and finally rinsed pounds of fur from its body before calling it good. The water drained slowly past thick clumps of fluff.

Sera wrapped 42 in a big beach towel. Now that all the caked crap was out of its eyes, and the fur was fluffed up rather than matted down, it looked just like a regular old dog. This didn't sit well with Sera, but a promise is a promise.

They sat on the couch, and Sera flipped on the TV, pulling her mom's blanket from the floor and up around herself. 42 snuggled deep into the blanket and pushed into Sera's side. Sera smiled in spite of herself. Quickly, she tamped it down. *Fucking idiot,* she thought. *This is your victim, not your pet. You can't even have animals! You don't even LIKE animals!*

A few minutes into some mindless rom-com, 42 began rubbing its eyes. Instinctively, Sera got up and found the eye drops.

She read aloud to 42. "Depending on the severity of the illness, administer two to four drops either every four hours or every eight." She rolled her eyes. "Super specific." She stood over the dog, wondering if she should kill it now or give it the eye drops. She kicked herself for not listening to that lady.

42 continued pawing at its eyes, and Sera's stomach rumbled.

It was like a light bulb turned on in Sera's mind. *The last meal!* That's why she felt so bad. Of course, she didn't want to kill the mangy mutt like this. It had suffered through a long string of animal shelter meals, and before that, who knew what it was eating? 42 wasn't long for this world, so this pupster should have a steak fit for a king. She knew exactly where they would get it. Maelini's. It's a hell of an expensive steak, but she figured it was the least she could do. After all, she was going to slash its throat. DoorDash to the (unlikely) rescue. She ordered a steak for her and one for 42. Then she returned to the eye drops.

She decided four drops every four hours for as long as the dog should live sounded fine. It might as well live pain free until she killed it. If the drops somehow did it in first, well, she wasn't above poison as a method of assassination. She held open its eye and raised the bottle. The parallels between her foiled knife attack and her medical pursuits were not lost on Sera. 42, however, seemed to think of them as entirely different things and squeezed its eyes shut and shook its head. Sera grabbed its head again, trying to pry the eyelids open. There was a low growl. Sera held its mouth shut with one hand and the eye open with the other, but she ran out of hands for the drops. She let go of the mouth and grabbed the bottle. 42 wriggled and squirmed until it broke free.

"Really, you're fine with the giant knife, but this is too much?" She snatched 42 up and forced its eye open and squeezed a drop out of the tube. 42 nipped at her hand. "Fucking mutt," she muttered. "Fine."

She wrapped her legs around all forty pounds of its body while holding its head back. The dog squiggled and wriggled its way free again. "Uh!" Sera cringed in annoyance at her wet clothes from wrestling the freshly bathed dog, but at least she smelled like peaches instead of sewer. Another attempt and another.

At this rate, she would most definitely run out of drops before she killed the stupid thing.

DING-DONG.

Sera sprang to her feet in shock and rushed to hide the evidence of her crime. *Fuck, fuck, fuck,* she thought, grabbing the butcher's knife. She realized she looked more guilty now than she had before. There was actually no crime to hide. *Shit.* She mentally scolded herself both for being stupid and for not having killed 42. She shook off the odd feeling she got when she thought about killing 42 and internally rephrased. She was an asshole for not having killed *it* yet. That was better.

DING-DONG

*Shit.*

She dropped the knife, which almost stabbed 42 in the back, but she swiftly kicked the dog out of the way. It gave a quick yelp.

Sera grumbled to herself, "Now I'm actively saving the dog. Idiot."

"Knock-knock. Everything okay in there?" A guy's voice came from the other side of the door.

"Yup. Totally fine, just dropped my knife." What the hell? Great. Now the delivery guy would be afraid of her.

Instead, he laughed. "That's a new one."

She opened the door and found him holding two steaks in a thermal bag. "Fit for a king," he said.

"That's what I thought," she replied, pleased.

He took in the scene around them: the old blanket with an older towel, the knife on the ground, half-empty eye drop bottle askew, and, finally, 42 wet and shaggy but clearly triumphant.

"New dog?"

"Something like that," she said.

"Want some help?"

She stared at him, confused. How could he possibly know she hadn't been able to do it? Even weirder, how could he possibly know that she was trying to *kill* it? And how was he *okay* with that?

"...with the eye drops?" he finished off her confusion.

The look flushed from her face.

"Oh! Yes, please! I can't hold her and do the drop things."

"I got it," he said, setting the steaks down to help.

Unfortunately, for all his confidence, he was actually worse at this than she was. He and 42 went through a few brief bouts of wrestling followed by 42 excitedly running around the living room. This was the closest 42 had ever come to play, and it was amazing. Sera chased as 42 dodged and weaved around the table and blanket. 42 started to think that maybe this place wouldn't be that bad after all. Sera wasn't so good with dogs, but she certainly seemed to be a black belt at playing. *Awesome.*

Soon it turned into a game of catch that 42 was decidedly winning, but on one sprint around the coffee table, she caught a sniff of the thermal bag and stopped in her tracks. Her tummy rumbled. She was so hungry she could taste the smell. It was delicious. Sera threw herself on the dog, tackling it and wrapping her legs around it again. She grabbed its mouth and forced one eye open.

"Now," she screamed, "now!"

The delivery guy adeptly squoze about twelve drops into the dog's eye.

"Other eye." She shifted her hands lightning quick, and he administered another healthy dose of the medicine.

For its part, 42 had moved on. The game no longer had her attention, so she hadn't been fighting. Instead, as they let her go, she sat perfectly still in front of the steak.

People always think they train dogs so well to sit and stay and do all these things, but really dogs are just showing their manners. Every dog knows it's polite to ask before you take someone else's food, and since very few dogs have jobs of their own, most are required to ask for food even if it's kibble. It's a large power imbalance. At some point someone should address it, but sadly, that point is not today.

"We did it!" The delivery guy practically cheered. "Unfortunately, I think your steaks are cold."

"I got them rare," she said. "I'll just pan fry them for a minute." She hesitated, and then, against her better judgment asked, "Want to stay?"

"Oh, no. You probably have someone coming over... for... the other steak. I wouldn't want to impose." But his eyes said he certainly did want to impose.

"That? That's for 42."

"42?"

"The mutt," she said. And that was that.

42 waited patiently for the bag's contents to be prepared. She didn't understand the hullabaloo. Everything smelled delicious already, but as the steaks hit the hot pan, she was pleased the humans had done it. The entire apartment filled with the

delicious scent. A drop of drool slid from 42's mouth onto the ground. Too late to catch it, she licked at her lips. It wouldn't do to be rude, but the people were chattering happily and hadn't seen her incivility. 42 chipped in with an occasional yip, which prompted Sera to swiftly turn up the TV.

"Careful, 42," she said, but she didn't say no, so she clearly wasn't as afraid as Sampson had said some humans were of sound. 42 made a smaller yip, which seemed like exactly the right amount of yip for the occasion in Sera's eyes. 42 made a mental note.

42 did not end up getting her own steak. Instead, she got giant chunks from both of their steaks and was able to sit with them on the couch. Having never had a steak before, this seemed like it was the normal arrangement. Steak was clearly a communal affair, and as she did not have opposable thumbs, someone had to cut her bites. She understood it. Left to her own devices, she didn't know if she would have been able to hold herself back long enough for everyone to have some.

They watched what Sera called a "very shitty rom-com," and 42 agreed with the assessment. This is not to say all rom-coms are shitty nor that dogs don't like rom-coms. 42 suspected she would very much love a good rom-com. Perhaps one where a dog brought two people together, and they all ate steak.

Soon, 42 fell asleep, chuffing and kicking her little legs, running in a dream where a thousand Frisbees flew through the air, and she was able to catch every single one.

# Eight

Sera awoke on her couch. 42 was snuggled in her arms like an over-sized plush football. *Oh God,* she thought and jumped up, *the delivery guy!* She scanned the apartment to find that not only had he not robbed her, but he had also left a note and locked the door behind him.

> *Thanks for the steak. Next time it's on me. 319-472-3983. Sorry to bail. Didn't want it to be weird in the morning. - Alex*

She picked up the remote to turn the TV off, but her finger lingered over the button. A row of three of the finest indie comedies streaming offered populated her Just Watched selections. After the first one, they'd laid off of the rom portion of the coms. None of the movies were great but making fun of them with Alex sure had been. She rolled his name around in her mouth. *Alex. Alllllllex*—the *l* felt smooth in her mouth. The *x* exotic in an invitingly childish way. She chewed on it for a second, *X, x, x.* She barely put any voice behind it. *I'm ridicu-*

*lous,* she thought, shaking her head to knock the foolishness away. *Just a random night. That's all.*

*A great night,* a voice from inside her corrected.

Sera clicked the TV off and picked up an empty pint of ice cream. Licked clean. Apparently 42 liked ice cream, too. For a moment, Sera was proud of herself. Not only had she made a connection with someone who did not seem to be an asshole, but she actually felt like herself. She felt *normal,* like the version of herself before she ever met The Bitch.

BAM-

Like a smack in the face, it all came crashing down. That stupid fucking Bitch. God! Why had she ever let herself get sucked into that chasm? As she started a truly impressive tirade of not just derogatory but damn near obliterating slurs directed squarely at herself, she heard whining. She involuntarily looked toward the door and found 42 doing a very urgent morning pee-pee dance.

Sera looped the sad-looking rope-leash around 42's head and took it outside. Although the dance had been quite urgent, once outside, 42 didn't seem to be able to select a suitable spot to relieve itself. As they paced back and forth on the small patch of grass, Sera's mind wandered.

Why had she allowed herself to fall in with The Bitch? She must have seen it coming. She had always had such strong gut reactions.

*That you ignore,* the voice in her head chided.

It wasn't wrong. Sera had practically made a study of teaching herself to ignore her inner impulses. Hanging out with friends, but they're doing something awful? No problem. Shut down the part of you that knows it's wrong. Doing something you're sure to regret in the morning? Just tell yourself that you won't do it next time. This time is a freebie. It doesn't even count. Friend making you feel like shit? *Anyone* making you feel like shit? No worries, it's probably just your imagination, or they're having a bad day, or their life was tough or, or, or—*Jesus, Sera. You don't even make them come up with their own excuses.* She hated herself, but most of the time she wasn't even sure what she hated herself for. Worst of all, she had to wonder—

Was it all The Bitch's fault?

Or...

No. Absolutely not. She was not going down that road. She'd done it a thousand times.

"It's not my fault," she said out loud, and 42 paused its sniffing to regard her with curiosity. Humans really did have too much going on in their brains *all the time.*

Sera didn't want to believe someone could be so awful, but—

But was The Bitch that awful? Was she?

The Bitch had systematically stripped Sera of her self-worth. She'd made her feel useless, stupid, weak, guilty, and worst of all, SELFISH. Sera had always thought of herself as a giving person, a caring person, a person that generally put others first most of the time, but she had been told in no uncertain terms that she was not only not that person but that she was the exact opposite. She was a greedy, selfish bitch. She was a narcissist.

Sera didn't think it could be true, but her mind couldn't help but return to it. She knew it didn't make sense. She looked back on her life, on all the times she sat with a crying friend, or even a crying stranger, and helped them. She thought about rides she'd given to people going miles out of her way. It seemed nice, but it also seemed like another way she'd let people she didn't even know walk all over her. The Bitch had changed her perception of herself, morphed the world and how she understood it. She took trust away from Sera.

*No, she didn't take it away,* Sera thought. *She threw a match on a pyre and burnt the shit to the ground. There's a lot of fucking trust required in every single day of our lives, and I have none left.*

"Jesus, 42. Just piss already," she barked. The dog looked up at her, and Sera saw that 42 had indeed pissed already. In fact, it had left quite an impressive pool of piss all over the sidewalk.

"Oh," she said. "Sorry." She felt chastised, though 42 clearly said nothing, which only fed into her guilt more. Was there something she should have done differently with The Bitch? Maybe if she'd stood up to her from the beginning, things wouldn't be like this? Maybe they'd be friends still? She looked at 42 and wondered how much of it was training. After all, Sera did train The Bitch to think she could get her way all the time. Every single time. Sera had trained her wrong...

But...*everyone else.*

No matter who it was, The Bitch somehow pulled the same strings. Sera had seen it before it happened to her. She hadn't understood how damaging it was. She'd seen friends come and go. Most of them had seemed to *want* to leave. Most of them had seen what this "friendship" really was, but even when they wanted to go, they slunk away with their tails between their legs, forever feeling smaller than they had before.

Sera was not going to feel small.

She looked down at 42 and knew she really did have to kill it.

She trudged back up to her apartment. Neighbors complimented her on her new pup in hushed tones and reminded her to hide it from their landlord. *It helps,* Sera thought, *all these people being nice.* But she questioned it too. Doubted it in the back of her mind. What was their angle?

Sera shut the door and sat 42 down on the towel. With the butcher knife in hand, she stared at 42. She willed herself to plunge the knife deep into the fur. She mentally pleaded with herself that this was the dog's entire purpose. Wasn't she putting it out of its misery? But bathed and fed, the dog no longer looked like it was on the brink of death. Sera plopped down next to 42. It was no good. Somewhere along the way,

42 had become a dog rather than an *it* and killing a dog seemed twisted.

*Seriously?* She was pissed at herself. It was the bath. The fucking bath and those damned eye drops. How could you care for an animal and then kill it?

Unfortunately, she knew better. Female serial killers actually had a long history of specifically killing those in their charge. In fact, most female killers killed those they cared for: patients, husbands, children. Somehow, Sera couldn't bring herself to do it. If she wasn't going to be a serial killer, there was nothing left. She looked at her reflection in the dull butcher's knife and had a come-to-Jesus moment. Even though she was fairly certain Jesus was just "some guy" and not "The Guy," she realized she was not "that kind" of serial killer. She was more of a tradesman. A craftsman.

In the arts, there are child prodigies, but there are many more artists that have to work and work to get to where they want to be. Some of those that struggle with the craft even become more prolific than the young talented ones. She hadn't put the time in. She wasn't a naturally talented killer. Of course she wasn't, but that didn't mean she couldn't still be an excellent killer. Who knows how many serial killers started out just like her, a woman with a dream? Or a man with a dream? *Damn. Seriously, is every profession dominated by men?* She grinned to herself, *No. Getting caught is dominated by men. Not killing.*

Serial killers that started at five by killing the neighbor's dog, well, those were prodigies. But serial killers that began later in life, perhaps when they were already adults, as was the case for her, were people that needed to labor at their craft. They couldn't kill a cuddly dog straight off. In fact, even most prodigies probably killed ants and beetles and all sorts of things that people didn't give a shit about long before they got to four-legged friends.

Sera had skipped a bunch of steps. No one gave a shit when you ripped the legs off of the eight-legged intruders in the basement, but it was still a transformational milestones. Yes, Sera was still becoming a serial killer, but she was going to start with a real mercy killing. Something that was already going to die. Something without fur.

42 whined softly, almost as if in protest, but when Sera looked over at it. She realized the dog's eyes had again begun to accumulate an impressive amount of goo. For a moment, she did want to kill the dog. It'd be easier than dealing with those damned eye drops again. She trudged back to the kitchen, where she traded the butcher knife for the medicine. The instant she picked the bottle up, 42 crouched into play position and darted around the couch.

Comparatively, murder would be a breeze.

# Nine

Sera sped down the highway in her hoopty of a Prius. She was on her way to nowhere. To the middle of it, to be exact, and she was going to get there fast. 42 sat in the passenger seat, blinking tears out of its eyes. They had come to an understanding about the eye drops. If Sera used about half a bottle, she was bound to get two to four drops in per eye. For her part, 42 struggled but did not bite. It was the least she could do, quite literally.

Sera was definitely going to have to go back for more medicine and probably read the other bottles the woman had given her. None of those seemed overwhelmingly important. In fact, one was just shampoo. She had shampoo already. She couldn't believe she'd been duped into paying for that. She shrugged. An outlandish animal donation seemed more than fair, given she had planned on killing the dog they had entrusted to her.

What was she going to do with the mutt now?

42's tongue hung out of her mouth, whapping the side of her head as the wind pummeled her. This is amazing, 42 thought. She had seen dogs do this but had never guessed she'd get to do it herself. It was a day of firsts for 42 and all of them were good, like the peanut butter she'd had for breakfast. If she could, she would ask for peanut butter for every meal. Unfortunately, she had begun to believe that people really couldn't understand Dogese. She wasn't 100 percent sure because Sampson had seemed to think people could understand them too, and so far, he had been pretty spot-on about everything. Previously, 42 thought people chose to ignore her because they thought she was below their station. She was aware that people were pretty classist and downright self-centered most of the time, so it tracked.

However, Sera didn't seem to have much class. She was definitely talking to 42 (fairly nonstop, actually), and she still didn't understand a bark 42 was saying. This was hardly the biggest of 42's concerns though. So, whenever there was a sad lull in the conversation, 42 simply offered a bark of reassurance. This seemed to reinvigorate Sera's talking, so 42 knew she was on to something.

In the outskirts of town, farms began to spring up. Mostly cornfields, but livestock roamed freely too. Soon, Sera came to the farm she was looking for. The Durmonts' place. They had a steady stream of pigs they set aside, raised, and slaughtered specifically for rich locals. It seemed a strange luxury because anyone can get pork from the grocer or butcher, but as with all things, if there's a VIP version, someone will pay for it.

She slowed as they approached the farm. Cattle roamed the open field, and Sera realized they must have expanded their operation. Still, near the farmhouse, she could see the corral full of maybe a dozen pigs. It was a large, enclosed square space. Nothing special really, but the pigs inside all seemed to hold their heads high. They weren't big for prize pigs, certainly, not compared to a normal pig meant for the butcher. She'd put the biggest at maybe 150 pounds.

"I guess the more you pay, the less you get," Sera said aloud, without realizing it. "Sounds about right." 42 waited for a moment, then barked agreement. She didn't know what she was agreeing to, exactly, but Sera sounded far more reasonable than she usually did. 42 hoped she was agreeing to something delicious or fun. She looked excitedly out the window. This would be an excellent place for Frisbee. She was sure of it, but Sera didn't pull over. Instead, she cruised past in the country version of what would make city folk look up for fear of a drive-by. She held her finger-gun out the window, took aim at the corral, and shot. *Easy as pigs in a barrel*, she thought, as the farm receded from sight.

They would have to wait for dark to abduct and murder their first victim.

"We have an errand to run, but first, lunch!" she said to 42, who perked up at the thought of another jar of peanut butter. She was glad it was going to be something delicious. There would be time for fun later.

· · · · ● · ● · ● · · ·

Sera had 42 jump into the booth opposite her yet again. It was trying her patience. It seemed to think it should sit right next to Sera, which led to a repetitive game of "No, 42. You stay over here. Stay. Stay. Good. No, 42. Stay. Stay there." This was another game 42 immediately loved that Sera could have done without.

"Miss, you can't have your dog in here," the server said as she walked up.

"Why not?" Since when did her farm town care about animals in restaurants?

"Boss says it's only for paying customers, and he ain't cleaning up after no dog."

"It's cleaner than most of the people in here," Sera said, nodding toward a man that looked like he'd rolled in dog shit moments before coming in. His was a pungent eau de poo-poo. "And it *is* a paying customer," Sera said. She hadn't quite come around to calling 42 a dog yet. She had residual objectification issues that were still working themselves out from her attempted murder of 42. 42 didn't mind. She also didn't know.

"All right. But you're gonna have to get that dog the works," the server said.

"Great. It will take two pork chops, a large Coke, and some garlic mashed potatoes." Sera said.

"Garlic will kill a dog," the server replied.

"It will?"

"Yup. Garlic, onions, grapes, raisins, chocolate." Sera stared at her blankly. "You're new to this whole dog thing, aren't you?" asked the server.

"What about fries?" Sera asked.

The server nodded. "And for you?"

"I'll have a bowl of water and a BLT. We're on a pig kick."

The server gave Sera a patented I-don't-give-a-shit-but-I-like-tips smile and walked away.

Sera looked at 42. "You are so easy to kill, and I couldn't do it. If I'd just ordered grilled onions with our steaks or had chocolate ice cream, I'd have killed you by accident. I am not shaping up to be a very fine serial killer at all. Not at all."

A middle-aged man from the next booth overheard this and joined in on her joke. "Nice day for a murder, isn't it?"

She smiled. "Yes, sir, it is."

42 cocked her head to the side and let her tongue dangle happily out of her mouth. It was a good day.

# TEN

Full of as much pork as they could eat, Sera and 42 strode into a hunting goods store. Sera needed a sturdy knife. She barely trusted her butcher knife when it was up against 42. She certainly didn't trust it against pig hide. In the back of her mind, she kept having this nagging feeling that she really ought to be planning better, but it hardly seemed necessary for a pig. She felt her wallet and sighed in relief at the thickness. She definitely had cash on her. That was good. She shouldn't leave an electronic trail if she could help it, and as it turned out, she could. They would quickly get a big ol' already-sharp knife and be gone before anyone even noticed them.

42 had other things on her mind though. She was in scent heaven. Her ears perked up to full-mast, and her nose tugged her this way and that. There were all sorts of conflicting man-made and nature-made smells. There were leather smells and shoe smells, hunting smells and gun smells. There was even a worms-in-the-dirt smell. It made no sense. As they walked past the bait stand, 42 planted her feet, refusing to go any further. It wasn't her fault. She sniffed the air and noted a robust earthy scent, but when she sniffed the ground, it was

cold polished concrete. She sniffed again. Maybe her sniffer was off?

"42, come on," Sera said, tugging lightly on the rope-leash. She knew she should get an actual leash at some point, but now was not that point. She didn't want to yank though, not because she didn't want to choke 42, no. She'd almost killed 42 mere hours ago, she assured herself. She was not concerned about a rough yank. She was on her way to becoming a cold, hard killer. She just didn't want to attract any attention. That was it. Hunters may not give a shit about elk, but they sure the fuck love their dogs.

A man pushed past Sera, sending her elbow hard into the counter's corner. She cringed and grabbed her funny bone, stopping herself from speaking up. *You don't want them to see you,* she reminded herself, but she shot daggers at his back, irked that he hadn't even glanced her way.

"It's like you're invisible," The Bitch had said once while they were out shopping.

It was a fancy store. Far too posh for the poly-blend hiking shorts and sneakers Sera was wearing. They were supposed to be halfway through a hike by now, but when Sera had arrived to pick her up, The Bitch insisted they "drop by" a store "real quick."

"Of course, we're still going hiking," The Bitch said in her wedge sandals and bright white top. "You don't need to change. It won't take five minutes."

They weren't going hiking. Sera knew it. The Bitch had changed her mind, but Sera didn't want a fight. She never wanted a fight. What was the point? She knew she'd go to the store anyway. Why bother?

Now, she wished she'd argued though. She wished she'd argued every damn time.

"They can help me," The Bitch said, standing defiantly in the dressing room. "You don't work here. You have to stop letting people push you around. Go grab me someone. Quick," she said, shooing Sera toward an employee without the decency of even noticing the irony. "Her."

"Excuse me," Sera said softly, raising her hand in the air as the woman rushed past. Her heart pounded in her chest harder than it should. She felt ludicrous asking for help she didn't need, but The Bitch was right. She needed to stop letting people push her around.

"Get her," The Bitch urged, but another clerk dashed past without glancing at Sera, knocking her hard into the wall.

"Shit," Sera said, grabbing her elbow. It stung. It stung more than the hit should have, but that's how some injuries are. They just hurt more.

"It's like you're invisible," The Bitch said happily. "Don't look at me like that. It's a compliment. You can blend into the background of any room. Everyone says so. It's like your superpower. I wish I could do it, but people always see me. Besides, it's not like you want to be a model or an actor or something. It's good you don't want one of those 'pretty people' jobs. Not 'cause you're not pretty, I mean—" The Bitch motioned to Sera's entire being in that supremely derogatory and dismissive way that she had mastered without thought. "You know." The Bitch finished by shrugging away any opinions Sera might have on the matter.

Sera wanted to say something. She did. She knew she should, but what was she supposed to say? What would have saved Sera's self-esteem and also not started a fight? She watched the looks on the employees' faces as they steered clear of her.

"I didn't know we'd be shopping," Sera said, glancing at her outfit possibly as an admission of guilt, or worse, as an apology?

The Bitch tightened up. Her energy shifted to defense as if chastising Sera with a short *This isn't my fault*. She didn't say that though. Even mentioning that it could be construed as her fault would be far more responsibility than she was ever going to take. Instead, she recovered and redirected.

"Please. Rich people all dress like trash," she said, passing her insult off as a compliment. "The worst dressed people are the richest people. Look at me." She posed for Sera to admire how poor she looked even though she'd obviously dressed up for this outing. "It's you. You're forgettable. Don't worry about it. It's okay that you can't grab them. Fetch me a size smaller," The Bitch said, turning and disappearing back into the dressing room without waiting for confirmation. Sera would do what she was told. Of course, she would.

"Fucking mutt," the man across the sporting goods store cussed at his dog, pulling Sera from her thoughts. She rubbed her still smarting elbow and watched as he considered, then decided that, yes, it was a good idea to kick his dog.

"Asshole," she muttered, scowling at him. She thought it was residual anger at the thought of The Bitch, or at him hurting her elbow, but no, she realized, it was a new anger bubbling up against a man who would kick his clearly complacent dog.

*Fucking asshole.*

"Kick that damn dog again, and I'll kick you, Clive," a gruff voice from behind the counter growled.

The man, evidently Clive, looked sheepishly back before grumbling an embarrassed "Sorry." He wasn't sorry he'd kicked the dog though. He was sorry he got caught.

"Guys like that shouldn't have dogs. Getting 'em for the hunt but not wanting 'em the rest the year." The clerk motioned like he was spitting on the ground, confirming his disgust. "Nice leash."

Sera had the good sense to look abashed herself, but then realized he was genuinely pleased with it. He had a no-nonsense look that spoke volumes. People shouldn't spend money on things they didn't need, and a leash wasn't a necessity if you had a perfectly good rope.

"It's the dirt," he said, but it came out like *is the dirt.*

"What?" Sera asked.

"Dog's smelling dirt for the worms." He nodded down at 42, with her snout high in the air, and opened up the worm box. He reached his hand in and lifted out a clump of dirt and worms. He held it in front of 42 for her to sniff, and sniff she did.

42 breathed in the cold, fresh earth and the squiggly brown buggers. That was the good stuff. The scent stirred something in her. It was somehow both invigorating and calming. She sniffed again deeply, and her tongue lolled out of her mouth. *Oh yeah, this is the life!*

"Good Girl." The man patted her head with his free hand, bringing an even bigger smile to 42's face. "Need worms?" he asked Sera, already dropping the handful back into the bin. He knew better, but it was only polite to ask.

"A hunting knife," Sera said defiantly. She could be here for worms. He leaned back and took a second to reassess her. The goal was in and out without talking to anyone, certainly without bringing attention to herself. What was she doing? Making a silent case for feminism in a hunting goods store was not the way to go unnoticed. "It's a gift," she quickly covered, but he did not reassess her a second time.

"Huntin' or protectin'?" the man asked, not completely dismissing his first impression. He'd seen the truth of her. She was tougher than she looked but not by choice.

*Please let me be forgettable,* Sera thought, hoping against all odds that The Bitch was right this one time, but the sheer act of hoping for The Bitch to be right struck her wrong. *I'm not invisible,* Sera thought, squaring her shoulders imperceptibly to get a little bigger.

"Hunting," she said resolutely. Invisibility would be better right now, but her body raged against everything The Bitch had ever said.

The clerk stepped a few feet over to the knife counter. 42 immediately followed him behind the counter. Sera considered pulling 42 back, but he didn't seem to mind. He reached under the glass, pulling out a few knives. His hand wavered over a particularly large one before he dismissed it, glancing down at her hands.

"Know what you're looking for? Fixed, folding, buck, Bowie?"

"Bowie," she said, jumping at the only hunting knife she knew. He reached under the counter again, and Sera found herself hoping it wasn't a folding blade. She had no desire to accidentally cut her fingers off. Luckily, it wasn't.

He pulled out a red leather handled blade.

"8-inch blade. Good grip. Works well in smaller hands," he said. Sera shot him a look, but he didn't flinch. "You don't want to be out there struggling to grip a knife 'cause you wanted to feel bigger than you are."

"It's a gift," she reminded him.

"They bigger'n you?" he asked, eyebrows raised. It wasn't a gift. She could keep her fantasy if she wanted. He had a daughter. A woman should know how to use a knife, but he wasn't going to worry about this city girl stabbing herself because she didn't want to hear she had small hands.

"Not much," she said.

"It's a good one." Again, it came out *is a good one*. He petted 42 lightly as he spoke, and she lapped it up. 42 didn't trust a lot of people, but this guy, he was good people.

Sera didn't doubt him. The knife did look like "a good one," but she was a bit more wary than 42. He had a confidence about him that made Sera both comfortable and uncomfortable. He seemed safe. Like he knew things she didn't. So, what was so off-putting?

*Jealousy!* It sprung to her like a bolt of inspiration, but the happiness that accompanied the realization quickly morphed to self-loathing. *Shit. Why the shit am I jealous of him?* She watched his smooth movements as he pulled another knife from under the counter. *Weird,* she thought, but it wasn't weird. It wasn't weird at all because he did know something she didn't. He knew himself. Of course she was jealous. She was the one person she'd been missing for years.

"If you need a second choice." He laid another Bowie knife down. "This one ain't half bad."

"But the first—"

"Is better," he confirmed with a tilt of his head. He didn't waste movements.

Sera lifted the blade. The leather. The balance. The weight. It felt good. Smooth, but easy to grip. Long and sharp. She took a deep breath in.

Her instincts hadn't completely abandoned her.

This was it.

42 watched Sera intently and mimicked her sniffing the air in short, fast whiffs. She wondered what Sera was smelling, but it wasn't something 42 could detect. She was certain she had a better sense of smell than Sera did, but still. Even when she breathed in as hard as she could, 42 couldn't smell anything other than all the delectable scents she'd already investigated. *Huh*.

Sera wasn't smelling so much as ingesting. She breathed the knife in like a piece of her long, dormant strength coming back to her.

"I'll take it," she chirped suddenly, drawing a curious kind of look from the man helping her. He couldn't help but soften at her open joy. He hoped she never had to use it, but if she did... He knew a good knife, and that was, in fact, a good one. She'd be okay.

# Eleven

Sera and 42 parked about a mile up the road from the Durmonts' turnoff. She could see the farmhouse across the flat land and the pigpen in front of it. If she'd timed this right, and she thought she had, then the family would be away at the county fair showing their prize cows. Still, it was important for her not to overplay her hand. She needed to be not just careful, but certain. It wouldn't do any good to get picked up for killing a pig when what she wanted to do was slaughter The Bitch.

The sun crept past midday and began to swing low in the west. It had been hours, and no one had gone in or out of the house yet. The pigs were sitting ducks. Few trucks lumbered past on the old highway, but Sera planned to wait until dark. She needed the cover of night to protect her from prying eyes and to allow her the time she needed just in case. Catching a pig and slitting its throat was no easy task. Catching a pig definitely wasn't an easy task; she'd been to enough fairs to guess that. And the skin was clearly going to be as tough as leather, making both stages of the plan difficult and unpredictable.

Sera rubbed her elbow, surprised it still hurt, and wondered if The Bitch considered herself one of the "pretty people." At the time, Sera had assumed The Bitch counted herself among the lucky few, but she suspected the truth was far more complicated. Perhaps, Mondays and Tuesdays she was among the pretty people, Wednesdays and Thursdays she was average, and the rest of the week maybe she might as well have been 42 when Sera first found her huddled in that cement cage.

Sera smiled at the thought and didn't notice that 42 leaned slightly away from her, not quite cowering, but certainly a far cry from comfortable. Sera's eyes focused on the door of the house. She silently willed someone to come outside. *I could start with a pig,* she thought, *or I could go straight for gold.* The world around her disappeared. There was only her, the stillness of the car, and the possibility of a victim coming out of that house.

The wind stirred, kicking up old chimes hanging from the porch. Sera startled as if she could hear them from a mile away. It was dark. Hours had passed. She was ready.

She was certain the house was empty and even more certain that she would be able to strike anyone that happened to surprise her with a swift and deadly swipe of her knife. *Being alive felt great.* She smirked at the ironic thought that snuffing out someone else's life force would make her feel more alive. Even the idea of life force made her smile. She didn't believe in that hogwash. Never had. But, on the precipice of her first murder, she realized the idea that an ancient warrior could harness the power of an enemy they had slain made perfect sense. You didn't steal some inner energy they had. Instead, you awoke a power that was locked away in yourself. There was likely no rush on earth like that of killing another. Similarly, there was likely no rush on earth like being faced with your own murder, but she didn't have to focus on that side of the equation. She was the hunter. She would never be prey again.

Night had fallen. Sera's car crept slowly up an access road behind the Durmonts' farm. Shingles needed replacing, and it'd been more than one season since the house had been painted. She remembered the shade of falling sky blue from when she had lived at her grandma's. Old Man Durmont had systematically run all the other pig farmers out of the area. While he kept this pristine pig patch for rich clients to select prize pigs from, he had a far more lucrative pig farm a few miles up the road.

It was the standard big-pork company that one expected. The kill floor was automated. The pigs couldn't turn left or right but stared straight at their troughs all day. They were enticed to eat constantly, and eat they did. Sera could have gone there instead. The pigs were all but hog-tied already, and a single pig missing would not sound any alarms. She told herself that it was smarter to attack here. At the big business, there might be security cameras or security guards, but she didn't believe that. No, she wanted them to know that they had been attacked.

Maybe she wanted her first kill on record. Maybe she wanted the small-town infamy that was bound to come from the senseless slaughter of a farmer's pig. Or maybe, she wanted to hit the Durmonts where it hurt and let them know that someone could fuck with them. They had strangled this whole town into submission, but someone could still go on a limb and fuck with them.

A shiver ran down her spine as she realized old wounds still festered.

She let the feeling pass, then started her car and drove the mile along the main road, watching carefully for other cars. There were none. She turned off her headlights and pulled onto the Durmonts' access road. She drove slowly, keeping noise to a minimum as she hummed "Uptown Girl" softly to herself. Dust kicked up around the car and combined with Sera's humming to fill 42 with sleepy excitement. It was way past her bedtime, but any place with this much dirt had to be awesome.

The cloak of night swallowed Sera's car even before the dust settled. She pulled off into a patch of bushes and parked further camouflaging her car from the road. Straight ahead, she could see the pigs who were blissfully unaware of the danger they were in.

She studied the layout, looking for her best approach. The pen wasn't large, but by food-pig standards, especially when compared to the Durmonts' other pig farm, it was huge. It was a square about 30 feet by 30 feet with three troughs full of constant feed along one side and a long watering station against the connecting fence. The constant water turned the entire pen into varying degrees of a mud pit.

Across from the food was the latch gate, but it hardly mattered. The rail-style fence was handmade with long horizontal logs locking into posts about four feet high. Separated by about eight inches each, the rails looked sturdy, which would make the fence easy to climb for any person, but impassable for a pig. The age of the wood gave the whole thing a natural feeling that was entirely unnatural. Sera considered the sorry state of animals that could so easily be contained. She had never before appreciated her hands and opposable thumbs so damn much. People were lucky.

*Poor fucking pigs.*

The pigs moved in a weird rhythm all their own. The group sort of thrived together in ebbs and flows as one pig moved to the trough and another to the water. One rolled in the mud, while another scratched its rump on a stump just off-center in the pen. It culminated in a surreal sort of benign choreography. The Porkcracker, or some ballet long forgotten, and possibly for good reason. Still, it put Sera in a sort of trance. She told herself she was finding their rhythm, but she was helpless against the transformative powers of the damn pigs. At long last, she looked at 42, who was fast asleep in the passenger seat. She quietly eased her door open and shut again. *All the better,* she thought. *42 shouldn't have to see this.* She also had no idea what she'd do with 42 while she was busy with the pigs anyhow. Problem solved.

Sera crept away from the car, cringing at the cacophony of sound that erupted from her every movement. She stepped. A twig snapped. She crouched, watching the pigs and waiting. An eternity passed as she ogled the pigs, making sure, but they never looked. They never suspected a thing. She tried to mock herself for this drastic bit of over-caution, but she couldn't do it. They were pigs. She knew they were pigs, and they were FARM PIGS. No person walking up to their pen was going to set off alarm bells for them. Still, she couldn't shake the need to exercise caution. They wouldn't know what had hit them until it was far too late. She *knew* that. That was the point of livestock, right? Docile and easy to kill. She'd heard pigs were smart though. How smart? She didn't know, but no matter how many times she told herself to walk faster or stop freezing when she made a sound, she couldn't do it.

As she closed the gap between her and her prey, she realized she was enjoying the hunt. She wanted to sneak up on them. She wanted to feel the rush of them, realizing some awful end was coming. She hoped that they would sense her deadly intent and squeal. She hoped she could savor the dawning of comprehension as the light drained from the pig's eyes.

She wasn't being cautious. She was savoring.

She stepped up to the wood gate and reached for the latch. A pig raised its head and looked at her. She stepped inside the corral, and all hell broke loose. The pig that had looked at her did squeal. It squealed so loud Sera's hands shot to her ears, protecting her from the sound. On cue, all the other pigs ran. Their coordinated animal farm ballet was dashed. Mud flew into the air. Pigs darted this way and that. Sera spotted a small one and ran for it. A trough fell over, clipping Sera's leg. She pulled her foot out of harm's way before it crashed down, but she'd have a designer bruise where it had grazed her thigh. She leapt towards the piglet. Her arms wrapped around its warm, pink body, but it wriggled and kicked its way free. Her arms and shoulders already ached from the attack. She grabbed again at another pig, focusing on holding the legs, but it squirmed from her grasp. The mud gave the pigs a definite advantage.

Sera darted this way and that. Exhaustion quickly set in. How did cowboys do this? It must be those damn ropes. For half a second, she considered going to the car for 42's rope, but this moment of hesitation gave the pigs all the opportunity they needed. The largest pig careened forward, pummeling Sera in the gut with its entire body. She swung madly with the knife but came up short. The pig rounded the pen, and the other pigs immediately cleared a path. This pig knew what it was doing. More than that, the other pigs knew what this pig was doing.

This pig was their leader.

*Is that possible?* It was. Sera *knew* it was. She took all this in and broadened her stance. This was not what she had in mind for her first murder, but a good serial killer rolls with the punches. Sera raised the knife above her head, glad the leather handle offered the superior grip it promised. The pig wheeled on her and flew towards her, kicking mud up in its wake. Sera braced herself and brought the knife down hard. The pig head-butted her with a force she didn't know was possible. The knife crashed into the pig's back, but instead of Sera stabbing it with all her might, the knife dug into it as a side effect of Sera curling in on herself as her ribs gave way under the pig's blow.

All the pigs stopped and stared at their injured ruler. Then a horrendous collective cry pierced the night. This was not the squeal of non-sentient beings. This was the death cry of a community losing one of their beloved. Sera tried to regain her footing, but she couldn't find the strength to stand. The screams assailed her ears, a damning accusation. A damning cry of guilt. Sera was not accused. She was tried and convicted. There was no court in the land that would see the aftermath of this situation and see her as anything but a monster.

The pig, the leader, lay on its side in silence. Sera was afraid to look as the shrieks of its kinsmen pierced her heart. What had made her think killing a pig would be blameless? Of course they were bound to die, but they didn't know that. She crawled through the mud to its side. The turned-up ground became a war-torn battlefield in her mind. She put her hand on the pig's chest. Still warm. She raised herself to her knees, wincing as her body unfolded from around her injured ribs. She reached for the knife and saw the pig's chest rise and fall. Rise and fall. The blade had tumbled to the ground, and blood dripped onto the mud. It wasn't nearly as much blood as she'd expected. The rise and fall of its chest. The rise and fall. She paused. The shrieks had ceased. A silence fell. Each pig leaned forward, looking onto the grisly crime scene, hoping their attacker would become their savior.

She saw the wound. Two inches by two inches and barely bleeding. Confused, she looked to the other pigs for an answer, and suddenly, the pig sprang up from the mud. Rising to its full height, it knocked Sera down again. This time she screamed. She screamed and scrambled, forcing herself to her feet, biting on the searing pain, and jumping over the wood fence. She heard barking and howling coming to her from a distance. She turned. Her car shook as 42 clawed and gnashed its teeth, trying with all its might to get to her, to help her. "I'm okay," she yelled without conviction. "It's okay, 42. It's okay." 42 knew better though and continued scratching and howling into the night.

Behind her, Sera saw the pigs gathered around their ruler. It was unlikely the pig was fatally injured, but it was again lying on its side. The other pigs looked to her expectantly. *You did this,* their eyes said. *Help us. Help him.*

"Shit." Sera grabbed her side as she hobbled back to her car. The clan of pigs stared after her accusingly.

She pulled open the car door and 42 hurled itself into the night ready to attack whatever predator had come to disturb their serenity. Sera knew she was that predator.

"It's okay," she cooed. "It's okay. Get in the car. 42. In." Then her voice rose, losing patience. "42, get in the car!" 42 tucked its tail and jumped inside, still wary of the evil lurking somewhere up the farm road.

Sera turned on the car and, instead of kicking it into reverse and getting the hell out of there like she knew she should, she drove forward. These animals shouldn't die because of something The Bitch did. She understood that now. So, she resolved to save them. In the distance, a cow mooed, and she realized she would have to save them too.

She backed her car up to the pigpen. Each breath hurt, but she climbed out and laid the back seats down. Now, all she had to do was get the injured pig in the car.

She opened the gate leading straight to her hatchback, but none of the pigs moved. They didn't investigate the car, and they didn't walk past it into the great unknown beyond.

Sera tried to lift the pig, but it was a heavy son of a...another pig. She suspected none of these animals deserved to be lumped in with The Bitch even in a colloquially meaningless saying. *Fuck*. She kicked at the pigpen, breaking off parts of the fence. 42 pranced around through the mud, inspecting the other pigs and determining that whoever the predator had been, they had obviously left. These pigs were both calm and smelled like an enchanting mix of mud, pig shit, and straw. 42 rolled on the ground, coming up near THE pig. Instantly, 42 knew something was wrong. Her frolicking ceased, and she laid down next to the pig, keeping it company. This pig needed someone right about now.

Sera used the boards she'd wrenched from the pen to make a wobbly ramp. Now, she had to figure out how to get the pig up it. She rooted around in the foot-wells in the back seat and came up with a crusty old beach towel. It had been years since she'd gone to the quarry. She hadn't been there since she and— Not now. She turned back and laid the towel on the ground. With all her might, she pushed on the pig, trying to roll it onto the towel. 42 joined in, offering more moral support than actual muscle. Then, low and behold, the pig itself rolled over as if it were a trained house pet. Then it laid on the towel and moaned. Sera couldn't be sure, but the moans seemed slightly put on. They were far from the horrified squeals of earlier, and she wondered if a pig could ham it up.

She grabbed the towel and pulled, her ribs burning with pain. There was no way. There was absolutely no way she was going to be able to get this pig up those beams. But then, the piglet stood up and walked up the ramp. It sat down inside the Prius and looked back at its community. It oinked a few times, and a ripple of understanding seemed to move through the drift of pigs. Sera yanked on the towel again, but this time a pig joined her efforts, pushing from behind, then another and another. When one would tire, another would push. *This can't be happening,* Sera thought as she awkwardly backed herself up the ramp and into the hatchback, still pulling on the towel, but it was happening. The pigs pushed while Sera pulled until the big pig landed in the car with a thump. Then all the other pigs followed up the planks behind.

Sera jumped out the back door and counted as every one of the ten pigs pushed their way into her small car. She hadn't intended to create a clown car of pigs, but she didn't have the strength to get them out. The tires sunk into the mud, but the car didn't give. 42 jumped into the passenger seat and barked twice. "Let's go!" 42 seemed to say, and Sera looked at her, her heart melting from the camaraderie, because in that moment 42 became the puppy she had always been, the puppy Sera had refused to see. Sera had done an objectively awful thing, but this dog was looking at her with love. Sera nodded. "All right, girl. Let's go."

The car groaned under the weight, threatening not to move. The mud might be too much, but Sera gave the gas pedal a slow and pleading push. She'd driven in snow. Slow and steady wins the race. She just needed the tires to grab hold.

"Please move. Please," she begged the car, and it decided to comply.

They drove up the road, and not one of them was surprised when Sera stopped at the gate to the cow fields and opened them wide. She didn't know where the cows would go or if they could get far, but she had to let them try.

The pigs all squealed, possibly in delight, 42 barked, and as they pulled away, Sera saw the cows beginning to trundle toward the opening.

# TWELVE

"Come on. Come on," Sera said aloud as her car bumped and trundled along. Prii are by no means zippy vehicles. Their impressive gas mileage leaves precious little space for all the horsepower that Americans of generations past, or farming communities present, adore. As such, Sera's one-horse Prius struggled to reach and then maintain the highway speed. She felt quite proud of herself when she got to the unimpressive 65 miles per hour the signs heralded as the limit.

A pig butt hit her in the back of the head, not for the first time, and not for the last.

"Excuse you," Sera said, and the pig farted in reply. "Ugh! Really?" She rolled down her window but dared not roll down the others. After all they'd been through, the last thing she needed was a pig trying to fly and falling to its death. Also, 42 was so excited at the prospect of everything, that Sera had no doubts the dog would immediately launch on an exploration of wind that might lead to her demise.

The smell was awful, not just the fart, but the pigs in general. However, the comradery was impressive. Never had Sera considered filling her entire car with livestock, but if she had she could not have imagined better results. Except for the slight stabbing, they were all doing quite well. Sera looked in the mirror. The pig leader laid in a heap in the middle of all the others. The other pigs nestled together in a close-knit circle. Three were in the foot wells with their friends, basically standing on their heads, but none of them seemed to mind. She was lucky the pigs weren't all as big as their Big Kahuna.

Sera had no idea what she was doing. She was racing toward a vet's office, but she didn't know how she would explain the injured pig, and her ribs were killing her. Even worse, she doubted that a pig vet was cheap, and a pig vet that had to give stitches, or more likely perform surgery, was likely to be drastically beyond her means. Also, she expected when the adrenaline of trying to save her first victim's life had worn off, she might pass out from pain.

The frigid air helped not just with the fart, but with keeping her focused and alert. All she wanted to do was pull over and rest her battered body. *You brought this on yourself,* she thought. She scoffed at herself and shook her head as if talking aloud. 42 cocked her head and then licked Sera's cheek. This human was indeed a sad sack.

Sera pulled up to the vet clinic and climbed clumsily out of her car. Half hunched over but trying to be the bigger person, Sera pressed on. She sighed heavily. How the hell was she going to get the pig *inside* the clinic? She opened the back door and slumped against the car. She needed a second to figure out her options. She should have brought the wood planks, but as soon as the door was open, an unfurling of pigs began. Each climbed out and down the others, using their brethren as a sort of pig ramp. Sera couldn't help but laugh. *What the fuck with these pigs?*

Finally, a path was cleared for the injured pig. It was the moment of truth, and a lot of truth was revealed as the pig stood up, climbed down the pigs that had remained in the foot wells, and stepped out onto the pavement. Sera's mouth hung open as the pig looked back, and the utility-stepping pigs oinked in some way that was informative to the injured pig, who then turned toward the building. Sera didn't understand how, but somehow this made it clear to her that those two pigs were planning to stay in the car.

"Here, piggies. Here pig-pigs," Sera cooed, trying to cajole them out, but they didn't budge. It seemed smarter to stay together, but her ribs hurt too badly to argue, and frankly, these pigs could take care of themselves. Her car would never smell the same again anyway. So, what did it matter? She was glad she hadn't rolled up her window, so she didn't have to try and sit back in the car to crack one for their safety. She shut the door and was surprised to find all the pigs and 42 awaiting her next move. They seemed to know what to do better than she did, but fine, Sera took the lead.

They were quite a sight. Sera, hunched over and afraid to look at her ribs for fear of bruising, staggered into the clinic, leading 42, covered in mud and pig shit, and a line of eight pigs that were equally filthy. The pigs sniffed the air, ground, other animals, and people just as much as 42 did. The people did not appreciate it.

The injured pig, undeterred by the intoxicating scents, walked straight up to the desk, doing perfectly well, and then flopped down onto its side, exposing his wounded shoulder. Sera tried to look sheepish, but in that moment, she wished she had killed the damn thing after all. How dare a pig make her look so bad? *They were all going to die, and then I brought them here*, she wanted to scream.

"I think I killed a pig," is what she landed on instead.

The receptionist recoiled instinctively at the sight (or smell) of Sera, and Sera gleaned that she was covered in as much mud and pig shit as 42 was. The receptionist collected her courage, and held her breath, before leaning forward to glance down at the pig on the floor with a very dubious look. It was abundantly obvious that she did not share Sera's concern.

"We have to see the vet, now," Sera asserted with as much strength as she could muster.

The receptionist raised an unconvinced eyebrow, but she was concerned enough about the many pigs that were still alive and dirty as hell to agree that Sera and her entourage should go next. All the patients seconded the decision with approving nods. This might have been because the sight was so strange, and it might have been because the smell was so bad. Sera thought she saw at least one plugged nose. In either case, Sera, 42, and the pig clan went right in.

"Right this way," the receptionist said, leading Sera's crew around the desk and toward the back. The pig rose from the ground and followed confidently, never wavering on its feet. When they reached the scale, it ceremoniously fell on its side again. This was no accident. Weak from pain, Sera didn't have the capacity to process it, but she instinctively knew something was up. After being weighed, the pig walked on toward the exam room. Following him, each pig climbed onto the scale, plopped on their side, stood, and walked on. No one was taking the weights of the subsequent pigs, but if someone had been, they would be amazed at how well that little Prius had held up under all that pork.

The pigs filled the small examination room pretty completely. They intently sniffed each nook and cranny. Luckily, they left the chairs open, so Sera plopped onto one. 42, after watching Sera, jumped onto her own. She decided to leave the investigation to the pigs. This was clearly a serious room, and 42 could be a serious dog when needed.

Sera briefly wondered if the vet was going to pull down the metal table that was built into the wall and try to get the pig to climb onto it. *The pig will probably jump right up,* Sera thought bitterly, but that thought ended abruptly when the vet came in.

"Your pig *fell* on a knife?" He eyed Sera suspiciously.

"You've seen him," she said. "Sometimes he's walking and then just sorta falls over, and I had...dropped a knife." She sat still, focusing on staying as upright as possible. She probably should be going to the hospital next.

"You keep your pigs in the house?"

"Just the one." That seemed less suspicious to her. "He's special."

"What's his name?"

"Pig." It just came out. She had to stop herself from rolling her eyes.

"Pig?"

"Pig seemed simple." She shrugged, starting to worry that the vet might think she was crazy, but in reality, this was way less crazy than the truth. *I'm sorry, senior vet, but I stabbed a pig because I wanted to practice my murder technique for my newfound love of serial murder. See, after my best friend— Best.* The thought choked her. Just the thought.

"And the others?"

She came back to the moment, taking a second to connect the dots. "I didn't name them."

"Where do you keep them? In the house?" It was her turn to look at him like he was an idiot.

"In a pigpen outside... Hence, the mud." He wasn't buying any of this, but it didn't really matter.

"Right. And why did you bring them with you?"

"Solidarity?" She stopped him before he could continue. "Look, I know this is weird. That's fine. Judge me. But can you please just look at the cut. I'm afraid he's going to die."

"He's not going to die. He's not particularly hurt. I'll clean it up for you—"

"But— all the blood? I stabbed him— the knife stabbed him— he— he fell pretty hard... on my knife."

"What blood?" he shrugged.

The vet had a lot of concerns. However, as it turned out, none of them were about the pig. It seemed that rather than stabbing it, Sera had grazed it, perhaps with a lot of force, but pigs have really thick skin. This pig was no exception.

She looked at the pig's wound and found that, indeed, there was barely any blood. There was, however, a fuck-ton of mud.

"I can't fucking believe it," she blurted out.

"All that mud does make it seem a bit more like Pig was in the pen outside when he fell on your knife," the vet said, looking at Sera meaningfully, but she said nothing. She'd probably get in more trouble for kidnapping the pigs than she ever would have gotten in for killing one. She wasn't going to make this any worse by telling a lie or by telling the truth.

"I'll clean it up, but I doubt he even needs stitches," he said as he swabbed mud off Pig's back. Pig, true to form, cried out in agony. The other pigs immediately joined in until the vet nudged Pig. "That's only water," he said, and Pig immediately stopped. "However, the alcohol may sting a little."

Pig affected a pretty convincing look of a stiff upper lip, and the vet dabbed him with the alcohol.

The vet gave Pig a big dog biscuit for being such a strong patient and then threw a handful of smaller treats on the ground for Pig, and Pig's friends. Politely, he also handed one big treat to 42, who patiently waited her turn from her chair. She had prime viewing real estate. Sera winced as she eased back in the chair.

"I should also take a look at you," the vet said.

She didn't know what else to do, so she raised her shirt, showing him her ribs. One could say years of conditioning made her oblige without thought. One could also say she was in a fuck-ton of pain and was hoping he could write her a prescription and maybe also assure her that she wasn't going to die.

He poked her ribs. She winced but didn't cry out in pain.

"It doesn't feel broken, but I'm a vet. You should probably go to a real doctor. That bruising is pretty bad."

"Like internal bleeding bad?" she asked.

"No, like see a real doctor 'bad.' And you probably need an X-ray 'bad.' So, how did that happen?"

This time she rolled her whole head in exasperation.

"Look, Pig fell. I fell. We all fell." She glanced at the clan of pigs, half expecting them to all drop to the ground. They did not. *Well, at least that seems normal*, she thought. "Are you gonna stitch Pig up or not?"

He raised his hands in surrender. When someone wanted to lie to him, he was only going to push so far. He ultimately gave Pig three stitches. All of them were to make Sera happy. He also filled a prescription for her in case "Pig" had any pain but proceeded to explain what the dose for a person might be. He advised her to get lots of rest. Pig, however, could do whatever he wanted.

As Sera stood, she noticed a glob of goop forming in the corner of 42's eye.

"Shit. Also, since I'm here. My, uh, other vet said 42 needs eye drops. I had some, but I kinda used most of them already. Could you..."

"Sure," he said as 42 climbed off the chair and unceremoniously dragged her butt on the ground, following the throng of pigs who were already exiting the room. "Got five minutes for another exam?"

"Uh—"

"No charge."

"Yup," Sera said, and then the metal table did come down. All the pigs waited patiently a second time, though, Pig was clearly their star patient. 42 was in good shape other than her eyes. It seemed all those other "meds" she needed were a load of BS. That lady really had taken Sera for a ride, or she'd been super aware of how supremely bad Sera would be at dog-ownership. *It was probably the latter,* Sera thought with complete confidence.

Much to Sera's chagrin, the vet easily put three drops in each of 42's eyes.

"You better let me do it like that," Sera said to 42, but 42 made no promises.

"You take it easy," the vet reminded Sera as she, 42, and her pig posse left.

Outside, she sighed in disgust as she realized she was going to have to get all the pigs back into the Prius.

*Take it easy, my ass.*

# THIRTEEN

Sera's Prius had groaned and trundled all the way home, but it made it. Sera thanked her dumb luck that the moon was behind a swath of clouds as the pigs burst forth from her car and squiggled along to the apartment building behind 42. 42 was thrilled to be leading such a prestigious group. Her big, goofy grin announced it to anyone who might see her. Sera really hoped no one would.

Bringing them here was an awful idea. Sera knew that, but she unlocked the apartment building and held the door wide open while 42 led the pig posse right up the front stairs anyway. They were quiet, or as quiet as a group of pigs huffing, puffing, and oinking their way up a staircase can be. Innately, they understood the need to sneak. These were some high-IQ porkers. Still, Sera knew if one neighbor opened their door on them, she was outta here. 42 was one thing, but the cast of *Animal Farm* was another.

She ushered them inside her apartment, shut and locked the door behind them, and breathed a huge sigh of relief.

*We made it,* she thought, ready to call it a night. Then she took in the sight of ten pigs circling her apartment. *Shit.*

She had no idea what to feed them, so she grabbed a box of stale Apple Jacks and sprinkled them all over the kitchen floor. She was definitely going to get kicked out. She also realized, with some annoyance, that she hadn't gotten dog food. The initial plan had been lunch, kill a pig, buy dog food, come home. Clearly, it hadn't worked out that way at all.

She pulled out a frozen pizza, double-checking that it was pepperoni *without* onion. It was, and she baked it for her and 42 to share. She dropped down onto the sofa with a sudden wince. She'd forgotten all about her ribs. She wondered if she needed to go to the hospital, but figured if she'd forgotten them, it was probably a good sign. She lifted her shirt. It looked awful, but she could press on her ribs pretty hard without wanting to die. She decided she was fine and took a dose of Pig's meds. Pig looked up at her as she did, but she concluded that was happenstance. Pig most certainly did not know she was taking his medicine, and even though she had freed them all and brought them to her apartment rather than killing him, she was certain there was no way Pig, or the others for that matter, had master-minded the event. It was a crazy night. That was all.

*Fuck.* In an instant, her thoughts darkened. She was definitely not a serial killer. She couldn't kill a dog, and she couldn't kill a pig. Not even a pig that was going to die anyway and had absolutely tried to kill her. Her heart sank. She felt tears rushing to her eyes. This goal had kept her going. If she wasn't going to kill The Bitch— she didn't know what she would do. Her body wanted to cry, wanted to fold in on itself, but she couldn't comprehend it. This couldn't be over. It couldn't. She'd been thinking about it for years. Not heavily, true. And, no, she never thought she would actually go through with it. Still, the idea of killing The Bitch, and anyone like her, had kept Sera going. She dropped her slice of pizza back on the table.

This was too much.

She sat like that for a long time. No TV, no food, just the oinking of her pig chorus and 42 salivating while staring at the last piece of pizza. Sera's head was empty. Absolutely, totally, and completely fucking empty. If there wasn't this, there was nothing. She wondered if she should kill herself, but she didn't want to die. She'd considered it. She really had, but she wanted to *live.* Life was good. She had known that before The Bitch, and she suspected it could be great after The Bitch too. B.C. and A.D. no longer held meaning for her. She would define her life as B.T.B. (Before The Bitch), D.T.B. (During The Bitch), and A.T.B. (After The Bitch). Three unique phases of life. She wondered if she should run away to some other state or country, but she knew The Bitch would still be there, in her mind. At this point, maybe it wasn't even The Bitch's fault. Clearly, Sera should have moved on and been able to sever ties completely.

But...

But somehow The Bitch always got her teeth back in. Sera didn't know how it happened. Not really. An invitation to an event where she knew everyone else too. Something found that she couldn't replace—how did The Bitch have all these things? Some obligation that seemed abhorrent to miss. Sera was, in essence, whooped. She didn't want to think about her anymore, but she did. She thought about her constantly. She didn't want to be filled with fear every time she ran into her at a store, or saw her name pop up on her phone. Even if The Bitch didn't reappear, she was still in her head. That was the real problem.

*Maybe a lobotomy would help.*

In her more rational moments, Sera knew she'd been conditioned. But it didn't make sense to her, what was there to gain? *Power,* her inner voice whispered. Had The Bitch really been some devious mastermind?

*Gaslighting is an impressive feat.*

A glob of drool fell onto her hand, tearing Sera from her thoughts. She reached down, grabbing the object of desire, and handed the slice to 42, who slurped it up willingly.

*Now what?*

She sat on her couch and thought all night long, but the only solution that came to her was being a serial killer.

It came over and over.

She tried to push it aside. She looked at 42, curled up so cozily on her couch, and told herself she wasn't a serial killer.

But the thought kept coming back. She began to drift in and out of sleep. Sometimes the dreams were happily full of murder and retribution. Other times the dreams were anxiety-riddled death traps where she could never say no again.

Pig nudged her, and she woke up covered in sweat. She looked at him and his three dainty stitches.

*Maybe I can't kill animals,* she thought, *but I don't want to kill animals. I want to kill people.*

Pig nestled up on the floor next to the couch, and Sera fell back asleep, scratching his head. This time, she had good dreams.

# FOURTEEN

Sera woke feeling refreshed and ready to take on the day. She stretched, wincing as her ribs reminded her that pigs were basically freight trains when they wanted to be. She climbed out of bed, though she didn't know when she'd made her way to her room. She didn't reach for her phone as she got ready. She didn't even want to. Shit was good. She threw on clothes and opened the bedroom door to find 42 sitting at a sleepy attention outside. Apparently, 42 had given up her bed in the living room for proximity to Sera. Then it hit her. Eau de barnyard. Sera might be fresh, but her apartment was anything but. Maybe 42 had moved for olfactory's sake rather than care's.

"Sorry 'bout that," she said, reaching down and scratching 42's head—an action that felt foreign to her, foreign but good.

She was going to have to figure out something to do with those pigs, and maybe... She realized, hand still nestled in 42's fur, that she hadn't actually decided if she was going to keep 42 or send her back. Sera's stomach rumbled.

"Come on."

She and 42 headed to the living room where Sera discovered the kitchen had become a makeshift pigpen. Although none of the pigs were confined there, they all seemed to want to be inside the linoleum lines. That was just fine with her. As long as they stayed there, maybe the carpet would survive, and she could get her deposit back after she was kicked out.

The prospect of getting kicked out suddenly became very real and very immediate. She had no idea what she was going to do. Where would she go? Would she stay in the city? Did she want to? In the past, she always would have gone to The Bitch's. Not now. In theory, she could couch surf, but that's not a great look on a 30-year-old. She had also spent a lot of time not hanging out with nearly every friend that was in some way an asshole or asshole adjacent. By now she could have an entirely new group of friends, that was apparent, but she was afraid.

Genuinely afraid.

Every person she met would say one wrong thing, and she'd find herself agonizing over whether they were a good person or not. She'd had an amazing gut when she was young, but she had told herself to stop listening to it. It would speak up, she'd hear it, and then she'd worry about how a certain someone would react if she were to say no. She hadn't even known it at the time, but she'd made all of her social decisions out of fear, and something that dominant eventually bleeds into everything else. It did for Sera. She'd loved helping people. Then she became the one everyone used.

She felt all used up.

She had felt all used up for so long she wondered if she would ever not feel used up—

She shook her head. All that was future Sera's problem. Right now, 42 needed a quick walk, and the eye drops. Sera groaned and her hand instinctively dropped to her ribs protectively, an action that was not lost on 42. In preparation, she popped one of Pig's pills, swallowing it dry.

Begrudgingly, Sera grabbed the eye drops, but to her great surprise, and relief, 42 leaned her head back and took it like a dog. Okay, Sera tilted 42's head back and held her eye open, but 42 basically took it as well as any dog could.

"Thank you," Sera said, and she really meant it. Her stomach growled again. She needed something to eat, and she was not stepping over all those sleeping pigs.

# FIFTEEN

Sera sucked down a giant Diet Coke. Sitting in the back of Carl's Jr., she picked on her fries while trying to define her criteria for murder. She had brought her favorite notebook for the task. It had remained empty because she never knew what was important enough to put in there. This was definitely up to snuff. She smiled at her own silly joke. A multicolored patchwork character stared at her from the cover. The colors were muted. It was a woman who'd been torn apart and put back together so many times that she was a shadow of her former bright self. At least, that's how Sera thought of it.

She knew how the girl felt.

She opened the notebook and jotted down:

Reasons to kill:

Then she thought long and hard. This ought to be a very high bar, but honestly, she didn't think it was. Not anymore.

Someone's an asshole

The words fell onto the page easily. *But what defines an asshole*, she thought. *Someone cutting you off on the freeway?* There needed to be criteria.

Maliciousness

It'd be a bit hard to prove definitively, but it seemed pretty straightforward. If someone was openly trying to ruin someone else's life, then fuck them.

Mindfuckery

She stared at the word for a long time. She wanted to cry. Her chest clenched up. The world shrank, folding in on itself. Folding in on her. She was hyper focused on the word and the thoughts crashing through her.

*How could she— Who was she— What did she— Why did she— Why had they— Had they— Did they— Would they— Didn't they—*

She couldn't breathe. Couldn't move. Awareness just outside her realm of focus. Everything was soft, almost blurry. Hard to see and harder to get a read on.

*Disassociation.*

*Association.*

She was so acutely in tune with the awfulness that took her over when she acknowledged that she had been had. She was a fool. *Not a fool,* her inner voice tugged.

Manipulation

Stillness settled over her.

This.

The world wanted to pull out of focus, but this wasn't a panic attack. It could have been. She lasered in on the page. She breathed slow and steady. Her breath didn't make it below her chest. She couldn't take it down to her diaphragm, or it would break her.

There's a stop. Everyone has one. Sera knew she couldn't let herself feel her entire body, couldn't stay completely present or she would crumble.

*A lot of people deserve to die,* she thought. It was simple and clear. There were bad people out there, and not all of them were murderers or rapists. Some of them casually destroyed those they were supposed to love by dismantling everything about who they were.

Sera had loved herself once upon a time.

Tears came to her eyes, but she breathed them away and took another drink of her now empty Diet Coke. She stood and refilled it. She left the notebook open. Some part of her wanted someone else to see it. Why? *Who knows,* she thought. *Who knows anything anymore?*

Now, the who. Who did she, Sera, personally feel deserved to die?

DING - A text popped up on her phone. Alyssa. Funny she should text now.

Sera threw out the rest of her fries and called Alyssa as she walked out to her car, taking another big swig of Diet Coke.

*Breakfast of champions.*

"Gross, you aren't drinking soda already, are you?"

Sera gritted her teeth. It's incredible how entitled some people feel. Was it really necessary to denigrate her for every decision she made? Especially before noon.

"Hardy har har. Are you drinking coffee?" Sera replied.

"Of course," Alyssa chirped with a holier-than-thou vibe.

"We both picked our poisons."

"Except yours really *is* poison."

Sera's blood began to boil. Instinctively, she hated herself for calling this person back, for inviting this energy into her life. She had to remind herself that this wasn't her falling back into some unavoidable trap, this was her luring Alyssa into her own trap. That helped. The idea that she had some form of control over this exchange helped. She wanted to tell her just how fucking rude she was being, but she didn't. This time she had a good reason not to, but people rarely ever did. Wasn't that how it was all allowed? The entire world was told to be good and behave, so the ones who really were just assholes were able to do and say anything they wanted.

Until now that was.

Sera was coming for them.

"How did you even know I was drinking soda?"

"Please. You're so addicted. You're always drinking it. So, are we going to hang out today or what? I was supposed to go out with Chelsea, but she got called into work. Boo. So, of course I thought of you." Alyssa prattled on without coming up for air.

Sera wanted to ask her how many other people she had texted, but she didn't bother. She knew the answer was everyone. Surprisingly, Alyssa would have actually said it. She would have said, "I texted Mark and Kalini, but I was really hoping *you* were free." That's where the lie lived, in her pretending it made any difference to her at all who called back. What she meant was, "I texted everyone I know because I really hoped someone would be free and keep me from spending time alone." Sera paused at this.

*Was she, Sera, an awful person?* If Alyssa couldn't bear to be alone, and The Bitch couldn't either, didn't that speak to some deep-rooted shit that they needed to take care of? Was she really allowed to blame them for taking things out on other people when they were so clearly messed up themselves?

*Allowed—*

That word caught her. Was she allowed to? This is how she thought, in absolutes and rights and wrongs. For her, the world was a place where she longed to live in the gray, where she allowed everyone else to live in the gray, but where she demanded that she live in the *right*, the *supposed to*, the *allowed to*.

*I'm so fucked. Yup, I am. And I don't ruin anyone else's life, so why should they be allowed to treat the rest of us like dirt?*

Sera knew it was debatable whether or not Alyssa meant to treat anyone else like dirt. In reality, it seemed like she just didn't recognize that she had the capacity to hurt someone else's feelings. She couldn't see past her immediate need for attention to realize that dismissing people out of hand, repeatedly, could be a problem. On the other hand, she was a hella smart woman that had emotional acuity when she managed to pay attention. *Stop trying to figure people out. It's pointless,* Sera reprimanded herself. *She's grown. She knows.*

At lunch, Sera ordered an iced tea. She did in fact want it, but she had to acknowledge that she would have ordered it regardless, because she didn't want to be judged by Alyssa. Not on something she could so easily sidestep.

"Laying off the Diet Coke, huh?" Alyssa commented anyway. Then to the server, "I'm fine with water." It was said with that impressively judgy tone. It asked for attention, validation. "You made a good choice, but I made a better one," it screamed.

"I'm glad we could meet up," Sera said and found she wasn't lying. She did actually want to meet up with her. She wanted to determine if it was acceptable for her to kill Alyssa. She noticed the irony in this, the idea that killing anyone might be acceptable. However, she also totally believed it was true. It was absolutely acceptable to kill some people. Not necessarily ethical or good or moral, but acceptable. Like, if you met Hitler, it was acceptable to kill him. If you met a klansman, it was acceptable to kill him. She agreed that it got complicated given that both of those people might also feel it was completely acceptable to kill someone else and that that belief was actually what made them awful people.

*Shit.*

She was going down the rabbit hole of what might be wrong with her, how her deciding it was okay to kill bad people might actually make her like the people she was going to kill. That wasn't great. But... well, it wasn't wrong.

*I am becoming a bad person. Wow.* She took it in. Chewed on it. Turned it around in her head. *I'm okay with that. For this, I am.*

She was. She knew she was. She wanted to. Wasn't that her goal? She wanted to kill people who were dicks so they couldn't torment others. That made her a horrible person, or it would once she'd done it, but it didn't make her believe in her goal less.

*Fuck.*

*I hope I'm better than Hitler.*

"Oh, you don't think so?" Alyssa asked, apparently taking the shrug for an answer to something she had just said. *Shit.* Now, Sera was being rude. Alyssa had been droning on and on while Sera ran through her own neurosis internally.

"Just an itch. Keep going," Sera covered.

"Oh. Good. I was like, how in the world could you side with her? She's so...I don't want to say *basic.* So, I won't, but everyone thinks it. Anyway, didn't something big happen with you lately?" Alyssa leaned in, suddenly super interested, and it dawned on Sera that maybe Alyssa hadn't texted everyone. Alyssa may actually have wanted to see her specifically. For a moment, her spirits rose.

"Yeah, I lost my job. So, that sucks."

"And wasn't it...you-know-who's doing?"

Sera's spirits fell. To get all the dirt. Alyssa wanted to see her to get the dirt. Sera wanted to kick herself. She knew she was coming here to see if Alyssa deserved to die, but somehow it still hurt when she realized that she didn't want to hang out with her at all. She wanted to be the one with the most up-to-date and the most straight-from-the-horse's-mouth gossip possible.

"I don't think so," Sera lied. She did it passably. It was easy. She lied all the time to these people. Not because she wanted to, but because she didn't want to be on trial for, well, for drinking Diet Coke.

Alyssa raised an eyebrow and leaned in further, not buying it. "You don't have to protect her. I won't tell anyone *if* you tell me not to."

Sera leaned in, upping the intensity. "Do you know something I don't? Do you really think she would do that? To me?"

She knew she'd trapped Alyssa with this. If Alyssa wanted dirt, she would have to dish first and then...well, then nothing Sera said could be used against her with The Bitch or anyone else. Fucking leverage. It was like being in a grown-up game of *Mean Girls*.

*What had happened to all of us?* she wondered. In the beginning, they were all on the same side. Weren't they? No. No. Sera was on the same side. The side of all of them, but each of them had always been on their own side, and somehow, "their sides" had always ended up being against her.

*They weren't all bad,* that's what she told herself, but most of them were. Now that her eyes were open, she couldn't seem to close them again. You don't hate sheep for following. You feel bad for them, but these sheep stabbed each other in the back. Even she had to admit the difference.

She was a sheep.

A real one.

It was why she hated herself.

It was why she tried so hard to justify the actions of others.

How had she gone from being a self-possessed, confident young woman to a sheep? Even the pig clan in her apartment was smarter than that.

*Well, they follow Pig. Hm.* She vowed to suss out if Pig was a benevolent leader or not. If not, he may have to die after all. *Huzzah!* She wasn't against killing animals. She was simply pro killing assholes. It felt like a small victory, but it was still a victory. She'd take it. Secretly, she hoped Pig wasn't an asshole though. That would suck.

"Everyone is saying it," Alyssa hesitated, "but I thought it was, you know, from you?"

Sera shook her head.

"Oh, well." Alyssa replied, leaning back, "I guess we can all still be friends with her, then." It was a test. A last-ditch effort. If Sera flinched now, Alyssa would take it as blood in the water and strike.

*Manipulation.* That's how she'd become a sheep. *No,* she thought, *I wasn't a sheep. I was a good friend, and I got fucked.*

"As if anyone would stop hanging out with her for me," Sera replied with a laugh. That was that. No flinch. No playing her hand. But it burnt. She tried to force herself to wonder if something in this exchange protected The Bitch. Was she inadvertently helping The Bitch? She could out her, but the thought dwindled even before it fully formed. This was not the worst thing The Bitch had done by a long shot, and somehow everyone still loved her? Liked her? Tolerated her? Sera didn't know. She couldn't understand. She thought somehow everyone was still trapped by her.

And before she could stop herself, Sera began, "I know it wasn't a great job, but I really needed it. I'm not actually sure how I'm going to pay rent. It's been super stressful, and I don't know what I should..." Alyssa's eyes wandered around the restaurant. She was looking for whoever or whatever might be the more interesting thing.

Sera stopped talking mid-sentence.

She let the words hang there like a noose.

Then Alyssa slipped the noose over her head. "Well, I'm glad you figured it out." She hadn't even tried to listen.

*Never show them the real you,* Sera thought to herself, but she was too sad and too tired to care. *No,* she thought, *I'm too used to it. Never say something where the simple lack of reply will hurt you.* Not for the first time, Sera realized the only way she might thrive in this world is to sew her mouth shut. It's awful being alone when you're surrounded by people. It's worse being alone when you're surrounded by people who are supposed to love you.

Sera regarded Alyssa like the alien she was.

"Look at that girl's jacket," Alyssa said. "So *weird.*" She said it as an insult. "I bet you'd wear something like that." She must use pain as fuel.

Sera didn't nod. She didn't anything. She just let Alyssa carry on the rest of the lunch conversation without her. She didn't need Sera's input or presence at all it seemed. A sadness came over Sera, and she realized she didn't want to be right. Not about this. She wanted to find out that, while quirky (or a total space cadet), Alyssa really was a good person and good friend. Sera was so naive, and she kept proving that to herself over and over again. *What is it with me and my perpetual benefit of the doubt?*

There had been a brief time when Alyssa had been a friend, or at least when Sera had thought she was. But it wasn't friendship. Alyssa had wanted something, and Sera had happily (stupidly) obliged. Ironically, she'd helped Alyssa get her job, her career, and now, Alyssa couldn't even be bothered to feel bad that Sera was unemployed, broke, and was absolutely going to lose her apartment.

Instead, Alyssa was ragging on her for the possibility that she could like a "weird" jacket. She did like it, actually. It was really cute. She'd give Alyssa that the jacket was *weird*, as in out of the usual, but it was amazing. It didn't deserve the side-eye Alyssa had given it. It was rainbow and patchwork. It was bright and disjointed. It was broken but ready to be happy. Before she knew it, Sera stood up and went over to the girl while Alyssa was still talking to herself. Sera looked at the girl sitting there, a woman really, probably 19, and sized her up. Yes, the jacket probably would fit.

"I'll give you a hundred bucks for that jacket."

The confused girl looked at her, "It's only twenty-five at H&M."

"Then you'll take the hundred?" Sera asked.

As she walked back to her table, Sera smiled at the gaping Alyssa.

"You're right," Sera said, pulling on her new armor. "I look great in this jacket."

# Sixteen

They walked out of the restaurant. Sera was strangely proud of herself. All she'd done was buy some broke-ass college kid's jacket, but it felt like an Alyssa-defying stand.

"Why would you do that?" Alyssa suddenly asked. Venom dripped from the words. "Were you trying to attack me?"

Sera's jaw dropped.

"Really, Sera, explain yourself. I'm in the middle of a conversation, and you get up and go buy *that jacket*. It's super...*weird*, like, it's not that cute."

Sera tried to collect her thoughts. It was hard to follow. She couldn't tell if Alyssa was more upset at the jacket or at Sera walking away. Sera decided to go with the more logical of the two arguments.

"I shouldn't have walked away while you were talking. You're right. It was rude." She paused. "But, you do that to me all the time."

"I walk away while you're talking?" Alyssa demanded.

"No, you just don't listen. You change the subject. You do anything you can so you get to talk nonstop and never have to listen to me."

"Please. I do not. We talked about your new job today."

"I didn't get a new job. I told you. I lost my job, and I'm going to lose my apartment and then you congratulated me on working it out because you weren't listening. You're never listening. Why is that?"

"Oh my God. I listen sometimes."

Sera widened her eyes at Alyssa's admission in disbelief. Did she think she was being funny?

"I mean," Alyssa continued, "I believe in you more than you do, is all. I know you'll get a job, so why do I have to listen?"

"Why do you *have* to listen?"

"I don't mean it like that. I mean, why is it about you? *You* walked away from *me*. She's right, you always change the subject to be about you." There it was. The moment where Alyssa twisted it and made her actions a result of Sera's lack of character, the moment where she used an absent Bitch to force her point. This moment came up every time they had any sort of altercation. It could be about where they parked, and somehow Sera was turned into the bad guy. She felt petty being annoyed by this, but she was ALWAYS made to feel petty being annoyed by this.

"No. I didn't change the subject and make it about me. The conversation was *why did I walk away*, and I'm telling you, I walked away because you don't listen to me, so I am under no obligation to listen to you."

"I listen to you—"

"Sure, if I'm dishing gossip or telling you how awful someone else is or how awesome you are. Why am I always supporting you, and you're always tearing me down?"

"I have never once—"

"No? So, my jacket isn't 'weird' and 'not cute?' Admit it. You only invited me here because you wanted me to talk shit, so you had more gossip to spread to your many tendrils of lackeys."

"Tendrils of lackeys?" Alyssa laughed. "That doesn't make sense."

"Like...like you're an octopus, and your lackeys are attached to you—" Sera stumbled over the words. She didn't know how to say it. Unlike The Bitch, who cultivated one group, Alyssa spread her feelers out among many. Her hold wasn't as strong, but it was just as insidious. Alyssa looked at her, triumphant and cold as ice.

"Ahhhhh!" Sera literally screamed, releasing her frustration. "Fuck you. You do this where you twist a conversation or catch me up on some small little completely unrelated detail like tendrils. Fine, your lackeys. You just wanted dirt for your lackeys. Does that make you happy? And when I didn't give it to you, you completely tuned me out and talked to yourself for the next thirty minutes."

"I was talking to you!" Alyssa shouted back. "So, you're telling me you weren't listening?"

"No. I heard everything you said because I'm a good friend. Jimmy might break up with Danny. Nina got a free vacation to Aruba, and you're hoping she takes you with her. Your mom is sick, but you're sure she'll get better, which, by the way, should have been the main thing you talked about. How is a possible trip to Aruba more important than your mom? I'm not saying I didn't listen. I'm saying you didn't notice that I didn't say one word for an hour!"

"I am worr—"

"Then you saw that girl's jacket and told me that it looked like my thing because it was *weird* which really meant ugly. So, I spent the afternoon being dismissed, ignored, and insulted. Actually, you even insulted me when I called you by making fun of my drinking soda. I know it's not healthy. I'm not a fucking idiot. I just have bigger things to deal with right now than a fucking caffeine addiction, which you also happen to have—just in the societally sanctioned form of coffee—which you drink with about a pound of sugar, making it just as bad for you." *Wow. Holy fucking wow.* Sera stopped. Alyssa's eyes were wide.

"If you don't want to be my friend anymore, you can just say so," Alyssa said, and just like that Sera knew she had somehow surrounded herself with a diverse collection of manipulative Bitch-worthy people.

"Fine." Sera raised her hands in surrender. "Ignore everything I'm saying and dismiss me as crazy or incoherent. I know you're going to say you didn't call me crazy to win. Don't bother. You win. You always win, but guess what? I don't give a shit. Not anymore. You can win this conversation and every other one we've ever had, because just being around you is a lose for me. I came here hoping to find... What? A friend? A support system? And I knew what I'd find, and now I'm mad I found it. Maybe this is all my fault. Maybe I expect too much. I'm too fucking nice, and I do this to myself."

"Nice? How are you so fucking nice? You asked me to lunch, and I came. I'm nice."

She was right. Sera had asked her out. Wait. Was she right? Maybe Alyssa hadn't even wanted to come. *Jesus.* Sera shook her head. *One fucking point in years of friendship, where I do exactly what she wants, and I'm going to make myself the villain? She wanted to come out, didn't she? She always did.* Sera was disgusted with herself. Nearly every encounter she had with her so-called friends made her hate herself more.

Sera nodded. "Fine. I did invite you. I'm sorry I made you waste your time with me."

They stood there in silence. If the shoe had been on the other foot, Sera would have gone down a rabbit hole about how it wasn't a waste of time, and she was sorry she'd spaced out. It would have been some grand moment of guilt. She would have carried it with her for years. For Alyssa, it wasn't. It was awkward, but it was clear that Alyssa knew she was in the right. Sera was baffled. How did she do that? How could Sera become that confident? Even worse, Sera felt the tug of an apology inside her. When had Sera become such a schmuck? How is it possible to question everything about yourself after every exchange you have? Even when you know that the other person is the asshole? She sighed.

"Okay," Sera said. "Have a good life. Bye." She headed back toward her car. Of course she had absent-mindedly been walking Alyssa to hers.

Alyssa scoffed but said nothing as she turned and unlocked her car door.

But, out of nowhere, something popped into Sera's mind.

"Wait," Sera called out. "Why did you text me?"

"I wanted to get lunch," Alyssa said, without realizing it. Then paused. *Did this mean that Sera was indeed being a good friend by going to lunch with her?* Alyssa ran the idea through her head and quickly dismissed it. *Sera should never have treated her this way.* She didn't deserve it, and Sera certainly had no grounds for grievance. Satisfied, Alyssa climbed into her car and immediately moved on. She sent a text to one of her many tendrils of lackeys and started her engine.

But Sera had seen it. The moment of hesitation, and Sera knew that, for once, they both knew she won. Sera had won. Even if Alyssa wouldn't admit it under threat of death.

Sera watched Alyssa pull out of the parking lot. She was animatedly talking. No doubt she had already reached out to someone else. By later today, anyone Alyssa knew would know that Sera was a decidedly shit friend and an awful human being.

Sera turned away, heading back to her car. How was it that every time she treated an awful person the way they treated her, she still felt like dirt? She wondered if Alyssa felt bad but dismissed it.

Sera was crazy.

Alyssa was right about that. Normal people didn't feel bad if they had to leave what they considered to be an awful person behind. They didn't question every thought they had because some dick said they were wrong. And right now, Sera knew that Alyssa was indeed an awful person. Maybe what stung was that she also knew Alyssa now considered her an awful person too.

Sera wanted to be self-possessed and confident enough to value herself above others. She didn't need to put them down, but she really wished she treated herself with the same respect she had treated these assholes with for years. Unfortunately, that wasn't her way.

*Being liked is a trap,* Sera thought unlocking her door, but it was a trap she willingly curled up inside of time and time again.

Sera slid into her car and thought about when she should kill Alyssa.

*Soon. Very, very soon.*

# Seventeen

Sera opened her door to a zoo of an apartment. The animals had decided that the carpet was not, in fact, lava, and that they were in fact perfectly fine with going on it. And go they did. Piss. Shit... It was a mess. Luckily, they seemed to like to keep their bathroom separate from their living space. Unluckily, they had decided that Sera's bedroom made a nice commode.

42 quickly ran to the door doing a potty dance and whining. In a heroic effort, she had held it. Sera shook her head in amusement, but beneath it, she was touched. The dog really was doing all she could to be a good roommate even in the face of all the pig shit surrounding her.

Sera leashed 42 up with the dusty old rope, and they headed out. The pigs all filed up behind, but Sera had to shut the door on them. It was true, she was probably getting kicked out with or without the animals being there by the end of the month, or maybe the first week of the next, but if the animals were found, she was getting kicked out that day.

Sera and 42 began a loop around the neighborhood. There were a lot of dogs out, which 42 adored, though Sera was less interested. She didn't want to have long, pointless conversations with every neighbor she had carefully not met before now. She didn't need to meet any more people that she would inevitably learn something awful about or who would treat her terribly. She didn't know how she attracted these people, but she did. Besides, she needed some time to clear her head and figure out how she was going to abduct and kill Alyssa.

Was she really going to do this?

The third dog in as many minutes came straight up to 42 with an excited butt sniff and a rapid tail wag.

*Why can't people be like that?* Sera thought, but maybe they were. Not all of them, but maybe she was.

Sera didn't know if she attracted awful people or if awful people were attracted to everyone and that she just had no filter. Not a verbal filter. She knew what to say and what not to say. No, Sera had no friendship filter. The second she walked up to a person and sniffed their ass, she decided they would be friends for life.

It wasn't an altogether bad approach to life. She met a lot of interesting people that others never would, but the people who immediately glom on are not the ones you want to keep around. Narcissists glom. Anyone needing loads of attention gloms. Anyone looking for a posse gloms.

Anyone seeking out a group of followers is not someone who should be followed.

That's how cults happen.

Sera worried that her all-in attitude had another side effect, one of desperation. Most "normal" people assumed that someone that eager to be friends must either be an outcast or a glommer.

*Maybe I'm a glommer,* she thought.

She hated the idea, but she didn't know how to change this. She didn't even know for sure if it was an actual issue.

Life is hard. Making friends is hard. Perhaps she wasn't cut out for it. For the game of it. It was entirely possible that, along with hermits and introverts, there was another subset of people who chose to be alone. Perhaps these were people who, under normal circumstances, thrived in a crowd, people who thrived so much in a crowd that they set themselves up for self-destruction at every turn. Sera might be one of those people.

Conversely, Sera could be a horrible person. She could be alone because everyone hated her except for the other horrible people.

Sera wanted to know if she was a horrible person. Did she end up being around these horrible people because she was also horrible, or was it, as she initially suspected, because she was too nice?

It was easy to be nice. It was also hard. Being nice takes a hell of a toll on a person.

When Sera finally realized that she had set herself aside in order to meet all the requirements of being nice, she found that it had crushed her day by day.

42 yanked on the leash, and Sera realized that she had been quite far away for quite a long time. They had looped the neighborhood and made it all the way back to her building. Dusk had arrived, and 42 was ready to go home.

Sera opened the door and wondered how much of what had happened to her was her fault for putting herself out and how much was their fault for taking advantage of her? Sera concluded that it was a very pointless question. Only God could know, and he wasn't talking.

# Eighteen

Sera and 42 sat on the couch underneath two heavy blankets. Every window in the apartment was open, and Sera had lit every scented Bath & Body Works candle she had. The effect was an overly romantic giant fire hazard. The mix of aromas was not pleasant, but it wasn't exactly unpleasant. What it definitely was was effective at covering up the ever-growing smell of pig.

Sera stopped flipping through options and landed on a docuseries on "serial murderers." The term bugged her. Why did they have to be PC about how they referred to killers? Sure, she planned to be a killer soon, and maybe using the lighter sounding "murderer" would help her if she was apprehended, but she didn't think so. Also, it just sounded wrong. Killers kill. It should sound harsh. It was harsh as hell. That's what appealed to Sera.

She hoped she could learn a thing or two about not getting caught or properly executing a crime, but she knew that was not likely. Most likely she would learn how murderers were not the most well-balanced people, which she already knew. It seemed like this should bother her, but it didn't. She wasn't balanced. She was fully aware. In fact, she'd been to a number of psychologists because she was so certain she was unbalanced. Ironically, all of them seemed to think she was far more stable than she did. She figured they must have pretty bad patients. Of course, she didn't tell them about her plans for murder. Outside of that, though, she was surprisingly honest.

Once you decide your life is so shit that you're willing to go away forever for murder, there's not much point in hiding things. It's not like you have to protect yourself or others... Maybe others, but Sera was sick of protecting them.

Sera was prepared to learn that the most important thing about being a serial killer was selecting victims that were in no way connected to you. That was what most killers did. Men, anyway. Women killed patients and husbands. And children. A lot of women killed their children, but Sera wasn't sure if they were considered serial killers. It was just as well. Sera had no interest in being lumped in with them if she was ever caught. Unfortunately, she knew there was a rather good chance she would get caught eventually because she was willfully ignoring that whole *don't pick victims who are connected to you* thing.

Rule 1 - ignored.

The pigs were clumped in a semicircle around the couch on the floor. All pig eyes were glued to the TV. It was a magic box of wonders to them. 42 didn't seem nearly as entranced. Sera wondered how much each comprehended. Was 42 less interested because she wasn't as smart, so she didn't follow the story or pictures as much as the pigs? Pigs were reportedly uber smart. Or was 42 so smart that she knew it was fake and might suck your life away? It really could go either way, and 42 was the only one who hadn't peed on her bedroom floor. Well, other than Sera.

Sera got up and went to the window. Each candle she passed offered her a small pocket of a different scent. Outside, dusk was waning, and Sera knew it was time. She should pull on her jeans and head out for an adventurous night of stalking, but her body tugged at her to sit back down. Habit was a son-of-a-bitch, and depression combined with habit was nearly impossible. 42 was definitely the smartest of all of them, she concluded. Luckily, the serial murderer on TV was far more interested in getting the documentarians to bring him a candy bar he remembered from his childhood than he was in exposing details about himself or his crime, which left Sera free to leave.

She wondered what his "type" was. Her type was... She paused to think about it. She wanted to say her type was "The Bitch," but she figured that wouldn't hold up as a large-scale classification. Profilers would never go for it.

Sera wasn't going for brown hair or blue eyes. She couldn't care less about college co-eds and their drunken debauchery. Slut it up. What was life without a little fun? Hitchhikers were boring, and she was far more likely to kill the John than any prostitute. Sex workers really needed better conditions. Each of them should have punch knives as part of their standard-issued uniform. A little brass knuckle dagger would save a lot of cops from a lot of policing, and they shouldn't be prosecuted until their third or fourth stabbing.

*Go ahead and assume the defenseless chick selling her body for money is innocent. Try it,* Sera thought. *It's not that hard.*

Sera's type was more insidious, less clear cut. She was all about those assholes tearing people down to build themselves up. The little shitheels wrecking peoples' self-esteem for fun, or because they could, or because they didn't care, or because they couldn't be bothered to consider anyone else in the fucking world. Manipulators. Gaslighters. Crazy-makers. *Fucking fuckers.*

It'd take a minute, but even the profilers would accept it as a category eventually. Every serial killer, or "serial murderer," had to have a type. It was a rule. Okay, maybe it was an unspoken rule, or a strong suggestion, but still, it was rule-esque.

Sera felt better realizing that this was one rule she was willing to abide by.

Rule (or strong suggestion) 2 - check!

Sera clicked off the TV, and a chorus of disgruntled oinks and chuffs immediately rose from the aggrieved barnyard on the ground. She turned the TV right back on. She was no longer resigned to the fact that she would need a new apartment. She was now excited about the change. Getting away from the stench covered by shopping-mall candle perfume would be a vacation, but that was no reason the pigs couldn't be entertained.

In her bedroom, Sera pulled a fresh pair of jeans out of her closet and remembered the yellow rope she'd used to strap The Bitch's mattress to the roof of her Prius. *It should still be in here.* She pushed aside shoe boxes, and memory boxes.

*Happier times,* she thought but didn't slow her search. It was definitely in there. Somewhere.

42 heard the noise and came to inspect the scene. Sera was potentially having fun, and she was potentially having it without 42. Unacceptable. 42 knew she was good at a lot of things, but one of the things she was best at was having fun. She figured she better go help so Sera would have as much fun as possible. Maybe Sera wasn't as good at it as she was. (42 was being nice, of course. It was clear 42 was way better at fun than Sera was.)

Ever watchful, 42 knew that the noises coming from the closet were Sera. Who else could it be? But it's in every dog's best interest to have a dash of caution surrounding their pure abandon. As a smart pup, 42 cautiously approached the closet. Her tail was still wagging, but it was tentatively wagging. It was ready to switch to full alert if needed. She crept forward. Wag, pause. Wag, wag, pause. Wag, pause, pause. It was caution, and it was a game. 42 really knew fun.

Sera threw some shoes aside, then shoved yet another box out of her way. How many memories did she have?

A lot of noise was coming from the closet, more than 42 expected Sera to make, so she slowed even further and poked her head in. Wag, pause.

Immediately, 42's tail switched to rapid-fire wag.

Wag, wag, wag, wag!

42 lunged into full play mode.

Sera was shoving boxes and fallen dresses from one side of the closet to the other. She chucked clothes out of her way, digging through them like her life depended on it. Sera didn't know why it mattered. She didn't even *need* the rope, but it mattered.

*I'm stalking,* she thought. *I'm not abducting or kidnapping. This is recon. I don't need the rope.* But it was killing her. Where was the damn thing?

42 jumped in to help and started to dig in the clothes too.

"42, no!" Sera yelled, stopping 42 in her tracks.

*Hm.* Sera had definitely not used that tone with her before, but she was doing exactly what Sera was doing. She was helping.

42 crept a paw forward and lightly placed it on a shirt on the ground. She looked up at Sera for clues, but all clues, including the mountain of clothes behind them, pointed to digging. It was the only logical answer, so 42 pulled her paw back at half speed, dragging the shirt along the ground, digging it into the pile where Sera had deposited all of the clothes she'd already dug.

"42..." Sera said, dragging her name out with clear meaning that was completely obscure to 42.

42 lifted her paw off the shirt in response. A test.

"Good," Sera said.

*Hm.* 42 was a good digger. She could definitely dig this stuff aside way faster than Sera was, but apparently that was not the game. *New game!* 42 realized and jumped into puppy-play position with her butt high in the air, ready for anything.

Sera tossed the shirt onto the pile, and 42 watched. What was the game?

Sera threw another shirt, and 42 jumped at it without touching it.

"Good girl," Sera said.

Game discovered! This was 42's very first round of Jump at the Clothes. She was amazing at it. She jumped at every item and didn't dig or bite a single thing. Well, she kinda got a little bit of the leg of one pair of jeans in her mouth, but they were awfully long, and she didn't bite down, so it didn't count.

However, Sera was getting frustrated. 42 couldn't imagine why.

Sera tossed the items aside and enjoyed the game of it with 42 more than she'd admit, but she couldn't find the rope.

42 was not looking for a rope. She knew having fun with what you had was better than searching for fun with what you'd lost.

*It should definitely be here,* Sera thought as she threw the last item out of the way.

Nope. It was just the back of the closet. Nothing to see here, folks. She shoved the pile back the other way with 42 springing after it. The dog had a huge smile. Sera didn't know if dogs actually could smile, technically speaking, but possible or not, this dog was definitely doing it.

Sera gave up. It was time to go.

She pulled on her jeans and grabbed her keys. 42 followed closely, grabbing her makeshift leash in her mouth and sitting patiently by the front door. The pigs did not line up behind 42 this time. They were too involved in *The Bachelor*. Sera did a double take, *how the?* But she saw Pig was mashing the remote buttons with his snout. Not ideal, but it was definitely working for them. Besides, maybe the "serial murderer" would get his candy bar and find something interesting to say. She didn't know if they'd care, but the pigs may not want to watch the same show twice.

She refilled their water bowls. The kitchen was littered with them. It looked like she had a Swiss-cheese roof and it had been raining nonstop. She didn't have access to a trough, though, so it was what it was. She also put out a few bowls of chips and cereal. She'd discovered she didn't need to leave the food on the floor, but she did need to leave it. Otherwise, they'd root through any part of the pantry they could reach. She really needed to pick up some pig feed. Whatever that was. She blew out the candles, cursing herself for almost forgetting. She didn't save their bacon just to fry them up now.

She looped 42's leash over her head and said goodbye to the pigs who couldn't be bothered to look up from their show. Who would the rose go to? The pigs had to know!

Sera led 42 down to the car, which had sat with its windows open all day. In a spot of good luck, she found that without physical excrement present pig scent wafted out of a Prius quite effectively. Sera winced as she and 42 climbed in. Her ribs were a lot better than she'd expected, but they were a long way from healed. She popped another one of Pig's pills. Only three left.

*They really don't give pigs big enough prescriptions. Probably worried about addiction,* she chuckled and immediately regretted it. She gingerly clicked her seat belt into place and thought for a moment about what would happen to 42 in an accident.

*Shit.*

Sera walked around to the passenger side and tried to wrap 42's leash-rope around her body and the passenger seat as a makeshift seat belt, but she needed a lot more rope.

*Double shit.*

Sera threw open the hatchback. She knew she didn't have any kind of harness, but she had to exhaust the possibilities. But there, shoved in the pocket of space behind the wheel well, was the bright yellow rope.

*Bingo.*

Sera pulled it out, happy she had cut it into different pieces to strap the mattress into place.

"Don't cut it," The Bitch had commanded too late. "I'll never use the pieces again." The Bitch was exasperated even though it was Sera's rope.

"Shorter pieces will be easier," Sera said as she cut it again.

The Bitch stiffened. "If you want to do it wrong, go ahead."

Sera didn't know what to say. The alternative was wrapping the rope around the mattress so many more times with only one knot for safety.

"I was thinking, the more knots the better?" Sera said, her tone asking for permission.

The Bitch shrugged. Wrong answer, but Sera had already ruined it. "We'll have to undo a bunch of knots instead of one."

Sera looked dumbly at the pieces of rope. She thought it'd be safer, but, yup, The Bitch was right. They'd have to untie all those knots.

When they pulled up to The Bitch's building, some of the knots had come undone. The Bitch's knots. Sera didn't say that though. Why be mean?

"I guess if you suck at tying knots, twenty ropes are better," The Bitch said.

She didn't give Sera a chance to say her idea had worked. Sera didn't have a moment to be happy the mattress wasn't left behind in the middle of the street. The Bitch wasn't wrong. Some of Sera's knots probably hadn't held.

"Guess we both suck at knots," Sera said, taking some of the responsibility to soften the blow.

"Mine held," The Bitch had said simply, and that was that. She jogged up to her building and left Sera staring at the rope.

Now, staring at the same rope, Sera wondered if all of her knots had held. *Hadn't they?* She knew at least some of the ones left were hers, for sure. Weren't they? *All of them,* her inner voice corrected. *All of them were mine.*

The Bitch saying something didn't make it true.

Sera grabbed the ropes and slammed the hatchback shut, startling 42. Sera used a strip of rope about eight feet long to create some DIY version of a safety harness for 42 before throwing the rest of the rope in the back seat.

It was not ideal.

Hog-tied to the front seat, 42 looked at Sera like she was crazy. They pulled out, and 42 yipped. How was she supposed to get her head out the window???

*Triple shit.*

Sera pulled over and loosened the safety contraption. 42 wouldn't go through the windshield, but she could move about and could definitely get her head out the window. 42 barked once in approval.

Next stop, Alyssa's apartment.

42 rode the entire way with her head out the window, ears flapping in the breeze. It was a perfect night, and both of them knew it.

# Nineteen

Sera and 42 pulled up to a looming Gothic apartment building. Alyssa had been so happy when she found it. Correction: when Sera told her about it. Alyssa was thrilled and then immediately told everyone how awesome the place *she* had found was. Sera had been really happy for her. Happy to help. It was a beautiful place.

Sera had actually considered it for herself first. For a fun afternoon, they had both fantasized about how great it would be to live in the same complex. But Sera's place was rent-controlled. Sera had dodged a bullet with that one, even if she hadn't known it at the time.

Alyssa's window was dark. *Third one from the left,* Sera thought. Even if she hadn't known which window it was, she would have recognized the bright pink curtains anywhere. Alyssa thought Sera's jacket was weird? Well, how about her garish thirteen-year-old Powder-Puff-girl apartment?

As Sera put the car into park across the street, 42 sat up at attention, switching her gaze from out the window to Sera.

*We're here. Time for a walk,* 42's body language screamed.

Sera pet her head and sighed. "Not right now. Sorry, girl."

42 already knew the tone of disappointment and laid down in the passenger seat. Sera loosened 42's restraints and absent-mindedly stroked her head as she looked up at the window. Alyssa would be home soon. After a few drinks at the bar tearing Sera apart to anyone who'd listen, she'd be back.

They were probably together, The Bitch and Alyssa. Wouldn't it be great if she were able to nab them both at the same time? She looked at the rope she'd tossed in the back seat.

*Reconnaissance,* she thought, chiding herself.

Was it enough to tie up two people?

The time passed slowly. This was not how it was supposed to be. She should be stalking Alyssa in some exciting alley, plunging a needle of who-knows-what in her neck and dragging her off to an undisclosed location. If Sera were honest, she had to admit there was something romantic about the whole thing to her.

42 whined slightly in her sleep, and Sera felt a ping of sadness.

*This isn't right,* she thought to herself. She looked over at 42 in the passenger seat and knew that she had to do this alone. More than that, she *couldn't* do this with 42. 42 was a good dog. A good, good dog, and Sera would not be responsible for pulling 42 into her awfulness. 42 deserved a better... What? Owner? Roommate? What? Owner was definitely wrong, but roommate seemed off too. Sera had never lived with any other roommates she *had* to shop for. She really needed to buy some dog food.

Should she return 42? Was that the right thing to do? But what if no one else adopted her? What if she never found a home? What if she was—

TAP-TAP

Sera jumped to find Alyssa staring in smugly at her with her fingernails still tap-tap-tapping annoyingly on the glass. 42 gave a low growl. She hadn't moved, but she was on high alert now. 42's entire body seemed held back. There was a tautness to her muscles Sera hadn't seen before.

Alyssa tapped harder.

*Fuck.*

Sera unrolled the window.

"Hey," she said lamely.

"Came to apologize?" Alyssa asked. 42's growl grew slightly louder. Smart dog.

"I-uh— I was in the neighborhood."

"You probably shouldn't have worn that," Alyssa said nodding at the jacket Sera still had on.

"You're right," Sera said. *I wouldn't want to get blood on it,* she thought.

"So. Go ahead." Alyssa looked at her expectantly.

Sera opened her mouth. An apology was going to fall out. An apology was supposed to fall out. That was the correct thing to do. Not correct. Smart. That was the smart thing to do, to protect herself, to embrace this lie.

"Why don't you get in?" Sera asked.

Alyssa looked at her and the still growling 42.

"Why?"

"Don't you think I should take you out?" Sera asked, recon quickly shifting to... To what? "It's the least I could do."

Alyssa considered, but Sera was right. That was the least she could do.

"Well," Alyssa demanded, "aren't you going to move your dog to the back?"

Sera opened her door and stepped out, but 42 immediately began barking.

"Sorry," Sera said, "she's never like this. Give me a second."

She went around to the passenger side and opened the door. To her surprise 42 immediately jumped out and lunged around the front of the car at Alyssa. Sera nabbed 42's leash just in time to stop her from taking Alyssa out herself. DIY safety harness be damned.

"Woah, 42. Stop. Stop." The dog calmed down, but barely. The makeshift leash was still taut under the strain of her weight pulling against it. 42 clearly could sense fucked-up energy.

"Jesus. You need to get a grip on that thing," Alyssa said, stepping back.

Sera gritted her teeth and bent down to 42. She whispered in her ear, "Don't worry. We're going to get rid of her." And 42 calmed right down. *Wow.*

Alyssa watched with awe. "What did you say?"

"I just told her that everything was going to work out."

Sera opened the back door and 42 hopped in. She didn't lie down this time. She sat at the ready, watching the back of Alyssa's head as she climbed into the passenger seat, kicking the useless yellow rope to the floor. A puff of dog hair flew into Alyssa's face as she sat down, and she sneezed.

42 looked at her, and a smug smile crossed her furry little lips. *I did that,* she thought to herself proudly.

Sera walked around to the driver's side. She couldn't believe how well this was going. *Everything is perfect*, she thought as she climbed into the car. *So what if it was supposed to be stalking only? A good killer improvises.*

Sera sat, creating another puff of dog fluff, and Alyssa sneezed again.

"Why did you get a dog?"

"To see if I could, you know, handle..." She trailed off...murder. To see if I could handle murder.

"What?"

"What?"

"To see if you could handle what?" Alyssa asked, annoyed.

"You know, I wanted to see if I'd kill it."

Alyssa stared at her blankly.

"By being a fuck-up, or whatever," Sera covered. "Responsibility. I needed to see if I could handle the responsibility."

Alyssa looked slightly on edge, but it was too late by a block or two. Sera had already pulled out, and they were on their way. Sera turned left, heading away from the bright lights of the city.

"Where are we going?" Alyssa asked.

"I know a great place where we can talk without interruption," Sera said.

"Ugh. If this is about you thinking I don't pay attention—"

"It's not," Sera said simply, and it was true.

The apartments turned to houses, and the houses grew dark as they drove further out. Sera imagined Alyssa was getting uncomfortable for a second, but then Alyssa broke the silence, diving straight into a story.

"I was with Alan tonight. That guy is such a wad. Did you know he broke up with Jackie? Like, seriously? Why would he do that? He was dying to have a girlfriend."

"Maybe he wasn't happy," Sera said. Alyssa considered this for a few seconds as if it was rocking her entire world view.

"No fucking way." She laughed. "That guy, he's lucky any girl would look at him, let alone Jackie. I think he was afraid that she would break up with him. I asked him about it," she said conspiratorially.

Sera hesitated. This was exactly what she was trying to get away from. Alyssa was still staring at her, her eyes pleading for Sera to pretend like everything was fine, to just keep the conversation going so she didn't have to face the silence.

*What the hell,* Sera thought, *I might as well have fun the last time we hang out.*

"You asked him about it? Of course you did. What'd he say?" Sera asked, and Alyssa's entire body relaxed.

*It's almost like we're real friends,* Sera mused to herself, and then it hit her. *Friends.*

She and 42 were friends.

Sera liked being around 42, and 42 seemed to like being around her. 42 didn't need anything from her. Okay, she needed that damn dog food, but she didn't need anything else.

There was no manipulation, no malice, and Sera wasn't trying to get anything from 42 either. Okay, there was that pesky attempted murder thing, but once they'd gotten past that whole "first victim" hiccup, Sera and 42 had really connected.

42 was Sera's first real friend in a while.

A wash of sadness came over her. She missed having friends. She glanced in the rearview mirror and was filled with joy when her eyes locked with 42's. She *had* missed having friends. Now, she had a new friend in 42. A best friend. An entire friend group if she included the pigs.

She wavered. They weren't there yet, she and the pigs. She knew that. Sera no longer became besties, or even friends, with anyone at the drop of a... *knife.* Not even her knife. It was bittersweet. She wondered how the pigs felt about her. *Necessary evil* sprang to mind.

More importantly, how did 42 feel?

In reply, 42's tongue lolled out of her mouth in a sideways sort of smile. It was all the answer Sera needed. She returned the smile and swung the car down an even darker road.

42 was happy Sera was happy. She wasn't sure what was going on between Alyssa and Sera, but she and Sera were good. That she could feel, but the air felt weird, charged. She could also smell the heat of anticipation dripping from Sera, which had been fine while Alyssa reeked of nerves, but Alyssa had suddenly stopped reeking of nerves. It confused 42. Now, Alyssa was happy, and Sera, still full of anticipation, was also happy.

*How could Sera be both happy and ready to pounce?* 42 pondered it for a bit, but dogs can't solve all the problems people have. Finally, she gave up and lay down. There was no immediate threat, and she was unaware of guile, so she couldn't conceive of exactly what was passing between these two creatures. She knew that Sera was the only one of them ready for action though, and that made 42 feel more secure. Still, she did not allow herself to sleep. She would stay vigilant, and each time Alyssa sneezed, her heart swelled with pride. Sera might be enjoying this lady, but 42 knew she was bad news.

# TWENTY

An hour passed before Alyssa came up for air. Sera was having a legitimately good time. If you allowed an attention whore to take the reins and entertain, it was entirely possible to be entertained. That was part of the problem, wasn't it? As long as their world was exactly what they wanted, Alyssa and The Bitch were great. The problems came when you shifted when they wanted you to stay still.

Alyssa wasn't the same as The Bitch though, was she?

The world outside the car had grown dark, and the streetlights had stopped appearing a few minutes ago. Sera figured this is what tore Alyssa from her monologuing.

"It's like we're going on a road trip," Alyssa said.

Sera almost felt bad for her. Somehow attacking her and kidnapping her seemed fine but tricking her into thinking she was safe felt a little dirty. She wondered at the morality of what she was doing again, but picking apart the morality of how she abducted someone before killing them seemed like a losing game.

She was becoming a bad person. That much was certain, and finding a thin line to walk, creating rules, and pretending she had an ethical code was a lie she wasn't interested in telling herself. She'd been manipulated enough by other people. She didn't need to do it to herself.

Sera sped past the Durmonts' farm, and 42 perked up behind her. She could feel 42's questioning gaze through the back of her seat. She hoped the dog wasn't judging her. It was an odd feeling. She immediately dismissed it as a reflection of her own concerns. She could still turn back. Soon she wouldn't be able to. She could turn off at the diner and buy a horrified Alyssa a cup of coffee and a piece of pie before dropping her off at home.

"Whoa, what's going on there?" Alyssa asked, pointing toward flashing police lights at the Durmonts' place. "Do you think it was something awful?" she asked. "Weird shit is always happening in these small towns..."

Sera knew the Durmonts must have returned from the fair to find themselves about 10 pigs short and who knows how many cows poorer. Sera hoped that pignapping was not a sufficient crime to warrant a large-scale investigation. She had done nothing to hide her tracks. Literally, she'd driven this Prius all over their place. Unconsciously, she sniffed the air, wondering if there was still a hint of residual pig.

"The smell, right? I don't know why you got a dog. So, where are we going?" Alyssa asked as Sera consciously decided to continue past the town's only diner and on to her intended destination.

"Remember how I told you my grandma left me a house?"

"Oh, yeah. It sounded like a real dump."

Sera held her tongue. As soon as the fun comes with someone like Alyssa, it's gone.

"No, I said it's out of the way," she corrected.

Alyssa raised her eyebrows. "Sure, that's what you said."

It had been... It had been exactly what she said until The Bitch, Alyssa, and everyone had begun ragging on the place for it being a farm. Then, Sera had joined right in. A little bit. A tiny bit. The tiniest bit.

It ate her up inside.

She had spent countless days on her grandma's farm running through the fields, picking crab apples, and helping her grandma bake pies, and she had thrown the entire place under the bus the second she had to fight to be heard above her nagging friends. Sera hated them for that, but she hated herself a lot more.

She was the villain. All she had to do was stand up to them. All anyone ever had to do was stand up to them. These words played in her mind, but some part of her knew it wasn't true. She had stood up to them. Not then, but eventually, and when she did, they had torn down her entire world. They had told her that she was the problem, and she had believed them.

Not all of them. Not all of them had torn her down. Some had stayed silent. Some looked away. Some were afraid.

"You're right," Sera said, surprising Alyssa. "I was a dick, and I was just going with the flow bagging on something I love. My grandma's farm is amazing, and I'm really glad I never took you guys there."

"Why?" Alyssa asked dubiously.

"You guys wouldn't get it."

"But you're taking me there now?"

"Yes."

Alyssa gave Sera a quizzical look that begged an answer, but Sera said nothing. And for once, Alyssa didn't press.

They drove on in silence. Sera watched the police lights fade in the distance, gauging how far a scream would carry. *Not far*, she concluded. *Not far at all.*

Sera smiled. She didn't even like pie, but she still loved baking them because it reminded her of her grandma.

*I'm sorry, Grandma,* she thought, sending the idea above her and into the ether as she pulled onto a small dirt road.

They were miles and miles from the police.

They were miles and miles from anything.

*I'm going to bake an apple pie,* Sera thought, noticing tree branches drooping beneath the ripe weight.

# TWENTY-ONE

Sera turned off the headlights, and the absolute darkness of the country enveloped them. 42 sniffed the air, feeling the life in it. When she did, 42 noticed that Alyssa had the slightly acrid scent of nervousness again. This calmed 42 slightly. She didn't much care whether Alyssa was nervous or not, but she liked the idea of both of the humans' scents matching, and now, they did. Sera was on the verge of something, and now, Alyssa was aware of it on a cellular level if nothing else.

Alyssa regarded the darkness with apprehension. She could feel the hair standing up on the back of her neck, but she misattributed its cause. Shadows offered hiding places for men and monsters alike.

"What do you think those cops were there for?" she asked.

"I don't know. Probably some stupid farm prank. Kids letting pigs out or something dumb. Country shit," Sera said.

"When was the last time you were here?"

"Why?" Sera didn't mean to let it, but a bit of enjoyment at Alyssa's obvious trepidation crept into her voice. "I just... I mean... Oh, Jesus. It's fucking creepy shit out here. Don't you think so? It's like there could be a serial killer or some crazy rapist or something out there."

"Or Bigfoot. We could catch him and make a million dollars. What do you say, Bigfoot hunt?"

Alyssa laughed despite her misgivings, and they melted away. "Okay, I get it. The city kid is scared, and that's funny. But you have to admit it is super dark," Alyssa said.

Sera flipped the headlights back on. "That better?" she asked.

"It'll kill your battery," Alyssa said. "Better use our phones."

*Idiot.* It hadn't even occurred to her that Alyssa had a way to call for help.

"Yup, we better use our phones." Sera hoped the batteries drained fast.

Sera opened the back door for 42, who tried to project her unease into Sera's mind, but Sera did not get it. So, 42 warily climbed down. Someone had to look out for her.

The unlikely trio walked up the short path to the porch. Sera fumbled for the hidden key as slowly as she could without seeming weird to help run down the phone batteries. It was ridiculous. She knew it. Ten extra seconds would never matter, but she kept praying to herself anyway. *Batteries die. Batteries die,* but they didn't.

She unlocked the front door and reached inside, hitting the light switch. Nothing happened.

"Shit," she said, remembering. "I didn't pay the bill. We can use our phones?" she offered, and for the first time since losing her job, she was glad she hadn't had enough money for all of her bills. Maybe Alyssa's phone would die.

"Should we go?" Alyssa asked hopefully.

Sera was at a loss. *What's the plan here?* she thought. It made sense to leave. Of course it did. But Sera always suggested things that made sense, and it never got her anywhere. *Did The Bitch listen when...* Bingo. *What would The Bitch do?* she wondered, and it came to her. *Get her drunk.*

"I have some killer moonshine," she coaxed. "You're gonna love it. It's made from blackberries and, basically, liquid death, but it's good. Strong, but good. Unless you want to go? We can go if you want."

Alyssa hesitated, looking back at the car. She listened for sirens in the distance but didn't hear any. Peer pressure was a sticky wicket. Sera hadn't called her chicken, hadn't even implied it, but if she wanted to go, was she? It wasn't that dark, she reasoned, and there were two of them. "I could use a drink," she said. "But I'm not going first."

"Afraid of the dark?" Sera jabbed only because she knew Alyssa would have. She stepped over the threshold, smelling the unmistakable scent of her grandma and the newer addition of dust. *Time heals all wounds.* She doubted that.

"Liquid death. You should call it that."

"I think I will," Sera said, shining her flashlight over the living room. *Grandma chic,* she had always joked. It was exactly how she remembered it. Wood-carved end tables, an oversized roll arm sofa, lamps that shed the perfect amount of reading light—when they worked, that is.

The darkness hid all the decorations in shadow, only making the desire to see it in the light swell in Sera.

*Tomorrow,* she thought and wondered what exactly she was planning to do tonight. *Some recon mission this turned out to be.*

Her flashlight flitted over the old furniture, briefly landing on the basement door. It was closed. It was always closed. When Sera was a kid, it was closed because "kids could fall downstairs." Then, when she was grown and her grandma was grown-er, it was closed because "old people could fall downstairs."

*Maybe I'll throw her down the stairs,* Sera quipped to herself, moving the light off the door and toward the kitchen before Alyssa could notice her hesitation.

"Moonshine's in the kitchen," Sera said, pointing. *Not push. Take. I'll get her drunk, and when she passes out, I'll take her downstairs. Then, I'll have time.*

Alyssa followed her inside, but 42 sat perfectly still just outside the door.

"Come on, 42," Sera said, reaching for the makeshift leash, but 42 took a few steps backward and sat down again. "42, inside." But again, when Sera stepped toward the dog, 42 stepped backward and sat. Defiance radiated from her, but she seemed nervous too. Could Alyssa be setting Sera up? Was it possible? She dismissed the idea but noticed that 42's defiant glare was not centered on her. It was focused squarely on Alyssa.

Sera felt the tickle of apprehension creep up her neck. She looked at Alyssa, weighing the danger, and 42's lips pulled back. She was not yet growling, but she was ready to.

"Don't look at me," Alyssa said. "She can stay in the car, for all I care."

Sera didn't know what she was looking for, but Alyssa had given her it. Whatever Alyssa had planned for tonight wasn't going to hurt Sera, not physically at least. Emotionally was a whole other question.

Sera didn't want to leave the dog outside, but—*but it's better,* her inner voice said. And it was. Who knew how 42 would react to this? Why had she brought her? 42 really did deserve better friends. Good thing they had the pigs.

"Want to go to the car?" she asked 42, and sure enough, 42 stood up and walked straight to the car, sitting down next to the passenger door waiting for Sera to open it.

Sera walked over and opened the back door for 42. 42 was not amused, but after a few seconds of silence, she climbed in. Sometimes you take what you can get. Sera shut the door, and 42 waited for her to walk around to the driver's side, but she didn't. She turned back toward the house.

*Nooooooo,* 42 howled abruptly. *Stupid human.* She scratched at the door, but it was no use. Didn't Sera realize that lady was bad news?

42 howled again, and Sera felt a pang of guilt as she continued toward the house. She really could bring 42 inside, but it was better. It was definitely better.

Sera walked inside and turned toward the archway that opened onto the small square kitchen.

"Follow me, madam," she said, shutting the front door on the howls emanating from her car.

# TWENTY-TWO

This was actually going to happen. Sera could not believe her good luck. She had planned to sit in front of Alyssa's apartment to—to what? *Collect data,* she thought, but she stopped herself. No point in lying. Not to herself. She had known she *needed* to collect data, but she had *hoped* to kidnap Alyssa. Wasn't that why she'd looked for the rope? She'd hoped she'd have a chance to grab her first victim.

*Well, her third "first victim,"* she thought. *Her first victim-victim.* She wasn't sure how to count 42 and Pig. She did not have a great victim track record. Did you count a victim that you never victimized? Maybe Pig. She did stab Pig, after all. Well, kinda. Okay, so victim numero uno.

She heard the water turn on in the bathroom. Alyssa would be back in a second. She wasn't sure how she felt about using her grandma's house for this. Her grandma wanted her to succeed, believed in her, wanted her to get new friends. Had she said that? Not exactly, and *exactly.* Her grandma hinting at anything was a full-fledged stamp of approval. Sera knew that. She wished she'd been smarter. If only.

Maybe it was okay.

It wasn't okay.

But maybe it was necessary?

Alyssa's flashlight bounced from the bathroom through the living room and to the kitchen. Her movements were bubbly, but the unnatural glow thrown around the house was from a cheap horror film.

She deposited her phone back onto the dining room table, where it joined Sera's pointing straight up at the ceiling. Pieces of sea green cabinets, red chairs, and the soft yellow patterned wallpaper were illuminated. In the grisly shadows, it was far from the inviting home her grandma had made.

Lighting made such a difference.

A piece of the kitchen door, a jutting corner of the window, the top of the archway leading back to the living room. Each entrance morphed into an escape route, promising demise. During the day, or even with the correct overheads, this kitchen could be pictured as 1957's home of the year, but not now.

*I'm gonna have to pay the electric,* Sera thought.

Alyssa didn't seem to notice though. She ran her finger through the sheen of dust on the counter and grabbed the moonshine.

"I'll pour," Sera chimed, taking the bottle from her.

Gagging a drinker's ability to consume liquor and continue to function is always a complicated task, but Sera found it particularly difficult right now. She was basically spoon-feeding Alyssa the equivalent of Everclear, and Alyssa didn't seem phased. Sera never would have called Alyssa an alcoholic. She would have called her a social drinker, a partier. She would have said Alyssa had a high tolerance. Now, five shots into the moonshine inside an hour while giving herself water, Sera was convinced that Alyssa was a high-functioning alcoholic.

"How often do you drink?" Sera asked.

"As often as I want. Woooo!" Alyssa hollered back, any semblance of nerves obliterated by the booze.

"Yeah, but really?"

"What kind of a bullshit question is that? I drink when I want." Alyssa gave her a pointed look. This wasn't the first time her drinking had been questioned, and she didn't like it.

"I didn't mean it like that. I mean, I'm almost falling over, and you don't even seem tipsy." "Oh. Yeah, I have a—"

"High tolerance." Sera cheered with her in unison, gaining back the frayed trust. The marching cry of those who were never without booze for too long never failed to unite.

Alyssa hugged Sera and lingered.

"You know I fucking love you, right? I wasn't really mad." Alyssa drifted back, and Sera thought if she kissed her very "straight" friend, she would instantly be kissed back. She reconsidered the light as the seedy pallor of a bad porn.

Sera grabbed the bottle of moonshine, shattering what might have been mistaken for a moment.

"To not being mad!" She poured another shot of moonshine for Alyssa and one of water from a bottle sitting on the formica countertop for herself. She was lucky it was dark. Alyssa would normally be all over being the bartender.

Alyssa stumbled a little as she slammed down the shot glass. Sera knew if she waited a little bit longer Alyssa would pass out. One, maybe two more shots and she would be putty in Sera's hand.

*Serial killer of the year, here I come.*

"Whooo-oo," Alyssa said, sucking down the sting of the alcohol. "This shit is weak," she slurred. "You're weak," she said and pointed an accusatory finger at Sera. "Did you know you're weak?" she asked, chuckling, and Sera lunged at her.

So much for waiting.

She crashed into Alyssa's torso hard, sending them back several feet into the living room. Alyssa fell to the floor, her head narrowly missing the edge of the dated coffee table, but Sera went down too, right on top of Alyssa, who'd grabbed her in a clumsy sorta bear hug.

Sera's ribs came to life, screaming at her for the sudden attack, and for a moment, all her energy was focused on breathing. The world shrank down to a pinpoint of light.

*Don't pass out. Don't pass out,* she thought.

But Alyssa wasn't thinking. There wasn't time. She clawed at the air, but her arms were still wrapped around Sera's torso, saving Sera's face from her finely manicured talons.

Alyssa was fierce, and she definitely had the advantage over Sera physically. They were a similar size, but Alyssa's drive to be in the limelight drove her to countless hours at the gym. She never did anything that might "bulk" her up, but Pilates can sure tone the hell out of a dedicated chick's muscles.

Sera gritted her teeth and raised up onto her knees, grabbing Alyssa by the shoulders. She slammed her back into the ground hard. This was her goddamned day. She kept pounding her into the floor. If she could just hit hard enough, Alyssa would be out, and she would be one step closer to being the killer she wanted to be. But Alyssa was not cooperating. She was lashing out like the cornered beast she was. She clenched her fists and swung repeatedly.

Sera grunted and groaned, her ribs and shoulder blades taking the brunt of the onslaught. Each hit a firework, fueling her rage.

Alyssa's head was still fuzzy as hell from the booze, but at the edges of confusion she began to process again. Fear surged her adrenaline, shoving the alcohol to the side. *Head,* she thought, *head.* And she began wildly slamming her balled-up fists into the back of Sera's skull. She couldn't punch, not from this position, but it was something.

Sera's head snapped forward over and over as Alyssa hit her. What the fuck had she done? Even as she fought to overpower Alyssa, she railed on herself for her idiocy. The whole point of the alcohol was to make this easy. If she had just waited a little longer. If she had just—

Her head flew back, and she yelled out in pain. Alyssa had a large chunk of her unruly hair clenched in her fist.

"You bitch," Alyssa screamed. "You fucking bitch."

And she fucking lost it, screaming incoherently.

A rally cry. A wolf's howl. A death wail.

Spastic, she yanked Sera's hair back and bucked her hips, twisting and turning in all directions. Sera was thrown into the air, then landed on her again, then into the air, and landing again, air, land, air, land—Sera burst out laughing. She was a kid again in a playground brawl. She lifted one arm into the air, pretending she was riding a bucking bronco.

"Yeeehaw!" she let out.

They could be fighting over Polly Pocket or Beyblades or whose turn it was to be the pizza delivery person, but Alyssa yanked on Sera's hair so hard it pulled her back into reality.

"Oouuuuuch!" Sera shoved Alyssa back down toward the ground and felt the hair beginning to tear from her scalp. She rolled back and to the side, desperate to free herself.

"Fuuuuck." She grunted.

But Alyssa held, locking Sera within reach. They lay in a position meant for sweet nothings but burst into the foot version of a slap fight instead.

*Slap, slap, slap.*

"Let go of my hair!"

Legs flailed about.

"This hair?"

They shielded their faces.

"Never!" Alyssa tugged, pulling Sera closer just as Sera's foot flung out, and it connected.

BAM!

Her hair was free!

Her ribs were fucked.

She definitely should have gone to the hospital.

"I'm gonna kill you!" Alyssa screamed, no trace of pain, and Sera realized the alcohol meant to hinder her might actually be Alyssa's superpower.

Alyssa pushed herself to her feet, wobbly but invincible, and flung all her body weight toward Sera. Instinctively, Sera threw her leg out in a desperate attempt at a side kick and connected!

Luck, the Gods, or the devil was on Sera's side, and clear projectile vomit spewed from Alyssa's mouth. She collapsed on all fours and puked again.

"Time out— Time out—" She gasped as her body expelled the liquid fire inside her. She groped in the dark for something, anything. "Garba—" Puke. "Ca—" Puke.

Sera scrambled to her feet, undeterred by the puke on her face and shirt. She looked for a garbage—

*Wait! What?*

She wheeled around. The lamp. A few feet away.

"My hair," Alyssa murmured, looking at a clump of vomit clinging to it.

Sera grabbed the lamp, and Alyssa pulled her hand down her hair, trying to get the vomit out.

"My hair—" And Sera whacked her on the head with the lamp.

Sera stood above Alyssa, who crumpled on the carpet in a pool of her own secondhand moonshine. It was safe to say, it could have gone better.

Alyssa wasn't even knocked out, but she couldn't form a thought. That was something. She murmured and tried to speak, but language wasn't at her disposal.

*There's a first for everything,* Sera thought and rolled her over onto her back. Sera wondered what was running through her brain, if anything at all. She looked down at her with an indifferent stare. She'd won.

It was all over, except the murder.

Sera grabbed her phone flashlight and walked out the front door to her car. 42 had climbed back into the front seat and curled up to sleep. The click of Sera opening the car door triggered 42, who immediately growled and barked at the figure looming over her from behind the bright light.

"It's me, 42. It's me," she said and moved the light.

42 stopped barking, but her spidey-sense was still up. Something was wrong. Sera was clearly... She paused. Sera didn't seem rattled. She seemed calm but rushed. In fact, Sera's distinct *lack* of *neurosis* is what had 42 wondering what was up.

As Sera leaned into the back seat, grabbing the rope, 42 smelled the acrid sweetness of vomit and the retreating scent of fear. She jumped into the back seat and out the door before Sera could stop her.

Something was afoot.

"42. Back in the car. Come on." But 42 just sat and watched her from a few feet away. "Please," she begged, but 42 simply stood and took a few steps toward the house. Whether Sera knew it or not, she needed 42's help. Something was off about that other human, and Sera was clearly not as aware of that as she should be.

Careful not to make too much noise, Sera sighed and pushed the door shut. Briefly, she wondered if noise was an issue. The houses were so far apart it shouldn't matter, but it could. She should have taken Alyssa to the basement. That was her plan. Get her drunk, take her to the basement to pass out and sleep it off, then tie her up. Unfortunately, Sera had a self-control issue.

"Who's weak now?" she asked the shadows as she stomped her way back to the house with the rope and 42 in tow. She didn't want to admit it, but she felt a bit foolish that she'd let her temper run her show.

*It could have cost the show,* Sera thought.

*But it didn't,* her inner voice replied.

*But it could have,* Sera affirmed, and then she saw that the kitchen was completely dark.

Alyssa's phone.

She dashed to the house with 42 racing at her side. Sera stopped at the kitchen door and listened. Nothing.

The phone's flashlight had been shining straight at the ceiling when she left. Hadn't it? Had it died? It was on, she was sure of it, but the room was dark now. Behind her, 42 tensed. Nothing about this felt right.

Sera held her light against her leg, blocking its glow and creaked the old door open. She stepped inside, reached to the left, and quietly eased a drawer open. She slipped a large butcher knife out, barely looking down. She was as ready as she could be. She crept towards the living room. 42 stayed a watchful foot behind her, helping, but not crazy.

There was mumbling.

*Shit.*

She tried to keep her focus ahead, on what was coming, but she couldn't help herself. She flashed her light at the table, and it glinted off Alyssa's phone.

Still on the table.

Dead.

She heaved a sigh of relief and heard the mumbling again, but it wasn't mumbling. It was Alyssa moaning softly. Alyssa was trying to force herself onto her feet, but it wasn't working. Sera went in and kicked her legs out from under her and began tying her up.

42 sat in the doorway, watching. She didn't understand what had happened. She knew evil though, and Sera was currently tying up the evil. 42 stifled a soft whimper. She wanted to leave. They should leave. They could leave the evil behind, but she also remembered getting caught and dragged to the cement cage. Sometimes evil came after you even if you tried to get away. 42 didn't know what to do. She hoped Sera did, but she could sense Sera still needed help. She needed lots and lots of help.

Sera noticed 42's eyes on her and felt the ping of guilt. She didn't feel bad for what she'd done, but she really should have made the dog wait in the car. It could never understand the need for her actions.

Sera instantly began buckling down her feelings. She could feel herself losing another friend. Feel 42 slipping away from her, and this time, it was her fault. It was all her fault. She would have to take it back to the pound. It. She hadn't called 42 "it" for quite some time now—It felt like years, though they'd only known each other for days. She, 42, would go to some other owner.

She looked over at 42 watching her with regret. Poor, stupid dog.

*Poor, stupid me.*

What now? 42 lifted her paw and batted limply at the air. Reaching. Sera's eyes softened. She dropped the half-tied rope and inched a few feet closer to 42, careful not to spook her. She held out her hand, and 42 put her paw in it.

Sera felt a swell of acceptance.

Behind her, a moan seemed to gain a level of coherence, and Sera released 42's paw.

"Go on, girl. Kitchen," Sera said, and 42 took the three or four steps backward into the kitchen and lay down, watching Sera to make sure she was indeed all right.

Sera turned around and shored up her knots. They would hold.

She turned the knob on the basement door and let it fall open. She looked into the abyss below and grabbed Alyssa by the rope tied around her hands. She dragged her to the stairs, and "Girls Just Wanna Have Fun" popped into her head as she *thump, thump, thumped* Alyssa all the way down the stairs.

42 did not follow. She did not want to, and she knew now that Sera was safe even if the crazy one was not.

# TWENTY-THREE

Moonlight shone through the basement's egress window, creating a measure of light below. It gave Sera the distinct impression that she was walking into the light rather than away from it as she trudged further and further into the depths, dragging her one-time ally and friend. It felt good. It felt sooooo good. This was how it was supposed to be. It should be her alone with the certainty of her thoughts, only her work before her—a series of actions devoid of the emotions that had held her back all these years. This moment simply was. She simply was, and Alyssa would simply be no more soon.

She deposited Alyssa at the bottom of the stairs, leaning her up against the wall. Sera put her there, in that strangely benign sitting position, without thinking about how little Alyssa's comfort mattered. Without thinking how little sitting up or lying down mattered. Simple.

Alyssa was both awake and not awake. Sera wondered at how long it took someone to really come back to consciousness after being knocked out. She glanced at her wrist instinctively for that watch she no longer wore, and for the first time, she remembered smashing her Apple watch to bits in a moment of panic without hating herself. It was a thing she'd done. It wasn't a sign of weakness. She had smashed the thing to bits after getting a text from The Bitch that demanded she give The Bitch her attention, that she wouldn't even have looked at if...

She breathed out slowly.

It didn't matter. It was nice remembering now.

She had thrown the watch to the ground in her tiled bathroom and stomped and clomped and jumped on it over and over again. She'd had to grab a hammer to finish the job, hitting it over and over until bits began to fly off. Well, to chip off, to crack apart.

*Smashing it should be an ad.*

She liked to remember it as springs and cogs flying from a torture device, but that wasn't the case at all. There were no springs, no physically satisfying components flying through the air, just circuits and bits that had been sealed together in an artificial feeling way.

Like super glue used to hold a wound closed.

That was when she'd realized something was irrefutably wrong with her.

Jumping on her watch. Screaming in her bathroom.

That was the day she discovered she had to change something about how she interacted with the world on a deep, deep level.

The world wasn't going to change, not for her.

People weren't going to change.

The Bitch wasn't going to change.

Instead of crying and flailing about in her mind like she'd usually done, she had sat down in the bathroom, leaning against the wall, much like Alyssa was slumped against the wall now, and had let the absolute blankness of her mind resonate for some time. A long time. There was nothing left. A husk of her former self.

What an expression. Like an honest lie. A husk of her former self, but completely full.

It was dark when she'd finally stirred. She didn't check her phone or turn on the TV. She had lain down in bed and curled up in her blanket. The red blanket from her mom.

*My almost murder blanket,* Sera chuckled to herself, glad she hadn't ruined it, glad it smelled of 42 and bits of her mother. Comfort.

Sitting on the bathroom floor, she'd known that things were going to change. Things were going to change, or she was going to kill herself. It wasn't sad or disturbing or anything, really. It just was. Much like this moment just was.

Empty and full.

Sera was home.

She looked up from her bare wrist and realized that most likely a very small amount of time had passed between when she'd struck Alyssa and now. Maybe three minutes, or five. It felt like a lifetime ago. It was true that the world slowed down in some high-pressure situations, or, in Sera's case, when you needed it to. She needed to take all the time she wanted, and the subjective nature of reality was offering that to her.

"Thank you," she said aloud to the universe.

A TAPPING answered her.

Confused, she looked for the source of the sound, but nothing was moving. 42 began barking ferociously before Sera fully registered the sound. Knocking, actual knocking at the door. She glanced out the window. Sure enough, the moonlight had been met with headlights.

Someone was here.

Sera glanced over at Alyssa. She wasn't going anywhere, but she could come to at any time. Sera yanked off her socks and shoved them in Alyssa's mouth. She rushed around the basement, looking for something to secure them with. Tools and rope hung on the wall behind a small worktable. The rope was too unwieldy, but something. She pushed around the crap that had collected on the table over years of use and Sera's half-assed attempts at cleaning up. No matter how many times her grandma said, "Put it away," she never did.

Electrical tape!

It was dusty and old, but it would hold. She hurried over to Alyssa and wrapped a long piece of electrical tape around Alyssa's head and the socks, securing them safely in her mouth.

KNOCK-KNOCK

Sera ran halfway up the stairs.

KNOCK-KNOCK

But remembered she had tied Alyssa's hands in front of her. She could pull the tape off.

Sera raced back downstairs and roughly pulled the rope off before retying Alyssa's hands behind her back. "There," she said to no one in particular.

KNOCK-KNOCK

"Coming!" she hollered and ran upstairs. A rush of blood reached her head, and she felt woozy for just a moment. She grabbed onto the banister, regaining herself and using her arm to help propel her upstairs.

She shut the door behind her.

"42. No. Quiet. Don't bark," she ordered to no avail.

She opened the front door an inch, careful to keep the disarray of the living room hidden.

"Sorry, my dog. 42, quiet." But the barking continued. "It's all right," Sera said and realized her tone was saying anything but. She bent down, petting 42, and cooed, "It's okay. We're okay." 42 calmed, but in doing this, the door opened slightly wider.

"Your dog's name is 42?"

"Yup." what an inane question. She looked up—

Fuck. A cop.

"Why not 43?"

"Because 42 is better." *Be nice, Sera.* "Just joking. I just like it."

"Ah," he found himself saying, a bit disappointed. He'd enjoyed her harsh initial approach. Being a cop had a way of inducing a fake niceness in people that he had come to loathe. He'd only been on the force a few years, but already he wondered if he could do this for the rest of his life. *Maybe it would be different in a big town,* he thought. *Maybe.*

"Your neighbors up the road, the Durmonts, seem to have misplaced some pigs. You haven't happened upon them, have you?" His eyes darted past her into the dark room. Surely, he wasn't looking for the pigs, but cops were always looking for something, weren't they? The dark room didn't hold many answers from his angle, but if he happened to come inside, the residue of her and Alyssa's fight would be clearly evident.

"Pigs? Like pig-pigs?" she asked lamely.

"Yup." He mimicked her delivery of the word. *What an inane question,* he echoed. Was he mocking her? "Like farm pigs," he added.

"Are they like farm pigs, or are they farm pigs?" she asked with a mischievous twinkle in her eye.

"They are farm pigs." He liked her. *Yup,* he liked her snide little way.

"No pigs around here."

"You sure?"

"I think I'd notice."

"You got a lot of land."

*Okay, I'll play,* she thought to herself.

"How many?"

"Forty-two."

A laugh burst out of her. She let go of 42 and quickly covered her mouth. Then she quickly reached back for 42, but 42 hadn't lunged or even growled.

"Good girl," she said and stood up. "I think I'd notice forty-two pigs, don't you?"

Their eyes caught for a minute. Lingered. But a moan crept up from the basement. A low moan. A faint moan, but a moan. Sera hoped he wasn't paying attention.

"Who's that?" he asked, more disappointed than concerned.

"My friend. She, ugh—" Sera stumbled.

"Been drinking?"

"What?" Sera asked, her mind racing for how that was illegal in this situation.

"Your shirt."

She looked down, and as her eyes landed on Alyssa's vomit, the smell hit her. She choked back a light gag. She hated the smell of puke.

"Oh, God," she stepped back, letting the door fall open further, and went into the kitchen grabbing a rag and coming back, wiping off the puke. She stopped dead when she saw him standing there.

He'd come a foot or two into the room. The door was still between him and the wreckage off to the side, but just barely. If he leaned forward even an inch, she was toast.

Another moan came from below. Louder this time. Stronger. Sera forced her eyes to stay on him, to not drift to the basement door. Was that natural? Should she look at the door? What was natural?

Suddenly, 42 snarled and barked, and barked again and again at the cop. He stepped back in a show of deference, and Sera relaxed, which made 42 relax. She quieted. She'd done her job. Sera was okay.

"She doesn't like me."

"I don't know if she likes anyone. I just got her."

"What's with the lights?"

"You mean the lack of light?"

"Well, yeah." Now his eyes were moving around the space inquisitively. He wasn't aware that he was suspicious yet, but he was. The hairs on the back of his neck had just begun to consider standing on end.

"I didn't pay the electric."

Another moan.

*Fuck!* Sera screamed internally.

"And your friend?"

Motioning to the puke on her shirt, Sera said, "She's sick. She drank too much. Waaay too much. I really should help her."

Before he knew what he was doing, he asked, "This isn't one of those serial-killer type situations, is it? Where it seems innocent, but then you invite me in, and you kill me to cover up the other victim writhing in agony in your basement?" A joke. It was supposed to be a joke, but it was dark, too dark. At the end. *What was that?* He floundered internally for a moment. *How do I back out of this?* he wondered but dismissed it. It was lost. Any moment he may or may not have had with her was gone. Long gone.

But she smiled. He'd basically landed on the truth, sure, but it was funny. More than that, it was *her kind* of funny.

"I hadn't considered that, but thank you. Now that I know how to get out of this awful situation, will you please come in?" It was strategic, but she would have said it anyway. She was enjoying the flirtatious words falling from her lips.

"If I value my life, I better not." He winked and took another step back and out the door.

"Shucks. Then I'll never get away with it."

He turned and headed back towards his police car. "If you see any pigs, call up the station." Then added, as if it were an afterthought, "My name is Clarence."

"Sera," she said.

She lingered in the doorway, listening to the sweet music of Alyssa's moans growing louder behind her as he climbed into his cruiser.

"She's the answer," he called out the window as he started the car.

"What?"

"To the universe," he said and waved as he drove away.

Sera looked down at 42 and scratched her head. "Yes, you are," she cooed. "Yes, you are." She knew she knew 42 from somewhere other than the kennel. How had she forgotten that? It didn't matter. Sera's subconscious knew even if she didn't.

42 leaned into the scratches. All was right with the world.

Sera shut the door.

A long moment of absolute silence enveloped them while Sera and 42 stood in the dark, letting the world wash over them.

*I should have done this sooner,* Sera thought, then reprimanded herself. *It's okay. You did what you did. You didn't know. You're here now.* She repeated these platitudes to herself, but she didn't believe them. *Should have* still tugged at the corners of her brain. It lurked in the dark. It sat, silently waiting. It didn't have to plan its return. It hadn't left. *Should have* had no fear that it would ever be forced to leave. Not really.

A small gurgle came from downstairs, and it struck Sera that silence might not be good.

"Uh-oh," she said, throwing open the basement door and running downstairs.

42 did not follow but looked into the dark pit with a feeling hovering between concern and self-preservation. Self-preservation won, and she posted up, facing the door. No surprises were going to catch her unaware because 42 was smart, and dark rooms with mean people were not smart.

Sera's feet hit the cold concrete floor, and she saw Alyssa lying on her back, choking. Sera ripped the tape off of Alyssa's mouth, and a pocketful of pressurized vomit shot the socks out, peppering Sera with granules of whatever Alyssa had eaten hours before. All the clear liquor had been expelled. This was the dregs of the dregs.

Sera gagged.

She urged herself, "Don't puke! Don't—" But puke she did. The bacon, and cereal, and water of her past few days coming up, and up, and up, mixing with Alyssa's clear liquor and pink stomach acid.

"Don't. You're done. You're—" Nope.

Sera wiped her face.

"Don't. Don't puke." But the thought of Alyssa's puke on her face or in her mouth.

And—

the thought of her puke.

And—

the smell.

And—

And, and, and—

And she puked, and she puked, and she puked.

Until she sat back.

Empty.

Puke everywhere.

She felt like shit.

This was not how—

*No—*

But she didn't puke again.

This was not how her first murder was supposed to go.

But was Alyssa? She looked up and confirmed that yes, Alyssa was quite dead indeed. A thin trail of pink puke spittle trickled out Alyssa's mouth and down her chin.

Sera looked down at their combined puke. It was like a Rorschach representation of their relationship.

*Well, shit. Or, well, puke,* she thought.

Now she had to do something with the body.

# TWENTY-FOUR

I t was a long fucking night. Alyssa wasn't supposed to be dead yet. Sera was supposed to have time to figure out what to do with the body. The cops weren't supposed to show up during her first murder for that matter, but that was life. Nothing ever went to plan, but did she have a plan? Did she *really?*

*Do better, Sera.*

There should be a meme. She could picture it now. There'd be a piss-poor hole in the woods and a body only half covered with dirt, one shoe missing. A killer, likely Sera, would be handcuffed near a tree with a *Home-Alone*-who-me? expression on her face.

The caption would read "Stop being racist, sexist, homophobic, transphobic. Oh, and do better at disposing of bodies. Come on, serial killers. Get your s*** together!" with three little clap emojis.

She could only imagine the comments.

Sera threw another shovelful of dirt over her shoulder. This was a solution, but it was not a *good* solution. She did not want to turn her grandma's yard into a graveyard. Besides, Alyssa didn't deserve to be buried near her pet hamster. That hamster was awesome.

She'd carefully chosen a spot far away from Plato, but she still wasn't happy about it.

She dug and dug in the dirt behind her grandma's house. She should stop thinking of it that way, she reprimanded herself. Behind her house. Her house. It sounded foreign. She could live here. If it came to that.

If—

It already seemed like it had come to that. Hadn't it? She hoped the pigs were okay. She hoped her apartment was okay too, but that ship had probably sailed.

She had no idea what to do with them. In a perfect world, she'd bring them here... In a perfect world, she'd let them roam free, but in this world, someone would find them, and they'd become lunch or breakfast. Breakfast was much more likely, she mused lingering on the thought.

*Mmmm, bacon.*

She was tired. Too tired to think clearly.

She should be wearing gloves.

Her hands were worn thin. Blisters had sprung up at the base of each finger, and her ribs hurt so much that the pain had ceased to exist. She didn't know that was a thing before tonight. She was afraid to look at her side.

She slammed the shovel into the dirt. Farm soil should be soft, but it wasn't. Neglect had dried it up. Her neglect.

*Fucking neurosis.*

She really wanted to suck less.

42 lay in the grass, watching Sera.

Maybe she really could keep them here. 42 and the pigs could run around the fields while she and Pig sat on the porch drinking mojitos and yelling for them to stop tearing up the cornfields.

She chuckled to herself. There hadn't been cornfields here in years. When she was very little, she remembered wandering through them with her grandpa, but it was an impression more than a memory. It was a feeling built up of having the memory told to her with love by him over and over again.

She could look up and see the sun glint off their entwined hands, then his smiling face obscured by the brightness of the full yellow sun and the blue, blue sky behind his head. She loved this memory. It was one of her most cherished. Even if it was a memory montage compiled from the memories of his love for his memories of them together in the cornfield.

He died too young.

So did her grandma.

So would she.

She wiped the sweat from her brow. The edges of the world were lightening, and the hole was not big.

Initially, 42 had dug with gusto along with Sera even if she hadn't necessarily dug where she should have. There was a small collection of a few inch-deep holes scattered around Sera's larger hole.

*42 would love it here.*

Sera stared at what should have been the black pit of a six-foot grave. Instead, it was a sad child-length hole of barely a foot deep. Alyssa would be inches from the surface. An animal would dig her up in five minutes. Hell, a bird could peck the earth and uncover her remains if Sera put her in this sorry attempt at a grave. Guess murder really was the easy part. Well, possibly because Alyssa had kinda sorta murdered herself choking on her own puke. Hm.

Sera stared at the hole.

*It's a garden,* she decided. She would buy flowers and plant them. Something her grandma would have grown. Hollyhocks. No one would ever know it was supposed to be a grave.

But she still had to get rid of the body.

# TWENTY-FIVE

Back inside the basement, Sera stared at Alyssa's body. Only a few hours old, and the stench of death had begun to set in. Or was that the puke? Sera took a deep whiff. She gagged. Definitely the upchuck. Luckily, she was too tired to puke again. Plus, there was nothing left in her stomach.

Bonus!

She grabbed a couple towels. She knew that killing would require a lot of clean-up, but her heart had been set on cleaning up blood and guts. Worst case, she expected some broken glass. She remembered the living room. Well, she might get to clean up some broken glass after all. Had the lamp shattered? She couldn't remember. Fatigue was coming over her fast, but she wanted to at least get the puke cleaned up and the body moved. Though moved where she didn't know. The grave was a dead end.

She sprayed some bleach and knelt to begin cleaning. She wished she'd brought some paper towels. She'd never feel clean if she used these towels again. She'd have to chuck them. She looked at the two she held in her hands.

*No way*, she thought, *I'm not cleaning up puke and throwing away my grandma's towels. Fuck you, Alyssa.*

She dropped them on top of the washer against the back wall. Even though they hadn't touched the vomit, she would absolutely wash them before using them again.

She looked back at the mess.

*Now what?*

She stared at the pool of cakey, drying puke and Alyssa's leg. Alyssa's knee was resting in vomit, and her jeans had a growing dark spot where they were absorbing as much stomach acid as they could.

*Hm.*

Half zoned out, Sera's eyes moved from the jeans, up Alyssa's leg, and to her shirt. She didn't even know what she was thinking until... Sera turned all her old shirts into rags. Was that too much? Too far? Was it wrong to clean up puke with a dead girl's shirt? Was it better if it was the dead girl's puke in the first place? Tough call.

*It really is the natural progression*, she assured herself.

Also, Alyssa's shirt was a lot nicer than Sera's was. Than any of hers were, really. Sera shopped almost exclusively off the Target clearance rack while Alyssa shopped at Guess or Express at full price.

She eyed Alyssa's shirt. Maybe she'd use her own shirt to clean up and keep Alyssa's. A shame puke had dribbled down Alyssa's face and chin onto it. Just a couple drops though. Her own shirt was covered. So...

If she didn't take it, she'd discard it with Alyssa. So, if she was already getting rid of it, what was the harm? It was basically recycling, up-cycling, being environmentally friendly. Right?

Also, Sera's T-shirt was bigger. She'd be able to clean up more puke more easily. It was basic mathematics.

But, did she really want to wear Alyssa's shirt?

*Hm.*

It was a hard sell ethically, but an easy choice. She'd killed her. They'd both puked, and she didn't want to throw away her grandma's towels, but she wasn't going to wear Alyssa's clothes. Not ever. So...

Serial killers weren't known for their impeccable ethics anyway.

She grabbed the shirt and pulled on it, struggling to get it up over Alyssa's head. She gently lifted Alyssa's arms even though she'd been bludgeoning her hours ago. Alyssa's arms were stiff, and her body kept toppling this way or that. It's true what they say, death adds ten pounds.

Done being gentle, Sera yanked hard on the shirt, which finally pulled free, sending her stumbling backward. Her foot hit puke, and she skidded. Her arms shot out to the sides as she slid through the basement on a rink of bile like a kid on ice skates for the first time. She came to a stop, still holding her arms out to the sides.

*Wow.*

Whoop!

She windmilled her arms, feet slipping forward and back until she came to a second stop.

*Double wow.*

Ever so carefully, she inched toward dry concrete. Careful, careful, and she made it!

*Gold! For the girl in the puke-covered shirt.* She lifted her arms, joining a fake crowd in cheering for herself.

*Huzzah!*

Her competition had not faired nearly so well.

On the floor, Alyssa looked like a mannequin made for a haunted house that had been through the ringer. She had toppled over, and her arms were crooked in weird ways, not quite falling to her sides, but not quite staying over her head. Seeing her there, in her florescent pink bra with graying skin in a pool of half-dried puke, it was hard to imagine she'd ever been a threat.

Murderer - one. Assholes - zero. Or, assholes all victories before tonight.

*Damn.*

Sera sprayed the puke with far more bleach than she needed. The floor was drenched, and bleach was seeping into Alyssa's jeans. Soon there would forever be a white stain where the bleach had burned away all of the vomit.

*Was it necessary to kill her?* Sera paused, watching the liquid bleach swirl with the vomit pathetically. She waited for a sense of sorrow or remorse. Real remorse. None came.

She had a twinge of something, a creeping sensation that something was drastically wrong, a ping of terror, but it wasn't guilt. It wasn't remorse. *Trained guilt*, that's what it was. That feeling where you feel guilty, but you know you shouldn't, and kinda you don't, but you also do, and you hate yourself, but you hate everyone else more, and you just don't know what to do, or how the world ever survives with all of this bullshit, and it's never ever ever going to end.

Phew!

Trained Guilt.

Now, it had a name, and monsters didn't have nearly as much power once you named them.

And it wasn't hers. In fact, right now, she wasn't feeling guilt or trained guilt at all. It was fear. Fear and certainty that Alyssa and, eventually, The Bitch would come and attack her for doing this. That, somehow, they would turn this into her fault.

She burst out laughing. Oh fuck, she needed therapy. This was her fault. No. *Fault* was the wrong word. Blame was a child's game. This was her choice. She had made it because of a thousand different choices they had made before. She had made it because... Well. It didn't matter.

*It did. It really, really did matter.*

She took a deep breath and tried to connect to her emotional core. What was she feeling?

*Fear.*

Okay. Made sense. She'd killed someone, and a cop had dropped by. But it wasn't fear of getting caught. It was fear of having to deal with The Bitch.

*So, if The Bitch has nothing to do with this, if she's not allowed to tell me how to live my life or have any type of influence over me, then what?*

*Nothing,* her inner voice whispered.

She checked in with herself again. The fear was behind a small wall. Still there, but controlled. Held at bay by the simple truth that no one else should get to live her life or dictate how she lived it. And... And... But the canvas was blank. Where emotions should be streaming down in reds and golds and greens, there was nothing. She didn't know how to feel what she felt.

That made her want to cry. She should at least know how to feel her feelings.

*Great,* she thought. *I have fear and depression.* But it wasn't quite right. The depression had been strong. It had been mixed with a lot of self-hate... *Depression is self-hate,* she thought. But no. Depression was often random self-hate. Her form of self-hate was specific. She hated herself for letting someone else come into her life so completely.

She wouldn't let herself think it.

She had been strong as a kid. Very strong.

*Therapy via murder. Not healthy,* she thought, *but not the most unhealthy.*

She wiped the bleach and puke compound with Alyssa's shirt. The material wasn't thick enough to hold up to the massive amount of liquid, and the scent came through with a harsh acidity.

She had been so strong.

She looked at what was now a rag, felt the liquid bleed onto her skin, and took a deep breath.

She was strong.

She didn't gag. She didn't even want to.

She rinsed the vomit down the utilitarian sink and wiped up more and more chunks. She washed her hands. Once. Just once. She was okay.

She pulled off her shirt rinsed it out and wrung it dry.

Now, she had to move the body.

She really hadn't properly planned for this. She needed a sheet. Again, she was unwilling to use her grandma's.

*Do better,* she smiled to herself, pulled back on her sticky wet shirt, and off to Target she went.

# TWENTY-SIX

Sera and 42 jumped back into her Prius and flew down the dirt road back onto the highway and toward Target. The red sign glowed before them like a beacon. Target, the goal, the bull's-eye, the destination. She swung into the parking lot and glanced at the clock. They had gotten there with breakneck speed.

She climbed out, and 42 jumped out after her, her rope-leash held between her teeth. Sera took it from her as they approached the store.

*We are kicking ass,* she thought. *I got twenty bucks cash, enough for some sheets with no credit card trail. If we're lucky, we'll have a few bucks left over for a bone.*

Sera was exhausted, but this was the easy part. Grab a sheet, wrap up a body, and...Okay, this wasn't the easy part. The murder itself was actually the easy part and the rewarding part, but this was a necessary part, *the* necessary part, really. All the rest she could do or not do. It was her choice. But she had to dispose of the body. She liked this version of herself. Kicking ass and taking names. Decisiveness personified.

They briskly stepped up to the automatic doors and— And nothing. They stopped. 42 looked up at Sera. She didn't know how this worked, but Sera seemed so sure of herself. Why were they facing a barred path? Couldn't she just open the door?

Sera waved her free hand over her head. Nothing. Then she saw the manual door, back on track. She briskly walked over to it, grabbed the handle and yanked— Locked.

*Shit.*

She looked inside. All the lights were on. People were walking around, pushing shopping carts. No, she realized, employees were walking around pushing shopping carts full of go-backs. She looked at the hours: 10 a.m. to midnight.

It was six-thirty. They had three and a half hours to wait.

*Double shit.*

She was awful at this. She didn't even know how she could be this awful at this. They really should get a move on, but she needed a sheet, a tarp? She needed something. Some kind of plan. She was trying to think, but her mind wasn't focusing. She was tired. Really fucking tired. 42 whined, drawing Sera's attention. First things first.

She took 42 on a loop of the parking lot until 42 found the exactly right, most perfectly-perfect spot on the seemingly all identical-looking, but most definitely not identical-smelling, grass to take a leak on. 42 was thrilled. That had taken exactly twelve minutes. A lot longer than it should have, but way less than the three hours they needed to use up.

Sera took 42 back to the car. She considered driving to another store, but in this town, Target was the only consumer-based big-box store present. It was the most likely to be open at this time and the one she was least likely to be noticed in. Target it was.

42 curled up on the passenger seat, and Sera leaned the driver's seat slightly back. She'd been awake all night. She needed to think, but she could relax a little as she did. Once she got the sheet, she would dispose of the body. Dispose of the... how

though? She didn't know. Where? A ditch or a ravine? Maybe down at the lake? She had no idea what she was doing. And, for the first time, Sera wondered not whether she could become a serial killer, but whether she could get away with being a serial killer.

So far, she was really bad at this. From victim selection, to kidnapping, to murder to body disposal. She kinda had sucked at it all. She didn't plan any of it well, and the one plan she had—getting Alyssa drunk and having her pass out—she had abandoned almost instantly. Sera realized, with some lament, that there was a really good chance that if she were a serial killer for very long, or maybe even just a killer, that she would get caught. Maybe she'd already get caught. She should have planned ahead. Planted a weapon. Got an alibi. Figured out how to dispose of the body. Planned an escape. Somehow, she had assumed she'd magically be good at this—really, really good at this, if she was honest. How had she not thought about what to do with the body?

• • • ● • ● • • •

"I don't want to go to the store!!!!"

Sera shot up in her seat, frantically searching for the source of the offending sound. She spotted a kid screaming at top volume as she was dragged past her car window. 42 glanced up from licking her crotch, as nonplussed as she could be.

11 o'clock. How had she slept until 11 o'clock? The parking lot was filling up. She opened the car door, and on cue, 42 began to whine. Her eyes were again caked in morning eye goop. Sera wiped them with her shirt. She should have brought the damn eye drops. 42 whined again, but it wasn't about her eyes. It was time to hustle up. Sera needed to go to the bathroom too, but she would have to wait her turn.

One exactly perfect pee-spot later, Sera and 42 were wandering the aisles of Target. She looked at the sheets. They were all more expensive than she thought, but the kids' sets were on sale. Minnie Mouse or Winnie the Pooh? She pondered over it for longer than necessary. After a few minutes of back and forth and comparing the feel of the identical materials, she thought she'd lost her mind. It was a burial sheet, for God's sake.

A shroud.

The idea popped into her head, and she couldn't shake it. This children's sheet was a shroud.

*Shit.*

Now the decision felt justifiably important. Was it really important, or did she just find an excuse to allow herself to puzzle over it unnecessarily?

*Decisive my ass.*

Decisive Sera from last night was apparently still sleeping.

*It takes time,* she thought, *time to undo years and years of self-doubt.*

"Fuck," she said aloud, drawing a dirty look from a mom and a snicker from a kid. She knew it'd take time, but she hated it anyway. *Okay. It's fine,* she thought. *I want to get the right sheets. That's okay. So...*

She looked at them. Minnie Mouse with her bright pink bow, or Winnie the Pooh with his honey pot? She liked Winnie, and the honey pot could be Alyssa.

*Oh, God.*

She wasn't even making good internal jokes. The four-hour nap had not done its job. She picked up the Winnie the Pooh sheets, walked about five steps, turned back around, and set them down. 42, watching Sera from her sitting position on the ground, hadn't moved at all. This was not the first time today Sera had grabbed a set of sheets only to return them. In the toddler aisle, there had been a perfectly price-appropriate set of

Paw Patrol sheets, but Sera had felt a little off about wrapping her murder victim in what amounted to a vestige of the law.

Minnie. She picked them up. Yes. She liked Winnie, which meant Alyssa almost definitely would have gone for Minnie. Plus, the pink of Minnie's bow. Duh. How had she been so blind? Also, she didn't think it would be great to think of Alyssa's dead body every time she saw anything related to Winnie the Pooh. Sure, she felt no guilt now, but she was a black belt at self-flagellation and had no reason to think this wouldn't do a number on her mentally at some point. She didn't think it would. She hoped it wouldn't, but...

*Am I going to hate myself for this?* She considered it or tried to consider it. She couldn't make her overactive brain spin on it. It didn't matter. She might hate herself, but it was the only way she could go on living.

*The Bitch.* The thought tugged at her. She needed to kill The Bitch soon.

Minnie.

She grabbed the sheets and decisively walked out of the aisle, leaving a surprised 42 scrambling after her. 42 carried her makeshift leash in her mouth. She was quite adept at walking herself. Sera smiled down at the dog. She did deserve a bone.

In the dog aisle, Sera found that animal supplies were even more ridiculously priced. Seven dollars for a dog bone?! It was literally the part of the cow that was going to be thrown away. Sera looked down at 42, her mouth watering already. It would just be cruel to come here and not get her a bone, but she didn't have enough cash.

Sera puzzled again. She was getting really sick of herself. She felt a tap on her shoulder and turned around to find Clarence smiling at her. She instinctively looked down. Her shirt was dry, but the spots left-over from her earlier pukefest were still visible. *Great.*

"You got a kid?" he asked.

"No," she replied incredulously. As if.

He motioned towards the sheets. "You're into Minnie Mouse and small beds?"

She almost hid the sheets guiltily but caught herself.

"A friend. A friend has a kid, and I thought." She shrugged. "Yeah, they're pretty dumb. I think I'm going to put them back."

"Don't skip them on my account. Minnie is great. Mickey too. Mice in general, unless they're in your house. Unless they're pets. Then they should be in your house. In a cage, most likely."

She smiled in spite of herself as he talked himself in circles. She felt like that was her secret superpower, one she worked hard to keep under wraps, and she was really enjoying someone else running into a burning building on accident. His flames fizzled out, and he stared at her dumbly for a second.

"I'll let you get back to it."

She watched him walk off, then looked down at the sheets.

Well, they were burnt. No pun intended, but she couldn't use them now. If they found Alyssa's body wrapped up in those, he'd definitely connect it back to her. Great. All she'd been hoping for at Target was some anonymity. Instead, she was famous with the town's goofiest cop.

That wasn't fair, she thought. She didn't know any of the other cops. Maybe he wasn't comparatively goofy at all. Maybe he was the town's most serious cop. That would be good for her. Very good. She hoped he was the town's goofiest cop of all though. To her, goofy was quite the compliment.

42 nudged her leg, leaving a wet spot where her muzzle had hit. The dog was starving. The sheets were useless, and she was hungry too. Well, no point in using cash. She ditched the sheets with the dog beds, grabbed a bone and a small bag of dog food.

42 would get something out of this trip to the store even if she didn't.

# TWENTY-SEVEN

Sera ate a Happy Meal in the parking lot of Mickey D's, though the small plastic toy was nothing to be happy about. She remembered when these things were real toys. Things that later became collector's items. Now, she'd be lucky if the toy survived the fifteen minutes it took her to eat the meal.

She tore open the bag of dog food and set it on the center console. 42 dug in happily. Sera tucked the bone in the driver's side door for a treat later. Veggies before dessert, and all that.

What was she going to do with the body?

Her phone rang. She glanced down and groaned, rolling her eyes. It was her landlord.

She gritted her teeth before picking up. She wanted to send it straight to voicemail but figured knowing would be better.

"Pigs?!?!" The apartment manager yelled before Sera'd even said hello. She should have hung up, but laughter burst from her instead, which only made her landlord angrier.

"N-n-n-no pets," he sputtered. "That's the rule. No pets. How in the hell do you justify having pigs in your apartment?"

She heard the scuffling and snorting of the pigs. The manager was *in* her apartment. Of course he was.

"Well..." Sera searched for some version of the truth. "They aren't really pets."

She could hear the exasperation exploding from the silence she was met with on the other end.

"They aren't," Sera continued. "They are—cattle. Sort of. Domesticated animals. Animals, but not pets. They're food, really. I mean, don't you eat bacon? If you're looking for a cheap way to feed yourself, you know, buying in bulk or better yet, going to the source and making your own meat is—ideal."

"I'm vegan."

"Oh. Well. Then. Not for you. But for me. I eat bacon."

"So, these are not pets?"

"No. Uh, correct. Those are not pets."

"They are animals you plan to slaughter?"

"Yes. When I got them, I planned to slaughter them."

"And now?"

"What?"

"Now?"

"Now what?"

"Now what do you plan to do with them?" he demanded impatiently.

"Oh. I didn't think you'd want blood on the carpet, so I figured—"

"You're fired!"

"What?"

"Fired! Fired! You have to—" He stumbled over the words trying to find the right one, knowing it was definitely fired—"get out. Leave. You're...fired!"

"Evicted?"

"Evicted! Yes! Goddamn it, you're evicted."

There was a brief silence on the line. Pig snorted in the background, breaking it.

"That's Pig," Sera said lamely into the void. "That pig's name is Pig."

"How do you—"

"I can tell. He sounds different than the rest."

Another tense pause.

"How long do I have?"

"The end of the day."

"No, no, no. You have to give me three days. That's the law. I know that's the law!"

"End of the day, or I call animal services, and Pig and the rest of them—did you name all of them?" He couldn't help himself. He had to know.

"What? Oh, no. Just the big one."

"Well, Pig and the rest of them will be scooped up and taken. I don't know where. A farm, maybe. What in the hell were you doing with all these pigs in the first place?"

"I told you, I was going to slaughter them."

"Right. And I'm the queen of Sheeba. Get your ass back here and get your shit, and the pigs' shit out of here. I mean it. I want the pigs' *shit* out of here."

CLICK.

The line went dead.

She wondered briefly if she should call someone. Should she tell anyone she was moving? Ask anyone for help packing? But there wasn't anyone left. Certainly, no one she wanted help from. Alex popped into her mind. She could text him, but what would she say? She wasn't going to ask him for help. She barely knew him, and she was not inviting him into her Pig Palace.

She shrugged. There was no one to call, but for once, she didn't care. That felt good. Really, really good.

"Guess we gotta get your friends," Sera said to 42, who looked a little blue around the gills. The bag of food sitting between them was nearly polished off. "42, that was for..."

How long was it for? She certainly didn't know. "A lot more than one meal. That's for sure."

Sera rolled her eyes. "I guess dogs binge too, huh?"

42 whined in response, and Sera took 42 on another walk around the parking lot, where she pooped the most giant puppy-poop Sera had ever seen. She also stopped three or four times, considering the possibility of throwing up her breakfast, but maybe after having had so little to eat since the bacon a few days before, she thought better of it. Who knows, exactly, but 42 managed to keep her food down. And Sera learned a valuable lesson about portion control.

However, 42 did whine and make Sera pull over for bathroom breaks three times between Target and her apartment in the city. Each time, the poop was more impressively scary than the last. Sera didn't clean any of it up. She had not signed up to be a dog owner. It had just happened. She certainly hadn't signed up to be the bathroom custodian. 42 was gonna have to pay her if she wanted her poop scooped.

42 didn't care either. Once the poop was out, she had no idea why anyone would want to pick it up, though she did smell it every single time. She assumed Sera thought she was getting buggy, but 42 was checking to make sure she wasn't sick. She wasn't. She had definitely gone wrong somewhere with her morning meal, though she couldn't figure out how, but she wasn't sick. 42 determined she should eat more bacon and less kibble. It only seemed logical.

# TWENTY-EIGHT

Sera got back to her apartment building but waited until she saw her landlord pull out of the parking lot to pull in. She had no interest in a run-in with him. If she could, she'd wait until the entire building was empty. She didn't think the neighbors who'd been so accepting of 42 were going to have the same warm fuzzies for the pigs. Plus, someone must have complained. There was no other way for her landlord to find out about them in the first place.

She wondered briefly if it was Mrs. Closome, but she knew better. They didn't talk much, but every now and then Sera would drop off a random fast-food meal or milkshake. She had a fondness for the old woman she shared a wall with, and she thought it was mutual. She even watched some of the same shows as Mrs. Closome to make the TV audio blaring through the wall less irritating.

Mrs. Closome didn't trust their landlord. She didn't trust any authority figure. Power went to people's heads. Sera doubted her neighbor would complain even if she fired a gun in the apartment. Besides, she probably wouldn't even hear it. There was no way she heard the pigs.

Mystery not solved, but it didn't matter. Sera was happy enough to know it wasn't Mrs. Closome. That left whoever shared her bedroom wall, or someone else in this hall, or someone below her, or above, or anyone that heard the pigs from the stairwell. It left pretty much everyone but Mrs. Closome, Sera thought. Good thing she wasn't trying to become a detective.

Sera and 42 slipped upstairs and into her apartment without running into anyone.

*Small favors.*

42 and Pig sniffed each other. 42 was simply saying, "Hey!" While, to 42, Pig seemed to be searching for something more important. She figured he wanted as much info about their adventure as possible. This was something 42 understood deeply, so she stood still for as long as Pig circled her.

Ultimately, Pig didn't seem to find what he was looking for, but his oink as he walked away implied he was happy he hadn't found it.

*Interesting,* 42 thought.

Sera stood inside her door, taking in the space.

She'd loved this place once.

The pigs had made a huge mess of the apartment, but let's be honest, Sera had already made a mess of it before they showed up. She had piles of stuff everywhere. She had both a clean and a dirty hamper. She'd given up folding some time ago. With fresh eyes, the apartment was very obviously the space of someone who'd given up on pretty much everything.

Leaving would be good.

It would take her more than a day to pack up all her stuff, get someone to help her with the furniture, and clean up both her mess and the pigs'. That didn't matter though. She was only taking the important things, and she had no intention of cleaning.

First things first, she needed to give 42 her eye drops. The poor dog kept rubbing her face with her paws every few minutes. She was getting better, but she was not healed yet. The docile dog Sera'd been met with last time was long gone. 42 darted around the apartment and the many pigs zigging and zagging with fervor. The obstacles only made the game more exciting. However, she noticed Sera winced as she tried to dodge a little pig, and 42 sat down. She was definitely ready for more play, but Sera couldn't play right now. Still, 42 appreciated her efforts. Sera could have just sat down, but she at least tried to catch her.

Sera joined 42 on the floor and wrapped her legs around her furry little body. She knew how this would go. 42 decided to allow it. However, when the eye drops went up, her eyes slammed shut and she turned her head.

42 didn't want anything going in her eyes. She decided the best defense was a good offense and buried her head in Sera's chest. That was met with a whole lot of petting which 42 assumed would stop the attack efforts. Unfortunately, the second 42 eased up a little, Sera sprung, finally getting a few drops in each eye and a lot more drops down the front of her shirt. 42 huffed audibly. She had lost this round, but now she knew better than to lift her head.

"Thank you, 42."

With that done, Sera went straight to her closet and pulled out a box of childhood keepsakes. She grabbed a photo album off her bedroom shelf and added it to her box. The more recent albums she abandoned. They were filled with pictures of her and the crew—filled with The Bitch. She was consciously choosing not to remember.

Besides, it seemed to her that The Bitch and the rest of them had practically forgotten all about her already. Why shouldn't she forget about them?

She should.

She should have forgotten already.

She knew she should.

But would she?

No.

No, they would probably always be there, in her head, clawing at her self-image and self-worth. She definitely needed therapy.

She stuffed a few garbage bags full of clothes. She had duffle bags, but she didn't want to take them. She had no idea why. Garbage bags felt like the right thing to do. Maybe it was just the romantic thing to do, but she was trusting her instincts. Wasn't that the point of this entire journey? It was like some scene out of *Fear and Loathing in Las Vegas*. She would abandon the past and disappear into an ending she chose. She was certain there was no garbage bag scene in the film, and suicide wasn't on her list of to-dos, but still. It was silly, ridiculous, but it fulfilled something inside her. She wanted this moment to be dramatic.

A shedding of her old skin.

She picked up her mom's red blanket, adding it to her meager belongings, told 42 to carry her makeshift leash (as was becoming habit for 42), and told Pig to rally the troops. The troops were already rallied, and the dirty dozen went down the stairs.

At the car, Sera went to stuff her garbage bags in the back seat footwells but got a snort and some side-eye from Pig.

*Where were his compadres meant to go?*

She realized her mistake and tossed the bags on top of the car. She grabbed another section of the cut-up yellow rope from the car and tied them down. The bags might not survive the journey, but she didn't care. She didn't really want the clothes. She just knew she had to wear something, so here they were. She also needed clothes she was fine with ditching while on her murder spree. These checked both boxes.

She carefully put her box of keepsakes in the passenger footwell and laid the red blanket on the front seat for 42. These were the things that mattered. 42 seemed to understand the importance of the artifacts as she jumped nimbly onto the blanket and made sure not to crush the box.

42 took her position as Sera's number 2 (or her number 42!), and the pigs climbed into the back, wobbling up two two-by-fours Sera had scrounged up for this purpose. Pig seemed to be counting heads, making sure none of his people were lost in the move, as he watched his friends get into the car. After everyone was successfully accounted for, he joined them in the Prius's impressively roomy, though very cramped with so many pigs, hatchback.

Sera had initially hated the hatchback, but she was wrong about that. How many times had the folding seats and under-estimated space saved her?

42 was not happy as Sera ghetto rigged her rope-leash into a seat belt again. Last time, it was no big deal, but now, Sera suspected, she was making 42 look uncool in front of her entire group of pig-pals.

"Sorry, 42," she whispered while securing the pupster any-way.

The single box seemed so small and insignificant. Surely, there was something else that mattered to her? Sera cracked the car windows and went upstairs to take a last look around. There was shit everywhere. Literally and figuratively.

She carefully stepped over piles of pig shit, crunching bits of cereal left over from what she had strewn across the floor. She had felt so free when she first got this apartment. Later, she had felt so trapped. Now, she felt great leaving it behind. A weight lifted.

The past lifted.

She took a mental picture.

She'd made a real mess of things.

Her junk was scattered all over the place. It was hard to believe she cared so little about any of it. She moved through the space for the last time. There had to be something else she wanted, but each item she picked up felt like a tether. Marie Kondo would have followed her with an ever-present "Does it spark joy?"

*No*, Sera thought to herself. *None of it sparks joy*. If she could, she would burn the entire place down. She didn't want to be tied to the version of herself that lived in this apartment, not at the end anyway.

She was Marie Kondo's wet dream.

Sera considered arson for a moment before dismissing it. She would certainly kill a lot of people—a plus in the serial killer column—but there was no way all the tenants fit her intended "type." Also, getting kicked out on the same day an entire four-story apartment building went up in smoke would definitely set off some alarm bells, especially if she had managed to get all her animals out just in the nick of time.

She wouldn't burn it down, but she did turn the gas stove on and blow out the flame. She hoped for some *Fight Club*-style vengeance without the thoroughly planned pre-game.

She headed out the door.

*Fuck*.

She sighed, annoyed with herself, and turned off the burner. She knew Mrs. Closome smoked which meant the place really might blow up, and if Sera blew Mrs. Closome up, she didn't think she could live with herself.

She settled on leaving the water running. It wouldn't do a damn thing except annoy the landlord, but that would have to be enough. She flipped off her door, more a symbolic gesture to the landlord since she had absolutely no problem with the apartment itself, and left.

She hesitated, then knocked on her neighbor's door. She was nervous Mrs. Closome wouldn't care that she was leaving, but she wanted to say goodbye anyway.

"News is on," Mrs. Closome shouted from inside. "Come back later?"

Sera smiled. Seemed fitting.

"You don't have to come to the door. Just wanted to let you know I'm moving out," Sera shouted.

"Moving? One sec."

"It's okay. You don't have to—"

"One sec!" Mrs. Closome shouted a second time before the TV paused and a chorus of old-lady-getting-up sounds arose from the apartment. Nothing Sera could say would stop her coming to the door anyway, so why try?

Eventually, the door opened. It was not "one sec," but Sera enjoyed every minute of her wait.

"Moving, huh?" Mrs. Closome asked, leaning on her walker.

Sera nodded.

"Better place?"

"My grandma left me her house."

"Good. You didn't suck," she said and laughed at her joke. They both did.

"You didn't suck either," Sera said. The old lady shrugged as if to say "maybe, maybe not." Her motion definitely left room for interpretation.

"No more milkshakes for me."

"Maybe I'll bring you some," Sera said, but Mrs. Closome waved her hand dismissively.

"Nah. Don't waste your time, but you have one for me. A chocolate one."

"Absolutely," Sera said, smiling. She was surprisingly close to having tears spill out of her eyes. She hadn't expected that.

"Bet some asshole will move in," Mrs. Closome said.

"If they do, call me," Sera said. "I'll take care of them." She meant it, but Mrs. Closome waved her off again. Never gonna happen.

"Gotta get back to the news."

"Have a good one."

Mrs. Closome's eyes met Sera's. They also sparkled with tears, tears and understanding. She held out one arm, the other still on her walker for support, and they hugged.

Mrs. Closome's body felt fragile, but her hug was strong. Sera's entire world disappeared in it. It was a hug that understood all Sera's pains and more. It was a hug that had seen some shit and was still kicking. It was the hug of one bad-ass woman.

And, for a moment, for a wonderful moment, the hug made Sera whole.

Then Mrs. Closome disappeared inside, and Sera left. Sera hoped her friend wouldn't cry, but she knew she would. So would Sera.

Outside, she clicked *Submit Order* in an app. Soon enough a burger, fries, and a large chocolate shake would greet Mrs. Closome.

Sera would miss her.

Inside the Prius, she, 42, and the pig posse headed into the night. With nowhere else to go, they were going back to exactly where she needed to be, her grandma's. She felt a little bit better about everything. Her past wasn't what she wanted, but no one's was.

*On to better things*, she thought.

She had a plan for her future, a bright plan—bright red, in fact. Blood red. She also had a body to dispose of.

Unfortunately, she had no plan for that.

Sera turned the musical stylings of Paramore way up, trying to drown out the pigpen noise. The posse was oinking furiously. She had spread the rest of 42's kibble around the trunk, but it had run out in moments, and she realized she hadn't fed them in nearly 24 hours. They were not happy.

# TWENTY-NINE

A t her grandma's, Sera released the pigs into the field. She expected them to wander away, to find their own special place in the wide-open plains. She was wrong. They stood there, staring at her like so many disgruntled workers. She had freed them, she had taken them from their consistent feeding schedules, she was to blame and needed to fix the problem.

*Let them eat grass*, she thought, and they begrudgingly did. Marie Antoinette was *not* onto something though, and Sera, again, resolved to buy pig feed the next day.

She headed toward the house and found a caravan of pigs following her. Letting them into her apartment had been one thing, but this was her grandma's house. They weren't going to run hog-wild here. There had to be ground rules, but how could she train a pig? The answer was with patience, but Sera didn't have any of that nor did she have the time.

So, instead of teaching them manners, she came to a different conclusion. The basement was made of cement walls and floors. It was virtually empty except for old canned goods, the washing machine, and Alyssa's body. They could stay down there if they wanted to. There was a storm door that led straight from the field to the basement, so they would have easy access.

*I'm so fucking weird,* Sera thought, looking over the land. *Why would pigs want to live in a basement instead of out here?*

It didn't make any sense, but she couldn't deny there was a line of hoofed friends behind her. They clearly wanted to come in.

They could come in, but first, she would have to deal with Alyssa.

Inside, she stepped onto the top step leading into the basement. The descent seemed more ominous than it had before. Was Alyssa really dead? Definitely? Sera cursed herself for not taking her pulse. Then, she remembered the cataract-looking eyes.

She was dead. She had to be.

The wood squeaked under Sera's weight. She looked back at 42.

"Come on, girl," she said, but 42 resolutely sat down in the living room instead of approaching the door leading to hell.

Sera took another step, and 42 began to whine and pace. She seemed to beckon Sera back to the living room, back to the light. Sera took another step. 42 growled slightly. Sera stopped and listened for any sounds of life below, though sounds of death may have been more likely. Zombies aren't real, right? That still wasn't a thing, right?

42 let out a pained howl, and Sera's heart skipped a beat. The thudding in her chest nearly drove her back up the few stairs she'd conquered. Was that the stench of rotting flesh? Would it smell already? She looked up at 42, whose eyes pled, *Please, come back. Please, come back.*

She looked down the stairway. If she didn't go now, she'd never go. She plunged into the darkness, taking the steps two at a time. If Alyssa was waiting for her, Sera would at least have some element of surprise on her side. She clattered to the bottom, and something moved.

Alyssa.

Sera flung herself at Alyssa before Alyssa could get the jump on her. She screamed and grunted, grabbing Alyssa's hands and pinning them down. She only stopped when she had successfully trapped Alyssa's arms and torso beneath her body. Panting, she looked down smugly, ready to kill Alyssa for the second time. A more satisfying kill. One where she didn't have to wonder if she was a murderer or an idiot bystander.

"Ha, ha! Gotcha, bitch!" she yelled in Alyssa's graying face, and then scrambled backward off the body. "Oh, fuck. Shit, shit, shit."

Alyssa was dead.

She was so fucking dead.

Her eyes had sunken into her head, not far, but far enough, and her skin had a thick, leathery texture.

But she'd moved. She had. Sera was certain of it. She nudged Alyssa's leg with the toes of her foot, hesitant to get too close to the body she had just aggressively straddled for fear of her life.

Alyssa's head fell to the side. A single drop of leftover stomach bile dripped onto the floor, and a few feet away, she saw a rat angrily scurrying back into a hole in the wall.

*Jesus.*

She gagged and shook her head, trying to get rid of the feeling of Alyssa's dead flesh and the fear that she was so quickly going to pay for her sins.

She was awful at this.

A hiss escaped Alyssa's body, and Sera retched at the thought of breathing her in. She turned and darted back up the stairs. Nothing came up, but she was afraid if she stayed any longer she'd be cleaning up her puke again.

She slammed the door behind her and sat next to 42, catching her breath.

42 wanted to bark *I told you so*, but knew it wasn't nice to rub sand in wounds. Sera was clearly pondering her mistakes. She knew better now. 42 didn't need to bark a word.

Sera could feel Alyssa's breath on her skin, as if she had exhaled some sort of sticky film that coated her. It wasn't real. She knew that. It didn't make sense, but that didn't help. She took another minute to gather herself, but as soon as she trusted herself not to puke, she went upstairs and climbed into a scathingly hot shower. She scrubbed off both her first and second layer of skin. Her clothes were rolled up in a plastic bag on the floor. She was unsure if they would ever be clean enough to wear again, so she was throwing them away.

*Step 1, figure out how to dispose of the body. All bodies,* Sera thought as she scrubbed, deciding this was the new most important step. It was more important than deciding who to kill, or where to kill them, or even how to kill them. She did not want to be trapped trying to get rid of another body or twelve. Fuck that.

As she got out of the shower, her skin all pink and red with the effort, her hair washed three times for good measure, she wrapped a towel around herself and realized all her other clothes were on top of the car.

*Fine.*

She walked into her grandma's room and found a close-enough-to-her-size flower shirt and a pair of elastic-band, easy-pull-on, old-person jeans. She yanked both on and aged herself by twenty years. It was an interesting portal to the future. On the bright side, she looked less like a killer than she ever had before.

She walked back into the bathroom and took the shower rod down. She pulled the plastic liner free and rehung the pole.

*This will do,* she thought and carried it with her downstairs.

In the basement, she laid the plastic sheet out and then rolled Alyssa's body onto it. She was prepared for her gag reflex to kick in, or her tangible disgust factor to creep up, but she was fine. The problem was not the dead body. The problem was rolling around in the dark with it like two lovers after a long-delayed reunion.

*There.*

The body lay dead center on the clear plastic. The arms and legs were spread into a star formation. This might be how serial killers got their weird rituals or their unique signatures—by accident. She wasn't spreading the arms and legs to make any sort of gruesome symbol or statement, but if Clarence had walked in right now, he certainly would have thought she had.

At the thought of him, she both bristled and was filled with butterflies.

*What a weird combo*, she thought. It wasn't a good time for a schoolgirl crush, and he was not a good person for it either. Maybe she should text Alex? Steak did sound good.

*THUD THUD THUD*

Sera jumped. The pounding came from the front door.

*THUD THUD THUD*

This was not the loud but respectful knock of an officer.

*THUD THUD*

This was the knock of someone who was willing to break her door down.

She raced up the stairs and quietly closed the basement door behind her.

42 was still sitting by it, watching Sera. *Humans don't learn.*

"Stay," Sera commanded, hoping that the presence of a dog would help deter her unwanted guest from trying to make their way downstairs, or into the house at all, for that matter.

Less than twenty-four hours in the countryside, and this was already her second visitor. While she thought the wide-open spaces would allow her plenty of room to kill and clean up on her own schedule, she found that perhaps the city, where no one wanted to talk to you even if they had to, might be more conducive after all.

She opened the door to find a large man with a large shotgun standing there.

"I think you stole my pigs," Mr. Durmont grumbled.

# THIRTY

Sera's eyes grew wide as she looked up at the large man with a shotgun. It'd been years since she'd seen Old Man Durmont. She expected him to seem smaller now that she was grown, but he seemed just as big as he had when she was ten. It wasn't entirely his height. He was considerably taller than her, almost a full head, but part of his perceived size came from his overconfidence. No one went against him. Ever. She considered lying about his pigs, but a few feet away they milled about, slowly eating the dried or drying grass. Clearly, he was right. She'd stolen them.

"I work for PETA," she blurted out. Well, she was going with lying after all.

"The fuck you do," he said and lowered the shotgun until it was level with her eyes. "Why'd you take my pigs?"

She was caught red-handed, and what was worse, she had a body in the basement. "Might as well tell me," he drawled. "I'm locked and loaded, and 'round here, I don't think people would be too upset if I killed a pig thief."

"I— I'm not a thief."

He raised his eyebrows and shifted his gaze to his pigs wandering around beside them. Pig wasn't grazing like the others. Pig was leveling his gaze right back at the farmer.

"Go on, git," Mr. Durmont yelled as he slammed the butt of his rifle into Pig's ribs. Pig backed up a few feet, but he did not *git*. The other pigs stopped their grazing and gathered closer to Pig, protectively. "Never liked that one. He looks at me funny." Mr. Durmont turned back to Sera and smiled a sleazy kinda smile.

He raised the shotgun slowly back to her face. He paced it for the effect. He wanted to scare her. His sleazy smile grew.

It wouldn't seem like it was possible to make a killer's skin crawl, but it was. All over her body, Sera's skin crawled with a million invisible bugs. It was trying to climb inside of her, into the dark parts that are hidden away from the world. She knew he was trying to scare her, but it still worked.

Sera didn't like Mr. Durmont. He looked at her funny.

"I took your pigs," she said. "What about it?" She stepped forward and shut the door behind her, instinctually protecting 42.

He licked his lips. "I think we can come to some sort of arrangement." Her mind jumped to rape, coerced rape, immediately, but his purpose seemed darker than that. A chill raced down her spine. It took effort to keep herself from visibly shaking it off.

*How many serial killers could live within a few square miles of each other?* she wondered.

*Out here, everyone could be a killer,* her inner voice answered instantly. *Who would know?* Sera swallowed hard.

"I took your pigs 'cause I wanted to see if I could kill one," she said. She didn't know why she offered up the truth, but it was clearly the right thing to do. His eyes lit up, and he lowered the gun slightly. He was surprised and a little impressed.

He looked at the pigs and counted each one out loud.

"One, two, three—"

"I didn't—"

"Shh. Four, five, six—"

"You don't have to—"

"Shhhh." He put his finger to his lips and shushed her with the same look a stalker might use when blowing his long-lost love a kiss.

"I'm counting. Seven, eight, nine." He looked Pig dead in the eye. "Ten."

He turned the shotgun on Pig and pulled the trigger, but Sera grabbed the butt of the gun, shanking his aim. She tried to yank the gun away, but she was no match for him. He easily stripped the piece from her and brought the butt up, sharply connecting with her chin. She stumbled back, tripped over a rock, and fell to the ground. She winced as a sharp pain shot through her ribs. Those damn, screaming ribs threatened to take her out of the fight just as it began.

"Stupid bitch," he spat out, then collected himself and stepped over the top of her. He stood astride her, his body blocking out the sun, and for a second, Sera couldn't see him or his gun for the glare around them.

"Too bad you didn't kill them," he said, giving Sera's eyes time to adjust to the light. "I could have at least respected that, but this—" He motioned vaguely around him, not noticing that the pigs had all moved behind him with Pig at their helm.

Sera was staring down the barrel of his gun, and he was itching to shoot. Her hands groped over the dirt. She had to find—

"The little girl wanted to kill a pig, and instead, instead"—he licked his lips—"she saved ten of their lives. Don't worry, miss. You'll all be dead by nightfall."

His finger danced on the trigger, and Sera found what she was looking for. She slammed the rock she had tripped over down onto his foot, crushing his toes. He screamed out, stumbled back, and lifted the gun to the sky as his second shot rang out. She curled into a ball, covering her ears and pulling her legs out from under him.

The shot was loud, louder this time than the first. Unseen, the pigs closed further in on them, forming a semicircle a few feet behind the farmer. Each one pointed toward the center, staring directly at Old Man Durmont. Sera struggled for a plan. He was going to regroup. This was her only chance.

She thrust herself at him from the ground and connected hard, cutting him down at the knees. There was a sickening pop, and he fell in the dirt, writhing in pain. His left knee bowed in, bending in the wrong direction.

Shock ran through her slowing the world. She cocked her head to the side, staring at the leg. She couldn't figure out how it could move that way.

*It doesn't look broken so much as crooked,* she thought.

A sudden *woosh* of air and warm bodies rushed past her, forcing her back to the present, as the pig posse descended upon Mr. Durmont, closing their semicircle in a frenzy, locking Sera outside of it. Frantic, she scuttled backwards on the ground, but they weren't coming for her. They only had eyes for Mr. Durmont.

She watched as the pigs tore him apart, limb from limb. A feeding frenzy. She felt suspended somehow. Outside. She noticed Pig was also watching. He seemed suspended too. Apart. Above. Pig sat on the sidelines, observing the work Sera was certain he had ordered.

Pig's ribs were red, where the butt of the gun had hit.

She didn't know what to make of this coordinated attack, but she felt sorry for Pig. For all the pigs. It was clear they had battered pig syndrome, whether it was a thing or not.

*Funny how life plays out,* she thought.

Slowly, a barking began to rise as Sera's senses relaxed. No longer focused on survival, the surrounding world resumed, but she hadn't caught up. She looked around, trying to find the source of the sound, and was filled with a moment of panic when she realized she couldn't hear the pigs gnawing at bone and tearing at flesh. The world was muted. The barking distant.

Very distant.

She looked toward the house and saw 42 barking and snarling in the window. Sera jumped up and ran to the door. The second she threw it open, releasing 42, audio rushed back to the world in a sickening mix of cries turned to gurgles, oinks, and indescribable pig snarls.

42 ran around the horde of pigs, barking incessantly, cheering them on. They had defeated the big bad. Then she raced to Sera and jumped on her over and over again. She was all right. Sera was all right. 42 had been terrified. *What would the pigs do if Sera were injured or worse...* 42 didn't want to think about it.

In the distance, a twig snapped as some birds took flight, and 42 came to attention. She stood protectively in front of Sera, guarding her from the dangerous world beyond.

*What would the pigs do if... What would I do?* 42 thought and quickly pushed the idea aside. 42 was a survivor. She'd always survived, but the pigs needed Sera, and 42 really wanted her around, whether she needed her or not.

42 understood with a new kind of clarity that she would have to protect Sera now. Whatever it was Sera was doing, she was obviously not good at. She definitely needed 42's help, and the pigs' help too.

42 locked eyes with Pig, and they nodded to each other, sharing a sort of animal understanding that would forever be beyond Sera.

# Thirty-One

S era watched from the window as rivulets of blood made
their way through the cracks in the earth, forming a new
sort of river. The dry ground drank up Old Man Durmont's
blood as if it could single-handedly revive it and all the parched
plants that were growing off it. One by one, the pigs wandered
away from their feast. There was almost nothing left anyway.

42 sat beside Sera on the couch, still on high alert. The poor
dog hadn't left her side since they came inside. She wondered
if she should call the police. She hadn't actually done anything
wrong, but what if they searched her house? On the other
hand, what killer would call the cops? So maybe... maybe it
would make it easier for her to hid in plain sight? He had a
family, so she knew someone would come looking for him, and
it was undeniable that she had ten pigs she certainly should not
have. She wondered if the pigs were branded. Probably. This
would lead back to her either way. If she tried to hide it, things
could get ugly.

She picked up her phone and dialed 911.

"A man. The pigs. He tried to shoot me..." she yelled into
the receiver, hoping she was hiding the absolute divine numb-

ness she currently felt with a veil of fear and disgust. It had been terrifying. Absolutely terrifying. She'd thought she was going to die. So why was she so calm?

42 watched her with confusion as she placed the call. The dog could tell nothing was wrong, but her voice...her voice told an entirely different story. 42 scooted closer to her and growled at nothingness in the corners of the room. Something was wrong with this human, and 42 needed to help.

Sera sat outside in the dirt much like she had during the pig attack. She didn't know what would be more suspicious, sitting out here on the ground, or sitting inside like nothing had happened. She opted for stunned shock that left her in the same place that she had begun.

She heard sirens go silent as they pulled off the main road. For a moment, she wondered if her hearing had gone again. Was this a trauma response? But she heard the gravel crunching beneath the tires as the cruiser pulled up with lights flashing. Her ears still hurt, but they were working. The cops must have silenced the siren. She exhaled in relief. Apparently, the idea of losing her hearing was scarier to her than her near-death experience.

The car parked. Inside, she saw Officer Clarence. She really should get his last name. She smiled. She was glad it was him. She also second-guessed herself for the first time. She shouldn't have called the police. If Clarence found Alyssa's body, what would she do? She would have to—

*Kill him.*

The thought dried her mouth out, but it was true. If he found her victim, she would have to kill him and flee. She would have to run away and either kill The Bitch as fast as she could or let her live forever while Sera wasted her life living on the lam, unable to do anything of any use for herself or anyone else.

Clarence smiled as he got out of the car. Sera couldn't muster a matching pleasantry. She was too busy trying to imagine what it would be like to smash his skull in. The shotgun was still on the ground.

*I could use that,* she thought.

Her dead stare seemed to remind him of why he was here, and he quickly changed his expression. Luckily for her, he mistook her look as trauma rather than homicidal ideation.

"Are you okay?" he asked.

She shook her head, yes, not trusting her voice. She wasn't afraid she would have the telltale quiver that belied tears. She was afraid she wouldn't have it. She was afraid that she would sound so cool and collected that he would immediately know something was wrong—not with the situation, but with her. He would see her for what she was, raise his gun, and shoot her.

*It wouldn't be so bad.*

She didn't want to die, not currently, but she had before. She had felt trauma and gaslighting run around her brain, making short shrift of her for a long time. She didn't want this to end, especially not before she finished her calling, but there was a sort of peace inherently present in the idea of death.

She wouldn't have to fight with herself anymore.

She wouldn't have to try and figure out why people wanted to use her up and spit her out.

She wouldn't have to—

He was staring at her. He must have asked something. Maybe she was traumatized. Was she traumatized? He certainly thought so.

He looked at the bloodstained dirt. Dry rivers of Old Man Durmont soaked deep into the earth.

She didn't want him to think of her as damaged, not because she cared what he thought, but because she didn't want to be damaged anymore.

She stood up.

"I'm fine," she said. "He showed up waving that gun around, and. Well. The pigs ate him."

It seemed like a lie, even to her, but it was the truth. *Truth is stranger than fiction*, she thought. Oh, how incredibly true that was.

"The pigs ate him?"

She wasn't sure if he believed her or not, but his eyes drifted from the mouth of one pig to the next, clocking the blood, and in some cases, the guts and sinew, that still clung to their muzzles.

"The pigs ate him," he said finally as a statement of fact. His hand had been hovering over his gun holster, but it relaxed now.

She thought he looked like he was in shock now, and she felt a bit better. Maybe he would be too busy dealing with his own horror to worry about whether she was damaged or not.

*I am damaged*, she thought, *but it's not who I am. I am amazing. A-MAZE-ING.* She drew the word out as she said it in her mind. *A-MAZE-ING. A - MAZE. I - MAZE - ZING. I maze.*

She talked to herself a lot inside her head. She wondered how much other people said to themselves. Some people, she had read, literally had no internal voice. None at all. She couldn't fathom this. It must feel so isolating.

But also.

So free.

If she were alone in her head, there would be no one there to second-guess her.

"Mind if we go inside?" Clarence asked.

"Aren't you afraid I'll kill you?" she quipped, then looked at the blood surrounding them. "Sorry. I meant, 'cause, 'cause you asked me, you know, if I was a serial killer, last time, and..." she trailed off. She should get an award for how not good at this she was.

"Yeah." He nodded, trying to muster up some type of mirth for her. He didn't want her to feel worse, but it was hard to fake a smile under the circumstances. Likely, she was in shock.

Things like this broke people. She didn't seem broken, but the insides and the outsides weren't always the same. He hoped she'd be okay. She'd probably be okay. She seemed strong. Maybe he'd give her the number to that therapist in town though, in case.

She nodded, and they walked inside.

As she shut the door behind them, her eyes fell on the shotgun in the dirt again. If only there was some way for her to bring it in that was inconspicuous. There wasn't, of course. She would have to hope that he didn't want to check the basement, and that, if he did, she was able to get the jump on him with a knife or a lamp.

*Why would he check the basement?*

Perhaps she could use the same lamp she had used on Alyssa. She liked the idea of that. It wasn't poetic justice, but it did sound poetic.

They sat in the living room, and he asked her about everything that had passed. It was pleasant. If only they'd been talking about their lives rather than Mr. Durmont's death, Sera would have said they'd had a genuinely nice time.

"That's about all I need from you," he said. "I'll call it in. A team will come out to assess what you've said and corroborate the details." She must have looked more concerned than she wanted to because he immediately followed with, "He was shooting at you. You hit him. Anyone would have done the same, and then the pigs went after him. There's no way you could have predicted that. Who knew pigs could eat a person?"

*I knew*, she thought. *I saw it in a movie*, but she hadn't known they would attack. And the movie could have been bullshit. She wondered if she should fear for her safety.

Outside, she could see Pig watching her from the distance. Was he watching her? She must be delusional, but he did seem to be keeping his eye on things.

"What will happen to the pigs?" she asked.

Clarence immediately came to her rescue. "Don't worry. Animal services will pick them up, and they'll probably go back to Mr. Durmont's wife."

"Could they stay?" she asked. He watched her for a long moment unsure if this was a joke or a test of some kind, but it seemed to be genuine.

"If Mrs. Durmont doesn't want them, I imagine they could stay. Do you want them here?" he asked, surprised.

"I don't know," she said. "It seems like they had a rough life."

"Pigs usually do," he said and stood up.

The second he stood, 42 also stood from her post in front of the basement door. Sera didn't understand why she had chosen that spot, but she was happy she did. Until now. He walked over and scratched the dog's ears.

"You hiding something down there, 42? Huh? You hiding something? Good girl." He smiled at Sera but saw a hint of trepidation in her eyes. He looked at the doorknob. "Old houses like these have some pretty amazing basements."

He was fishing. She knew he was fishing.

She shrugged. "It's about usual, as far as I know."

"The new ones hardly have any basement at all. You'd think they'd get bigger over time, you know, better building methods, but it doesn't seem to be the case." He paused, waiting for something, but she had nothing to give him. "I'd love to see it sometime," he poked.

"I'd love to show it to you sometime. When do you think you'll be back?" she asked.

He stood, taking the hint. He wasn't sure what was behind the door, but he was definitely curious.

"Whenever you'll have me," he said, following her to the front door. "You sure you're okay?"

Years of training said she could be hiding something, but it could be something else entirely. People always acted like they could be hiding something from him. That's the trouble with being a cop.

He looked back and noticed that 42 hadn't moved. *Strange dog,* he thought, but then again, most dogs were strange in their own way, and that dog had definitely been through a lot today.

He eyed the pigs as he walked to his cruiser. They didn't seem any different than regular pigs. Except for the big one. The big one seemed to be thinking something about him. Sizing him up maybe.

"You sure you don't want me to have them take the pigs away?" he asked.

"If Mrs. Durmont wants them back, I get it. I have to give them up, but it feels like they saved my life, you know?"

He nodded.

That he understood, and the whole thing fell into place. Of course, she wasn't afraid of the pigs. She'd had them for the past week. She was afraid of the man that had tried to take her out with a shotgun.

*Makes perfect sense,* he thought, but his eyes drifted back to Pig one last time before he started his engine and pulled away.

# THIRTY-TWO

*Shit, shit, shit.* Sera shut the door behind her, listening to Officer Clarence pull away. They were going to come back. They were going to come back with a team, and she was going to be fucked. She was fucked.

She was fucked already.

She was already fucked.

That washed over her like a tidal wave.

She had completely fucked herself by killing the wrong person. Twice! Not twice, exactly, but...but twice adjacent. Yes. Fine, Alyssa was great practice, and sure, that guy was clearly going to kill her if she didn't kill him first. Well, if they didn't kill him first. She couldn't exactly take credit for that one. It was obviously the pigs' murder. Great. She was going to go down as some petty girl who killed a friend while they were drinking rather than as a woman who had been pushed too far and consciously decided to become, and succeeded at becoming, a serial killer.

They wouldn't even know she'd killed Alyssa on purpose.

It was going to look like they'd gotten drunk, passed out, and Alyssa had choked on her own vomit while Sera choked on fear and tried to hide the body instead of calling the cops. She was just gonna be some stupid girl who went to jail for second-degree murder, or maybe just manslaughter or criminal negligence, because she was afraid of the cops.

This was a nightmare. All her plans, her hopes, her dreams were being flushed down the toilet like so much shit from these people-eating pigs would be later.

*Think*, she commanded herself. *Think.*

*The body.*

With a bolt of genius, she realized all she had to do was get rid of the body, and the shower curtain...but that was it. One body. One shower curtain. Done and done. Easy peasy.

The pigs.

She ran outside, with 42 hot on her heels, and tried to herd the pigs down the outdoor steps to the basement door. Unfortunately, the pigs were far more interested in sunning themselves and resting after their feast.

"It's Pigsgiving," she encouraged them. "There's more feast downstairs. Dessert!"

She put her hands on one pig's rump and pushed and pushed to no avail. Pigs were a lot heavier than she gave them credit for. It's those jaw muscles, she thought. They can chew through bone. They must weigh a lot.

42 was running around the yard, playing with Sera, having a grand ol' time. This was great. The pigs were happy. She was happy, and best of all Sera was finally playing. Sera needed more play in her life. 42 knew this to be true intrinsically, and she wasn't wrong. Sera did need a lot more play in her life.

She just didn't need it right now. Right now, she needed—

"42! Herd the pigs. Herd the pigs, puppy. You can do it." She motioned for 42 to follow her lead. Sera went behind a pig and barked, trying to urge it forward.

42 just cocked her head and stared at Sera. What if she had gone insane? That could happen. If a person sees too much, they could go insane. 42 wondered at how much knowledge

she had acquired in such a short time. It seemed like a million years ago that she lived on the streets alone, and, thankfully, like a million years since she had been caged and hosed off like a criminal.

Sera barked again down on all fours.

*She's playing!* 42 realized, and she ran over to play along with her.

42 took prime puppy-play pose and barked back at Sera. The pig moved forward by a few inches. Sera cheered, and 42 understood. Sera wanted her to bark at the pigs.

42 leapt to her feet and sprinted around, barking at all the pigs indiscriminately.

"No, no!" Sera yelled, and 42 stopped. The dog was watching her closely. 42 knew she was supposed to be doing something. She just didn't know what yet.

Sera barked at a pig and then ran toward the stairs leading to the basement, still barking. 42 trotted alongside her, confused.

Sera barked again at a pig. 42 looked at her, and then barked at the pig. The pig stepped forward. Sera barked again. 42 barked again, and the pig stepped forward again. Sera cheered, and 42 raced around in another excited circle.

Sera called her back and began the cycle again.

She barked. 42 barked. The pig stepped forward. She barked. 42 barked. The pig stepped forward. In between, Sera showered 42 with praises of "Good girl," and "You're so smart."

42 was thrilled, and once the first pig got to the stairs and she gave a good bark, the pig ran all the way down to the basement door.

"Yes!" Sera cried. "Good girl! Good girl!"

Sera ran down the stairs after the pig and quickly opened the door. The pig wandered into the basement and back out of the basement bemusedly. Sera hoped that pig legs were long enough to go up these stairs as well as down them. These weren't the short little stairs of her apartment building. These were the steep cement stairs of decades ago. It hadn't occurred to her, but she'd need to get the pigs out of the basement too. Fuck it. If pigs couldn't climb stairs, it was future Sera's problem. Not hers.

Sera raced up the stairs and encouraged 42 to herd another pig down them. This time, 42 caught on and fulfilled her task with alacrity. Soon, she had gotten each and every pig downstairs, except for Pig.

42 looked at Pig and bounded over to him, but when she got there, she paused and thought better than to bark. She sat down in front of him on the ground and wagged her tail. He considered her for a moment and walked a few steps towards the stairs. 42 took a few more steps and looked back. Pig glanced at her unamused and, with a huff, quickly walked past 42 and down the back steps.

"Wahooooooo!!!!" Sera whooped with excitement. All the pigs were down there. Surely, the body was almost gone by now. Alyssa wasn't even half as big as Mr. Durmont was.

She and 42 followed Pig down the stairs but found that the pigs were rather dumbly wandering in and out of the basement.

42 sniffed the air and sat on the landing outside. She was not going in there. Sera seemed to understand because she said nothing. Instead, she watched the pigs.

The pigs would go onto the stair landing outside, look around, and go back inside. Then they'd walk the perimeter of the basement, determine there was nothing particularly interesting for them there, and head back to the landing. They had not yet gone back upstairs which either meant that Sera's fear of their short legs was accurate or that the steady stream of their compadres had kept them underground.

Sera led pig after pig to Alyssa's body, but they didn't seem to notice. Maybe the meat was too old. Maybe they were just so full they couldn't do it. She had no idea.

Sera went upstairs to the kitchen. It'd been an hour since Clarence had left. He was probably already almost back with his team. Now, she had a decision to make. She could either herd the pigs back upstairs and hope to keep the cop squad out of the basement, or she could try and convince the pigs to eat her friend, former friend, somehow.

She grabbed a bottle of barbecue sauce and the saltshaker. She had to try something.

Downstairs, she poured barbecue sauce over her friend's body liberally. Then salted the hell out of her. If the cops found the body now, Sera'd look like a deranged cannibal.

*Better than a scared girl that accidentally killed her friend,* she thought, but it might not be.

She stepped back from her culinary masterpiece. This might be too much, even for an aspiring serial killer. She wanted to puke, but a pig sniffed the air, walking over to Alyssa's body. It licked the barbecue sauce.

Sera held her breath.

Nothing happened.

"Please, please, please, eat my friend. Pretty please." She clasped her hands, as if praying to some higher pig power, and it worked.

The pig took a big old bite out of her decomposing friend.

"Yes!!!" Sera jumped in the air, cheering.

Then, as the other pigs began to eagerly partake in the barbecue, the stench of a day-old body along with the very vivid scene of the pigs eating said day-old body hit Sera. She lurched forward, barely stopping herself from throwing up all over them and Alyssa. She wove through the pigs to the sink basin and hurled over and over again.

42 sat on the outside landing, listening to the sounds of a pig feast and Sera losing her lunch and breakfast. 42 was not entirely certain that this was the best thing for any of them, but who was she to judge? She had rummaged through garbage many a time.

Next to her, Pig oinked once and nudged her gently toward the stairs. 42 correctly took this as a sign that she didn't need to see all this and headed back to the yard, where she lay watching the stars come out until one by one the pigs returned. Eventually, Sera came out in yet another flowery shirt with minty-smelling breath.

They all laid down and fell asleep under the night sky, one big happy dog pack.

# THIRTY-THREE

B lue and red flashing lights woke Sera. *It must be past midnight,* she thought as she yawned and stretched, scratching her arms on the dry grass. She stood and headed toward the car. With luck, they wouldn't realize she'd been sleeping outside.

She hoped Clarence had come with his team, and indeed he had. It was him and two other cops with black lights, print kits and all sorts of measuring devices and yellow tape. They looked around for a moment, confused.

"There's no body," Officer Lyza said.

"Nope," Sera said, keeping her happiness under wraps. "You won't find any bodies here."

The forensic investigator looked to Clarence for guidance. "What exactly do you want me to mark up for a crime scene?"

"It's not a crime," he said. "It's— I don't know. It's a farm accident or something, maybe. I told you all this."

"So, I should just put the crime tape..." she trailed off.

He shrugged and indicated where the blood had soaked into the soil, darkening it.

"There. Put it around the blood. And then follow the pigs for any other evidence."

Officer Boyle looked up at him, surprised. "You mean?"

"Yup," Clarence said. "Every last morsel."

Sera smiled apologetically, though she wanted to laugh, and led Clarence inside to make him and the other officers coffee. She brewed an incredibly awful pot, but he choked it down without hardly making any face at all. Mostly.

42 had reclaimed her perch in the living room, guarding the stairs that led down to the basement. Clarence eyed the dog warily. Something was off. He knew it, though he didn't know what it was or why.

Someone died here today, he tried to tell himself. The sudden death of a person very likely would make him feel like something was out of whack in the universe, but his gut told him that wasn't the issue. It was odd that the dog wasn't joining them in the kitchen. Dogs love being near their people.

Sera watched him eyeing the door, pretending to be looking at 42. She sighed internally and decided, why not? She'd done all she could. She wasn't exactly known for her housekeeping abilities, but she'd been meticulous. This was not how she'd get caught. Besides, not showing him the basement would be way more suspicious at this point.

"You want to see my basement?" she asked.

He laughed, caught. "Sorry. Yeah. If you don't mind. Just to get a feel for the space, you know."

"Sure," she said.

They stood and walked toward 42, who crouched a little lower and growled at Clarence. "It's all right, 42," she cooed. "It's okay." 42 eased up, though her muscles remained strained and at the ready.

Sera opened the door, and when Clarence's foot hit the first step, 42 began to bark ferociously, though she didn't step forward or lunge at him.

"I don't know what it is with her and the basement. Maybe it's haunted," Sera said, trying to laugh off 42's behavior, but the hairs on Clarence's neck stood at attention.

He drew his gun.

"I don't think you need that—"

*Shhhh*, he mimed to Sera with none of the malevolent undertones the same gesture had when performed by Old Man Durmont. He really thought someone might be down there. She hoped he'd turn right back around when he saw the empty room.

He moved his finger from his lips back to his gun, and Sera marveled at how different an action could be depending on the person—protective, or full of artifice and threat. That was the whole thing though, wasn't it? So many times, The Bitch had said some perfectly acceptable thing that oozed with an undercurrent that convinced Sera she was less than human. Less than worthy.

*People are scum*, Sera thought.

Clarence slowly descended the stairs, gun at the ready. Sera didn't follow initially. He was protecting her. It was sweet if a little misguided. He was protecting her from the potential bad guy in the house, but she was the bad guy in the house.

*He might not be a good cop,* she thought, *but he was a good person*. A sense of relief washed over her. He was a good person. She knew it. Her spidey-sense was not completely broken. It was simply dormant.

His foot hit the cement landing below, and he swung the gun around carefully in the dark. First one way, then the other.

"What are you looking for?" she whispered down to him.

She heard the lights click on, but he said nothing.

He swept the basement, moving into corners, under the stairs, even looking behind the washing machine. He saw everything there was to see. What he didn't see was everything Sera had cleaned up. Every bit of blood the pigs had spilled on the plastic shower curtain that she had washed down the utility sink. The bleach she had used to clean the curtain and the sink before rehanging it in the tub upstairs. She would throw it away later, but right now, all that mattered is that he saw clean cement.

"It's clear," he said. "You can come down." But as he holstered his weapon, he looked down and saw a single hoofprint. The print itself was odd, but what was odder was that there were no other hoofprints leading up and out of the basement. Or down into it, for that matter. If a pig had come down here, how had it gotten out? Did she carry it? Did she carry it down and up? Could she?

She came into the basement, holding her hands in the air in a sign of surrender.

"Weapons up?" she asked.

"Weapons up," he said, also raising his hands.

He hoped she wasn't up to something. He also hoped she wasn't in trouble, but that part he suspected he knew. Why else would she suddenly decide to move to a house that she had left empty for nearly six years?

"I talked to Mrs. Durmont," he said, his eyes still tracing the room, looking for something he might have missed.

"And?" Sera asked.

"You can keep the pigs. She claimed they'd tried to kill Mr. Durmont more than once, and she didn't want them coming after her next," he said. "She also offered to slaughter them all immediately, if you'd rather." He watched her closely, trying to gauge her response. He wasn't sure what he was looking for. He hoped he'd know it if he saw it. "Do you think I should have them killed?" she asked. She looked just like the city girl she was with no understanding of country life, and a genuine sadness at the idea of killing a pig, even though she probably ate meat every day.

"Are you a vegetarian?" he asked.

She laughed out loud. "No. Actually, I love bacon, but don't tell the pigs." And just like that, the tension shattered.

"I don't know if I'd keep them," he said. "But if you trust them...Be careful. They're clearly a risk." He had to consciously stop himself from looking down at the hoofprint. He didn't want to alert her to it. He didn't know what it was, but it was something. Maybe Mr. Durmont had come down here? Had forced his way in? He couldn't figure out why she'd lie about that though, and she didn't care that he was in here. She'd invited him down.

"Better head up," he said. Was there a flash of relief? Even if there was, did it mean anything? Of course she'd be relieved when tonight was over. Who wouldn't be?

They joined the other officers, who were finishing up outside. Their coffee cups had been abandoned, still full.

The cops had taken stool samples from a number of pigs, but all of them expected to find the same thing—the pigs had eaten a whole lot of human flesh and bone. Past that, it was anyone's guess.

The most disturbing thing was the pigs. They all seemed so calm, calm but watchful. Perhaps that was throwing Clarence.

"You sure about keeping them?" he asked one last time before climbing into his cruiser.

"I'm sure," Sera assured.

Sera watched the officers drive away, figuring it was a job well done. She hadn't noticed that Clarence saw a hoofprint in the dust. She hadn't realized she'd missed a spot on the floor. She didn't want it to look too clean down there, not like she'd just cleaned, but she had also had to clean. She'd dusted and kicked the dust around. She'd cleaned and spread the dirt.

She waved, both hoping she'd never see Clarence again and kinda hoping she would, under different circumstances though. Definitely under different circumstances.

The pigs wandered the yard, making camp wherever they saw fit. There wasn't a lot of night left, but there was enough.

Sera and 42 went inside to lie on her grandma's overly broken-in bed. 42 nuzzled into the blankets, smelling the scent of one of the nicest old ladies ever. Sera breathed deeply as well, doing the exact same thing.

# THIRTY-FOUR

S era stretched out, languishing in her new bed. Why hadn't she moved here earlier? Oh yeah, The Bitch. She'd made the place out to be some sort of demented haunted mansion.

"You're not going to sell it? In the middle of nowhere. Haven't you seen any scary movie, ever?" The Bitch asked. "*House of 1000 Corpses* much?"

*She was probably just jealous.* The thought blipped into Sera's head randomly, but it felt good, evolved. Was The Bitch jealous? Could that be it? What drove The Bitch to do the things she did? This kept Sera up at night. She couldn't understand why. What was the motivation? If The Bitch was straight-up evil, it made sense, but she seemed to want friends. She seemed to— Yeah, Sera realized. She did want friends, but not friends-friends. She wanted patsy friends. She wanted a collection of people that would do her bidding. She wanted control.

It was the wrong era, and the wrong country, but Sera thought what The Bitch really wanted was to be a queen. The Queen. Infallible. With unlimited resources and minions that gathered around her. In modern times, The Bitch needed to trick her followers into believing they were friends, but that was doable, wasn't it?

The setup had worked for her, for a long time. In fact, it still seemed to be working for her with most people. The only downside for The Bitch was that she could see the seams, and that drove her crazy. She needed to shore things up, keep people in line, but friends were allowed to have opinions. Other plans. Friends were allowed to do a whole slew of things that were off-limits to underlings, which put cracks in the foundation The Bitch had worked so hard to lay.

It's what led to the downfall of her and Sera. The Bitch couldn't allow there to be seams. There could be no gaps allowing unsanctioned change to take place, and Sera, along with many other things, loved change. She thrived on it. She was constantly striving for better, more, different. Change was, in fact, the only thing that made Sera feel comfortable.

Ironically, if The Bitch had ignored the few things Sera was doing on her own, nothing big probably ever would have changed, but The Bitch couldn't stand idly by. Just a fraction-of-an-inch shift in tectonic plates has big consequences, and that's for giant mountain ranges. Imagine a fraction of an inch between itty bitty people. The Bitch never stood a chance.

Sera never stood a chance.

She wondered if knowing The Bitch had made her embrace change? Had knowing her and witnessing the isolating effect of constant control led Sera to want constant chaos? She wanted to embrace that theory. To embrace any theory that explained why she was how she was, but there wasn't an answer. There isn't always an answer, and there is almost never one that is packaged up nicely with a bow.

Sera also knew she couldn't hold on to the idea of constant chaos as her guiding principle. Not at all. She loved change, sure, but she had an intrinsic fear of choosing wrong. This was, in and of itself, a kind of control. She had to be right, or, more accurately, she realized, she couldn't be wrong. Wrong was dangerous. Wrong had ramifications.

This came from The Bitch.

This came from instant consequences every time she had ever chosen "wrong," in The Bitch's opinion.

*Mental abuse is a sticky wicket,* she thought. *It is a sticky fucking wicket.*

She was going to get rid of her fear of choosing wrong. Fuck it. She'd rather choose wrong and go down living than never choose at all and die of fright.

Sera reached the stairs to the basement holding an armful of clothes. She was prepared to bid 42 a short adieu, but to her surprise 42 willingly trotted down the stairs behind her. Sera shrugged. Apparently, no body, no problem.

Downstairs, she threw her clothes in the washer, cleansing herself of the memory of the pigs' murder. For the pigs, was it murder? Self-defense? A senseless animal attack with no concept of right and wrong? She considered and dismissed the last one.

The pigs may have no concept of right and wrong, but it was certainly not senseless. And she was pretty sure that Pig, and probably the others, if he had taught them anything, had a very strong sense of right and wrong. Pig just clearly knew that he was in the right and Old Man Durmont was in the wrong. He was very much in the wrong.

Sera dropped a sock, and when she bent to pick it up, she saw it. The hoofprint.

*Shit.*

She walked over and knelt down near the offending dust. Behind the hoofprint was the unmistakable crescent moon shape of the toe of a boot, and it wasn't her boot. It was a big boot. Not giant, but larger than even her rather-large-for-a-female foot.

Clarence.

It had to be.

The print was so close to the hoofprint.

She tried to convince herself that he didn't see it. What were the odds that he looked directly at the ground by his feet?

*100 percent,* she thought. *The odds were 100 percent.*

He had thought something was up in the basement, and let's be honest, something was up in the basement, AND he was there on a call about a bunch of stolen pigs murdering a man. She wondered, if she had told Officer Clarence that the pigs had followed her out of the pen on that first night and were safely in her apartment, if all of this could have been avoided.

Probably.

Probably Mr. Durmont would have pressed charges, and instead of him lying dead in a ditch—well, in ten pigs' stomachs—she would be in jail never having been able to murder anyone. Well, Alyssa would still be dead. Her body count would be the same, but she wouldn't have been able to get rid of the body. So, she would have started in jail as a pig thief who claimed the pigs followed her into her Prius like they were wandering onto the ark, and she would have ended up in jail with second-degree murder charges.

Her brain hurt already. Was there a pill for this? To stop these thoughts? Probably, but being half comatose would also have downsides.

The print.

She stared at it and stopped being neurotic for a second. Everything else fell away. She let it fall away, only focusing on what mattered. She stared at the hoofprint and the crescent moon boot shape smiling above it.

She had to kill The Bitch now.

She didn't have time.

Clarence might not suspect anything, or he might think that she was somehow more involved in Old Man Durmont's demise than she had said. She doubted he suspected about Alyssa, but did he ask Sera about her yesterday? She couldn't remember. If he had, it could be innocent. Any cop would ask about the drunk girl he'd heard groaning in the background. Or the print from human-eating-pigs could be a huge red flag, and so he might ask about her friend from a growing sense of unease, or worse, a theory. Or...he didn't ask about her at all. Sera couldn't remember. Even if she could, she didn't know if not asking was better. That might mean he didn't want to tip his hand by showing her what he was thinking.

Likely, he had nothing. Likely, he hadn't seen the print... He had. She knew he had. But he still had nothing. A pig had been in the basement. Had she left any other clues? She glanced around. Nothing she could see. Fucking hell. Either way, she had to kill The Bitch now if she was going to be certain she had the chance. How to accomplish that?

She hoped to do a good old-fashioned stalking, but maybe just calling her and picking her up would be better. No. There would be a record. And if she dropped by, The Bitch would surely want to take her off on one of her own adventures or chores or... And The Bitch would definitely text someone, anyone, likely *everyone* saying that Sera had crawled back and was finally ready to apologize for being such an awful human and friend.

Sera's blood boiled.

She would not apologize.

42 whimpered a little and nuzzled into Sera, which made her smile. 42 took that as a sign of encouragement and jumped up on her, enthusiastically knocking her over. She laughed in spite of herself. She was getting a ravenous dose of face licks. She laughed and laughed as 42 pinned her down, undeniably the top of the dog pile. When she'd finally had enough and lifted 42 off of her, she noticed that both the hoofprint and the boot print were gone. Their rolling and the dust from years of disuse had washed away all traces.

*If only this had happened yesterday,* she thought, and 42 jumped on her again, starting the licking match all over. Clearly, 42 agreed. This should happen every day.

Sera let herself be knocked down this time. She needed to go kill The Bitch ASAP, but a few minutes of play would do them both good. Besides, Sera was pretty damn happy about the day that was ahead of her. Why shouldn't she celebrate?!

# THIRTY-FIVE

Sera went upstairs with a new sense of purpose. 42 chased her the entire way, sniffing the corners of the stairs as they went. They were clearly onto something. She didn't know what, but she'd bet Sera did.

Sera knew she needed to kill The Bitch ASAP, but she also needed a plan. She didn't want to get caught. She'd already made mistakes, more than she should have, but that would stop now. With any luck, Clarence wasn't really onto her, and without any luck... Well, without any luck, she had today to grab The Bitch and take her down.

This was not ideal.

Neither was going to jail before she'd had a chance to off her nemesis.

Nemesis? She wondered if that was right. They'd never been rivals. At least, Sera didn't think so. She had certainly not been The Bitch's rival. She wanted to scream "What the fuck did you do to me???? Why would you do this? What did I do to you? We were FRIENDS!!!!!" Instead, she tore open her grandma's junk drawer.

A plan.

She needed a plan.

This was not the best mindset to plan in, but fuck it. All these years, she'd been so careful trying to tightrope walk around everyone. Never make anyone mad. Never upset anyone. Never hurt anyone's feelings. It's fine, she'd told herself time and time again. You're fine. You don't need the space, the time, the love, the break, the acceptance, the ability to be you. The compassion. You don't need your help. They need your help, and they'd confirmed it. With every action. Every request. Every unacceptable thing. Everyone else needs you, but you, you're fine. You should sit in a fucking drawer and hand them their socks.

"Ahhhhhhh! I fucking hate you!" Sera screamed at herself.

42's ears immediately fell, and she tucked her tail.

"Shit. I'm sorry. Not you. Me. I hate me. Come here. It's okay. It's okay, 42."

42 tentatively tippy-tapped her feet in place. She had no idea what she'd done. Had she done something? What was wrong with Sera? Her friend needed her, and 42 knew, she knew with a deepness that cut to her bones, that she could not help. She couldn't help at all.

Sera sat and wrapped her arms around 42, and 42 nuzzled her head into Sera's shoulder.

"I'm sorry," Sera said it to 42, and she said it to herself. Sera was broken, but she didn't want to break 42. She didn't deserve this, but 42 really didn't.

"It's not you 42. It's me. It's all me." And for the first time in the history of all the times that that phrase had been uttered, it was completely true. It was definitely not 42. It was absolutely positively 100 percent Sera.

*Maybe 42 shouldn't live here,* she thought for the thousandth time.

She threw her hands up in the air. Not again.

*I'm going to kill The Bitch so fucking hard. She took everything from me. She's still taking things from me.*

42 whined, pulling Sera back to the now. She couldn't do much, but she could let Sera know that she was here for her. Whatever was going on, she was here for Sera.

Sera hugged 42 and buried her face in the fluffkin's neck.

"Not you, right, 42? She's not going to get you."

42 leaned into Sera hard, confirming that no, whoever *she* was, *she* would not get 42.

*Why would she?* 42 thought. *No one gets me, but me. I'm my own dog.*

But she knew she'd share her awesomeness with Sera for a good, long time. Forever, maybe. 42 imagined them running through a field playing Frisbee. She tried not to think about it too much. She'd been given so much in the past few days, but she still wanted a Frisbee. She didn't need one. She had friends and this beautiful house and field Sera was sharing with her, but man oh man, a Frisbee sure would be nice. She didn't know, but she bet the pigs would enjoy a Frisbee too. They could have an entire Frisbee tournament. 42 thought she'd win, but she might let the pigs win sometimes, except Pig. Pig could handle the loss.

42's body relaxed as she thought about Frisbee which made Sera relax.

Sera hadn't broken 42 after all. She'd scared her. She hated that, but she didn't break the little pup. The pup had probably been through a lot in her day.

*All the more reason to not get caught,* Sera thought.

The pup was probably stronger than Sera was, but Sera was getting stronger and finishing this would make her even stronger. She knew that, but she had to do it first.

Sera patted 42's head, stood up, and dug in the junk drawer. 42 was still watching her warily, but it was a lot better than having her cower.

Finally, Sera found what she was looking for— a pen covered in about fifty years of dust and drawer grime and a small notepad. Her grandma had these pads stashed all over the house. The paper had a small watercolor painting of flowers and a butterfly printed in the corner. It was a free gift for donating to the Paralyzed Veterans of America. The image was a painting a vet had done after coming home. Likely, it was part of their therapy to help with PTSD. Sera looked at the next page. It was a different watercolor. There were five different watercolor paintings in all. Each done by a different vet. Each a variation of some type of garden flowers and wildlife. A blue jay, a hummingbird, a bumblebee. Soothing, pleasant images. Things that could fly away.

Maybe she should take up painting.

She looked at the pad. She was an idiot. Why did she even get the paper out? She couldn't write any of this down.

*No, Mr. Officer, I didn't plan to kill anyone. That list is household supplies. Honest. Of course I need rubber gloves, bleach, and a rope at home.*

Even Clarence wasn't that stupid.

She paused. She could actually have all these things on a perfectly legitimate list. These items were things it was 100 percent likely someone would have at home. The rope would maybe raise some eyebrows, but even that wasn't weird. It would only raise eyebrows after someone had been kidnapped. Also, she'd just moved—Moved! Ha!—She'd just fled her last apartment before her landlord could have her and her friends unceremoniously kicked to the curb—having rope was a necessity for strapping stuff down, and she'd had it on hand. Sera wondered how many people were out there buying supplies for murder on the daily without anyone ever suspecting?

The number must be higher than she'd guess, higher than anyone would guess, though that would probably create a lot more missing persons than there currently were.

Would it?

How many missing persons were there?

*Well, I'll be,* Sera thought. *Here, I thought I was being original, and it turns out I'm just like everyone else.*

Of course it made her just like everyone else. The majority of the world seemed to be out for themselves. She was playing catch up, and her unwritten list of murder supplies was one more breadcrumb leading her to normal. She decided to gather up the basics. Gloves, rope. She should tie her hair up. She wouldn't want to leave DNA evidence. Her hair was probably still all over The Bitch and her apartment, but you could never be too careful. Her new knife. That was important. That was the most important.

She went and grabbed it from the bedside table. She stroked the red leather handle. It reminded her of blood, but in a romantic cinematic way. It was a beautiful piece. She rolled her eyes at herself. Yeah, that list would be real suspect compared to stumbling through the hunting goods store and buying a knife from some dude you talked to for an hour.

No wonder so many people thought serial killers "seemed so nice" and were "just like everyone else." Honestly, the ones that "kept to themselves" were probably the ones that stood out.

*Good,* she thought. *All my fuck-ups might be camouflage.*

They weren't, but she couldn't get hung up on that now. She'd done what she'd done.

*Mr. Durmont wasn't your fault,* her inner voice piped up, giving Sera pause.

He wasn't. He wasn't her fault at all. She did have to defend herself, or at least, she'd had to defend the pigs. She couldn't be expected to do nothing when he shot at her pigs—well, at his pigs, but still. Why did she always blame herself?

Because she'd been taught to.

"Everyone knows not to do that," The Bitch had said because The Bitch never made a mistake.

Different versions of "You knew you shouldn't," "You're not that stupid," "So, you only ruined mine?" "You thought that was okay?" and "Mm-hm. Sure" played through Sera's mind. It went on and on, because Sera wasn't allowed to make a mistake, and because Sera was blamed, and because Sera was there, and because Sera was easy to blame, and because Sera let it happen.

Let.

She was still making it all her fault.

She was letting it be all her fault.

It wasn't the job. It wasn't losing her friends. It wasn't learning that so many of the people she had surrounded herself with happened to be narcissists or, at the very least, users. It was that Sera didn't think she would ever be free of The Bitch.

Her brain had been hijacked.

Rewired.

Broken.

Fried.

Left.

And she was supposed to pick up the ruins and make them function again.

The things all seemed so small. She knew they did, knew they were individually minuscule. Each incident. Each statement. Each look. Each tantrum. And each time the effect on Sera was small. So, she let it happen. And it happened. And each and every time, it built on itself.

She still couldn't understand how she had been so weak. She was so strong. She'd always been so strong.

*Grooming,* her inner voice chimed in. *Manipulating. Gaslighting.*

All these words that meant nothing and everything.

*She broke me, broke my reality.*

That was *The Thing.*

Sera pulled a silk kerchief out of her grandma's closet and tied the scarf around her hair. She paired the pink and teal scarf with beautiful driving gloves she found in her grandma's drawer. She'd be the most stylish serial killer out there, she chuckled to herself. Well, stylish for someone in their nineties.

She looked at her reflection.

In jeans, an old T-shirt, a headscarf, and driving gloves, she looked like she was the fanciest woman to ever clean a house. The Bitch wouldn't recognize her, but she'd stand out in any group of people. She dug through her garbage bag of clothes and pulled out some black yoga pants and a black hoodie. It was not more stylish, but it was about functionality and anonymity, not beauty. Sera wanted to nab The Bitch in the dark, and black would be harder to spot. Yoga pants were also a lot more comfortable to fight in than jeans. She hoped there wouldn't be a big fight, but The Bitch wasn't going to go easily.

Sera reconsidered the driving gloves and kerchief too. Everything she was wearing would have to be thrown away. She pulled them off and put them neatly back where she'd found them. She didn't need to think of her grandma during this. More than that though, she wanted to keep these. They were important to her.

Besides, there was a reason black on black was all the rage in Serial Killer Vogue. A black hoodie and black sweats was basically serial killer chic.

# THIRTY-SIX

Sera walked out of the house feeling woefully underprepared for a murder. She carried all her supplies in one hand. They didn't seem sufficient at all. She knew there was something she was missing. Something very important.

*An alibi.*

*Holy shit.*

She had completely forgotten about an alibi. That was basically Murder 101, and she hadn't even considered it. Over the past few months, she'd spent so much time making sure she didn't hang out with anyone that wasn't awesome that the idea that she might *need* to hang out with someone had never occurred to her. It felt ironic that she hadn't considered an alibi since hanging out with assholes was single-handedly what led her to decide to be a serial killer instead of a simple one-off murderer. Fucking people.

How did people normally get alibis?

Normally? Did that word apply here? No one should normally get an alibi. She would need to though. So...

*Friends that would lie for you,* she thought. That's how people normally got alibis.

Did that make them good friends or bad people? Huh. Would she have lied for The Bitch? Would she have been an alibi? She hoped not. She hoped that would have been a line in the sand.

The best way to get an alibi was not to have someone lie. It was to hang out with someone just after you'd committed the crime but to make it feel like you'd gotten together earlier. Like scheduling a late lunch for, say, 5 p.m. Then when they were asked what time you'd met up, they'd remember lunch which was generally way earlier than 5. Bingo bango, you had an alibi and the time to kill someone!

None of this mattered.

Sera didn't have an alibi, and she didn't have anyone to ask to hang out to create an alibi. Sera was utterly alone. She'd set it up that way. She'd gotten rid of everyone, but it still stung. It stung every damn time. She didn't even know if she could function with friends anymore. Even when people weren't straight-up assholes, she had an extremely tough time trusting them. How could you know, for sure, that they weren't about to be an asshole? How could you tell that they weren't just super good at using you? And every small thing they did wrong suddenly became the possible tip of the iceberg. It was too much. Too big a risk.

The Bitch stole her trust.

It's impressive how many things one person can ruin.

It didn't matter. Not right now. She needed an alibi. Someone she could hang out with... Alex. He was the first person who came to mind. The *only* person. It was sad that he was the one she thought of. She barely knew him. She less than barely knew him. She didn't know him. Not really. She only even knew his name and number 'cause he'd left a note.

Still, she had had fun with him, and she had ended up so comfortable that she fell asleep with him in her apartment. He was the one.

*Not "The One,"* she thought, *but the one, the one to be her alibi.*

Well, maybe a pseudo alibi.

She had no idea how long a murder would take, and she didn't have time to walk through the potential scenario.

Fucking hoofprint.

Did it really matter? Was Clarence onto her?

She honestly didn't think he could know enough to do anything. He couldn't arrest her, not yet. A hoofprint proved nothing. He hadn't even taken her into custody after Old Man Durmont's demise. He obviously didn't think she was a criminal mastermind, but if he suspected anything, anything at all, he could make it impossible for her to kill The Bitch. She should have killed her first. Why hadn't she? Why did she start with Alyssa?

Wanting to get shit right always got in the way. Just decide and do a thing. When did she become such a perfectionist? This was not her. At least, it didn't used to be.

*Fuck it.*

She opened the passenger door and shoved her hunting knife and some rubber kitchen gloves in the glove compartment. For the first time ever, the glove compartment seemed aptly named. Touché. Then, she pulled out her phone and texted Alex.

Hey. Not sure what to say, but if you want to hang out tonight lmk.

Then—

This is Sera BTW. The steak girl.

She wasn't sure how well an alibi would hold up from someone she barely knew, but maybe it would be better. It probably would be. If he were questioned, he'd have no reason to lie, so they'd believe him. Cops, a jury, a judge, they'd all believe him. He'd never talk to her again, but she wouldn't be in jail, which was something. She sighed. She was just a little disappointed that they wouldn't be friends.

*Chill, Sera. He hasn't even texted you back. Your friendship isn't over yet. It doesn't even exist.*

She glanced down at her phone. Still no text, because five seconds is only a super long time to wait for a text in the most subjective of ways. She wanted to hang out with him, but she hoped he was busy. She couldn't actually see him today. That was beyond her capabilities as a newly dawned murderer. She wanted a pseudo alibi. Someone to attest to her trying to hang out and thus sorta being busy, or at least not being out planning a murder, but if he actually could hang out, she'd have to cancel cause she was busy committing a murder.

*No wonder alibis fall through so often.*

She looked back at the glove box. She could probably fit the rope in there too. At least some of it. Or maybe she'd put it on the seat? It seemed smart to have it on hand in case, but it could be suspicious if she got pulled over. She wasn't going to speed. Only break one rule at a time. She knew that. Still, she begrudgingly decided to leave it in the trunk. She walked around the car to see if she had enough and to confirm it was there. She wasn't neurotic. Not at all. Three Ziplock bags full of yellow rope bits seemed a little ridiculous, but it was functional. She stared at the trunk for a moment. That was it? That was all she was bringing for the biggest day of her life?

Was it—the biggest day of her life? No way to know.

Oh! She suddenly remembered the rope she'd seen in the basement. Inside, she took the stairs two at a time. Behind the worktable, she grabbed the long blue coiled rope. Scraps and bits were all fine and good, but having a solid backup wasn't a bad idea. She ran back up the stairs, taking them two at a time for about two steps. Then she switched to single stairs. Taking stairs up at double speed was not Sera's strong suit. Working out was definitely in her future. Single stairs be damned, she kept running. Every step was one step closer to the totally fit serial killer she wanted to be.

Back outside, she added the rope to the trunk. The pile of supplies did not increase much. She untied the hoodie from her waist and dropped it on top. That was something. It didn't really seem like there was much else she'd need. Still, what if she needed more? Was there something else? Could she use a shovel? Or?

She went around to her grandma's back shed, only to find it was padlocked.

*Shit.*

Inside the house, she rummaged around in the junk drawer one more time, eventually pulling out ten different keys of various shapes and sizes. Seven of them seemed like they could possibly go to the padlock, but only four seemed likely to go to it. She pocketed all ten. Might as well try.

By this time, 42 had given up on Sera promptly heading out, so rather than patiently waiting by the car, or following her back and forth, 42 was hanging out with the pigs. She'd begun by sitting with Pig because 42 was, after all, also a leader and master of her own fate.

Unfortunately, even though Pig was super smart, he was also a little boring. He preferred to sit and survey the land. 42 guessed he was looking for security risks, but that seemed a little strange out here. Still, that giant evil farmer had shown up out of nowhere. Pig was probably right. So, 42 sat with Pig for *forever*. Then, after about five minutes, 42 decided that her talents would be better put to use investigating the field. She got up and joined the other pigs. She smelled the grass. She smelled the mud. She smelled one pig, then another. All in all, she was doing her part to keep the place safe.

Back at the shed, Sera shoved key after key into the lock. None of them worked. 42 came and smelled the lock and keys in Sera's hand.

*Never can be too careful,* 42 thought, but the keys were fine. She continued making her rounds to each and every pig. It was important work, and she was up to it.

Sera stared at the padlock. There could be all sorts of useful stuff behind the door. She could break the lock, but the key would be around here somewhere. She was sure she could find it, but... was she stalling? Her brow furrowed.

She was.

She could feel it.

Her heart was thumping in her chest. Not racing. Not panicked. Slowed somehow. It was like her heart was trying not to beat but was having to beat anyway. Having to keep her alive, whether it wanted to or not.

Her breathing slowed.

Panic attack?

Her hands weren't numb though. Weren't tingling.

Not yet.

"Did you ever think about me?" she remembered The Bitch asking her once.

"I—" Sera had stammered. She had. Of course she had. It was when Sera decided she didn't want to go to Cabo with the group. The Bitch was all she thought about. She didn't know how to put into words how worried she was that The Bitch would be upset if she didn't go. *If* she didn't go, because she knew she could still be talked into going. Her hands had gone numb. It was hard to focus. She was almost dizzy. She was definitely lightheaded. It was the opposite of being drunk on power. She was drunk on impotence.

Another friend, a childhood friend, had laughed at her. She couldn't believe Sera was going to go because she thought The Bitch would be pissed if she didn't, because she didn't want to confront her. That was ridiculous. Sera had never had a problem talking to people. She had always stood up for people, for herself.

Sera struggled to remember that version of her. Standing up for others? Sure. Standing up for herself? Had she? She remembered she had, of course, but that was an entire "The Bitch ago."

She didn't know if it wasn't worth it. She didn't want to face the confrontation. Didn't want to go through it.

"Go through what?" her friend had asked.

It was impossible to explain. She tried, but her friend kept acting like Sera was insane. She knew that she, Sera, would be in pain if she didn't go. She couldn't make it any clearer because she didn't understand it herself. It didn't make sense. Her friend was right. She tried to explain. The Bitch would be pissed, hurt, upset. She'd be...

Sera had felt like a child without the correct vocabulary. The Bitch had never really told her what to do, right? Sera expected everything would go to shit if she tried to talk to her, but she hadn't actually tried to talk to her, had she? She had, but at the time it didn't seem like it. It seemed like it was all her fault for not bringing things up. The Bitch told her so.

"You sound like an abused housewife," her friend had teased. It wasn't funny. "It's not that big a deal. If this girl is your friend, she'll understand. If not, fuck her."

She would understand broke.

Would understand had to work.

Would understand burnt out.

Would understand I don't want to go.

She would understand it was perfectly acceptable for Sera to not use all her vacation days and put a trip she couldn't afford on her credit card, again.

"I *need* this," The Bitch had said.

"You'll have fun with Alyssa and Mindy," Sera had offered.

"I want to have fun with you. Why are you doing this to me?"

"I'll help you pack."

"I don't want you to help me pack. I want you to pack your own bag and come."

Sera'd practiced. She shouldn't have to make the case, but she had practiced the case anyway, because she knew. Sera had always known she'd have to make the case.

Standing in front of the shed, facing her grandma's house, Sera looked down at her hands and felt the tingling start, felt the absolute complete helplessness that she always felt.

She was stalling because she didn't want to confront The Bitch. She was going to kill her, and she still didn't want to face her. Sera wiped away a tear she suddenly felt on her cheek.

*I'm better than this. I'm better than this,* she closed her eyes and chanted.

*Then why'd you let it happen in the first place?*

Sera didn't have an answer.

She knew the answers. She'd researched the answers. She'd learned the answers. But she didn't *have* an answer.

How had she become a victim of abuse by a friend?

She didn't need what was in the shed.

*Fuck that.*

Whatever was in there wasn't going to help her anyway. She didn't even know what she was looking for, she certainly wasn't going to miss it if she didn't have it.

She headed back to the car with long sure strides. She was Sera.

S-E-R-A.

She was the Sera she wanted to be. She was past all that bullshit. She was putting it behind her. She had to kill The Bitch because The Bitch deserved to die, and she, Sera, was stepping up.

She saw the shovel she had dug the world's shallowest grave with and decided to take it with her. The shed would have been full of various yard tools. Now, she had as much as she would have had if she'd gotten in there.

Sera was prepared.

From across the yard, 42 saw Sera grab the shovel and knew exactly what they were going to do, *more digging!*

42 raced to the grave and started digging at the edges. She shifted from spot to spot, pausing only to find that Sera was

not joining her. She ran around the house as Sera closed the hatchback with the shovel inside. 42 cocked her head.

*Hmm. Guess we'll be digging someplace else.* 42 darted after Sera.

With everything all set, or as set as it was going to be, Sera went back inside the house to grab two cans of Febreze that she'd found under the sink with the gloves. No need to suffer while she was on her stakeout. She sprayed a can and a half of Febreze into the back of the car before the cans ran dry. Good ol' Grandma for the win. The cans were probably ten years old, but Sera just thought that made them more potent. It might have also made the fumes more intoxicating, but she could only worry about one problem at a time.

Now, she was all set.

The pigs lined up, ready for their next adventure, but she shook her head and told them no. This time, they willingly obliged, which surprised Sera. The pigs didn't seem like they'd listen to anything she said without Pig's approval, but she hadn't tried to kill them in days now. Maybe they were moving forward. They wandered back to the field, completely unphased, and Sera realized they probably liked the field better than the back of her Prius anyway. It had nothing to do with her.

If she didn't get arrested, she might need a truck.

*Shit.*

She'd forgotten all about food. They might be hungry and thirsty. Too late now. The grass would have to do for food until she figured out where to get pig feed. For water, she ran back inside, grabbing every bowl in the house, and filled each with hose water. She littered the yard with them. If anyone came, it would look like she thought the sky was leaking, but that was fine with her. Let them think she was crazy. She probably was.

42 was a dilemma though. Taking her with seemed nice, for Sera, but it didn't seem like it would be so great for 42 or for the mission. Inside, Sera slid the plastic cover out of the dog

door. That way 42 could go in and out at will. She figured 42'd probably want to hang out with the pigs, but if she got tired or just needed a minute to herself, she could go back inside. Sera paused. *Do dogs need "a minute to themselves?"* she wondered. *Yes,* she concluded. Every living being needs a minute to themselves. Imagine being a bee living in a hive with about a billion other bees. There's probably a reason most bees are seen flying around alone. They need a minute.

She put a large bowl of water down in the kitchen for 42. She felt bad that she didn't have any dog food—or human food, for that matter. Sera had not properly prepared. Surprise, surprise. She threw open the cupboards until she found an old bag of Doritos. They were stale, but they weren't poisonous. Sera tried to give one to 42, but 42 did not look impressed. Sera poured them in a bowl and set it on the floor. Maybe that would help? 42 did not think it would.

42 followed her to the car and sat down expectantly, waiting for her door to be opened. Why had Sera even put the chips down when they were leaving? Sera wasn't sure how to break it to the pooch that 42 was staying home. She was also worried about the pigs, whether she would admit it or not. That farmer could have come while she was out. If he had, who knew what would have happened? About ten feet away, she saw Pig sitting and watching them both.

*Pig knew,* Sera thought, and her shoulders relaxed a little.

She bent down and took 42's head in her hands and scruffed her behind the ears.

"42, I gotta go, but I need you to stay here and take care of the pigs. I need you to keep them safe. Can you do that for me?"

She figured the pigs probably didn't need looking after, but also, they might wander too far or get distracted. However, given that they had murdered a man, it was possible someone might come looking for them. In that case, Sera hoped 42 could stall them with a pretty impressive bark until Pig organized his troops. Ultimately, anyone going against those pigs was going to have a bad fucking day, but giving the pigs an edge wasn't a bad idea.

Sera also thought 42 would enjoy taking care of them. She could run around all day with an excuse to buddy up with the pigs. She knew this request could also go right over 42's head, but she thought the dog would get the gist of it, if not the exact meaning. 42 cocked her head to the side, and Sera wondered if she'd understood when she did not get the patented two-bark yes 42 was known to give.

42 had completely understood. She was simply considering the magnitude of the request. Ten pigs are a lot of pigs to watch after, and strictly speaking, 42 had never formally watched after anyone, pig or otherwise. She knew that Pig would take care of himself, which was a big help. Still, it was a lot of field to cover, and nine pigs she had to keep in order. It was important to consider everything before blindly saying yes.

She was up to the task though. 42 didn't know how it'd go or what she'd have to do, but she knew she'd figure it out as she went. She'd never formally compared herself to other dogs, but she thought she'd do well if she did, which gave her a strong chance of success at most things, particularly considering even average dogs were pretty doggone smart. This would be a piece of steak.

42 bounded across the yard to tell the pigs that she'd be helping them out today. She didn't want them to think of her as "in charge" so much as there in an emergency.

Sera watched 42 running from pig to pig and realized if anything happened to her there would be no one to look after the pup. She'd been in a sorry state when Sera had initially picked her up, so sorry in fact that Sera though killing her would be a relief.

*Shit.*

*Eye drops.*

That would go on the list of things to do when she got back. She wasn't great at this. At least 42's eyes weren't masses of goo anymore. That had to count for something.

She walked over to Pig and sat down next to him on the grass.

"So, I've got some stuff to do today. I should be back tonight, late, but…" She'd never really worried about if she got caught or even considered what would happen if The Bitch somehow overpowered her and she ended up on the wrong side of the murder stick, but she did now. It was unlikely, but it wasn't impossible, and now she had friends—well, animals she thought of as friends—who depended on her. "Well, some of what I'm doing is kinda risky, and—"

Pig oinked a low oink. She didn't need to go into the details. He got it.

Sera looked him dead in the eye. He was right. Just the important stuff.

"If anything happens to me, I need you to take care of 42. She'll help take care of the other pigs, but she's not *seasoned* like you or I are. Would you do that?"

Pig held Sera's gaze for a good, long time. He wanted to be sure that she knew he understood, and then he nodded assent. She hadn't needed to ask, but he was glad she did. She was a wild card, but she had a responsibility to that animal. He was glad she recognized it.

"Thanks, Pig."

Weird or not, she knew Pig would watch over 42 like she was part of his pig clan. Maybe she was.

42 saw Pig and Sera sitting together and raced over to join them, tongue lolling out of her mouth as she panted. She sat near Pig, proud of being part of the big kids' club, and Pig straightened up slightly, a subtle sign of respect to 42. Sera smiled.

42 was definitely part of Pig's clan.

# THIRTY-SEVEN

Sera got in the car and drove away, well, inched away. She'd never had so many animals free roaming near her car, and while she had intended to kill each of them at one time or another, it was certainly not on her to-do list now.

Finally, she hit the highway and turned onto the road without noticing that Officer Clarence was approaching from the other direction. A few moments later, he turned down her drive. Perhaps he didn't realize that it was her red Prius out in front of him on the empty highway. Perhaps he knew full well it was her and was thankful for the unexpected opportunity to poke around alone. Either way, Sera drove onward with the radio blaring, blissfully ignorant of the cop headed to her abode.

As Sera drove, she saw the glaring flaw in her plan... The whole plan bit. She was an idiot. She had tools but not an actual plan for the abduction. Where was it going to happen? How was she going to do it? She couldn't grab The Bitch and tie her up in broad daylight, could she? No. She most certainly could not even if the look on The Bitch's face would be priceless. Having a memory of that look would almost be worth going to prison though—Me! You dare to come after *me*?—Not quite, but almost.

Sera considered her options. She could go to Law Abiding, The Bitch's favorite bar, and try to drug her or drink her under the table, but there wasn't time to get drugs, and The Bitch could outdrink her in a second. Plus, the fact that it was The Bitch's favorite bar meant it had, at one point, been Sera's favorite bar too. She would be recognized. Not just seen with the potential to be identified later, she would actually be recognized in the moment. Name and all. There was also 0 percent chance that The Bitch would go there alone.

Sera needed her alone.

And she needed to get her phone away from her. Killers in the '70s had it so easy. Even the '80s would have been a stab! She'd been lucky with Alyssa. She wasn't counting on that twice.

She was currently driving to The Bitch's place. It'd been the next logical step. Need to abduct someone, go to their house. Duh. But she didn't live in a house. She lived in a building, a building with a billion other people. Everything seemed so public all of a sudden. Didn't anyone value their privacy anymore?

Nope. Social media had proven that with little room for debate.

She could check her profiles to see if she had any plans. It was risky though. They might be able to track that. Plus, time was of the essence. Tonight was THE night, whether Sera liked it or not. She did like it. She liked it a lot, actually. She was finally doing it. She just wished she had a surefire way to get The Bitch alone, and into her car, and back to her grandma's without being seen, or followed, or caught. Right now, she'd even settle for the relative ease of the '90s.

Nothing for it. She'd just have to stalk her and pounce when the opportunity presented itself. It wasn't ideal, but Sera clearly did not go in for the type of ideal hospital-clean murders that led to long-lasting serial killer careers. She was going to have to blunder her way through murder number two and hope she made it to number three.

*Who would that be?* she wondered. She'd been concocting an internal list, but nothing was set in stone.

"Not now," she chided herself. She couldn't afford distractions.

It was settled. She'd go to The Bitch's house and wait for her to come out, hopefully alone, and then she'd follow her until the opportunity presented itself. Maybe it'd be in a parking lot, or an alley—Dare she hope for an alley? If only she could be so lucky. Sooner or later, an opportunity would present itself. It had to, she realized, or she was screwed.

Sera was more confident than she had any right to be. She was well aware. She didn't believe in the universe providing, or the power of one, or mind over matter, or any of that crap. Things weren't meant to be. If you made a wrong turn, you simply needed to flip a bitch. But every now and then, for no reason at all, things would line up, and Sera was convinced she'd get the opportunity to do this.

She would. She knew she would because she was willing to wait and work and make the opportunity. The universe's approval was unnecessary. For a second, she wished she did believe though. It would be nice to have someone looking out for her for once, even if it was someone as distant and uncaring as The Universe.

About an hour later, Sera parked outside The Bitch's complex. She lived in a brand-new high-rise condominium complex. The Bitch liked to call it that—the whole thing. She didn't say "my condo." She said, "my high-rise condominium." It reminded Sera of how British people said *aluminium,* pronouncing every syllable precisely and with that extra *i*. Extra for Americans, at least. She was willing to concede that it was their language first. Though, somehow, *aluminium* made her smile while condominium made her physically ill.

There was no way to tell if The Bitch was home or out. Her windows faced the central courtyard, and her parking spot was in the gated garage below. Sera could ask the doorman. Yes, The Bitch had a doorman, even though it was a small city, whether people in the country called it "the big city" or not. Sera couldn't ask him though, because he would remember her. Not only would he be able to give a description, but he literally knew her. They chatted about his family all the time. Only when The Bitch wasn't with her though. The Bitch never had time to talk about anybody else. She was always in a very large and very important rush, unless she was talking about herself. Then clocks didn't exist.

The Bitch wasn't particularly fashionable or important, outside of her own mind and, perhaps, the lives of her lackeys, but she reminded Sera a bit of Meryl Streep in *The Devil Wears Prada*. She wasn't sure why. She didn't dress like that, and she wasn't mean in that same outright obvious way, but she did seem to think she was the end all be all and that she could, and would, determine the fates of those around her with a nod of her head. Sera liked the movie. She wondered if she would be able to watch it without thinking of The Bitch again. So far, it hadn't come up.

*In prison, it won't matter much,* she concluded and glanced at her phone. Still no text from Alex. So much for an alibi.

She watched the building for hours. Stalking made for boring work. Though, she had to admit, she felt more like the good guy, more like a cop on a stakeout, than a criminal waiting to pounce. She wasn't. She was under no illusion. She was a bad guy. Fine. Still, The Bitch was a bad guy too, and who was to say which of them was worse?

Sera mused for a minute. She was. She was to say, and she decided she was definitely a bad guy, but in this situation, she was the better guy. It was not as good as being the good guy, or even a good guy, but it was better than being the worst guy. The Bitch, she had to admit, was not the worst guy either, or gal. Worst gal. She was not the worst gal. She was just a bad gal. Sera was better though. Sera was going after The Bitch, who was a bad gal, while The Bitch went after everyone and had shown a strong propensity for going after good gals—or good people—at least she didn't discriminate based on gender. Ipso facto, if The Bitch went after everyone, and Sera only went after bad people, Sera was, indeed, the better gal. Not by much, but she'd take it.

She wondered, once she killed The Bitch, would she be a worse person? Not *The Worst* Person, but worse than The Bitch? She might be. She wasn't sure. You'd have to weigh the potential damage against the potential good, and it was really hard to weigh future shit accurately.

She should have gone into philosophy. She had so many questions, but never any answers.

Morality was a temperamental fucker.

Plus, she was the one making the judgment calls on good vs. evil, so while the system was inherently flawed, it was working in her favor.

She looked at her dashboard clock. Fifteen minutes had passed. This was going to be a long day. Maybe she should have brought 42. Suddenly she realized, 42's bone was in the door.

*Shit.*

She looked down, and sure enough, she could have given her a real treat instead of stale chips. Sera was batting a thousand. Her average better improve, or 42 wouldn't even get crappy Doritos.

Sera leaned back and tried to clear her head. Then, she saw movement at the front door. A woman with long dark hair came out. She leaned forward.

*Let it be her. Please let it be her.*

But it wasn't.

It was just as well because broad daylight was no time to stalk unsuspecting people—or suspecting people, for that matter. Seeing the woman had piqued Sera's interest. It had focused her. She leaned forward, arms resting on the steering wheel, and watched the front door and the garage gate.

Her mind no longer leapt from thing to thing. She no longer had to determine her value in relation to every other living thing on God's green earth—or even just this earth, given that she was an atheist. She sat and watched. Purpose allowed her to be herself again, and it felt good.

# THIRTY-EIGHT

Officer Clarence pulled up to Sera's house. He was right. She had just left. He didn't know how he felt about snooping around while she was out. He was a cop. In a sense, it was his job, but also, he kinda liked her. That complicated things. He couldn't be sure if his gut instinct was telling him to be wary of her, or if his butterflies had falsely triggered a gut instinct alert. It had been a long time since he'd liked a girl, and it had been never since he liked a girl he met while on the job.

42 pranced out of the field and bounded up to him. The pigs were all scattered here and there. Except Pig. That one was watching him again. He wanted to walk up to it, to talk to it, ease its mind, but he was being silly. He knew he was being silly, and yet—

"I'm just checking things out," he said too loudly to be talking to himself. "Making sure everything and everyone is okay."

He glanced at Pig. Pig's eyes didn't shift away from him. He knew pigs were smart. He'd grown up out here, so he'd seen their brains in action. Pigs would easily get out of pens if not closed properly, would watch and learn, remembering things like where the feed was kept even if it was not obvious. He also had to believe there was some sentience to these pigs' decision to kill Mr. Durmont. They'd tried it before, Mrs. Durmont said. *Twice.* That wasn't a coincidence. When he'd reported the death to her, she hadn't been surprised it was the pigs. She hadn't even requested Sera be looked at. She knew these pigs, and she had no doubts they'd done it. She had also been relieved he was dead and had shown no interest in hiding it, though she had double-checked three times before allowing the feeling to settle into her bones. Clarence had never seen her smile before.

He didn't know if Mr. Durmont was abusive or if he was just ornery, but he would guess that Mrs. Durmont could have put up with more than her share of orneriness if she had to. Maybe she didn't care if the pigs had done it, so long as it'd been done. If he stopped by Mrs. Durmont's place today, he fully expected to see her lugging all of Mr. Durmont's belongings to the curb already. He wondered if she'd sell the house or keep it. It was hard to get enough money to move out of this town from a sale, but the house might also be a reminder of everything that had gone wrong in her life. He hoped their pig farm up the road went to her. If so, she could go anywhere she wanted, but he wouldn't put it past Mr. Durmont to give it to someone else. A man. Or put some conditions on it that trapped Mrs. Durmont. Clarence had never liked Old Man Durmont. Death by pig was harsh, but he didn't think anyone was crying over it, and no one would miss the man.

Clarence turned his full attention to 42, who was thrilled to see him. She wagged her tail and offered him an impressively solid gnawing stick she'd made good use of. As soon as he grabbed it, her feet started tippy-tapping as fast as could be. She was more than ready for a roaring game of fetch. Clarence took her up on it for a turn or two before heading to the front door. He knocked. It was for show more than anything else.

He didn't know who it was show for exactly, but he could still feel Pig's eyes on the back of his head.

Was he really afraid of a pig?

A pig? No. A pig that had taken part in tearing a man limb from limb? Yeah, he was afraid of that pig. He realized he should be afraid of all of them, but he wasn't. He wondered again if it wasn't the right thing to do to call animal services, but he'd reported the incident to his captain. The captain never seemed to care much about anything, and he also hadn't cared much about this.

"She wants the pigs, and Mrs. Durmont doesn't want the pigs? Let her keep 'em," he had said. "One less pig on my plate." He'd laughed a big full-belly laugh. He always laughed full-belly laughs at his own jokes. Clarence couldn't fault him for that. The captain's jokes were lame, but they were funny in that dad sort of way. Plus, this job was equal parts boring and stressful. Everyone in town acted like you were against them, even when they weren't committing a crime, and the crimes were the most boring crimes he'd ever heard of. Maybe that's why he was here. This was the most interesting crime he'd ever heard of in this town. He wondered if maybe he should move away and do something else, but he did like being a cop. Well, he liked the idea of it.

He pushed that aside as he knocked on the door again. Like it or not, he was a cop right now.

"Sera," he called out to no reply.

42 sat next to his feet on the ground, with her tail wagging, patiently waiting for the door to open. Apparently, his presence had wiped the fact that Sera was gone from her mind.

He reached for the doorknob, and 42 growled.

*So much for her forgetting Sera wasn't home*, he thought.

He was hoping the door would be unlocked and decided to test it. He tried to turn the knob. 42's growl dropped an octave, and she lowered down into ready position. He lifted his hand in submission, and she immediately sat up, tail wagging.

Didn't matter. The door was locked. Now what? He could jimmy it open, but he didn't think 42 would take kindly to that, and he wondered if Pig might not charge him if he did. Also, breaking and entering was not a good look for a cop, though that seemed less important than 42 and Pig—especially Pig—at the moment.

Clarence had gotten too used to country folk. They always left their doors unlocked no matter how many times he told them they shouldn't. He hadn't even considered a plan B, but no reasonably intelligent city girl would leave her door open. At least she wasn't dumb. He liked that.

He figured he'd take a look around the property instead. He didn't need to go inside. He just needed to get a feel for the place. After all, he had no idea what he was looking for or why he was looking.

He peeked in the windows but saw nothing out of the ordinary. He'd been inside the house, so he wasn't sure what he expected to see from here that he would have missed from there, but it was worth a shot. The living room had a thin layer of dust over most things. It looked like she'd moved a lamp recently, but not much else. No harm in that.

The hoofprint kept coming back to mind though. How had a hoofprint gotten in the basement? More importantly, why had a human-eating pig been in the basement? Or, had a pig just wandered down there? Did it just wander down there, and she cleaned up after it like anyone would do? It gnawed at him.

He crouched down, looked in through the basement window, and saw the print was gone. There were scuff marks on the floor where he was sure it had been. Did she wipe it away? He looked at 42 and smiled. As if he'd given a command, 42 lunged at him, tongue at the ready, knocking him down. Clarence guarded his face, but 42 managed to dart her tongue around his defenses every time. Finally, he lifted her up and away from himself. He stood up, dusting dirt off his pants, and looked at the mess of evidence he'd left about his snooping. Then he looked back in the window.

She hadn't cleaned it up. Dust was smudged about randomly. A sock still lay on the ground where she'd missed it. He suspected she'd had a similar attack to his own. He released 42 and kicked the dirt around on the ground. It would be obvious someone was here, but he didn't need it to be too obvious.

*Why not?* he wondered. Did he really suspect something?

42 joined in the fun, digging rather than kicking. He pulled her away a few times, but, in the end, he decided that the best defense was no defense and a hole dug by a dog.

He continued around the perimeter.

42 followed.

He rounded the house, finally stepping out of Pig's view. He let a small sigh of relief escape before shaking his head and chuckling at himself, but the relief was short-lived. He sensed something, a presence, and turned around to find that Pig had adjusted his position and once again was watching Clarence as he lurked.

Clarence decided it would be in his best interest not to linger too long, but, as he was about to leave the back of the house, he spotted the grave. He didn't know it was a grave. It was a long and low hole. It didn't look deep from here, but his bristles went up. It was just long enough and narrow enough that it could have been for a body.

He unsnapped his gun from its holster instinctively. He studied his surroundings. He was still alone. He knew it, could feel it, but just in case.

He approached the hole for a closer look. He scanned the area for any clues he could find. He didn't see a shovel, or any drag marks, or anything else unusual. What he assumed were Sera's footprints were in the vicinity, but they were in the vicinity in a general way, not in a right next to the hole digging sort of way. Was the ground disturbed around the hole? Kicked up? Covered?

As he walked up, he could tell the hole wasn't deep. Not deep at all. No one would have any luck hiding a body there, but if they'd been interrupted... If, say, a group of pigs had decided to eat the body first. He couldn't place any reason on why Sera would have wanted to kill Mr. Durmont though. For the pigs, maybe, but did she really want them that badly? Bad enough to go to prison for life? He doubted it.

As he came up to the hole, his shoulders relaxed. It wasn't a hole. It was a series of holes all linked together with a whole lot of dirt wildly spread around the sides. 42 must have been digging here too. As if on cue, 42 began to dig. She worked hard at another hole connected to the big hole and to all her other holes, making it a bit longer. It became a bit more grave-like as it approached the length of a human male, but it was a lot less scary when Clarence saw each individual pockmark style hole.

He watched 42 dig for a minute. He didn't stop her. It wasn't his place. But he imagined Sera was going to have a few choice words for the dog if she kept going at it like this. He snapped the holster back over the butt of his gun and turned to walk the last leg of the house. He was no longer on high alert. He simply continued because this was the route he had been taking.

What he didn't see was the approving nod Pig gave 42. She had done a good job. A very good job.

# THIRTY-NINE

For the last thirty minutes, Sera had been wondering when she could take a piss. She'd wanted to run to the store or a restaurant hours ago but had forced herself to stay put. The Bitch could come out any minute. Now, as twilight was approaching, Sera realized she had no choice. She really had to pee. So, as the world grew incrementally darker, she decided to take her chance. She would jump out, pee behind the closest bush, and be back in no time.

She was going to have to risk it. About an hour ago, she'd begun considering every bottle in her car, but she'd known with a sad certainty that it would lead to hands covered in piss. She didn't want a car that smelled even worse than the leftover barnyard scent covered with stale Febreze that surrounded her now. Plus, if she got too much pee on her hands, she knew she'd end up going somewhere to wash up.

She might not be cut out for police work after all. If this was any indicator, maybe so many serial killer victims were victims of chance, not because the killers wanted it to go that route, but because after a handful of stakeouts, or stalker sessions given their side of the law, it was likely that they decided, "Fuck it. I'm not following a person and peeing in my car. I'm just grabbing the next person I see."

It might also explain the disproportionate number of male killers working the roadways. If she'd been a dude, she would have whipped out her dick and stuck it in a bottle hours ago.

Maybe women killed based on proximity to the facilities.

It wasn't the least likely possibility.

In any case, it was time. She didn't want pee on her hands, but she wanted pee in her pants even less. She jumped out and dashed behind the nearest bush. She crouched down, staring straight at the building's door, holding her lowered pants out of the way of the splatter. It'd been a long time since she'd been camping, but she still remembered the rules of roadside peeing.

She wondered if they could check pee for DNA? That would definitely be one of the top five most embarrassing ways for a serial killer to get caught. It'd be right up there with accidentally signing your taunting letter to the cops. It'd be just her luck too. In jail, the other serial killers wouldn't even let her hang out with them. She'd be the lame serial killer that even regular killers didn't want to be friends with. Regular killers!!!! She'd have no friends! Absolutely none. Pee-pee Patty. That'd be her nickname. Real name be damned.

"Pee-Pee Patty! Pee-Pee Patty!" they'd chant over and over again. She could hear it already. She wouldn't even get invited to any of the gourmet microwave ramen parties, and she was actually quite the bad ass when it came to ramen.

If this got her caught, she was gonna kill herself. It'd be easier.

The doorman opened the front door with Sera's eyes glued to him.

"Don't be her. Don't be her," she whispered, squeezing her eyes shut for a moment before she forced herself to look.

He held the door open wide as she'd seen him do so many times today, and for the first time, she wasn't praying for it to be The Bitch. Then she saw the unmistakable pink leggings.

Sera tried to pee faster, but there was only so much she could do. She shook her booty, urging the pee to exit immediately, hoping the wind would dry her off a touch. She cringed as pee spray got on her hands. Of course it did. All that waiting so she wouldn't pee on herself in the car, only so she could pee on herself out here.

She was going to have to become a dirtier person if she was going to make it as a serial killer.

The last drop hit the grass, and Sera was immediately pulling her pants on her ass. No time for air-drying. She stood, and The Bitch stepped completely out of the building and into the dying light.

Time froze.

Her dark hair was messy but not overly messy. It was normal. Her pink leggings were louder than anything Sera would expect her to wear, but still normal. Sera also knew that The Bitch had gotten them *because* they were loud. She needed them to stand out. She wanted credit for every workout she did, even if it was by absolute strangers whose eyes were simply caught by the bold pink.

"Cranberry," The Bitch had called it, correcting Sera. "It's not pink. It's cranberry."

It was a deep pink, Sera allotted, but it was still pink. Sera had wanted the leggings, actually. It was the kind of thing she would wear, but once The Bitch had grabbed them it felt like she would be copying her. She had seen them first, but still. Part of her suspected the real reason The Bitch had bought them was so Sera couldn't. It might also be the real reason she wore them so often.

If Sera had bought them, they wouldn't have been cranberry, they would have been fluorescent pink.

The Bitch pulled her hair into a ponytail as she walked. It was her nightly stroll. Sera didn't know how she had forgotten about it.

The Bitch passed by her on the opposite side of the street, completely unaware of Sera and the danger she was in. Sera was struck by how incredibly normal The Bitch was. The normalcy grabbed her by the heart and squeezed the pumping blood to a standstill. With her chest constricted, Sera watched as The Bitch rounded the corner. Sera's body was on full alert, but her brain couldn't connect how such a benign and utterly unimportant person could be so dangerous, so, well, important.

As The Bitch disappeared from view, Sera jumped into action. It was like being released from an evil spell. She popped open the hatchback, grabbed her sweatshirt, and threw it on. She'd frozen. Now, she'd have to walk double-time to catch up, but that was okay. Moving felt good. Definitive actions felt good.

But why had she frozen? It was just for a second. It could almost be considered hesitation instead of freezing, but she knew the difference. Why the fuck did she freeze? It didn't sit well with her. She should have been all piss and vinegar. She should have just—

Just what? Sprung into action? That would have been dumb. The Bitch might have seen her. So, it was smarter to freeze, wasn't it? Maybe instinctually she knew that if The Bitch had seen her, she couldn't follow her, couldn't stalk her or abduct her, couldn't eventually kill her, but it still didn't sit well.

Or...

Or, if she'd seen her, maybe The Bitch would have willingly gotten into Sera's car just like Alyssa had. What was wrong with that?

Sera rounded the corner. Ahead, she could see The Bitch a little over a block away. She zipped her sweatshirt all the way up and yanked the hood low over her eyes.

Would it have been better if she'd picked The Bitch up? She wanted to tell herself no, wanted to convince herself again that she needed to formally abduct The Bitch. But why? Why did she need to abduct her? Her getting in the car would have been better. Of course, it would have been.

Obviously, Sera couldn't have invited her out. She couldn't leave a phone record of texts or calls of plans being made, and she would have made sure that The Bitch didn't have a chance to text anyone. Sera would have needed to make sure that it was last minute, that they ran into each other somewhere randomly, but even right in front of her apartment technically would have worked. She'd have to deal with The Bitch's phone, but wasn't she still going to have to deal with the phone? Now, there might be other people around. A car could drive past, a person could be out walking their dog. Could Sera be sure to get her alone?

No one would be suspicious of a woman getting into another woman's car, but everyone would be suspicious if Ms. Cranberry Leggings was dragged kicking and screaming into a car.

The easiest time for a murderer to get caught was during the abduction.

Was that true?

Okay, maybe, technically, the easiest time to get caught was after the crime had been committed because there were unlimited time and resources—okay, resources were always limited, but there were some resources. Regardless, during a murder, from the moment it was planned to the moment the knife hit the heart, yes, the highest profile moment, if it was planned even the tiniest of bits, was the abduction.

*Fuck me,* she thought. *It doesn't matter.*

And she was right. She was doing it this way now. Right now. Not later, not tomorrow, not next week, right now. Still, she'd frozen. Was that a sign that there was a better plan out there? That she should be going about this another way? That this was bound to end in failure?

*Stop it, stop it, stop it!* she railed at herself. *You froze, for like half of one second. You're about to commit a murder. A MURDER. You're fine. There are bound to be nerves.*

*There weren't with Alyssa,* her inner voice piped up, and Sera pursed her lips and screwed up her face, vowing she was not talking to herself—her inner self, to be more specific. Not right now. She was busy, and, well, her inner voice was being kinda bitchy, not like "The Bitch bitchy," but kinda bitchy, nonetheless.

The Bitch rounded another corner. Sera followed her soon after. She was closer now and had to be careful not to gain any more ground. She had a lot of energy, but she couldn't let herself get too close too soon. That could blow the whole thing. Besides, she knew where The Bitch was going. The Park. They'd walked there many a time. She could duck onto a side street and get ahead of The Bitch, meet her in the park. They would be alone. The park would be mostly empty now, and even if it wasn't, there would be gaps, sections. There would be—

*The woods.*

Sera knew the path The Bitch would take. She'd taken it with her more times than she could count, not because she was a bad counter—though losing count was really easy to do—but because they did it that often.

It'd become a ritual.

The idea of ritual appealed to Sera. It hadn't always. She loved change, but recently, there was something about the meditation of ritual that she was getting curious about. It was this new serial killer thing. It had to be. Serial killers got very into rituals. It was a way to drown out the doubting voices. Not thinking about the next step meant not questioning it, and questioning everything was fucking exhausting. Sera imagined all serial killers big or small, all serial killers prolific or not, all serial killers child savant or dedicated craftsperson had those same doubting voices.

A serial killer without those voices was a CEO.

Sera turned again, savoring the fading light and the bright fucking pink of Ms. Cranberry's leggings.

*Follow different paths each day*, the advice from a self-defense class, rose from the recesses of her mind. It was true, absolutely true following the same path everyday was definitely more dangerous. The self-defense teacher had intended it as a strategy to ward off strangers who could learn your patterns, not against best friends turned enemies turned serial killers who knew exactly where to meet up with you.

Sera hesitated as she considered taking a side street, but she didn't turn. She wanted to savor this moment. She wanted to remember every step of stalking her prey. Her feet felt so good against the pavement. She felt so alive. Also, what if The Bitch turned a different way? It was unlikely, but there was a chance. There was always a chance, and it'd been a long time since Sera had walked with her. It'd been a long time since Sera had been face-to-face with her.

Her heart was beating so fast.

It shouldn't be.

They weren't walking that quickly. Quickly? Sure. The Bitch never walked slowly. Never ever. But they weren't walking fast. For The Bitch, they were positively *strolling*. Still, Sera could feel her pulse at her neck, at her temple, in her wrist. Her heart was going a mile a minute.

*Excitement,* she thought.

*Nerves,* her inner voice offered.

*Both,* they confirmed.

This was it.

It was finally happening.

Twilight was fading. Soon, she'd be alone with The Bitch in the dark and could make all her dreams, The Bitch's nightmares, come true. Sera was thankful it was late in the season.

The dark would be on her side. If it were summer, she would be in full view of anyone for hours to come. The chill in the air also helped her, less people out, less eyes on her. She'd always loved early fall.

Those damn pink leggings worked against her though. If those were kicking around in the air, someone was bound to notice.

She would make sure they didn't.

She would make sure no one saw.

The Bitch glanced behind her, and Sera's heart leapt into overdrive even as she forced her steps to slow.

Did she see her? The hoodie wasn't a great disguise. It was better than nothing, but not by much. Maybe she should have worn her grandma's kerchief after all. It would have been a better disguise, better—camouflage? Was that it? Camouflage? She wasn't really in a disguise. She was just herself walking down the street, trying not to be seen by—

*By her.*

The scarf would have been better. She knew it. Even The Bitch wouldn't have known it was her without a serious double take, without a good, long look. Scarves weren't really Sera's thing which would throw her off. Silk scarves definitely weren't. The Bitch wouldn't see her coming.

That wasn't the point though. Was it? She didn't want The Bitch to see her, of course not, but sooner or later The Bitch *would* see her. What she couldn't have was any passersby seeing her, couldn't have them notice her, couldn't have them remember her.

When the cops interviewed people—*If*—she didn't want anyone to remember that "nice young woman in that beautiful scarf," thank you very much. She wanted to be "some dude in a black jacket." Okay, she'd never be mistaken for a dude. She'd worn yoga pants, for Christ's sake. She should have worn bulky sweats, but she wanted to disappear into the night. "Some chick in black," that was the hope. Some random-ass chick in black.

A chill ran up her spine, and she knew that wasn't the reason she hadn't worn it.

Not the whole reason, anyway.

Not *the* reason.

She'd left it at home because she didn't want one more thing tainted by The Bitch. Not now. Not ever. She wouldn't have it. Wouldn't let it happen. Couldn't.

People have a way of seeping into things over time.

The Bitch had a way of seeping into everything and never leaving. She'd seeped into things Sera'd loved, now tinged. Things she'd cherished, now doubted. Things she'd keep forever, now left behind in that pigsty of an apartment.

She'd seeped into Sera's mind.

New memories added to old, and bad generally outweighed good. Things were that way, for Sera at least. She didn't like it about herself, but she *knew* it about herself. She hadn't always been that way. She hoped she wouldn't always be that way. For now though, even if she was intending to make this her best memory of The Bitch ever, she couldn't take the risk. She wouldn't.

The Bitch turned back around and headed into the park.

She hadn't seen Sera.

Sera was safe.

*Safe.*

That was it, she realized. She had wanted to wear the scarf as protection against The Bitch. She'd wanted to use it to hide from her specifically. She had to remind herself that The Bitch would be dead. Everyone else was the problem. The other people were who she needed to dress for.

But...

But The Bitch was who she didn't want to see her.

The Bitch was who she was hiding from.

"Not anymore, Bitch," Sera said aloud.

She jumped and looked around as if someone else had scared her, then laughed at herself. She was the murderer here. There was nothing to be afraid of.

Sera followed The Bitch into the park.

# FORTY

I nside the park, a sort of excitement overcame Sera. It was all rush and no fuss as she trailed The Bitch. A flood of happy endorphins washed over her. A bit of bright orange clung to the clouds left over from sunset. The air was crisp. The moon already visible, but not yet creating light.

It was a beautiful night for a walk in the park.

It was everything she'd been hoping for. The culmination of all her practice. Well...the culmination of all the botched attempts over the past few days.

She had hoped she was ready before, hoped she would be ready. Now, in the moment, there was no doubt in her mind. She was ready. Maybe not fully planned and carefully crafted, but ready just the same.

Her murdery skills were not yet 100 percent evident—that wasn't fair. They were evident. They just weren't refined. But no killer was refined straight out the gate. That's why most practiced over and over again on animals. She tried to be mad at herself for not killing 42, for not killing Pig, for not killing *any* pig, but she couldn't manage it. Those animals had her back in a way she couldn't quite describe and definitely couldn't believe.

She didn't need the practice. All she needed was confidence. She had that now. It would all fall into place. Besides, she'd killed Alyssa, or she'd killed her enough. Alyssa was dead, and it was thanks to her. That much was certainly true.

Tall trees threw deep shadows onto the asphalt, making the black path even blacker. The bright green grass of day turned to a dark forest green.

Sera primarily watched the ground as she stalked The Bitch. She knew the steady, rapid movements of The Bitch's steps. She kept stride but was careful not to gain on her. Not yet. She'd wait until they were near the woods. She'd grab her there. She was certain she could overpower The Bitch, but if anyone saw, or if there was a struggle, she wanted the certainty that she could pull The Bitch into the woods or disappear through them herself if needed.

*Not too fast,* she thought, allowing her pace to quicken slightly.

If The Bitch saw her face, she wouldn't get a second chance, but she needed to be close enough to pounce when the time came.

High in the sky, the beautiful moon began to glow faintly as the light waned. That would hurt her. It was easier to be seen and harder to sneak up on someone. She wasn't deterred though. She'd thought about this a long time.

She wondered if killers tracked the phases of the moon. There could be an entire group of astrology-inclined killers who began tracking the moon solely to aid their endeavors but ended up loving the illogical fortunes the various faces of the moon promised. Was there a most opportune time to kill someone?

*Tonight,* Sera thought, smiling at her own joke.

Then she heard it.

Unmistakable.

Awful.

Soul crushing.

"Yeah...but..."

The Bitch was on the phone.

*No!!!!!!! For the love of God, no!!!!* Sera screamed internally. This was awful.

She wasn't a religious person by nature. Aspirations of being a serial killer didn't go hand in hand with hoping for a heaven, but she prayed to God, capital G, that she was wrong and that The Bitch was not on the phone.

However, as anyone who has ever prayed to God for something of an immediate nature is likely to know, God does not often answer prayers. He certainly does not answer prayers that will end with a swift knife to the heart.

"I waited in line for thirty minutes. Thirty minutes. At the dry cleaners. Can you believe that?" she asked, not waiting for a reply.

Sera audibly groaned before she could stop herself. This could take hours. There was nothing The Bitch loved more than listening to herself speak, and the phone was the perfect outlet for that. Yes, everyone spoke on the phone, but there was no visual feedback, there were no clues that The Bitch had to pretend to miss. She could just talk right over people without any sort of pretense. Did she have bad hearing? Was it a bad connection? Who knows, but it all amounted to the same thing. A lot of monologuing.

This put a real wrench in Sera's plans. The woods were coming up soon, and she could talk forever. Literally forever. If she didn't need to eat and pee, she'd never stop.

Sera was happy she'd opted for comfortable shoes. No self-respecting serial killer would wear anything else to a kidnapping—was it kidnapping?—to an abduction, but still. This little grab and go might now extend into the wee hours of the night.

"Then, when I got home, there was a stain on my shirt. I had to go all the way back, and when he looked at the stain, he said it wasn't their fault. He said he'd told me when I dropped it off that they wouldn't be able to get it out. He charged me. No refund..."

A brief pause ensued, and Sera could see The Bitch roll her eyes from here. Her head actually half circled, as if whoever she was speaking to was an absolute imbecile. Sera had been that imbecile. How ludicrous a person must be to go against The Bitch.

She imagined the perfectly logical other side of the conversation.

*If he told you he wouldn't be able to get it out*— Getting cut off.

"Yeah, but you'd think he'd care more about repeat business than that."

*Sure, but why did you leave it if he couldn't*— Getting cut off every time.

"Not even store credit. He could have given me store credit. That's good business."

And the equivocating acquiescence. This conversation must have been going on for a while to be here already. Or, or this new Sera knew The Bitch well. But then—

*He could have given you store credit*— Why not give in?

"See. And I drove across town for that. Twice. Like I didn't have anything better to do. Do you know what I had to do today..."

Apparently, new Sera didn't know The Bitch as well as Sera did. By the time you knew her as well as Sera did, you didn't speak. You nodded, even over the phone. You gave an "uh-huh" or a "hmm" whenever it seemed your silence *could* be noticed.

Sera tuned her out. She did know what The Bitch had had to do today. She did know the ever-present list of tasks because it had been her job, her promotion actually. She bristled at the idea that The Bitch would turn all the parts of the job that Sera enjoyed into battlefields. She knew perfectly reasonable small tasks were now arduous work things.

She knew how The Bitch worked. It wasn't about the job, or the money. It was about the acclaim, victimhood, and the acclaim she garnered through that.

It killed Sera.

Suddenly, her feet sped up, though she didn't want them to. It wasn't time. The Bitch was still on the phone, droning on, and they weren't yet to the woods, but suddenly Sera was running to grab The Bitch, to get her, she was running, she could see herself bulldozing The Bitch over, slamming into her, taking her down, phone flying, this was the moment, Sera was running, gaining speed and then...

Then...

She ran right past her.

She just ran past. She didn't hit her, didn't slam her, didn't even smack her on the back of the head.

*What the fuck, Sera?*

But she didn't know. She didn't know why she'd done it. Why she'd *not* done it. How she'd kept going. Something was wrong with her. It was smarter. Of course, it was smarter, smarter to not strike The Bitch while she was on the phone, but—

Ahead, a kid was playing. A kid with their mom. The dad was sitting on a nearby bench.

*Holy shit.*

She'd almost fucked herself. She'd jumped the gun and almost gotten herself caught. If she was ever going to be a successful serial killer, she was going to have to get her emotions in check. That's why serial killers seemed so stone cold. That's why they could smile while in a trial that could end on death row. That's why they could look at a dog and not see a dog, but see practice.

Sera didn't know if she'd ever get there. She doubted she would. Her entire reason to kill was because of emotion. Maybe she wasn't a serial killer. Maybe she was a contract killer. She almost laughed out loud.

*Because contract killers have so much more emotion than serial killers.*

So, she wasn't stone cold. So, she wasn't able to smile while her world fell apart. So, she'd adopted 42 and an entire army of pigs because she was unable to hurt an animal. That didn't make her any less of a serial killer. Some serial killers were stone cold, but most were also fucked up because they'd been abused—and were sociopaths—though Sera chose not to focus on that part.

Her lack of body count was what kept her from being a serial killer, plain and simple, and she was going to remedy that.

No one had noticed her. She was lucky. The dad was looking at something on his phone, pretending to work, probably scanning Facebook or flipping through articles. He laughed, but he wasn't laughing with his kid and wife, he was just laughing.

Now was when the self-flagellation usually kicked into high gear, but it didn't. Instead, she kept jogging as if that's what she meant to do. She'd have to double back because she'd jumped the gun, but she couldn't do anything in front of the family anyway.

She saw a drinking fountain and stopped at it. She could wait. She'd get a drink, fake tie her shoe, and soon enough The Bitch would pass her by. Then, she could stalk her in peace again. She heard a laugh. She was still on the phone. Well, she couldn't stalk her in peace, but she could properly stalk her again. The Bitch was getting louder. She was getting closer.

Sera couldn't let The Bitch see her as she walked by, which meant she couldn't look up from her shoes. She'd have to stay there with her head lowered toward her feet until after The Bitch passed. What if she turned? What if she stared at the weirdo tying her shoes for twenty minutes? What if she stopped to say hello?

This was no good. She should join the dad on the park bench, or she could loop around? Would she wear herself out? She wasn't exactly not fit, but she wasn't looking to run a mile before she attacked a woman who was, by all accounts, very concerned about appearances and thus went to the gym quite frequently.

*I should have brought 42,* she thought.

She could simply be playing at the park with her dog. They could sit and watch The Bitch. They could do anything. The Bitch wasn't looking for Sera, and she wouldn't expect Sera to have a dog. It would have been good cover. Not great cover. Someone walking a dog was the perfect person to talk to. The Bitch would do it, start a conversation with anyone, complain to anyone as long as they would listen.

*As long as they were captive,* her inner voice corrected.

Okay, so 42 would have been good cover so long as The Bitch was on the phone.

"Store credit would have been so easy," The Bitch said, walking past Sera. Her sharp voice pierced through all the crazy in Sera's head, and she snapped to.

Well, The Bitch was back in front of her now.

# Forty-One

It was dark now, though the full moon was out. The family had long since gone, and Sera and The Bitch were on their second loop of the park. Still, Sera had to wait. The phone call was never ending, and if the caller on the other end heard anything, Sera was toast. Best case, they'd call the cops. Worst case, The Bitch would yell her name, and it would be all over for her.

She kicked her shoe against the pavement as they walked. She no longer worried that The Bitch would notice her. Honestly, at this point, it might help. Documentaries never made the stalking part seem so damn long, or boring. It was sooooooo boring. Killers always jumped out, grabbed their victims, threw them in a van, and were off. Sera had never considered how much they were leaving out. How many times did they have to circle the block, following their victim because there was no parking? How many victims did they have to give up because the victim found a spot, and they didn't? There had to be a more efficient way.

The conversation droned on. Familiar names flew about. Dee was still in a shit relationship. Mitch had never managed to ask that girl on a date. Sera was still a bitch... That last part she imagined, but it made her bristle anyway. She was sick of listening to The Bitch, sick of it tonight, and sick of it overall, but she wanted to have it out with her. She realized she was listening with the *intention* of having it out later, as if she were on the other end of the line and was finally ready to fight.

Her whole body tensed. A swell of anger raced through her, but hot on its heels was the paralyzing fear that so often gripped her. The anger she had expected. The fear she hadn't counted on. She should have. She was always struck with fear even in the most mundane of conversations with The Bitch. It had taken her years to name that emotion. It wasn't fight or flight, it was freeze to survive. Evolution had tricked her into thinking she could play possum to survive. Evolution was wrong.

She would finally say anything she wanted. Everything she wanted.

She was going to torture The Bitch, she realized. Not with bruises and cuts, but with words. Sera was going to tie her up, gag her, and make her listen to everything she had wanted to unload on her for the past few years. Sera was going to make The Bitch see herself through Sera's eyes. She was going to make The Bitch see who she was on the inside.

Then, she was going to kill her.

The fear drifted away.

She didn't have to be afraid of what The Bitch could do, of what she *would* do. The Bitch would be dead, and Sera would be free. All of them would be. She wondered what the others would think, but her musings were abruptly interrupted.

"...It was just a quick...All right...I'll let you go...bye."

And Sera was off.

She was sprinting faster than she had ever sprinted before. The Bitch raised her phone, poised to dial. Sera had to get there before—

SLAM

Sera hit into the unexpecting Bitch with the fury of a freight truck.

The Bitch's phone went flying, and her body hit hard into a tree trunk which saved her from face-planting. The tree kept her on her feet, but she wasn't safe. The Bitch's mind reeled. The weight of Sera was on her, pressing her into the tree, pushing her toward the ground. When The Bitch finally caught up to the moment, she started to kick and scream.

"Fuck you. Fuck. Get off. I hate you! I hate you!" The Bitch landed on the phrase, pummeling her fists into Sera's back. "I hate you!"

Had she been seen? She hated her? Did she know it was Sera? But as Sera held her pinned to the tree, the onslaught continued with the same generic "I hate you" over and over. Sera marveled at the phrase. How telling that The Bitch considered "I hate you" threatening enough to use on an attacker.

"Get off me, you asshole," she yelled, finally changing it up. "Do you know who I am?"

And Sera cracked.

She knew. Oh, she fucking knew.

Her fists flew of their own accord, finding purchase on The Bitch's cheek, her brow, her neck. Frantic arms swung, like kids in a slap fight, no logic to the placement. It was blind rage.

This wasn't what she was here for. She had to grab her, had to pull her away. But once Sera traded her bear hug for fists, The Bitch pushed off the tree, trying to run. Sera was still there, her black clothes hard to see in the dark, the element of surprise on her side, and the bright pink leggings helping Sera see The Bitch's every move.

The Bitch kicked wildly. Sera easily side-stepped the pink missile, and The Bitch stumbled, struggling to stay on her feet. Sera kicked her in the stomach, hard, and The Bitch fell to her knees. She looked up now. Now, she saw.

Her eyes went wide, and Sera struck her over the head with a tree branch before The Bitch could utter her name one last time.

Sera dragged The Bitch's unconscious body into the woods. The dark would be enough cover for a few moments, so she dashed back out and grabbed the phone, careful to lift it only with her sweatshirt. She didn't see anyone in either direction. She'd been lucky. That was much worse than expected. The Bitch was loud as hell, and as for herself, well, she was uncontrollable. She knew she'd had a fire in her before she met The Bitch, and she knew that fire was back. What she didn't know was that there was an angry mob controlling the fire sometimes.

She'd have to address that. She couldn't have herself going nuts with every murder, though she suspected she might not. This one was special, so it was likely an anomaly. She hoped. Future Sera would definitely have to look into that shit. It's hard to get proper mental care as a serial killer. She had to get this under wraps tout fucking suite.

Right now, she had to cover her tracks though.

She smoothed the dirt over as best she could. She was moving at full tilt, going fast but being precise. Her heart thumped against her ribs, but it was a good thumping. It was the thumping of effort and decisiveness. With any luck, this wouldn't be discovered as the abduction site for a few days, but for that to work, the phone couldn't be found here. She decided to carry it with her, just until they got back to the car. Then she was struck by a gigantic problem. How was she supposed to get The Bitch back to the car with no one noticing?

She stopped what she was doing, trying to puzzle it out, but she was at a complete loss. There was no way. She had a body and no way to move it. Inexplicably, she started chuckling. The corners of her mouth pulled into a grin even as she tried to stop them. Her body started shaking. Then the sound came. It began low and lost and grew to a full-bellied laugh. She was a smart person. She knew she was a smart person. So, how had she managed to be so incompetent with the car? Every murder was giving her an alternate version of 42 with the eye drops. If she didn't put her ten-thousand hours in soon, she was going to jail. Nothing for it. She'd have to trek all the way back to The Bitch's place to get it.

*Fuck.*

*Okay, one thing at a time,* she told herself and took a deep, calming breath.

The laughing had helped.

She ducked back into the woods and grabbed The Bitch by her shoulders and shook her. She probably looked like she wanted to wake her up, but she was gonna make sure The Bitch was not just unconscious, but hella unconscious.

She could hit her again. Should she? It seemed harsh, which made no sense, but it felt a little cringy to clobber a woman who was completely out. Instead, she grabbed her under the arms and dragged her behind a bush. Besides, if she made her bleed, she'd leave more evidence, and if she killed her by accident, there would be no—

*No confrontation.*

*No torture,* her inner voice corrected her.

Yes, she really did want to do the torture part. The Bitch should understand exactly what brought them to this point. Secretly, Sera wanted to understand it too, but she didn't know that.

She dropped The Bitch's phone in the dirt and lifted the branch. She quickly swept away the drag marks, then carefully wiped the branch off with her shirt. She had no idea if a tree branch could hold prints. Probably not, but what if? She didn't know for sure, so she cleaned it. She was sure she looked like a crazy person. First, she sweeps the ground. Now, she cleans the trees. Crazy was her new fashion statement. Sera thought à la insanité might be very en vogue in a year or two when everyone else came crashing down as she had.

She turned back and looked at the bush The Bitch was hidden behind. Even knowing she was there, she was invisible. Sera pulled her sleeve over her hand and lifted the phone again. At the very least, she would move it to a different part of the park.

Sera wondered for a moment if maybe she was a really, really bad person. The thought hung there. She was unable to answer it adequately. She shrugged. Maybe she was, but if she was, she had been made this way by other people. She couldn't blame it all on The Bitch, but she could hang a hell of a lot of it on her currently slumping shoulders.

That look. Oh, that precious look she had given Sera just before the branch came down on her head with a satisfying thud.

Sera would be able to sleep well tonight.

But first, she had to ditch the phone.

She glanced back at the woods. The Bitch better not wake up. If she woke up, Sera was dead.

She stepped back out onto the path with the Bitch's phone still held in her shirt. She pulled her hood up and began to jog. She rounded a bend and saw a man throwing a Frisbee for for his dog in the moonlight. The dog was wearing a glow-in-the-dark vest. The vest had pockets. This was a risk and an opportunity. Sera ran right up to the dog and petted it.

"Good boy," she said, hoping the man was too far away to see her well.

He waved, and she waved back without lifting her face. She clicked The Bitch's cell phone to silent and dropped it into one of the dog's utilitarian pouches. The dog would carry it home, wherever that was, which would hopefully add some confusion to the search. With any luck, the man wouldn't even check these pockets tonight. She doubted he checked them often, if ever. Why would he? The dog tried to give Sera the Frisbee, but she patted him on the head and continued jogging.

Once she thought it was safe, she slowed to a walk and headed the way she had come. The man threw the Frisbee over and over again. He wasn't watching her now. He probably hadn't paid attention when she jogged off either, but if he had, he'd think she went the other way. Another jogger stopped to pet the dog. More hands. More pets.

*Good*, Sera thought.

The man would be questioned if he didn't report the phone soon. He might remember the woman who petted his dog after dark, but hopefully, some other joggers would come by too. She'd love to be forgotten among the crowd. With luck, she was already forgotten. Maybe she wasn't the first person to pet his dog tonight. Maybe she was the third or the fifth. Fifth sounded good. A nice, odd number. Like she was odd.

Her eyes flicked back towards the woods. Well, maybe more joggers wouldn't be a good thing. The park clearing out completely would be great too.

# Forty-Two

After ditching the phone, Sera returned to The Bitch. She was still unconscious, still stashed behind the bush, and Sera wondered if she had accidentally killed her. She pressed her fingers firmly against The Bitch's throat to feel for a pulse. She imagined slicing it for a second, but that wasn't what she was here for.

Plus, her Bowie knife was in the car.

There was a definite pulse, a strong one. Sera had assumed it would be limping along at best. No such luck. She wouldn't die before Sera moved her though. That went in the plus column.

Moving her went into the minus column though. It was a big ol' minus. Sera stared down at The Bitch's limp body and wished she had both accidentally killed her already and that The Bitch hadn't seen her face so she could just leave her here. Did she want to leave? No. Not at all, but she really didn't want to lug The Bitch to her car either.

No wonder serial killers were always so trim.

She was going to have to join a gym.

There weren't great options for moving the body. She absolutely could not drag her through the park and down the street to her car the way they'd come, though it was fun to imagine. She'd smile and wave as she passed young lovers, small children, and suicidal teens who'd skulked away from their houses. She imagined it would make the teens' nights, and they'd go home happy if not mentally healthy. So, in a way, it would really be a public service.

If only she had remembered these dumb walks, her car would be closer and she wouldn't have to leave The Bitch for as long, if at all. She could have parked on the other side of the woods. *Holy shit!* That was it. The other side of the woods! If she'd thought of this sooner, she wouldn't have had to waste her entire day.

42 was probably so bored. Would she be? Maybe. Or she could be tearing up the yard with the pigs without a care in the world. The yard needed work anyway, so Sera hoped they were having fun. She wondered if 42 would have helped her move the body. She could buy a sled, and 42 would drag future bodies through the woods.

*Over the river and through the woods.* She smiled to herself.

Even with moving a body, it was going to be a good night.

First, she had to get The Bitch to the other side of the woods. Then she had to get her car. Her stomach grumbled. Yeah, this had taken a lot longer than she thought. She wouldn't risk it, but a drive-thru sure sounded good. She was going to have to make a Smart Serial Killer List. It would include things like "close getaway car" and "pack lunch."

Sera looked into the dark woods. She'd always had a healthy reticence about going into them after dark, but she didn't think any bad guys were going to bother her while she dragged a body through them. Would the bad guys call the cops? Hard to know. It probably had more to do with whether they were about to commit a crime or if they had just committed one.

It was decided. Sera was going to drag her through the woods. Then, she was going to leave her there to get her car, and she was NOT going to stop at Burger King on the way back.

She heard a laugh. Her eyes shot to The Bitch, but she was fast asleep.

*The path.*

She crept to where she could see the park through the leaves. Yup. The after-dark crowd was out. She'd taken too long. There were less of them, but they were as much of a problem as the daytime folks. She considered leaving The Bitch here while she ran to get the car. She could do that first, but it was too much of a risk. If she woke up this close to the park, she'd 100 percent get away. Also, if Sera parked the car on the other side of the woods with no landmarks and no idea where to cut through, she wouldn't be able to find her way back here.

She casually strolled out onto the path, looked both ways, and saw no one. Okay, she would move her in small stints between people.

She made her way back to The Bitch and grabbed her under the arms. She hoped that would make the least noise and began to pull. Twigs cracked and snapped under Sera's feet, and leaves crinkled under The Bitch. Sera groaned with the effort, and after every inch or two, she froze listening for sounds of someone coming through the trees to see what was the matter.

She heard a skateboarder ride past, and some teens posted up on a bench to smoke pot.

This wasn't gonna work.

Sera and The Bitch were hidden by the trees, but the noise of dragging her wouldn't be. She'd have to wait. It'd been a long night, and it was going to get longer.

Her stomach growled.

"Quiet, you," she whispered and sat beside The Bitch.

Snacks were definitely going on the Smart Serial Killer List.

The ground was cold. It held more of the early fall chill than the air did. She pulled the sleeves of her sweatshirt over her hands and wondered if The Bitch was cold. She used to give The Bitch her sweatshirt if she got cold. That one wasn't even her fault. Sera had just done it.

Sera was a nice person, or she had been. She knew that was a big part of what made all of this possible, but being nice shouldn't be a crime. Murder should be though, and as luck would have it, it was.

Sera was happy with her choice anyway. She was even happy to be in this moment, sitting in the dark with the worst person she knew, hoping to not get caught. She hunkered down. She couldn't quite relax, but she could get close.

"Remember being friends?" she asked The Bitch, but for once, The Bitch wasn't talking.

They sat like that, in silence, for a long time. People grew further apart on the trail, the high teens stopped screaming, and the moon moved across the sky.

Normally, Sera's mind would be full, flitting from this to that, racing to make her pay for any mistake she had ever made, digging to uncover the dirt others would use against her, clawing for air even as she suffocated herself.

Tonight was different.

Tonight, she didn't sit in silence while her brain wailed. Tonight, she *was* silence. Even the bugs sang as if she were one of them.

Murder was slower than she expected.

Sera looked down. She had adjusted The Bitch's position, laid her down more naturally. Anyone who caught a glimpse of her through the trees would think she was sleeping. That was what Sera wanted. Looking upon her one-time friend, she was struck that even unconscious she still appeared pained. She still appeared poised and ready to refute, debate, and demean.

Sera yawned. Soon, she'd have to move The Bitch in the moments between people whether she liked it or not. She couldn't fall asleep out here. Who would have ever thought an abduction would have enough downtime for a nap? If she got The Bitch far enough away from the path, people would assume it was an animal. They wouldn't investigate.

Sera spotted a worm poking its head up through the dirt. She gently picked it up and plopped it onto The Bitch's forehead. This tickled Sera. She grabbed a stink bug, then another. They went right on The Bitch's cheeks, the red of the bugs acting like blush on her pale skin. She moved the worm from her forehead and placed it on her lips, shaping it into a sort of squirmy Halloween smile. If she could have, Sera would have taken a picture.

*Click,* she thought as she blinked her eyes.

The Bitch hated bugs.

Weighty clouds drifted in front of the moon, blocking out its light and cueing the odd straggler in the park to go home. Sera watched from behind the bushes.

The man and his dog were the last to go.

The second they were gone, Sera sprang into action. She hadn't realized, but she was poised and ready to go. She grabbed The Bitch by her wrists and dragged her further into the woods. The stink bugs fell off, but the worm simply shifted into a crooked frown. Sera smiled and decided not to move it. If The Bitch woke up, a worm would fall right into her mouth. What a great surprise—for Sera, at least.

She grunted as she pulled.

"Putting on a few pounds, huh?" she asked.

The thump of The Bitch's butt against the ground acted as confirmation.

She would have to cover these tracks on her way back to her car, but for now, she had to drag the body to the far side of the forest where the trees butted up against the road. It was heavy work. An unconscious Bitch definitely weighed more than a conscious one. She was careful to move big sticks out of their way and avoid any sharp rocks. She didn't need to leave fabric or a blood trail behind them.

The Bitch's head lolled to the side, and the worm fell off.

*Damn,* Sera thought, but she didn't stop to replace it.

The Bitch moaned dully, and Sera instinctively whapped her against the temple with the heel of her palm. She'd surprised herself with the quick work. It did the trick, and the moaning ceased. Sera's palm throbbed though.

It didn't usually seem so far to the road, but dragging a body would do that, she supposed and trudged on. She really must have hit The Bitch hard. She couldn't imagine her not waking up by now. Could she have put her in a coma? Was that possible?

Headlights broke through the leaves, dappling her and The Bitch with light. Sera dropped The Bitch's arms, leaving her torso and head to *thunk* to the ground. It was unlikely a car could see them through the trees, but if they did, she didn't want them to see her dragging a body. They were coming to the road.

This had probably taken thirty minutes. Less, she hoped, but it could be more. Also, they had sat waiting for people to clear out for a long time. How long? She had no idea. She had to go get her car, but leaving The Bitch here was a terrible idea. What if she came to now? Sera checked her pulse. There was nothing for it. She picked up another branch, hoped she didn't kill her, and hit her on the back of the head again. The Bitch's body jumped reactively as if Sera'd been checking her reflexes. "All good here," a doctor would have said. Sera checked her pulse again. Still strong. At least she hadn't accidentally killed her, yet.

*There's still time,* she thought, remembering her impressively accidental murder of Alyssa. *Best laid plans.*

Sera wiped her prints off this tree branch too. She knew she was being silly. 99 percent likely, she was being silly, but there was that 1 percent. That was all she needed to make herself ridiculously careful in the realm of prints on tree branches.

*Never mind all the silly mistakes I've made this week*, she thought. *No branch prints, no crime.*

She was ridiculous. She knew it. This had to be an instance of too little too late, but she couldn't help the times her paranoia took over and the times it didn't.

She peered through the dark, trying to find something she could use as rope. She longed for all that perfectly good rope in the car where it was useless.

Thin, dark vines climbed their way up a tree, clinging to it for dear life or strangling the life out of it, depending on whose perspective you chose. Sera chose the tree's, grabbed a section of vines, and yanked. They came away from the tree easily but pulled through her fingers, giving her vine-burn rather than breaking. She rubbed her hands on her pants. No cuts. That was good. She shook the sleeves of her sweatshirt down over her hands and gripped the vines again, using the thick cloth as a kind of glove.

She heaved, separating a large chunk of vines from the tree. The vines weren't ripping though. She tugged and tugged, digging her heels in, three feet away from the tree, then five feet away from the tree, but they wouldn't give, they were simply loosening. Light danced through the trees, and Sera let go, falling square on her ass, afraid of being seen. Fucking vines. Suspended oddly in the air, no longer anchored to the tree, the vines were a sure sign of some weird struggle. She pressed them back against the tree. It didn't help much.

New tactic.

She took a single vine in her hands and twisted it over and over again, then yanked, then twisted, then yanked. Jesus, at this point The Bitch would wake up and help her before she broke one free.

*Fuck it.*

She brought the vine to her mouth, but just before she began to gnaw on it like a wild animal, she remembered the existence of DNA.

New tactic.

She searched the ground for a sharp rock, kicking unlikely helpers out of the way. Most of them were rounded via years of erosion, but one, one that was about half the size of her head, had lots of sharp bits. She held the vine on another rock, picked up her sharp rock, and hammered and sawed at the vine.

*Shit.*

Rock-cut. She looked down and saw a dew drop of blood springing up from her finger. She sucked the blood dry. But it was working. The vine was almost cut. She sawed again, with her sweatshirt over her hand, protecting her and catching any extra blood. She hoped she hadn't dropped any blood. She'd have to cover her trail very well in case. Finally, the vine snapped. Wahoo! Now, she just had to do that seven more times.

*Fuckity-fuck, fuck, fuck.*

The rock made quicker work of the vines than her first attempt indicated, and soon she was tying The Bitch's hands and feet. She told herself that in future, she would carry some rope in her pocket. Not much, just a little. She could even get yarn, so it was less obvious, some kind of thick yarn, if that was even a thing. Onto her Smart Serial Killer List it went. The vines wouldn't hold long, but if The Bitch woke up, they would buy her a few extra minutes.

Sera stood up, then immediately dropped back to the ground as car lights pierced through the leaves. She was filthy. So was The Bitch. Her cranberry leggings were more of a mud-plum color now. Sera stood again, grabbed a large branch still covered in leaves—it was really more of a small tree—and was about to leave when she realized how much time had passed yet again.

"Sorr—" She consciously stopped herself from apologizing. She would not apologize to The Bitch. Then she whacked her upside the head again. If she ever woke up after all these bumps on the head, it would be a small miracle.

# Forty-Three

Sera ran back over their trail, dragging what amounted to a small tree behind her. She held the branch with her shirt again. It was for prints, sure, but it helped with minimizing blisters as well, which she would be happy about later. Plus, her rock cut still hurt, and the shirt shielded that.

*Running while dragging a tree is harder than it looks,* she thought. *Well, it might be exactly as hard as it looks.* She realized as she ran, well, jogged, with the branch bumping along behind her. She'd never actually seen anyone run with a branch, and she highly doubted if she ever would.

The leaves and twigs of the branch acted as a broom behind her, but she kept having to slow down and go back over sections. She wondered if *broom* should be added to her Smart Serial Killer List but figured it would leave a pretty distinctive trail.

She stopped, yet again, when her branch snagged on a bush. The drag marks were still very much marks, but they weren't nearly as bad as they had been. Just in case it would help, she ran with the branch over an alternate section, then carried the branch back to the main path, carefully leaving no trace. She did this from time to time. It felt like insurance, but it was probably a waste of time.

None of it looked pristine, but the woods in general were crisscrossed with tracks from all sorts of park-goers. All she could hope for was that her trail would get lost in the mesh of everyone else's. Dragging the branch across it would help. She was sure of it. So, after her short respite, she covered her hands, hoisted her branch, and continued her midnight jog.

She reached the bush she and The Bitch had hid behind and was proud of her time. Not wearing a watch, she had no idea what her time was exactly, but it certainly seemed faster than dragging The Bitch through the woods had. She circled their bush and a few others with the branch still bumping along behind her. If they never found the beginning of the trail, they would never find the trail.

Hopefully, The Bitch's doorman didn't remember she'd left. Was that something doorpersons kept track of? She'd never noticed. She silently cursed herself for not asking more questions, but even if she had, she didn't think this particular issue would ever have come up.

At long last, she ditched the branch and was ready to fetch her car. If only that wasn't another mile or so away, she would have felt up to the task. Fortunately for Sera, and serial killers everywhere, feeling up to it had nothing to do with anything when there was an unconscious person stashed in the woods.

She began what she sincerely prayed would be her last run of the night. As she passed the entrance to the park, she had to actively stop herself from scanning for the rental scooters that were often abandoned in the parking lot. Scanning her Apple Pay would render dragging a tree through the forest obsolete.

*Almost there.*

She took a different route than the one they'd followed earlier. She didn't know if it would give the po-po more chances to find traces of her or if it would make it more likely that she too had just parked in front of The Bitch's apartment to go for her own, completely separate, nightly jog.

When she finally got back to her car, she was sweating though the night was no longer cool, it was cold. She didn't take off her sweatshirt anyway. Getting into her car with her license plate, the hoodie offered extraordinarily little anonymity, but she decided it was best to take what she could get.

She reached into her pocket for her key fob, but it wasn't there.

*Fuck. No, no, no, no.*

She began patting down all her pockets, once, twice. Then, luckily, she remembered she'd tucked it in her sports bra for safekeeping. She pulled it out, and not for the first time, nor the last, she thanked the key fob gods that a sweat-drenched fob was still a fob that worked.

BEEP-BEEP

She opened the door to her car.

"Sera!"

She heard her name before the presence of another human registered.

She looked up, half sick to her stomach, and became completely sick to her stomach. It was the doorman.

Sera waved back. There was no use pretending it wasn't her, there was no use pretending she didn't see him, there was no use doing anything. The first thing she thought was *I dragged that fucking tree through the woods for nothing.* Then she waved.

He came about ten feet closer to her, and she knew she had to meet him where he was. He couldn't leave his post, and it would be both weird and rude if she didn't go say hi.

"Hi," she said as she walked over.

"So, you two are back on?" he asked, and Sera was flummoxed.

They were not back on. They were extremely far from back on, but maybe she could use this. Maybe she could get him thinking The Bitch was upstairs.

"No. I, uh—" she stalled, while manufacturing a lie, but his look was sympathetic. He didn't suspect her. "I was grabbing my stuff." Then she realized she didn't have any *stuff* with her. "But"—she wasn't sure he'd buy it, but she tried anyway—"she got rid of it."

"All of it?" he asked. He seemed both surprised and not surprised. "I'd guess you have quite the wardrobe up there."

*What was his name?*

"All of it, Phil." She produced it at the last second. "I went up, but none of it's there. Or she says it's not. I don't know."

"It's too bad you two don't get on—"

"Yeah."

"For me, that is." He cracked himself up. "I miss seeing you."

"Yeah, I looked for you when we got here…"

"Musta stepped off for a minute," he said, making a smoking gesture with his hand.

"Still quitting?"

"Every damn day. I'll let you get to it," he said, motioning back to her car. "If you're ever in the neighborhood…"

"With bells on."

He walked inside, and she watched him go. She might actually drop by again. She wasn't sure if that was really smart or really, really stupid, but for the first time in a long time, she realized she missed chatting with people. Not all people. Only good people. And he was good people.

With the panic of possibly being seen erased from the equation, Sera climbed into her car, started the engine, blasted her AC, and closed her eyes for a few moments. She was no longer sweating, and that exchange had gone about as good as it could have gone. Old Phil might even count as an alibi given The Bitch's body would not be found in her "condominium."

*I left her place around...* Sera glanced at the clock: 2 a.m. *Shit.*

She better get a move on. She kicked her car into gear, turned on the headlights—no use hiding now—and pulled out.

# Forty-Four

Sera drove her car around the loop behind the woods. All she had to do now was pick The Bitch up and kill her. Easy peasy. Well, it would be easy peasy if she had any idea where in the fuck she had left The Bitch to begin with. She could kick herself for not having marked the location. What was she thinking? She pulled over and walked into the woods. Fifteen feet. Then twenty. Nothing.

This wasn't her first stop. It was her third. She worried that perhaps The Bitch had up and walked away. She could have. She could have woken up and stumbled to the road or stumbled back to the park or simply stumbled into a ditch, and there'd be no way for Sera to know. The cops would come looking for The Bitch's assailant and find Sera dumbly pulling over every fifty feet, searching the woods for the victim who was now a survivor.

Sera had no desire to make The Bitch a survivor. She would fucking love milking that.

She drove further up the road and stopped again.

The night was even darker now. The stars had all come out, but the moon had set already. Where the fuck had she left her?

It was a comfort that none of the places she'd checked looked familiar yet. Whether The Bitch had walked away or not, Sera couldn't be sure, but she did know none of the spots she'd checked were THE SPOT.

There was still a chance.

She climbed back into her car and began to drive. Ahead, she saw a large rock, a boulder. Maybe. Could it be? And sure enough, headlights from an oncoming car bounced off the boulder and lit up a dazed and confused Bitch.

*Shit.*

Sera held her breath until the other car passed and its taillights receded in the distance. A moment before, she had been ready to curse the moon for its absence. Now, she was ready to pay tribute to it. If the moon had still been out, that driver would have certainly spotted the bumbling woman.

She turned off her headlights and coasted to a stop. It seemed like the smart thing to do, though she didn't know why. The Bitch certainly knew she was coming, and she did, in fact, have to come. There was nothing else she could do. She had to make it to her before she made it to the street and another car came.

Sera tried to creep up the steep ten-foot hill into the woods, but it proved more difficult than it looked. She had to get The Bitch, and she had to get her *now.*

*Fuck it.*

She ran up the hill and into the woods, not heeding the noise she was making. A loud grunt came from behind her in accidental warning, and she ducked just in time to evade a branch meant for her head.

*Clever girl.*

Sera wheeled around, ready for combat, but The Bitch stumbled and fell to the ground. She'd freed her hands but hadn't yet untied the vines around her ankles. No wonder she hadn't run. Sera had made it back just in the nick of time.

She grabbed her in a bear hug from behind and began to drag her through the woods, kicking and screaming. Sera was terrified a car would come, terrified someone would hear. She covered her mouth with her hand, but The Bitch bit, and when Sera replaced her hand, she licked, big drooling open-mouth licks. She pulled her hand away and wiped it on her yoga pants.

She preferred the bite.

"I knew you would do something stupid like this!" The Bitch yelled frantically, flopping her bound legs like a useless mermaid fin.

Exasperated, Sera couldn't stop herself. "Are you kidding me? You knew I was going to—"

"Yes." Even in this situation, she was so sure of herself. "You are so extreme. We aren't friends anymore," she said, then shrieked like a frightened animal. "Move on!"

And Sera cold-cocked her right in the temple with her bare fist while still holding her in a one-armed bear hug from behind. It hurt like a mother, and it was not a successful KO.

"AHHHHHHHHHHHHH!" The Bitch wailed and flailed. Arms and hands flung about wildly. She twisted this way and that. She wasn't so much trying to escape as she was trying to keep Sera from holding onto her. The Bitch was losing it, because she did not lose. She was a four-year-old throwing a tantrum in Walmart. The goal was not success. The Goal was chaos. And chaos it was.

The Bitch got free and immediately fell to the ground. She mermaid kicked and flailed her arms. Sera darted in, dodging one way, then the other. Reason had left her. She tried to grab an arm here, or block one there without getting hit, without looking at the bigger picture. She wanted to evade the inevitable blows which rendered her completely ineffective. Finally, with no other option and logic prevailing, she accepted the beating she'd get and dove headfirst onto The Bitch.

"Ugh." The Bitch grunted and doubled over on the ground.

Sera quickly pushed her on her stomach and pinned her down with a knee in her back. She yanked her arms behind her and pulled out a handy dandy Ziplock baggie of rope.

*That's right, motherfucker, I brought rope!* she thought, but what she exclaimed was "Fucker rope!"

She pulled out one piece, then the next.

Damn short pieces.

The Bitch still struggled, but her heart wasn't in it. She probably had a concussion. Her motions were slowing in a way that didn't quite track. Then her hands went limp.

*Fuck.*

Sera leaned back, moving her knee.

*I killed her. Oh, no. I killed her. Shit. Another murder turned accidental death.*

The idea nearly had Sera beside herself, but—

She put a finger on her throat.

The Bitch was still breathing.

Sera realized her knee must have slid up and been cutting off her air supply against the ground. Didn't matter. Accidental advantage Sera. She quickly tied The Bitch's hands behind her with a longer bit of rope. She hadn't come to yet, but if Sera's childhood games of Down Under were any indication, she wouldn't be out for long. She had to move fast.

"Asshole," she muttered to The Bitch as if it were an intentional KO rather than a happy accident.

Apparently, accidents were a murderer's best friends. At least, they were for Sera. Preferably, time and a little practice would fix that right up.

She hauled The Bitch the last fifteen feet to the edge of the woods.

She could see her car parked on the street. It was only about seven feet of open air, but it petrified Sera. She couldn't traipse The Bitch right out in the open. A car could come around the bend at any moment. She hadn't come this far, worked this hard, and suffered at the hands of The Bitch for years only to come up short now.

She'd left her car unlocked. It would only take a second to throw open the hatchback, but then she'd have to hoist the body in.

Sera dropped The Bitch and sprinted to her car. She threw the hatchback open and ran back to the safety of the tree line. Phew! She grabbed the rope again and stood panting from the effort. She watched the street.

Black.

Darkness.

Still black.

*Go, go, go!*

She took The Bitch by her ankles and schlepped her to the car, head thumping on the ground the whole way. There, she hefted her up, dropped her, and hefted again.

*FUCK!*

The Bitch's torso hit the matte in the back of the Prius with a heavy thud, a puff of caked pig-mud, and an accompanying groan.

Sera quickly shoved her legs inside. They were still tied with vines, but she was outta time. She pulled the privacy tarp over her and slammed the hatchback shut.

It bounced open.

Another moan, louder this time.

*Shit.*

Her feet weren't all the way in.

Sera stuffed the offending body parts inside and checked more carefully before slamming the door again.

*Bingo!*

She went to the driver's side, about to climb in, and realized she had to clean up the woods. Sera locked the car and hurried back into the dark. The tarp would do nothing if The Bitch started to move, so she didn't have much time.

Their fight and the ensuing drag-a-thon left a mess. She kicked some leaves around and raked a branch over their trail, but she knew it was pointless. As soon as the police found this spot they would know, and if they never found this spot, then they'd never know anyway. Would they know? They must, right? How much could they really tell from woodsy ground. It was probably all about fibers. She couldn't do anything about that.

*Kids*, she thought. It might fool any kids who would otherwise be suspicious and report it. Hikers? Maybe, but she doubted it. Not if they were paying attention at least, but...did hikers get suspicious? Did they really? Did kids? There was no blood, there was no—

*Rope.*

She dashed back to where she had made The Bitch pass out and found the two short scraps of rope.

*Bag,* she thought, but she reached into her sweatshirt pocket and happily found the Ziplock was still there.

It wasn't her best, but it was the best she could do right now.

She raced back to her car just as she saw the familiar glint of headlights. She jumped behind the steering wheel, started it up, and took off without the lights on. She was gone by the time the other car crested the bend.

After the next turn, when she was sure she'd dusted the other car, she flipped on her headlights. She adjusted her rearview mirror and glanced behind her. The tarp wasn't moving, no one was following her, and the car was silent. The Bitch was either completely out or completely dead. Either was a win.

Sera set her sights on the road ahead of her.

*Over the river and through the woods...*

Wait. Where was she taking her?

The plan had always been her grandma's house, but that felt like a bad idea, not because of the other bodies, not because of the cops or any possible suspicions—though those did all make it an absolutely terrible idea—but because she didn't want to have any memories of The Bitch in that house. Not one. She already hated that she had ever even told her about it. Sera wasn't going to give The Bitch the chance to tear down one more of her favorite things as she exited this world. She wouldn't let The Bitch taint her grandma's with even the shittiness of her spirit.

No.

The Bitch would never set foot there. She would be taken and killed somewhere else. Somewhere she had already ruined.

Sera's childhood playhouse.

# FORTY-FIVE

Sera's heart was pounding as she rounded the next bend. She looked behind her again. The other car was nowhere to be seen. Ahead, the freeway on-ramp called her name, and she answered by speeding up it without a second thought. It was east, not west, but right now it didn't matter. It was smart to get the fuck out of dodge. She didn't know where dodge was, exactly, but she knew she didn't want to be there if that car had seen her.

She didn't think they had. She was pretty damn sure they hadn't, actually, and was even more certain that if they did see her, they would have simply seen a woman getting in her car late at night. Not exactly brilliant, but not suspect in and of itself.

Now that she knew where she was going, she just had to get there. In a few miles, she'd exit the freeway and flip around. It seemed smart to go the wrong direction for a little while, especially since she was here already. Any effort to hamper the future investigation was energy well spent. She passed a second exit and wondered how far she should go. Her car hit a pothole, and an unconscious groan answered her from the trunk.

*Not too far,* the groan implied. She didn't want The Bitch to wake up.

Sera watched the speedometer carefully. She was going five over the speed limit, only five over. She wanted to go one hundred miles per hour to match how she felt inside. Even two hundred miles per hour wouldn't have felt fast enough. She was flying.

*One rule,* she reminded herself, *one.* She wondered, not for the first time, how much that really mattered, but she figured, with a body in the trunk, it mattered a great deal. The irony of the size of the rule she was breaking versus the one she was upholding amused her. It amused her a great deal.

The next exit was a small one, primarily for farmers. Sera took it. It'd be less likely to have cameras, so if anyone ever did decide to check them, they'd be less likely to see her car. With any luck, anyone looking for her would keep on going east for a while.

*Well, with any luck,* Sera thought, *no one will be looking for me at all.*

At the bottom of the exit ramp, she flipped her blinker on to head up the opposite ramp, but the old country road beckoned to her. She wasn't sure which was riskier, the freeway or the old road. She was certain one of the two was definitely the worse choice, but country road it was. This was the choice she made. She didn't deliberate for an hour or even five minutes. She simply thought, *Hm. I want to do this. Is this smart? I don't know.* Then she shrugged and did it anyway. This brought her great pleasure. And pride.

She was proud of herself for making a decision.

It was silly. She knew it was silly. That didn't change a fucking thing. She knew there was no way to know which choice was better, so why stress it? And she didn't. She didn't stress it at all. It wasn't like there was a serial killer tips Reddit group, though now that she thought of it, there might be. Regardless, that would not be full of successful serial killers, not for the most part anyway. There might be one or two on there, but she didn't think she could trust the kind of serial killers that posted about it on Reddit. Besides, she didn't think serial killing had any one size fits all solutions.

Whether the country road was the smartest choice or not was hardly the biggest choice she'd made this week. It was certainly not the most problematic.

Off the freeway and headed towards her final goal, Sera rolled her window down. The breeze hit her, cold air mixed with the familiar scent of hay and dirt. She smiled. This was the feeling—free-floating, life-living, dream making—this was the feeling she wanted to keep. This is where she wanted to live. She wasn't greedy. She knew living there constantly would be overshooting. No one gets to live in heaven 24/7, but some people get to live there 7/24. Sera was on her way. She was making her dreams come true.

She had missed the simple satisfaction of *living* for a while now, a long while, but until recently, she hadn't known how to get back to it. Right now, the lost time didn't cost her anything. The lost time was the path that led to here. It wasn't how she wanted to get here, it wasn't where she wanted to go, but it was somewhere.

Dorothy didn't know where she was going when she went over the rainbow either. There was something inviting in that.

She wasn't far from the turnoff for her hut. From there it was just a quick hike—she'd worry about how to accomplish that once they got there—and then victory was hers. "The Hut," as they'd all called it, wasn't exclusively hers, but she thought of it that way, her hut. Maybe all her childhood friends did, each of them claiming ownership of their own little piece of it. She hoped so. She liked that idea. Like they were all still together somehow. For a moment, Sera didn't feel so alone. She flipped the radio on, turned it up, and picked up speed.

Tonight was her night.

# Forty-Six

S era pulled up to a patch of dense woods and a trail that was tucked into the trees so well it was only visible if you knew where to look. In appearance, the woods weren't dissimilar to the ones Sera had just left. She breathed deeply as she stepped out of the car. She could smell the brook even before she could hear it.

She loved this place.

*Is it the right place?* she wondered and breathed in deeply again. She was so incredibly, perfectly calm.

It was.

She had brought The Bitch here years before. She had led her through the woods and past the brook. Every ten feet or so, she mentioned another thing she loved about the place, and every ten feet or so, The Bitch told her why she was wrong. Why this place was awful. Why everything about her fond memories were flawed. She didn't say it like that, of course not. She cloaked her sword and dagger. She said simple things like, "Oh, I thought it'd be prettier." Ouch. "Wow. There are so many bugs." Yes, sure. It's the woods. "You had to come all the way out here to *get away*. It's so sad you felt you had to *get away.*" No, I wasn't trying to escape. I just liked it. "Uh-huh," and a deceptively sneaky nod that said, sure, yeah sure you liked it.

And when they had finally come upon the old, dilapidated shack that she and her friends had painted and decked out, The Bitch said, "I'm so sorry your childhood was like this. You must be so damaged." Damaged. She was, Sera realized later. She was very damaged. Exchanges like that damaged her. Allowing this woman to take over her world so completely and abuse her so easily damaged her, not her childhood.

Sera had wanted to share one of her fondest memories with the person she thought she was closest with. Well, unfortunately for her, with the person she was closest with. Like it or not, The Bitch had been her best friend for a while. Sera hated herself for it, but things like that clawing at her mind were what drove her to her newfound purpose.

*The good with the bad*, her grandma would say. Sera just hadn't realized there was so much bad.

She stepped around a large oak tree and walked about ten feet deeper into the woods. There the path waited for her, overgrown and inviting. As much as she'd like to walk the path alone once more, she knew there wasn't time and went back for The Bitch. The screams reached her before the thumps did.

"Help! Help me!" The Bitch's muted yell came over and over as clunky thuds emanated from the hatchback. Sera imagined her mermaid kicking the hatch door awkwardly, with vines still binding her feet. Apparently, she hadn't realized the only thing between her and sitting up was a cloth privacy screen. This tickled Sera more than it should.

As if on cue, The Bitch suddenly sat up. Dazed and confused, her screams stopped. She took in the surrounding woods, and Sera could almost see her trying to puzzle together the situation. Had they moved? Were they in the same spot? Was anyone else there? What time was it?

Sera actually wondered that too. It was still dark now, but eventually it wouldn't be.

The Bitch locked eyes with Sera and froze. A deer in headlights. Sera lifted her arm and gave a small wave. She relished the moment. This was part of the torture. Simple, effective, unplanned. She couldn't stage a moment like this, and as with most memories, the best ones were spontaneous.

As Sera walked calmly to the car, The Bitch panicked. She suddenly jackknifed herself over the back seat, trying to get to a door to escape, *or maybe to lock it?* Sera wondered. Neither would work. She had a key, and The Bitch was in no condition to run even if her feet weren't still tied which, as she struggled over the seat, Sera saw they were.

She stood in front of the window waiting for The Bitch to right herself, then she rapped on the glass.

"Can I come in?" She waited for a reply. The answer itself didn't matter, but she was curious. How could she not be? Impulse or fear might reduce The Bitch to simply saying "Come in" out of habit. Wouldn't that be fun? It did not. Instead, she stared at Sera, her mind racing, trying to find the right thing to say. Neither yes nor no was it. She knew that. The Bitch was no fool. The problem was that there was clearly not a correct answer. This was unprecedented territory, and The Bitch didn't like unprecedented territory. *New* left things to chance. *Different* left things to chance. *Out of her control* left things to chance. The Bitch curated her life. She curated the actions of those around her. She had not curated this.

Only, she had. Sera was living proof that curating people was a bad idea. A very bad idea.

The Bitch's anger flared up. Sera could not do this to her. Who did she think she was? "Just do whatever you're going to do!" The Bitch screamed. When in doubt, she usually, subconsciously, went for the I-dare-you tactic. It was surprisingly effective with adults as well as kids. People have simple brains, and it was one of the simplest manipulation tactics, whether

The Bitch knew it or not. She'd force her hand. That's what she'd do. As soon as Sera realized she had to do something or let her go, she'd let her go. It was just like her to not think things through. "Just do it!"

Sera cocked her head to the side and smirked. *What a versatile slogan. Whoever came up with it ought to be a millionaire.* They probably weren't. They were probably making 60k a year. Life wasn't fair. She watched The Bitch, with her head cocked like that for a minute, just like 42 would do, and The Bitch squirmed. Nothing like silence to unbalance a talker.

For her part, The Bitch would have preferred if Sera lashed out at her, if she yelled or hit or cried. Any reaction caused by her screaming would have put her more at ease than Sera's stupid fucking smile. She was fumbling for some semblance of control, and Sera wasn't playing fair. She wasn't playing *right*. Sera let the outburst roll off her like so much fog, unnoticed and sans weight. That did not sit well. The Bitch started twisting and turning her wrists behind her back. She had to get out of here. She had to break the ties that bound her.

Sera opened the door.

"Do you remember that rope? It's the rope we used to tie your mattress down. The one all cut up in pieces. I guess my knots hold after all." She paused for effect. "You never thanked me for that, by the way."

Confusion stopped The Bitch. "What?"

"For helping you move. You never thanked me." It bugged Sera. More than it should. Certainly, more than mattered in this exact instant.

"Yes, I did. I'm sure I did."

"No, you didn't. Want me to help you out of there?" she asked, meaning the back seat.

"I thanked you. You just don't remember it. It was a long time ago."

Sera shrugged. "Nope. I waited."

"What?"

"I was paying attention. I kinda suspected you didn't usually. Thank me, I mean. Or anyone, probably. So…" Sera shrugged. "I paid attention. Not that day, not the next, not the next week."

"That's what you're mad about? I didn't even know." The Bitch twisted it. How could it be her fault if she didn't know? It was Sera's fault. "You should have said something."

Sera watched the moment. Watched the blame shift. Watched it become her fault. There was a time she would have believed her, believed it was her fault that The Bitch was rude because she didn't call her out at the exact right instant.

Silence did not sit well with The Bitch. She shifted.

"You should let it go."

"You should say thank you," Sera said flatly, grabbing her by the arm. Sera yanked to pull her out of the car, but The Bitch leaned back, bracing herself. Sera made no headway. She couldn't move The Bitch with her weight planted, pushing her feet into the floor of the footwell, leaning her shoulders back and away from Sera. She wasn't fighting back. She was playing Stiff as a Board. Sera grunted and tugged and tugged and grunted. Then let go.

"You should say *please*," The Bitch said, and that did it. Sera lunged into the car, wrapping her arms around The Bitch's legs. She pulled them out of the footwell, turned around, and ran forward. She wasn't playing.

"No. Stop! Stop. I'll get out—" The Bitch screamed as her leggings easily slid across the seat.

*Thump!* Her ass hit the doorframe.

"Ow. Stop—"

*Thump!* Her head followed.

"Ohhhhh," she moaned. The dark night went bright white with the sharp shock of pain. Colors swam in her vision.

Sera dropped her legs and turned around. The Bitch lay on the gravel, her head resting against the car.

"Are you gonna stand up? Or do I have to convince you?"

The Bitch struggled trying to get to her feet, but it was no good. The vines held her ankles too close together for her to get any leverage, and she couldn't use her hands with them tied behind her back. She stumbled and fell. Sera reached out to help her, instinct trumping her plans. Luckily, The Bitch went down before Sera caught her. She tried to stand again with the same results. The second time, Sera didn't help, but it was pathetic in a way that didn't sit well with her.

"Okay, okay. Wait a second." Sera went to the glove box and pulled out her Bowie knife. She came back around. She was trying to be nice, but she realized that seeing it must have made The Bitch realize she was in big, big trouble because she sat docilely and watched while Sera cut the vines from around her feet.

The Bitch had known she was in trouble since she'd been hit in the head with a branch, but something about seeing a sharp hunting knife really drove the point home. She was many things, but she was not stupid. She could play along if she had to. Sera was going through something, and she was taking it out on her. Of course this would happen to her. Bad things were always happening to her. Fine. She'd get out of this. She always did.

Sera was certain The Bitch's mind was spinning, trying to find the angle, the weakness, the vulnerability that would bring Sera down. It wasn't there. She was certain it wasn't there. It couldn't be, not after everything that had happened. It definitely wasn't there, but she could gag her. In case, sure, but did she really want to listen to her blather on for the entire hike? Did she? Of course not. It wasn't a bad idea. In fact, it was actually a smart and completely appropriate idea. What if someone else pulled up and took this path? What if someone heard her scream? What if she managed to run and... Sera wouldn't let that happen. She'd stab her in the back before she'd let her run away.

Still.

They were parked down a system of small roads, but it wasn't unheard of to see hikers here. In the middle of the night, it was unlikely, but unlikely was probably what got a lot of serial killers caught.

That decided it.

"Don't move," she warned and got up to search the car for a gag. How had she not brought a gag? Gag was going on the Smart Serial Killer List. It was such an obvious omission that Sera felt stupid. She was smarter than this. Wasn't she? She set her knife down on the dash to search. The list was getting quite long. How had she overlooked so many things? Plus, her alibi never got back to her. Not that she should be worried about that right now. She wasn't. But still.

"What are you going to do to me?" The Bitch asked, watching her from the ground.

Sera detected a hint of reticence in her voice, like she was afraid to ask. It almost made her want to talk to her, to ask her what was wrong. She felt the familiar pull. Old habits die hard. She kept her attention on the search though. There had to be something she could use. Even an old paper towel would help.

"Do you *know* what you're gonna do?" The Bitch exercised restraint, but it was strained. There was something unsettling about her voice, but Sera couldn't quite put her finger on it.

Sera dug under the front seat.

"Ah-ha!" Sera exclaimed as she pulled an old dirty workout tank top out from under the passenger seat. It was gross, but it would do. She opened the hatchback to grab tape and realized, yup, another fucking item on the list. She had learned nothing from Alyssa. She pulled out her Ziplock baggie of rope and opted for a piece a few feet long.

"Open up," she said, turning to The Bitch, whose eyes went wide.

She had to be able to talk. She had to be. She felt a weight in her chest. It was a deep-seeded need, a fear, though even

The Bitch didn't know that. What she did know was that she couldn't talk her way out of this if she couldn't talk.

"I'm not going to scream," she said.

"Yes, you are," Sera said, in no uncertain terms, and tried to shove the shirt in her mouth. The Bitch pursed her lips together and turned her head away. She was still pressed firmly against the car, and Sera was standing over the top of her, so she didn't have a lot of leeway for escape.

"Open up," Sera taunted and grabbed The Bitch's nose. She'd force her mouth open. Sooner or later, she had to breathe. If someone saw them now, maybe they'd think it was all a prank. They certainly looked stupid enough. The Bitch shook her head, pulling free from Sera's grip. She quickly grabbed her nose again. There had to be a smarter way. How did people do this? Her knife. *Shit.* She'd left her advantage in the car, but the Bitch parted the corner of her mouth to breathe, and Sera jumped at her chance. She shoved her fingers into the opening and wriggled them between her teeth. She was going to pry her damn jaw open if she had to.

CHOMP!

"Ow!" She yanked her hand back. "You *bit* me."

She sat down, straddling The Bitch to get more leverage. Knife forgotten. She would make her open her mouth.

She winced. Her ribs were getting worse, and both vets' meds had worn off long ago. She hoped The Bitch hadn't done real damage when they were fighting, and now, she was quite fucking lucky The Bitch hadn't kicked her again. She must not have been thinking straight. Kicking was the obvious answer or, Sera thought, maybe she was thinking straight. She was tied up. Did she really expect to win this? What was she up to?

"Enough!" Sera yelled. It came out more feral than she intended, and they both froze.

Their eyes locked.

Sera didn't yell. Ever.

The Bitch opened her mouth.

Sera balled part of the tank top up and put it in her mouth, trying to leave enough space that she could easily breathe around it. They had a hike ahead of them after all. Also, she needed The Bitch to be willing to walk. Her ribs hurt more and more, and she was not up for dragging her through the woods. She picked up the rope she'd dropped and tied it around The Bitch's head, securing the gag in place.

"Okay?" she asked, expecting The Bitch to look small being beaten and tied up with a gag in her mouth, but she didn't. She looked furious. She nodded her head curtly, and then, after a beat, looked down.

Using her sweatshirt sleeve as a glove, Sera picked up the vines, untied any knots, and threw them into the underbrush. Eventually someone might find them, but she didn't think they would be recognizable as anything other than bits of vine. Plus, kids tied vines into all sorts of things, and the vines grew here as well as in the park, so she was safe on that front. They wouldn't immediately scream, *Here! This is where The Bitch was taken.* At least, Sera hoped not.

She grabbed the long rope from the car, happy she'd brought something useful. She tied it around The Bitch's waist as a sort of leash and grabbed her knife from the dash. The Bitch's head was still bowed slightly, making Sera wonder if she was docile or if she was trying to look docile. She could be planning Sera's death, just like Sera was planning hers.

# Forty-Seven

Sera followed The Bitch through the woods. She made her lead to eliminate the likelihood of funny business. She was acquiescent now, but Sera suspected she was devising some type of escape. So, she stayed vigilant. She carried the hunting knife carefully in front of her. It had never occurred to her that she might need a belt to carry it on. She'd even left the leather sheath at home. Why would she need to put it away? It didn't matter. Without a belt, she still would have been carrying it.

Belt went on the list, and she decided it might be the Don't Be an Idiot Serial Killer List rather than the Smart Serial Killer List. She was trying to hold off on her final judgment though. Trudging through the woods with a victim was no time for self-doubt.

They'd been walking for maybe fifteen minutes, and the incline was getting steeper. The Bitch sucked in a big pull of air and then coughed around the gag.

"All right. Slow down." Sera yanked on the leash, and The Bitch jerked to a stop. She doubled over, coughing harder. She wasn't choking yet, but she might. Sera didn't want another Alyssa on her hands.

*Shit.*

She rushed up to her, holding the knife up as if she needed it to control her. However, The Bitch was so focused on trying to breathe, she didn't even seem to notice the blade.

She did though. She did notice it.

Sera dropped the leash and tried to untie the knot, holding the gag in place. It was no good, not with one hand.

The Bitch coughed harder. She was choking now. Just a bit.

*Double shit.*

Sera wasn't going to lose another victim to choking. If they choked to death, she was going to be strangling them, dammit! She bent to set the knife down to free up her hands, but she thought better of it. *Not here.* She jogged about ten paces away and put it down behind a rock. Then darted back.

"Okay. Calm down. Calm." She tried to untie the knot holding the gag, but The Bitch kept leaning forward and back. Sera couldn't get it. Finally, she grabbed her whole damn head with both hands, as if she were going to plant a kiss on her, and tore the rope down around her neck, popping the gag out. So much for untying. Sera shoved the shirt in her pocket.

"There." Sera looked up at her and

SLAM

The Bitch head-butted her.

They both bounced back, rebounding from the impact. The Bitch undoubtedly had more head injuries, but Sera hadn't been expecting it. She stumbled and nearly fell, catching herself on a tree.

The Bitch's eyes frantically searched the ground. *Where was the knife? She needed the knife.* But it was nowhere, and she had no time.

Sera righted herself, already feeling the goose-egg forming on her forehead.

*That fucking BITCH,* she thought and looked up as That Fucking Bitch ran into the woods with the rope dragging behind her.

*HA!* Sera stomped on the rope which yanked The Bitch back. Her feet kept going and went right out from under her, and she fell smack dab on her ass with nothing to break her fall.

"Oooof!" She gasped open-mouthed, literally trying to catch the breath that had been knocked out of her.

Sera bent over to grab the rope. Bad idea. Her vision swam, and she sat on the ground. She had no other choice. She wasn't going to pass out. Not here. Not now, she'd come too far.

They sat like that, The Bitch on her ass, hands bound behind her, facing the woods, and Sera loosely holding the rope, watching The Bitch's back for motion. It took a few seconds, but Sera recovered faster and looped the leash around her hand a few times so The Bitch couldn't pull it away if she decided to run again. Once she was sure she wouldn't faint, Sera stood.

"Are you done?" she asked, trying to sound fierce, though it came out shaky and weak.

The Bitch was still focusing on gulping down air, though, and didn't notice. First the gag, then the ground. The last few minutes had not treated her kindly where breathing was concerned.

Sera gave a quick tug on the rope. She didn't trust herself to ask again. Not quite yet.

"Wait!" The Bitch screeched beside herself. How had she blown that? She knew better than to run. Sera was an idiot. She was weak. You didn't run from weak, you mentally overpowered it. The Bitch was a thinker, not a fighter. "Don't gag me," she shrieked desperately. She needed to be able to talk. "I couldn't breathe. I had to run. Come on. I'm your *best friend.* What are you doing?" She kicked her legs, as if in panicked frustration or a child's tantrum, but it was a sales ploy. She was advertising falling apart.

Sera watched the deep rise and fall of The Bitch's back and shoulders. *I should feel something,* she thought, but she was spent. She was over feeling. It hadn't helped.

"Are you okay?" The Bitch asked in response to her silence. A hint of hope belied her position. "Sera?"

"How do you spell my name?"

"What?" The Bitch was totally confused now.

"You said you're my best friend, so how do you spell my name?" Sera felt nothing. She knew that a few months ago, she would have felt hope or fear swell in her heart at this question. Maybe even a few weeks ago. A few days... Now, she didn't. Instead, she felt the heavy nothingness that came with the certainty that her *best friend* wouldn't know because once upon a time, The Bitch had asked her the same question and then decided she didn't like Sera's answer.

"My best friend would know how to spell my name," she said, watching as The Bitch's back stiffened as Sera, yet again, studied her *friend* in the dark for clues.

The Bitch's mind raced. She knew the answer. Of course she did, but this was a trap. It was so obviously a trap, but she didn't know how it was a trap. There was only one answer. The Bitch knew she had to come across as confident. Any sign of hesitancy would be used against her. She knew that because she would do it. She would use anything against anyone if she needed to. She squared her shoulders.

"S-A-R-A-H, Sarah," she said, waiting for praise and an apology. Even in this situation, this ungodly, uncharacteristic, bewildering, insane situation, she knew she was correct. Being correct is what she did.

Silence.

More silence.

The Bitch started to panic. She turned around to look at Sera and saw that she wasn't smug, she was...deflated? *Good. Good,* The Bitch thought. She was right. She knew she was right, and she was. She had to be.

"No," Sera said. "S-E-R-A. Like that song—"

"You're lying." The Bitch cut her off with a shrill edge to her voice.

"—The one from the Nicholas Cage movie," Sera contin-ued without pausing.

"If you're going to lie, I can't win. No one can win with you." The Bitch had always suspected SARAH would go to any lengths to be right, and now, she knew it. Lying about her own name? Ridiculous.

Simultaneously, the weight of certainty settled into Sera's chest. Then, she shook her head almost imperceptibly and stood up.

She expected it to sting. It didn't.

The Bitch would never change.

*It's all over but the murder,* she thought again. Maybe that would be her new mantra. Mantras seemed fun.

"Get up. We're almost there."

"Where?" The Bitch asked as she stood.

"My favorite place in the world." Sera laughed mirthlessly. "Double or nothing. What's my favorite place in the world?"

"Why? You're just going to lie about it anyway," The Bitch said.

"Go on," Sera said, indicating the path. Why argue? She'd never be right in The Bitch's eyes.

The Bitch came back to the path, then paused, for the briefest of moments, as she remembered the knife. She quickly stepped forward, hoping against hope Sera hadn't noticed her hesitation. Sera had noticed, but it could be attributed to a thousand different things. Unfortunately for Sera, she did not attribute it to the forgotten knife waiting for her safely under a rock, so they walked on without it.

It was The Bitch's turn to smile.

<br>

# FORTY-EIGHT

The woods grew thicker as they walked. Sera could almost taste The Bitch's blood from here. Soon, they'd be there. It was almost time. Sera wondered if she could go through with it. If she'd have the strength for the most important murder of her life. She would. She knew she would. Purpose had carried her through the last few months. Purpose saved her. Once The Bitch was gone, she could go on with her life as before. Though, she wouldn't. She would never be able to live as she had before, and that was a good thing.

Nice was her past, not her future.

"Your hut," The Bitch said out of nowhere. "That's your favorite place. Not that it matters. You're going to kill me regardless, I imagine." She said it without malice or anger. She said it as a simple fact, which it was, but still.

Sera didn't respond, and The Bitch's gut sank a little bit. She was going to kill her.

For her part, Sera was lost in thought. The Bitch knew what her favorite place was? It seemed almost impossible, but shouldn't she? Sera had brought her here before and made a huge deal out of it. Also, if she knew what it was, why hadn't she answered before?

Because she loved putting people off-balance.

"I didn't see the point," The Bitch said, as if reading her mind, "in mentioning it before. You were pretty mad."

She hadn't been. Sera hadn't been mad at all. That's how The Bitch knew she was serious. That's why The Bitch had waited until now to speak. Sera was waiting for an apology. She expected an apology from The Bitch for not knowing how to spell her name, but she didn't get one.

Always leave them wanting more.

"I bet sunrise here is beautiful." The Bitch tried to get Sera talking, but still, nothing. "The way the trees are. Over the quarry, it'd be beautiful too. The quarry is right over there, I think."

Sera kept walking, taking careful, steady steps. She felt like she was on slightly uneven ground.

"Have you ever seen sunrise here?" If Sera wasn't going to answer her, The Bitch was going to at least force her to see that *she* was the one not answering. The Bitch was trying.

Sera thought back, had she ever seen sunrise here? Not that she recalled. Sunset, sure. Sunsets here were beautiful. Sunsets in any part of the woods were beautiful, but this place did feel singularly hers, making the sunsets somehow more impactful, more memorable, more personal.

"I'd love to see one," The Bitch said, and Sera's eyes shot up to the back of her head. The Bitch didn't turn around, but she felt the eyes on her.

Sera didn't say anything. She knew there was an angle. It wasn't hard to figure out. The Bitch wanted to convince Sera to let her watch the sunrise. But there was something else. Of course, there was something else. *Fucking bullshit.* But was it? Was it bullshit? It wasn't, not really. Of course, she wanted to convince Sera to let her watch the sunrise. The alternative was death. Who would want that to happen sooner? *Suicidal people,* Sera thought, but The Bitch had never struck her as suicidal. She liked herself far too much... No, that wasn't it. She thought too highly of herself. That was it. She was far too good to kill herself. That's why The Bitch would never do it.

Also, suicidal and ready-to-be-killed seemed extremely far apart in a practical sense. Sera was uncertain that one would equal the other in any situation.

The trees became even denser, harder to see between, and the path cut abruptly uphill. The Bitch turned to follow it.

"To the left," Sera said. "Around that tree."

The Bitch hesitated. That couldn't be the way. There was no trail.

That was part of what Sera loved about this place. It was a home away from all others. Serenely quiet, blocked even from the trails. You had to know to look for it, or you'd never see it.

"Keep going," Sera confirmed, and The Bitch kept walking. About fifty feet further in, there was suddenly a small shack. It wasn't in a clearing, but the trees immediately around it had been cleared once upon a time. The trunks were thinner. The trees younger.

The Bitch stopped, as if taking in a beautiful sight, but her act was lost on Sera because Sera actually was taking in the beautiful sight.

*Now,* The Bitch thought. "I'm sorry," she said in a careful, deliberate way that got Sera's attention. Sera watched her. She stood off to Sera's side, about seven feet away, and they both looked at each other for a minute.

A long moment.

A shitty, fucking sucky, suck, suck of a moment.

It sucked hard because Sera wanted those words to be true. Even now. Even coming up here to kill her. Sera wanted The Bitch to apologize for what she'd done, for everything she'd done.

"Come on," she said and walked ahead of The Bitch to the hut. She had to shimmy the rickety door open, but it was easy enough to do. She knew being in front of The Bitch was a risk, but it didn't matter. Part of her wanted The Bitch to jump her. Force her hand. It'd be easier.

The Bitch did not. Instead, she followed at a substantial distance behind Sera. Her spidey-sense was up. Sera wasn't engaging. People always engaged with her. She was fucking charismatic, or at the very least, she always dominated a room.

That bit was true. Charismatic or not, she did always bowl over the entire room through her sheer force of will.

The door popped open, and Sera found that the back wall had been almost completely disassembled. Deteriorating boards had been pulled off and kicked out. It created a picturesque view of the trees beyond through a dilapidated rustic frame. Behind those trees sat the quarry. It was completely hidden, though Sera knew it was there. The fresh scent of water hung imperceptibly in the air. Sera took a deep breath and smiled. The logs and chairs she and her friends had dragged up here twenty years earlier were still around. Still functional. It felt good. Artifacts from another time grounding her in a better reality. A reality where she was strong. Where she could do anything.

At this point, the chairs were more rust than metal, and the logs were completely smooth from wear, but they were the same ones. Sera's initials were carved into the bark, proving it, though she had no doubts. She dropped the rope.

"Sit down."

The Bitch did, and Sera reached at her waist for her knife.

*FUCK!!!* Her fingers fumbled for a moment, but she forced them to continue back to her hips as if that was the plan. *The knife!!!!* Had she really left her knife sitting behind a rock? She had. She had fucking fucked herself, and now she was up here with The Bitch, and she was ready to kill her, but she didn't have any kind of weapon at all, and The Bitch probably knew that. She'd probably noticed her reaching for it.

*The Rope.*

She glanced down at it, lying there on the ground. She wished she hadn't dropped it. The Bitch was sitting. She wasn't making a move, but the rope was connected to her. In a strange way, that suddenly became an advantage. She was connected to the only weapon they had.

*But her hands are still tied,* Sera reminded herself. She still had the upper hand. Now, it was time for answers.

She looked at The Bitch sitting on a log, hands tied behind her back, looking up at Sera. Sera had all the power, still her mouth grew dry.

The Bitch sat there, waiting for Sera to do something. To say something. Sera could feel her eyes on her.

What did she want to say? She started making a list in her mind, but realized she didn't have to. For once, she was in control. She could go ahead and say it all out loud. Imperfections and all. Though she couldn't, not really. She knew any imperfection would get picked apart. *Fuck it,* Sera thought, *I'm not being careful with my words around a walking corpse.*

"Every time I said something positive, you'd tell me I was wrong. Or mock me. Every time I had a win, like when I first got the marketing job, you'd immediately ask me why you couldn't get the job if I could. How I got it, when you didn't, as if I was never as good as you. All you ever needed to do was say congratulations first, and then bitch. That would have been annoying, but at least better."

The Bitch stared daggers at her but didn't say a word. She was challenging Sera to go on. Even tied up in the middle of the woods, she thought she was better than everyone.

Sera's heart was racing. She could feel the panic rising up in her chest. She wanted to break, to cry. What in the absolute fuck was wrong with her?

*Grooming,* her inner voice whispered. *Conditioning. Years and years of it.*

Sera kept going though. She wasn't being quieted. "Every time I'd say I didn't want to do something, you'd badger and badger me until I'd give in and did it. If I didn't give in and do it, I'd never hear the end of it."

The Bitch shook her head no. This was all bullshit. Everyone was always against her, and now even her best friend was.

"You sound like I was your abusive husband. I didn't make you do anything." The Bitch practically spat the words out.

"Every time I disagreed with you, you'd ignore me. You'd punish me. You act like my opinion is always your opinion, or tell me it's not valid—"

"Give me one example," The Bitch said. She wasn't going down for these fantasies.

"It's not about one time. It's about all of them. It's a state of being."

"See, you can't do it. You can't do it, can you?"

"I already did," Sera countered. She could feel herself losing ground, confidence. "Fine. When I got the marketing job."

The Bitch motioned with her hands, as if to say, "What about it?"

"You didn't even say congratulations."

"I said Congratulations." The Bitch sneered.

"No, you didn't. You immediately cut me down." Sera knew a jab would come soon. She knew something would. Why was she doing this to herself? Why was she trying to have this conversation when it was impossible?

"I'm sure I did." The Bitch rolled her eyes.

"No, I remember very specifically."

Sera was having this conversation because she had to. She was going to kill The Bitch, and she would never again be able to confirm that The Bitch was as awful as she thought. She needed to know 100 percent for sure that it was her fault that Sera had lost her shit.

"Well, you and I remember differently."

Sera was going to have to pick her words more carefully if she wanted to win this. She shouldn't have to pick her words, but she did have to. Well, she was right about that.

"I don't remember. I know. I was paying attention. I knew you never said it, so I was waiting for it—"

"So, you set me up?" The Bitch asked.

"What?"

"You set me up."

"I didn't set you up."

"Yes, you did. You just said you were telling me to see if I'd say congratulations. How do you know I didn't suspect that and not say it because you were setting me up?" The Bitch asked.

"I didn't say that."

"You just did."

"No, I said I was paying attention to see if you said it." Sera could feel the ground slipping. She hated this.

"Right, so you said it in a way so that you knew how I'd respond."

"Because that's what you always do. You never say congratulations."

"Never or always, what do I do?" The Bitch twisted.

"Never—"

"Because you set me up."

"It's not even about that," Sera said, exasperated already.

"You brought it up." The Bitch shrugged. *I rest my case,* she thought.

Sera stared at her. It was fucking dizzying.

"Never mind," Sera said.

"I didn't bring it up, you did."

"What about everything else?" Sera asked. Would she have an answer for all of it?

"What else? You haven't said one other thing."

"I did. I just said a lot of other things."

"Give me an example," The Bitch said, as if Sera hadn't brought up a single other issue.

"Oh, my God." Sera sighed. This was how The Bitch won. How she won at every fucking thing. It was impossible to talk to her. She wore people down when she wasn't bowling them over. "Fine." Sera shrugged. This was what she'd come for, right? "You, you make everything about you."

"You're making everything about you *right now*," The Bitch said with a sarcastic lilt.

"You think everyone's lives have to revolve around you."

"I do not."

"Yes, you do. You think you're the most important person in the world."

"Come on." The Bitch was so annoyed. "Everyone thinks they're the most important person in the world."

"I don't."

"In your world? You don't?" The Bitch challenged her, phrasing it just so, but Sera didn't budge. "Everyone should think they're the most important person in their world."

"You think our lives have to revolve around you."

"'Our' who's in on this 'our?'"

"Fine. My. You think my life has to revolve around you."

"I never said that," The Bitch said simply.

"You didn't have to. Everything you do says it."

"I can't fight about things that you assumed."

"I didn't assume." She was losing this. Sera knew she was. She was right, and she was still losing because that's what The Bitch did. If it hadn't ruined Sera's life and wasn't making people crazy, Sera would have had to tip her hat to her. The Bitch really was skilled at double talk.

She should have been a politician.

"Name one thing," The Bitch said again as if nothing had been said.

Sera sat very still.

It was that logic. The circles. Was she right? Sure, if she phrased everything just so and ignored giant parts of an argument, it was easy as hell to be right. Was she wrong? Absolutely, but not to her. The Bitch was God. God wasn't wrong, and if anyone else wanted to be right, well, they should have phrased their argument better, shouldn't they?

Sera hated her.

In the past, she would have wanted to scream. She would have wanted to yell and punch and throw a tantrum because it was maddening. But Sera wouldn't have said anything, because The Bitch knew exactly what she was doing, and because Sera could also never be 100 percent sure that The Bitch did know.

In life, the only thing that's certain is there is no certainty. Someone great probably said that, or something similar. If they hadn't, Sera thought they should.

"You can't. Can you? If you can't name anything—"

Sera held up her hand to stop The Bitch. The Bitch couldn't stand silence. Silence was where people caught her, but she'd already been caught. The rope around her waist should have told her that.

The Bitch hesitated, then continued. She would not be slowed by Sera's fucking hand. "If you can't name anything, then what are we even doing here?"

*If you stop, you die. If you stop, you die.* Sera watched The Bitch, watched her thoughts, or lack of thoughts, and knew that her lizard brain was chanting, *If you stop, you die.* Her shark brain. Sera had felt like she'd die if she stopped moving. She'd felt that very, very potently. It launched this journey. Her purpose. But now, Sera was ready to stop. Ready to stop all of this. Wasn't that what it was all about?

"Stop talking," Sera said, and The Bitch did. She looked at Sera's cool, calm demeanor.

"Look, I don't know what you—" The Bitch revved up again. *If you stop, you die.*

"Stop talking," Sera said again.

"But I—"

"Stop, or I'll gag you."

The Bitch stopped. The rope still hung around her neck, a dangling reminder, and the tank was tucked in Sera's pocket.

It wasn't an empty threat. It didn't feel like an empty threat. The Bitch opened her mouth anyway. Then she licked her lips. Then again. She had to remind herself every few seconds not to say anything. Not to talk. She licked her lips again. *This is crazy. What the hell is this?* she wanted to say, but Sera was out of her mind. She was completely out of her mind. She opened her mouth again, and Sera raised her hand to stop her. The Bitch licked her lips and pressed them closed.

"Facts, then," Sera said.

The Bitch opened her mouth—

"Ah-ah-ah. My turn. You had your turn for the past ten years. My turn. Fact, you made me feel like shit, and every time I told you that, you blamed me—"

"I couldn't help your emotions—"

Sera held up her finger. "Fine," she said. "That includes my emotions. Okay. Fine. It is a fact you disregarded my feelings and blamed me for it, but fine. Fact. You decided to change how my name was spelled."

"I spelled your name *wrong*. It's different, and I already—"

"Apologized for that. Thank you, but it's a little late. You told every new friend how to spell my name and that I had confirmed that. It was fucking ludicrous."

"I did not—"

"Levi showed me the text chain. So did Alyssa. Don't lie—"

"I'm not—"

"You are. Fine, not lying is tough. I get it. At least don't lie on things you can get caught on. You should be good at that."

"I don't remem—"

"Doesn't matter. It quite honestly does not matter if you remember doing it. That is not an acceptable excuse. You still did it."

"That doesn't excuse you tying me—"

"Ah, ah, ah." Sera wagged her finger in the air. "Still me. There's a lot of unimportant things. There's a lot of things you'd pick apart—"

"I'm not going to sit here while you—"

"Shut the fuck up!" Sera closed the gap between them in a flash, forcing her hand over The Bitch's mouth. "You never let me talk. You are going to let me talk, or I am going to kill you right now. Is that clear?"

The Bitch nodded.

Sera paused. She considered saying "Thank you." It danced on her lips, but she didn't want to. She wouldn't thank The Bitch for letting her talk when she always should have. It was simply good manners.

"Good," she continued. "There are a lot of things I could say, but a lot of those things you'd twist." She felt The Bitch flinch. "You would. You'd twist them. You twist anything that might feel subjective or emotional, and there are a lot of things that feel subjective or emotional, or that you can make subjective or emotional. I'm not going to lie to you and say there aren't—"

Wow! She was on fire. She felt it. Her brain and her body were finally both coming together to do what she wanted. It felt incredible. She had no idea where it came from, but she wanted it to last forever.

*Not trying,* her inner voice prompted. *That is what this is.*

Sera knew it was right. Not protecting, not being nice, not saving everyone else. Being honest and letting the chips fall where they may.

*Why was this usually so damn hard?*

"You lie to me, but I'm not going to lie to you. Not today." Sera removed her hand from The Bitch's mouth and stepped back.

"I didn't remember. It's different," The Bitch mumbled. Sera gave her a look, and The Bitch licked her lips and firmly pressed them together. Apparently, she had absolutely no idea how to be quiet for even a minute.

"Facts," Sera said. "No emotion. Just facts. You stole my job and got me fired."

The Bitch's eyes widened, but she didn't immediately say anything. Sera could see the gears turning. She looked like a deer in headlights.

*Holy shit,* Sera thought. *The Bitch hasn't come up with an excuse.* Why else wouldn't she immediately jump in? Sure, Sera had just told her in no uncertain terms to shut the fuck up, but The Bitch would defend herself on this, the one irrefutable 100 percent concrete thing that Sera had said, regardless of threats.

"Go ahead," Sera said.

"What?" The Bitch asked.

Sera shook her head, and a small chuckle escaped her. "Tell me what happened. Tell me I'm wrong."

"Oh, so now I can talk?" The Bitch asked, covering for her silence. Sera did not react. "Why? You think you know, and no matter what I say, you aren't going to believe me."

"Don't you want to tell your side of the story?"

The Bitch licked her lips, pressed them together, and shook her head no. It was impressively defiant. Sera had to give her that.

"Okay. So, I'll just kill you now, then," Sera said.

"The apology would be forced. You know that. You're not stupid. Anyone would apologize right now. But I'm not apologizing for something I didn't do," The Bitch said. She was panicked, but not panicking. There was a significant difference.

"Right," Sera said, taking another step back to her original position. She was close to the rope and close to The Bitch, but she wanted it to feel like she was giving her space. She genuinely wanted to hear what The Bitch would say about this. "I didn't say apologize."

"It's what you meant. Look, if I made you feel bad, I am sorry," The Bitch said, trying desperately not to emphasize *if.* "But I can't help your emotions. Maybe if you'd told me about all this stuff when it happened—"

"I did," Sera said.

"I would have addressed it. I didn't know," The Bitch continued, as if she hadn't heard Sera. As if Sera hadn't spoken at all. "Look, I don't think I can defend myself to you. You're clearly going through something, and I'm sorry I didn't know it, but you didn't tell me—"

"I did," Sera said, low and calm. She was watching The Bitch, watching her onetime friend.

"I wish I had known. I really do..." The Bitch kept going.

Sera wanted to be able to see the story weaving, the lies coming together, the truth being transformed into something else entirely in real time, but it was impossible to distinguish. Because she believed it. Each thought came into The Bitch's head a lie and left her lips as the God's honest truth.

"I'm sorry, if things got..."

If. I didn't. You should have. All bullshit. All convenient. All word tricks. Was she even capable of the truth? Did she even know the truth? Was everything with her lies and manipulation?

*Degrees of truth,* Sera realized, that's what The Bitch would have thought. She's not lying. She's never lying, but it's all manipulation, all versions. And that was the crux of it.

It wasn't about the job, or about the name spelling, or about The Bitch saying something mean every time Sera had a win. It was about all of those things and every other cut or trick. Every single one of those things adding a gram of weight to a back that could only take so much before it broke.

Suddenly, Sera realized if The Bitch was honest, truly honest— no manipulation, no tricks— about just one thing, she would let her go. *The job,* she thought. *If she's honest about the job, I'll let her go, or the name, or manipulation or...* And she would. Looking at her friend in this sad state, dirty and tied up in her cranberry fucking leggings, she decided that yes, if The Bitch was honest about any one thing, she would let her go.

Honesty would mean she was capable of change.

It would mean Sera was wrong, The bitch wasn't evil and they just weren't meant to be friends. It would mean Sera was crazy, and she shouldn't have done any of this. It would mean all the things she had replayed in her head were... were what?

She was so fucking tired of this.

If The Bitch was capable of honesty, true honesty, Sera would let her go.

There would be some logistical issues, sure. Big, crazy logistical issues, but the whole reason she had embarked on all of this was because The Bitch could not change. Because The Bitch was a horrible fucking person. If she was honest, even under duress, it would be a step forward. A tiny, minuscule itsy-bitsy fucking step, but a step.

Would she really let her go?

Yes.

She would, but just as suddenly, she realized she had only decided to let her go because there was no risk of it.

In this moment, as The Bitch apologized for everything that they weren't talking about—for Sera's mental health, and not having noticed it even though it wasn't a thing to notice, for Sera not telling her things—as she apologized for everything that she was clearly saying was not her fault and nothing that could even slightly be construed as her fault, as she apologized for all of that, Sera knew with a sinking certainty that The Bitch could not change. She could not be honest.

But Sera had changed.

Until that exact moment, Sera had not understood that she was still holding onto some tiny vestige of hope. She hoped she was wrong. She actually hoped that she was crazy and that her friend wasn't, in fact, The Bitch but that she was just a bitch. One among many.

*Why do I want to be wrong so badly?* she wondered and discovered she wanted to be wrong about this because she still loved The Bitch, she still cared for her, and because, most of all, she didn't want to have been wrong for the 10 long years of their friendship.

Sera changed because not only did she suddenly accept that she was wrong, that she had been wrong for a decade, but she also forgave herself for it.

"I never meant for..." The Bitch was still going. Still not talking about the job.

It would be a process of forgiveness. A long one, something she would have to do over and over again. But for now, for right now, Sera forgave herself because she couldn't have known. No one could know that hadn't been through this before. Because grooming is insidious and secret and diabolical. Some might get lucky, some might dodge, but if they knew they would warn others. And no one had warned Sera.

If The Bitch was honest, Sera would let her go.

"Tell me what happened with the job."

A pause, imperceptible to anyone who didn't know The Bitch, and possibly, to many who did, but The Bitch didn't pause. Ever.

"Linda called me and said she thought I'd be a good—"

"From the start. From my presentation."

No pause this time. The Bitch was good to go. Whatever mental gymnastics she had needed to do, she had apparently done. Usually, her gymnastics were done on the fly. The pause was probably only because she had to do really well since her life was on the line.

*Does she know I don't have the knife?* Sera wondered, but there was no way to know without asking, which would give it away. Probably. Probably she knew because Sera wasn't waving it around. *With any luck, she thinks it's in my back pocket*, Sera thought, but who would think she had an eight-inch hunting knife in her back pocket?

Someone who thought she was an idiot. That's who. So, Sera knew it was possible. It didn't matter. Sera would happily strangle her, though it was a shame to buy the knife for nothing.

"The day of the presentation *we* prepared…" The Bitch had stood in the room while Sera put it all together, but she had chosen a font. So, Sera gave her a pass on that one. "So, we presented the new ad campaign, as you know because you were there, and they loved it. And later that day, Linda called me and offered me the promotion. I didn't know you wanted it this bad, or I would have turned it down—"

"Rewind. In between those two things."

"Between the presentation and the job offer?" The Bitch asked, pretending she didn't know what Sera was talking about. Sera nodded. "I went and got lunch with Alyssa, and while we were out, she said that you had told her that you were super sick of the job anyway. And I thought you were. You bitched about it all the time." Here, she paused, trying to nudge Sera into defending herself and thus into admitting that she did hate the job, but Sera didn't say anything. "Don't you remember how, when Keagan got the Anders account, how you said you didn't even know if you'd stay with the agency?"

She hadn't said that. The Bitch had said that. The Bitch had been pissed.

"Anyhow, Alyssa and I got lunch—"

"Who picked the restaurant?" Sera thought she knew, but she wanted to know if it had been a setup or a happy accident.

"Alyssa. She texted to see if I wanted to go to lunch, so I don't know for certain, but Alyssa probably did. She likes that place. It's a little posh for me." The Bitch was always pretending she was so grounded, but she wasn't. Sera still suspected The Bitch had picked the place, but she couldn't be certain. The Bitch continued, "There wasn't really much that happened. I don't really remember what we talked about…" Sera knew there was a big, old gap though, because Alyssa had invited her to lunch too, because Sera had said she couldn't make it, because Sera's meeting canceled and then, suddenly, she went to the restaurant. "After that, I went back to the office. You and I debriefed on the presentation, and then Linda called."

"And you hadn't spoken to her before?" Sera asked.

"I saw her at the presentation." *Sneaky Bitch.*

"But not after?"

"We didn't have any other meetings that day. She called and I accepted the job—" *Sneaky, sneaky Bitch.*

Sera had to hand it to her though, she didn't say no. She wasn't officially lying, though she knew exactly what Sera meant. The Bitch always knew what everyone meant, and she always said exactly what she wanted to anyway. It was a lie of omission. Intentional omission.

"Why'd I get fired?"

"Did you? I didn't know. I mean, I knew, after, but I don't know why. They never even told us at the office that you did. They told us that you decided to pursue other opportunities, and—"

"And when *I* told you I got fired?"

"I mean, I knew. Of course, I knew. But they didn't tell us anything official. I did hear some people saying that they thought they'd seen you drinking a lot, and, well, you do. You know. I mean, we all do. Together, of course, but you do."

"Wow. *I* drink a lot?"

And The Bitch latched on, misinterpreting Sera's rhetorical question for engaging in gossip. "Yeah, I don't know who said it first. Do you think that had something to do with it?" The Bitch asked innocently, leaning in as if gabbing in an abandoned shack with her hands tied behind her back was just the most normal thing in the world.

"What did you say to Linda when you saw her at the restaurant?" Sera demanded. Point blank was really the only way to go with her. No wiggle room.

"When? Oh, I ran into her the next week at—"

"The same day. I was there." Sera wanted to see The Bitch's face fall, see the panicked recontextualizing of what she had just said, but she didn't have the satisfaction. The Bitch was shameless. She hadn't just lied. Of course not. The Bitch was never wrong.

"You're probably remembering some other time when we went to lunch together. It was only me and Alyssa," she said confidently. Apparently, Alyssa hadn't mentioned inviting Sera. Not surprising honestly. With the two of them together, why would anyone else ever come up?

"Some other time where you told her that you made the entire presentation?" Sera asked. Now, The Bitch's face blanched but only for half of one second. After it was gone, Sera couldn't even be sure she had seen it.

"I didn't say that. I'd never say that. I probably said that *we* had done a lot of work on the presentation. I mean, I couldn't very well tell her that all I did was pick fonts, if I did run into her, but I'm not sure. Are you sure it was that day?"

Sera nodded.

"I don't remember it."

"You seem to remember everything else really well," Sera said.

"Only because I knew you'd grill me on it," The Bitch countered.

"Why would I grill you on it?"

"I don't know. Why would you tie me up and drag me into the woods? I don't know why you're grilling me on it, but I thought you might, and you are, so I was right," The Bitch finished in a huff. The magic of circular logic.

"But if there was nothing to grill you on, why would you think that I would?"

"I didn't think anything. You're just dramatic sometimes, and you grill me on stuff. Everyone says it. You do it to them too. I mean, isn't this all a bit dramatic, Sera?" The Bitch asked, looking around, and Sera had to admit that it was all a bit dramatic. It was also exactly what she needed to do. "Besides, if you were there, why don't you tell me what you heard, and I'll tell you if I remember it," The Bitch said. She wasn't going to bury herself. This way she could counter anything, deny anything. *How could I possibly remember that?* she'd probably say.

"I heard you say that you made the entire presentation." Sera was playing along now. She'd heard a lot more, but would The Bitch admit to this? Admit to anything?

"I don't know. I may have run into Linda. I'm not sure about that day, but yes, I remember telling her I did the presentation, but I didn't mean that only I did the presentation. I don't think she took it that way. I don't know how she could have, but if she did, I'm sorry. I can tell her that you did most of the presentation, if you want. It's not that big of a deal," The Bitch offered, using a tone that implied she would be completely willing to do this one small favor for Sera without a trace of shame about creating the problem.

"It was that day. You told her I drink. You told her you did the whole presentation because I was hungover, when you were the one who was hungover. You said you thought I got high. I don't get high. You know I don't get high. I was in the fucking stall listening—"

"You were spying on me?"

"What?"

"That's so. That's low, Sera. That's so low." The Bitch was going a mile a minute now. There was no breaking in. "And weird. I can't believe you would do that. To me? You were my best friend. I thought you were still my best friend, until tonight, and you were spying on me? People said you were getting weird, clingy, but I told them that was bullshit, but I guess—"

"I wasn't spying on you—"

"You waited in the bathroom to, to what? Hear my conversation if I went in there? Oh, my God, were you already planning on kidnapping me—"

"No, I wasn't planning—"

"I had no idea. Sera, look, we can get you help. I can. I'm sure I can talk to Linda and get you your job back. I tried, you know. If you'd returned my calls you'd know I talked to Linda and was trying to get you your job back, and I think it would have worked too, or at least, I could have gotten her to let me have you as my assistant."

Sera's eyes were wide, her mind reeling. What was happening?

"You should have answered my calls. I could have helped you. I know now. It's probably good you got fired. I mean, not good-good, but good. You know what I mean. Now, they'll never know that you had this little meltdown. I'll take care of it. Are you sure you aren't drinking? Like, not at all? Maybe just sometimes? Some people can't handle that. I can, but some people can't."

Sera's mouth hung open. She... They... The Bitch... What the fuck? What had Sera been—?

"We are so lucky you weren't at work when this happened. It's okay. I can take care of it now that I'm in a management position. You would have gotten fired anyway with all of this."

Sera'd been talking about the—

"Untie me, and we'll take care of everything. I'm so glad you're back. I completely get why you weren't calling now. Why you haven't been around. I thought you didn't like me anymore. Didn't want to be friends. Can you imagine? You have no idea how much I missed—"

"The fucking bathroom!" Sera exploded, having waded her way through the mush and gunk back to what she'd been saying. "I wasn't spying on you—"

"Not spying-spying, but eavesdropping. Listening. You're the one who said it—"

"No, I didn't, I—" The Bitch opened her mouth, but Sera wasn't having it, not this time. Instead, she got louder. She played The Bitch's game. She screamed. "I was in the bathroom because I needed to use the bathroom, and you came in with Linda and were shit-talking me. Stop trying to say I don't know what happened or don't understand or that you did me a fucking favor. You didn't do me any fucking favors. You're a liar and a cheat and a fucking NARCISSIST!"

"Whoa." The Bitch leaned back, as if the assault were completely unwarranted. "If you aren't even going to talk to me like a real person, then I'm not having this conversation," she said, completely throwing Sera off. She was not going to lose. Her brain couldn't even fathom losing. The problem was it wasn't about winning. It was about accountability, and that was a concept she couldn't comprehend.

"Look, I'm sorry to be the one who has to tell you this," The Bitch went on. "But you aren't a nice person. You aren't. I know you think that you're a do-gooder or that you're so sweet, but you're pretty selfish. You've been a bad friend to me, and to everybody else. And it hurts. You know? And now this?" The Bitch said, meaning the abduction. She said it soft, and low, and planned, and perfect. It was crafted to make Sera question everything, but all it did was make her realize that The Bitch was right. Conversation was pointless.

The Bitch had to die.

Sera dove for the rope, but The Bitch lunged for Sera.

The Bitch had gotten her hands free.

# FORTY-NINE

Sera dove for the rope, coming up with the end, as The Bitch's outstretched hands circled her throat. Sera kicked her off, maintaining her grip on the rope, but immediately remembered the other side was still tied to The Bitch. She'd gotten her hands free, but Sera didn't have time to wonder about that now.

Sera jumped towards The Bitch, holding the rope out in front of her like a bow staff. The Bitch met her in kind, holding the rope up, though it was still tied around her waist. They dodged in and out, but Sera realized she'd do far better to knock The Bitch down, so she turned and sprinted in the other direction. She was hoping she could take her feet out from under her again by yanking on the rope around her waist.

Instead, The Bitch raced after her. They ran out the back of the hut. Nearly an entire wall was missing, so it wasn't hard.

Sera sped forward, but The Bitch kept pace. Unfortunately for Sera, it was clear The Bitch had realized her plan. She screeched to a halt, and The Bitch ran right into her outstretched rope. It hit her in the chest. Sera quickly spun around, bringing one hand over The Bitch's head as if they were swing dancing—

The rope was exactly where she wanted it. Right around The Bitch's neck. She pulled tight, but The Bitch spun, and Sera reacted out of instinct, spinning the opposite way. They spun again and again, trying to both catch and evade each other, and just like that, they were tangled together back-to-back.

Sera still held her two rope ends and pulled tight. From the squawk-choke sound that The Bitch emitted, she guessed it was still around her neck. And it was.

It was hard for her to get a good grip though. And The Bitch bent forward, lifting Sera's unsuspecting feet off the ground. She dangled there, on The Bitch's back, like two kids on the playground.

She had no leverage, but she yanked on the rope again. The Bitch stumbled forward a foot, and Sera tilted to the side, trying to fall off The Bitch's back. The Bitch pulled on the rope in response, and it closed around Sera's neck too.

She shot her hand up to block it, but that just released the pressure from The Bitch's throat, giving her a chance to breathe and find her footing.

Sera pulled the rope that was strangling her up to her forehead, trying to get it over her head. She fought to maintain her grip on both ends of the section she was using to strangle her foe. She couldn't do it though. She had to choose one. She chose strangling The Bitch. She'd rather they both die than The Bitch live. She lowered her arm, and The Bitch's end of the rope slid back down her face, over her eyes, past her nose, and into her—

She bit down, hard. The rope was in her mouth. It wasn't ideal, but it was a damn sight better than around her throat.

The Bitch pulled tighter, using the leverage from bending over. Sera made strange grunting, gurgling, choking sounds around the rope in her mouth. The Bitch smiled. She was doing it. She was choking Sera. She was going to win!

But Sera pulled violently as she held the rope fast in her teeth—not that she had to hold it. It was wedged now, rubbing against the corners of her mouth, tearing at her lips. She hoped her cheeks didn't cut, didn't break. The pressure was immense. She bucked her legs, trying to get her feet back on the ground. Writhed this way and that. She needed stability if she was going to strangle The Bitch. A few more tries, and *voilà!* Touchdown! Her toes hit the ground—

And then they bounced right back up again as The Bitch redoubled her efforts.

*Shit.*

Sera tried to tighten the rope but couldn't get it tight enough without—

*Oh no*, she thought. She had to choke them both. The only way to pull the rope tight enough was to cross it in front of her which would put it squarely around both their throats.

She kicked again. If she could just get her feet down—

But it wasn't happening. The Bitch staggered forward. She didn't know it, but they were getting closer and closer to the edge of the quarry. Sera knew it though. She could see how far the hut was behind them as she rocked her weight forward. It was glimpses as The Bitch staggered further and further away from it. She didn't know how far they had left, but it wasn't far.

Sera wanted to hope against hope that The Bitch would see the drop, but her gurgling gasps suggested she was focused on something else. Also, the woods went right up to the cliff edge from this side. They'd have about a foot for The Bitch to realize they were going to go over, and by then Sera knew it would be too late.

They might die either way, but at least by strangling them both she'd have a chance. She heaved with all her might. She crossed the rope in front of her throat and changed her grip from one side to the other. It was a tricky maneuver, but she made it. Then she pulled. Sera coughed, and The Bitch tried to suck in air. It sounded unsuccessful. Was it unsuccessful? Sera would have to hope so. But the rope pulling at her mouth tightened, and she knew The Bitch was still in the fight.

They stumbled another few feet forward.

"Ur- Ur- Trrrr-" *TURN!* Sera screamed, but it came out gurgling vowels. "Cuuurrr—" *Quarry* was even less intelligible.

They kept going.

Lurching toward the ledge.

Sera twisted the rope, tightening it about both their throats. She turned her head as much to the side as she could. If she could just keep the rope off her windpipe—

It might not be enough though. The rope yanking at her mouth kept her from making big moves in any direction. She wrenched and twisted more and more.

Twist. She felt the pain in her throat. Pain trying to force her to release. Losing her air, trying to force her to release. *Tighter,* she kept thinking, and she did—she pulled tighter and tighter and tighter.

The Bitch stumbled forward.

Her gasps weren't gasps anymore. Her sucking air wasn't sucking. It was all shallow, ineffective clicks and clugs. Sera's eyes swam.

The Bitch stepped forward—

Onto rock—

Sera felt the difference. Heard the difference. Knew the difference. They were on the edge, her feet dangling, hanging from The Bitch's back. She kicked, kicked, writhed, but as The Bitch lost air, she leaned further forward rather than straightening up.

Kick. Kick. She had to get her feet on the ground.

Kick, twist. Stars.

Twist.

Air. Twist.

A loosening. Her mouth burning suddenly with the release of the rope, and she moved.

She could turn her head.

*Oh, fuck. Quarry. Quarrry!*

Air filled her lungs the second she turned her head, helping her brain catch up.

She twisted, hard. Yanked with all her strength—

Kicked her legs forward, and then—

They fell.

# Fifty

Sera's knee hit the ground. Hit hard rock. She'd won. They didn't go over, and Sera would pull them back. Would pull them back from the brink.

But the rock under her knee. They were close. Too close.

There was no motion.

No motion behind her. No motion from the woman she wore like a turtle shell.

Her brain was behind her body. Her body knew she had to let go, let go of the weight that threatened to take her over, that had always threatened to take her over.

One finger, next finger. Mentally, she pried her grip open. Physically, she pried her grip open.

More air. Sera breathed deeply.

*What if she's not dead? What if she's just passed out?*

Sera froze, petrified by fear. Nothing. No breathing. No rise and fall. No rasp of an angry esophagus.

Sera just had to stand up and drop her off her back into the quarry. *She'll fall down into the quarry.* Atlas shrugging the weight of the world off his shoulders.

She strained, trying to come up from the deepest, weighted lunge she'd ever been in, and The Bitch's weight shifted on her back—

The ropes shifted.

Not moving. Dead weight—

Dead weight tied to Sera.

Dead weight that pulled. Pulled her backward. Pulled her toward the ledge. Dead weight that would take her over the cliff and into the quarry below.

*Fuck.*

Her brain was foggy.

She couldn't stand. She needed to think, so she stayed there like that. Kneeling on the ground, with a body on her back.

*A bodypack.* She smirked. *Okay. Sense of humor intact.* She just had to loosen the rope and drop the body. Drop the body back over the ledge. Not great. She had to dispose of the body, and while it might sink in the quarry, it also might float. It was far more likely a body in the quarry would be found, found quickly, and found with pieces of Sera's hair, Sera's skin, and maybe even traces of Sera's blood on it. Had the rope cut her? She had no idea. The corners of her mouth were raw. It had to have, but the rope itself could also be tied to her.

No. Both Sera and the body had to stay there. But her legs were getting tired, compressed under the dead weight of her friend. Ex-friend. Frenemy. Enemy. Why be nice?

*Dead.*

*Dead weight.*

*Dead.*

*She's dead!* Sera realized, with a rush of endorphins. She wanted to scream. To cheer! But she didn't want to send herself over the cliff. She had lost so much oxygen her brain wasn't working right, but she was catching up now. Her friend was dead.

The Bitch was dead.

And Sera was—

*Free.*

Her body shuddered. A release of everything she'd been holding onto rushed through her. No more second guessing, no more crazy making, no more crazy maker! No more mental "Is she right? Am I right? Am I an asshole? Is she an asshole?" No more manipulation or lies—or truths that were bent and forgotten and replaced by lies that The Bitch believed that Sera had believed that, luckily, Sera had stopped believing.

But her legs were so tired, she was going to—

*Fall over,* she thought. *That's the answer. Give in.*

She glanced to her right, at the rock and gravel on the ground, making sure it was safe, clear, far enough from the edge. Then she released everything she held onto and fell on her side.

She heaved a sigh of relief as the pressure on her lungs receded. A body is a heavy thing. Her feet and legs were numb. They'd fallen asleep. She wiggled her toes and rolled her ankles, bringing the feeling back. The blood rushed to them, and the tingling began.

"Ow, ow, ow, ow." So bad, so bad, like stars exploding in her feet, and she couldn't stand, couldn't walk it off. She had to grit her teeth and bear it. Sharp inhale. She squinted her eyes shut. It would pass. This too would pass.

She hated it when her feet fell asleep. She breathed out through pursed lips and in again through clenched teeth. The pinpricks were dissipating. She lay like that, breathing in and out, for another minute.

The body. She had to free herself from the corpse of her dearly departed Bitch.

Well, then.

She set about the business of untangling herself. She started with the rope around her neck, which was easy enough to cast aside. The problem was, with all their spinning, they had effectively wound themselves up together, so she needed to unroll them. But how do you unroll yourself with a body that won't move at the edge of a cliff?

*Okay.* She pushed her feet against the ground. She was going to turn them so they were parallel with the edge, and then she'd just roll them toward the hut. *Easy peasy.*

Her ribs screamed as she moved, scraping them against the ground. She was on her bad side. Her worse side. Both sides were bad sides currently. She drove her feet into the ground again, slowly propelling them sideways. She wished she had fallen to the left. She hadn't really chosen though. The weight of the body and the lunge of her legs had decided that whole deal for her.

Nothing for it now. She couldn't just flop to the other side like a fish, but oh how she wished she could!

They swiveled on the ground, Sera and the body of her friend. She couldn't help but think of Homer Simpson. *S-M-R-T... This should be morbid,* she thought, but she couldn't wipe the grin from her face. *S-M-R-T. Smart, smart, smart, smart. Maybe that's how you spell Sera.*

It was weird, like something that would happen to Pugsley in *The Addams Family.* Wednesday would have gotten him out of it though. Too bad no Wednesday was coming for Sera.

They arrived.

*Perfect. Houston, we have position!*

And she rolled. Well, she tried to roll. She rocked, and rocked, and heaved herself over onto her stomach, with The Bitch ending up on her back, but that's where the rolling stopped. The Bitch's weight wanted to go back the way it'd come, but Sera needed it to continue forward. Her ribs bellowed, "Get this Bitch off us!"

Rock. Rock and—

No roll. They flopped back onto their sides the way they'd come. Sera needed more *oomph.*

"All together now," she said aloud, rallying herself. "And a one, and a two, and a threeeeee." And Sera rolled faster. She landed face down in the dirt, but speed propelled them, and the weight of The Bitch went over her and then took her onto her other side.

*Victory!*

Now facing it, she looked out over the edge of the quarry. It was beautiful. Dawn was breaking.

*Shit.*

She needed to hurry. Plus, they'd been a lot closer to the edge than she'd realized. Another inch or two back and even falling on her side would have put at least half of The Bitch's body over the edge. She wiped her brow. There was no sweat there, but she needed to release a big, giant "Phew!" She had almost accidentally launched herself over a cliff.

*Sera, 1. Cliff, 0. Thank God,* she thought, but again, it seemed unlikely God had anything to do with this. He, She, They were unlikely to be on her side in this particular endeavor— though, maybe God knew what an absolute bitch The Bitch was. She was talking about God after all. Well, thinking about. Well, stalling, she realized as the prospect of The Bitch's weight crushing her ribs into the ground for a second time suddenly became very real to her. Welp. Nothing for it.

"One, two, threeeeee."

She rocked them, and they rolled over yet again.

"Wahoo!" she actually yelled aloud, before catching herself. She had her rhythm. It was worth celebrating.

"One, two, threeeee."

They rolled, and Sera looked behind for the unraveling rope... Where was the—?

*Shit.*

She'd rolled the wrong way. She'd positioned them the wrong way. They were rolling with the rope. They were rolling how they'd roll to keep the rope nice and tight. She was winding them up. She looked back toward the cliff and considered rolling back. She couldn't. It wouldn't do. Two revolutions were unlikely to undo enough rope, and who was to say they'd cover the same distance? They might just go right over the edge.

*And squiggle.*

She planted her feet into the ground, spinning them the opposite way so that they could again roll toward the hut.

*S-M-R-T. Yup, that was exactly how you spelled Sera. She didn't get an A.*

*Fucking ribs.*

Again, she looked out over the cliff. The sun would be coming up soon. Hikers might be coming soon. Cops. Cops would be coming as soon as hikers found her with a body tied to her back. She'd plead self-defense, The Bitch had kidnapped her! But it didn't seem like that would work. It certainly wouldn't work after hearing about Mr. Durmont's accident and once they discovered Alyssa was also missing.

Well, The Bitch could have killed Alyssa too. Mr. Durmont wouldn't help her case though.

"And a one, and a two, and a three- Ah-ah-ah!" She was getting loopy.

They rolled, and one revolution of the rope was left on the ground, trailing behind them.

"Again!"

And they did roll again, and again, and again.

The rope unraveled, and Sera jumped up. She was free! Free again. *Free!* She was killing it with this serial killer crap, but she still had a whole body to deal with.

Bodies were the bane of serial killers everywhere. She didn't know this was true, but she suspected it was. No body, no crime, right? *Was that a real thing?* she wondered. Or maybe that was a movie thing. No way to know. Googling bodies and crime was completely off the table for her.

She looked back and noticed that the sun was rising. Breathtaking. Sera sat next to her onetime friend and watched.

The Bitch had been right about one thing. The sunrise was beautiful.

# Fifty-One

The sun was up now. Barely, barely, but Sera had to get a move on. She stood up and did the only thing she knew to do. She dragged The Bitch's dead body back into the hut. Inside, she stashed it behind the log chairs shoving them back, hoping the body was sort of hidden between the wall and the wood. It was not a super successful hiding spot. Maybe she should leave her in the bushes?

Unfortunately, there wasn't as much in the way of low-to-the-ground dense brush here as there had been in the park. Here it was thick, dense woods, yes, but those thick, dense woods were primarily trees. She didn't need a hiker to see an injured comrade only to find they'd stumbled upon a strangled comrade. And the strangling was clear.

There was no version of this that could be misconstrued as an accident the way Alyssa could have been. The way even Mr. Durmont sort of was. The rope was still tied to The Bitch's waist, and a rug burn was permanently etched into the skin of her neck. It left bruises, but they were mild purple on the now-pale skin. The bruises of a dead person rather than the bruises of a vibrant young woman.

Vibrant. Sera never would have described The Bitch as *vibrant*. It was just as well.

She stared down at the body between the logs and the wall. Sympathy could have crept into her then, regret, or remorse, but it didn't. Instead, she regretted the lack of a blanket, or sleeping bag. If she could lay her just right and cover her with a blanket just so, it would quite convincingly seem like a homeless person had established the hut as their new domicile. Hikers would steer clear, and hopefully animals would stay away. In either scenario, she hoped animals would stay away, at least until— Until...

Well, then. Until she figured this out.

Sera stepped back and looked at her work. It was clear she had very successfully killed The Bitch, and she was not wrought with guilt. All of this she took as a good sign. A very good sign.

42 and the pig posse aside, she had the makings of a serial killer after all.

This had not been a problem. It had been a release, an experience. Well, she had wavered for a moment, but then she'd doubled down. But did she waver? Not really, she reasoned. She had decided to let The Bitch go if she did something Sera knew she was unequivocally incapable of doing.

Of course, in the actual moment, The Bitch had lunged at her, so Sera had to defend herself had to— No. She took a deep breath and calmed her nerves. Sera lunged at the rope *before* The Bitch had. Before she knew The Bitch was free. Had she had to defend herself? Sure, but victims were bound to fight back. *Huh.* She had never quite considered that before. The practicality of that. Serial killer was a dangerous profession, and no one got hazard pay.

She was proud of herself. She had set out to kill The Bitch, and now, she had.

She would never have to listen to The Bitch say how awful she was again. Ever.

She felt that hit her, strike her to her core.

*Wow.*

The silence sat there with her. Poured over her. Stopped her from acting. Allowed her to just be. Demanded she just be. And she was. She just was.

The absolute perfection of nothingness.

How does one describe nothing? No one can, and, for the first time, Sera understood Buddhism. Not to say she was a Buddhist—the corpse refuted any claims to that—but she understood the Zen of it. The nothing. The enlightened state where you can detach from everything. She tasted a piece of it and knew why those who thought they could achieve that in even a semi-permanent way might try.

It also made her understand why serial killers were serial killers. In a unique way. A new way. The noise that had attacked Sera when The Bitch came into her life must be a fraction of the noise that attacked serial killers all the time.

They were bad people. They were the worst people. But she knew something of the noise now, and something of the silence.

The feeling of the silence stayed with her. The memory of it. A piece of it that she could recall. But she had to go now. She had a lot to do.

Sera had officially become a serial killer. She was able to do it. She had done it.

And she was good at it.

Well, she had done a pretty shoddy job of prep and a lot had gone wrong, so all things being equal she was actually not, in fact, *good* at it. She had accomplished it though. Even with everything that had gone wrong, she had somehow still made it to the finish line. *Well, the main event,* she thought. *There's still the cleanup.*

She looked around, taking a mental picture, and decided she could linger in the aftermath for a few moments longer.

If someone caught her in the next five minutes, she was going down regardless.

Her heartbeat quickened when she saw a necklace. Her necklace. The Bitch was wearing it. Sera had tried to get it back so many times, but somehow it never worked out. She considered taking it. It wasn't a normal souvenir. It was already hers, but she knew better.

Someone could know The Bitch still had it.

Souvenirs were a one-way ticket to life. Perhaps a one-way ticket to the electric chair. She had not done a fantastic job of covering her ass, but she certainly wasn't planning to turn herself in. Besides, the "Sarah" who let The Bitch keep the necklace was dead too, and Sera didn't want any part of her back.

She did, however, need to cover her actual tracks. Again, she grabbed a branch and swept it over the ground between the hut and the edge of the quarry. In the early morning light, she could see the long drop and the water below. She wondered, if they had gone over, would there have been any chance for survival? Not tied together. Not at all. She'd been lucky. Incredibly lucky.

Inside, she draped that branch and a few others over The Bitch's body. She was no longer visible. However, the curious pile of brush might attract attention. There was nothing for it. Hopefully, people would simply walk by. *Hopefully, they wouldn't even come up here,* she thought. The path had seemed very overgrown last night. The hike back would give her a better idea of that though.

She exited the shack, pulling the door shut and wedging a small handful of sticks and twigs in the hinges. It wouldn't stop anyone determined, but it might stop a random lookie-loo or a family of hungry raccoons.

She trekked back to her car in her mud-caked sneakers and dirt-covered yoga pants and sweatshirt. It looked like she'd rolled around in the dirt, which she had. She was quite the sight. Like an extreme backpackers' ad gone wrong. She really deserved some new clothes. *Too bad I don't have a job.* She smiled as she thought it. She'd never been less sad about anything. Getting fired had changed everything about her life for the better.

The path was indeed overgrown. She'd been too distracted to worry about it last night, but in the light of day, it looked more like an abandoned trail than a current one. *Good.* She didn't need a group of Boy Scouts to find her prize. She didn't expect to come across anyone as she walked, but part of her hoped she did. This was the part that wanted to gloat. The part that wanted to give someone a big high-five like she'd just finished a marathon or won the lottery.

That part wanted credit.

That part was stupid.

Killers who corresponded with the press or kept in touch with the family were idiots, but now she understood it. She was learning a lot today. They wanted props, not for some horrible deed, but for the most incredible thing they had ever done. It was sick and twisted. She thought all of them were awful humans, but she was happy as hell to be among them. Hopefully, the fact that she killed awful people helped her morality, but she didn't think now would be a good time to delude herself. She'd set out to become an asshole so she could no longer be taken advantage of, and it seemed she had succeeded past any normal model of success.

*I need a psychiatrist,* she thought.

*Little late,* her inner voice piped up.

*Hm.* It'd been a while since she'd heard it. *Interesting. Very interesting.*

She saw her car ahead. Suddenly worried, she fumbled around in her yoga pants pocket for her key fob. The pants were tight though, and the key hadn't gone anywhere. She could feel that there would be an impressive bruise on her thigh where she'd dug it into her leg over and over. She pushed her thumb into the soft flesh. It ached as a beautiful reminder.

She clicked her key and heard the familiar beep of her car unlocking. She climbed in, not noticing the pair of preteens that were staring at the muddy crazy lady from between the trees.

She pulled out, wondering what she should do with the body. She needed a plan. She might have pulled off two (two point five if she wanted to count Mr. Durmont) successful murders, but she was pretty awful at disposing of bodies and even worse at planning ahead for them. She couldn't leave it in the hut, but dragging it out through the woods was an impossibility. She decided she needed to add "figure out body disposal practices" to her Smart Serial Killer List, or perhaps, add it to a second list. She needed one list for supplies and one list for ongoing education.

*Where does one find the time?* she mused, but maybe that was why so many serial killers lived in their parents' basements. *Was that true?* She wasn't sure. She didn't really think so. Not at all. They did often seem to be poor, but it was probably a ruse. Maybe they lived in poor neighborhoods so the residents couldn't get a rise out of the cops. That was it. It was all quite fucked up. Resources would help with any hobby. Of course, that extended to serial murder. *Plus, lawyers*, she thought. She might need to up her bank account.

That wouldn't help her in the short-term though. What was she going to do with The Bitch *now?* The easy solution of the pigs had gone out the window when she changed venues...or had it? The trail wasn't steep, and the pigs were in decent shape. If she could manage it with injured ribs, she was sure they could. 42 would be thrilled to go on a hike.

Looked like they were taking a field trip.

# FIFTY-TWO

She pulled up to her grandma's and found Pig sitting directly in front of the front door. This was weird behavior, even for him.

"What is it, Lassie?" she asked excitedly. "Timmy fell down the well?" Pig cocked his head. This was not a joke.

He stood with no further acknowledgment and led her around the side of the house to the basement window. *Hm.* Something really was up. She saw a hole that 42 had dug. A lot of holes. It was obvious it was her as she bounded over to say "hi," then stopped and looked ashamed as Sera puzzled over the holes. Sera petted her head and cooed, "Good girl," which put an immediate end to the shame. Excited that digging could become their new game—Sera had started it, after all—42 began happily digging again. Sera didn't join in though. Instead, she looked from the holes to Pig and back again. She knew she wasn't getting Pig's point. Pig wouldn't care about a few holes. Not in the least.

*What am I looking at?* she wondered. The dirt was pushed around, and there was a footstep leading away from the messed dirt. There were a lot of footsteps, actually. She followed them with Pig and 42. They led around the house in an obvious circle. There was no effort to hide or cover them up. It was Clarence. She knew that, but why wouldn't he hide his tracks? And why wasn't Pig showing her his actual tracks? They completed the circle, landing back at the window.

*Oh. Oh, shit.* It dawned on her. Why would he hide his footprints by the window and nowhere else? Because this was the place he didn't want her to know he'd lingered. Because of the hoofprint. He'd seen it. He'd definitely seen it, and he came back to look in the basement again. But— But what? But he saw it, looked in the window, and then walked all over her yard without trying to hide it from her in any real way? Was he that bad of a cop? Honestly, maybe.

He was there during one murder and right after another without raising any flags. She supposed Old Man Durmont couldn't be considered a murder. It was a killing, but she didn't think animals could be given the descriptor of "murderers." Still, he was there for one murder... Well, sorta murder. Alyssa *could* be called an accident or, at best, accidental death on the verge of homicide—if there was a category for that. Man, Sera really had been quite awful at this whole serial killer thing. She did better this morning, but she imagined Bundy or Gacy would still think she was quite the hack.

*Oh, fuck, the knife!!*

Okay, she was very much still awful at this.

Pig oinked at her, drawing her attention back to the matter at hand. The dirt at the window. She didn't know what to do, and honestly, she was too tired and too damn sick of all the games and strategies. She'd tried everything over the years to make things work with The Bitch, and it was exhausting. Trying to figure out people and their motivations is what got Sera into trouble in the first place. She never should have given The Bitch any benefits of any doubts. So, she decided to ask him. That was the least suspicious and most logical thing to do. Pig snorted and walked away, as if he had read her mind and was in agreement.

Sera bent down and looked in the window. So, he'd come back here to peek into the basement again. What did that mean? The hoofprint was gone, snuffed out by 42's attack yesterday. Nothing else seemed to be amiss. She hoped she was right.

The second she walked into the house, her body started to yearn for another long shower. Killers really aren't water conservationists, but she didn't have time. It was already daylight, and she needed to get everything cleaned up ASAP. Honestly, she should have cleaned it up before she left. If she'd had a way, she would have.

She readied a go-bag of cleaning supplies, and garbage bags. She didn't know what she'd need, but her ever-growing Smart Serial Killer List implied she ought to overprepare. She would definitely need things she hadn't thought of. She considered changing clothes, but figured she should only leave fibers from one outfit rather than two. She didn't know if that made identifying her clothes more or less likely. But as far as she could guess, the less chances the cops had the better.

She walked outside with her bags and found the pigs all sitting around the car waiting for her. She was touched, and maybe a little creeped out. It was so thoughtful, but also strange that they seemed to know where they were going. It was also slightly suspect that they had no qualms about the whole thing. They were a weird pack of pigs, but who was she to judge?

She petted a pig's head as she made her way to the car and wondered if she ought to name all of them. The pig looked up at her with big pig eyes, and it suddenly seemed silly not to name them. Pig was the leader, but they all had personalities. She decided that would be tonight's after-murder-cleanup activity.

42 would be thrilled.

She opened the car and laid a piece of plywood she'd found on the side of the house across the back seats. She was up-grading her skills. She then laid two pieces of 4x4 down as a ramp. One by one, the pigs climbed in. 42 stood by her side, watching like her second-in-command, which she obviously was, and headed to the passenger door when Pig, last of the bunch, was safely inside. With footwells and all usable empty space now stuffed with pigs, Sera shut the back and let 42 in the passenger side. She stashed the gear at 42's feet.

As they drove, she called Clarence. It would seem really innocent if she called a cop the day that her friend died, right? Not quite an alibi, but certainly better than nothing. What had happened to Alex?

*Oh well*, she thought, not wanting to admit to herself how big of a bummer that was.

"Hey. Sera. How can I help?" Clarence picked up, sounding a little hurried. She wondered if she was imagining it, but his voice definitely had an edge to it.

"I saw you were poking around my house," she teased. "I fig-ured, maybe we could just grab some food and have a conver-sation sometime instead." She said it as a date, but she didn't know if she meant it like that. Wasn't it pretty stupid for a killer to date a cop? Or was it the perfect cover? Was this the same as befriending the family? As following the investigation?

She wasn't sure where his jurisdiction would end and an-other's would begin. She hoped he wouldn't be on The Bitch's murder. Then relaxed. No way. She was abducted in the city. *It'll be the city's case. For sure*, she assured herself.

"Absolutely," he said, the tension dropping from his voice. Maybe he felt guilty about poking around? Maybe he just didn't want to be caught, so once he was caught, it didn't matter? She had no idea. She marked it down in the column of questions to ask.

She smiled. She really was back. Willing to ask questions, unafraid of the answers, and, she realized with an enormous sense of accomplishment, she hadn't second-guessed herself all day. It was only, she glanced at the clock, 8 a.m.? Damn! She was making good time. Still. Every decision she'd made between yesterday morning and today might have been wrong, but at least they were her mistakes to make, or more likely, her mistakes to damage control later.

"Tomorrow?" she asked.

"7 p.m. at Dante's?"

"Is that the diner? I only know the diner," she said. He chuckled. His laugh sounded good. Inviting.

"There's a whole town, you know. Don't worry. I'll show you it."

They hung up as she pulled off the highway and onto the dirt road that led to her favorite place. Once parked, she dropped her phone into the center console as she got out and stretched. She didn't need it. She didn't even want it, and, because she was so in the moment, she didn't even notice when it finally chimed with a text from Alex.

Instead of being controlled by a *DING* or soft *BUZZ*, she walked around the car and opened the backdoor and her caravan of compadres traipsed out of the car.

She looked like a circus ringleader.

She loved it.

Joining in the fun, 42 climbed into the back seat and followed Pig out. Then they began their hike. Sera led a long line of pigs through the woods. This, she thought, would definitely get more attention than even leading The Bitch through on a leash would have. 42 ran up and down the line, making sure all the pigs stayed in formation. She didn't need to worry, but she liked her job. Plus, she was great at herding pigs. Pig, who allowed her to think she was amazing at herding, knew the pigs didn't need any help to stay on the path, but who was he to ruin the dog's fun?

Sera slowed them down each time they came to a few larger rocks to search for the knife. It wasn't an overly rock-laden trail which, she assumed, would really help her out. Still, it was a bit frustrating. How could she have been so stupid?

Each time Sera looked behind a rock, 42 joined her. She looked, sniffed the ground, sniffed Sera, sniffed the air. She just generally sniffed for anything that could be important. Sera, who was certain that they had already passed the rocks where she must have left the blade, began to worry. Maybe someone had found it. If someone had found it, what were the chances they had found The Bitch? If they'd found The Bitch, what were the chances she was leading herself and her found family straight to the cops?

Suddenly, 42 started barking and howling ahead. Sera dashed forward, unsure what sound the dog would make if she were genuinely in trouble. The pigs all paused, waiting patiently. They understood the sounds of barks and howls better than people do. They were not afraid.

As Sera raced up to 42, she saw the dog sitting next to a large and extremely familiar rock, with her tail wagging back and forth at breakneck speed. 42 had found the knife. She was awesome. 42 got about a billion *good girls* and pets on the head. Then they continued up the trail. 42 continued sniffing everything just in case, but the knife was the only thing that seemed to be of interest to Sera.

They reached the shack in less time than Sera expected. Partially driven by fear and partially urged on by the line of hearty livestock behind her, Sera felt like she was faster now than she had been yesterday. Of course, she was also not slowed down by The Bitch's foot dragging.

The sun was high as they walked through the trees to the hut. It had the effect of making the shamble of a building appear both ominous and inviting. Sera looked at it and saw the two sides of herself: the good girl she had always been and believed she needed to be, and this new person who wasn't afraid to let the dark out. She wasn't certain who she was, light or dark, but she suspected the truth would be far more complicated whenever she discovered it.

Pig and 42 walked up alongside her, each taking a side. She scratched 42's head and nodded at Pig. "Maybe I don't have to pick," she said aloud to no one in particular, but 42 knew she was talking to her and barked twice in quick succession.

*That's right!* she seemed to say.

Sera looked back at her army of hungry pigs and felt both a sigh of relief and a pang of guilt that she hadn't been able to feed them properly earlier. *They'll eat now*, she thought and hoped they would be happy to go back to pig feed between killings. She planned to have a lengthy career, but a body a day seemed like an impossible pace to maintain both for her and for them.

She told 42 to go play, then opened the shack's door and stepped inside. The familiar flood of relief washed over her again. The Bitch was dead. She was still dead. Sera hadn't known, but there had been a small part of her still wondering if maybe, just maybe, she had left her alive.

A metallic tinge scented the air. She was happy they'd made good time. The body would decompose faster out here than Alyssa had in her basement. Plus, the smell would draw animals.

She moved the branches off The Bitch. If Sera had to describe her expression, she would have said that The Bitch wore a look of condescending shock. Quite the expression for a corpse, but her face had the placid implication of "How could S-A-R-A-H have bested me?"

Sera pushed a log aside and dragged the body out into the center of the circle of hodgepodge chairs. She pushed the logs back into place. She didn't know why, but it felt off to have them not in their long-standing 'round-the-campfire positions. The body with logs and chairs around it was like a sacrifice at a mini-Stonehenge. Sera walked over to the body and knelt down next to it.

She placed her fingers against The Bitch's throat, feeling for a pulse she knew she wouldn't find. It was unnecessary. If she were alive, by some miracle, the pigs would take care of that right quick. But she didn't want them to. *If* she were alive, Sera wanted to handle it herself. To an onlooker, it would have looked like concern, or, perchance, remorse.

It wasn't.

Kneeling like that, she did feel her heart break again, but not because of guilt. How could she have loved someone so much who had nothing but contempt for her? How could a heart break for the same reason so many times? She was going to grieve. She knew that now. She would have to grieve for all the things she had thought they were. All the things they should have been.

She removed her hand.

There was no pulse. She was certain of that.

There was only freedom. She was certain of that too.

Sera turned her back on The Bitch and walked away. Right out the front door.

Pig, knowing his cue, went inside on her exit. His friends followed in single file behind him. They circled around the body, like taking hands before a feast, shared a brief pause, and then stepped forward. It wasn't choreographed, but it wasn't *not* choreographed either.

Outside, Sera kept walking until she came to another smaller path. A path she had taken many times as a child. A path she had taken The Bitch down long ago. Sera hadn't followed it since. She'd tried a few times, but it had always felt tainted. It was washed clean now. The sacrifice was successful, and the living were able to spend another year of bounty after a long curse had been lifted.

42 trotted up beside Sera, joining her best friend. Eventually, they came upon a secluded clearing where a small waterfall fell into a sparkling pool below.

"Do you like to swim?" she asked 42.

42 cocked her head to the side as if to say she didn't know.

Sera pulled off her clothes and said, "We'll find out."

She waded into the water as 42 leapt and yipped tentatively, then happily, from the shore. Finally, 42 concluded that it was not a bath at all, and she would very much like to try it. At that instant, 42 ran in at full throttle and quickly learned that running turned to swimming in a flash. It wasn't quite a Frisbee, but 42 was enjoying the water immensely anyway.

*Besides*, 42 thought, *a Frisbee would surely be in her future, because they were going to be together for a long, long time.* Sera splashed 42, bringing her back to the moment, and 42 bit at the water and swam after her.

They stayed like that for the rest of the afternoon. They were best friends, and Sera didn't have to worry about the next murder until later.

The moment was now, and now was perfect.